TIGRESS IN A CAGE

Striding into his cabin, Hawk demanded, "Have you finished your tantrum, wench? It isn't every day I have to imprison a woman in my cabin. Usually my bed companions come quite willingly, even gladly."

Bethlyn stiffened and spat. "You're an arrogant, conceited man. I assure you that I'm not like your other women and won't become a mewling kitten for your pleasure."

A deep laugh escaped him. Hawk found her amusing, a beautiful and headstrong young woman despite her low station. Then he gazed at her voluptuous figure and flawless features and hot blood flowed through his veins. He growled, "I have no wish for a kitten, my sweet, but a wildcat. So, come now, and make this voyage a memorable one."

He swiftly advanced towards the innocent Bethlyn, and catching her unaware, pulled her into his embrace. His hands stroked her lush curves, his tongue traced her rosebud lips and—despite her maidenly protests—the lusty Hawk sensed the svelte beauty in his arms respond to his touch . . .

PIRATE'S BRIDE
Lynette Vinet

ZEBRA BOOKS
KENSINGTON PUBLISHING CORP.

ZEBRA BOOKS

are published by

Kensington Publishing Corp.
475 Park Avenue South
New York, NY 10016

First printing: June, 1989

Printed in the United States of America

As always, to Martin, Jason, and Jared . . . and Catty, the most beautiful and sweetest cat in the world.

To Potsy and Champ Vinet—my husband's wonderful parents.

A special note to Brenda Bone and Robin Lee Hatcher—I love your letters. Corresponding with you both means a great deal to me.

And to the Historical Group—I love you all.

Author's Note

The attempted kidnapping of Benedict Arnold is a fact. One other such attempt was made but also ended in failure.

I have used factual information in *Pirate's Bride* about this incident. It is true that General George Washington was so enraged by Arnold's treachery that he enlisted the aid of Sergeant Major John Champe, who was a Virginian under the command of Major Henry Lee, to carry out the plan. Washington specifically ordered that Arnold not be harmed or killed but brought directly to him.

Originally, John André was to be exchanged with the British for Benedict Arnold, but it is believed that the plot for recapturing Arnold was most probably already in the works before André's confession. However, André, a man whom Washington personally liked and pitied, hastily confessed to his part in the whole affair. Thus, Washington had no choice but to order his immediate execution as a spy.

This only increased Washington's desire to hang Arnold. So, Champe pretended to desert the American side and made contact with Arnold, winning the traitor's trust. However, the plot failed because, on the date the kidnapping was to take place, Arnold moved to new quarters to be nearer the embarkation point of troops for his Virginia expedition. Champe was ordered to embark with the rest of the legion and spent the night set for his great exploit aboard a transport, which he was unable to leave until Arnold landed in Virginia. Major Lee knew nothing about this, and he waited with a cavalry detachment at Hoboken with three horses: one for Arnold, one for Champe, and one for a mysterious associate of Champe's, a man whose identity has never been discovered.

Needless to say, General Washington was quite upset over the failure of this plot.

I have tried to be faithful to the events of that night. Because Arnold's attempted kidnapping was such a fascinating and little-known incident in American history, I knew I wanted to use it as a part of my story. The problem was how to do this. It wasn't until I discovered that Champe had two nameless associates (one to help in the kidnapping and one to ready the boat for the trip to Hoboken) that *Pirate's Bride* took root in my mind. I knew that one of these associates would become my hero, Ian Briston.

This is the only way I've tampered with history.

I wish to believe that this unknown associate was daring, venturesome, and as handsome as the hero in *Pirate's Bride*, and on that night as he waited in the shadows to aid his country, his life may have changed, too.

I do hope it ended as happily.

Prologue

The captain's cabin
The Black Falcon,
1777

If he touched her, she'd kill him.

Emboldened by such a brave thought, the beautiful young woman clutched the small jeweled dagger in the palm of her hand. The ruby-encrusted hilt cut into her soft flesh she held it so tightly, and the cold steel of the blade resting against the thin material of her gown gave her a degree of assurance that she could adequately defend herself.

Within the cabin, all was quiet. Except for the slight pounding of the waves against the hull of the ship, she heard nothing. Earlier that evening, the voices of the piratical rebels and the women who were their captives had drifted through the solid plank door. She'd heard singing, hearty male laughter, feminine giggles, and then these same voices had grown louder as the men and women shuffled through the passageways to seek pleasure in each others' arms. Now an ominous silence pervaded the ship, and she somehow knew that the man who had placed her here earlier would soon return.

"Animals! Doxies!" the young woman cried softly. In the dying candlelight she pirouetted sharply, her honey-brown hair fanning out and then swirling around her shoulders in long, graceful tendrils. The other women

9

might take delight in being ravished by these colonial upstarts. She, however, wasn't one of these women, these whores transported across the seas for the pleasure of the British soldiers quartered in Philadelphia. Never would she eagerly open her arms and legs for any man who'd have her. Not even for the captain of this notorious band of men, masquerading as privateers.

"Captain Hawk." She mouthed his name with such vehemence that her eyes flared and resembled twin torches in the dying candlelight.

A shiver slid down her back. For a moment she wasn't certain if she felt repulsed, frightened, or excited by the prospect of the man's presence . . . of his touching her. No man had ever intimately touched her. She'd been properly kissed by some and fended off many an overamorous man with her friend Jeremy's presence. She kept her heart and body as her own, never having dispensed with either of them . . . not even to her own husband.

The thought floated through her mind that since the hour had grown late and all was silent, perhaps the arrogant captain had found comfort in the arms of one of the other women. A small hope rose within her that the man, masked to conceal his identity, wouldn't bother with her. Perhaps, just perhaps . . .

The click of the latch on the door brought her up sharply. A broad-shouldered shadowy form, whom she instantly identified as Captain Hawk, stood in the doorway. Quietly he closed the door. With the sound of the latch being locked into place, her heart knocked wildly against her rib cage. Hugging the dagger closer to her body, she realized the irony of killing the man with his own weapon.

Captain Hawk stood with arms akimbo, barely five feet from her. Candlelight emphasized the broadness of his shoulders in the white open-necked shirt, the close-fitting black breeches, and knee boots. Her gaze moved upward to the black mask in the shape of a hawk which covered the bridge of his nose and his eyes, his hair being covered by an ebony scarf and tied in a queue at the back of the neck.

Indeed, he struck her as a powerful, awesome figure, a man who inspired fear in those less brave. At the moment she felt more than cowardly as her legs shook and threatened to buckle, but she wouldn't let him see her fear. She raised her shoulders, straightening her spine. This fearsome privateer wouldn't bully her with his arrogance. She'd faced much worse in the form of her father, and she'd survived him!

"Have you finished your tantrum, wench?" Captain Hawk asked with a trace of amusement in his voice. "It isn't every day I have to imprison a woman in my cabin. Usually my bed companions come quite willingly, even gladly."

She moved forward a bit, hiding the dagger in the folds of her skirt. "You're an arrogant, conceited man. I assure you that I'm not like your other women and won't become a mewling kitten for your pleasure."

Hawk laughed deeply. "I have no wish for a kitten, my sweet, but a wildcat. You seem to be of the latter persuasion, and my blood grows warm at the sight of you." His gaze settled on her face and moved to her breasts, causing her to grow heated. "I do admit that you're the most comely doxy I've ever seen and quite refined, too." Making a move towards her, she escaped him by rushing to the opposite side of a table. This action stopped him in his tracks and once more, he laughed. But the sound was mellow, laced with passion.

"Ah, so you wish to play the reluctant maid, I see. Fine with me if playacting pleases you . . . Beth. That is your name, I believe. So, shall I play the lecherous duke and you the beautiful but virtuous serving girl? Or perhaps you'd like to be . . ."

"Stop your filthy ravings!" she cried. "I want none of you. Come closer to me and I'll kill you."

"Good, good," Hawk began and took off his belt to hurriedly throw it upon the floor. "I'm to be the lecherous nobleman. I always did want to pretend I was a member of the aristocracy. Spices things up a bit."

"Stay away from me, I beg you. I'm a married woman . . ."

"Wonderful. I've always loved dallying with the married ones. They're so much more passionate than the timid virgins. I applaud you on your creativity, Beth."

11

Flashing her a smile, Hawk made a dash for her. For a second she eluded him, thinking that she'd somehow escape him and convince him he'd made a horrendous mistake. She wasn't a doxy sent to the Colonies for the soldiers' amusement. But she couldn't tell him the truth about herself, couldn't admit to him who her husband was. Such a notorious man might use her true identity against her, and she couldn't bear for anyone to know she'd been at the Hawk's mercy . . . or, God forbid, his woman. She must fight this man, fight the sudden rush of excitement she felt by his very presence.

She started to protest anew, but a long arm slithered out and grabbed her about the waist, pulling her towards him and turning her to face him. The man breathed hard. His breath hotly touched her cheek and she caught the whiff of brandy, the acute masculine scent of him. Through the slits of the mask, his eyes were an indistinguishable shade, so dark that somehow they seemed to blend in with the mask, forming a whole.

His hand reached into her bodice and lightly twirled a nipple between his fingers before embracing the ivory mound fully, "God, you're beautiful," he whispered, his voice hoarse and thick with desire. "Let's quit the playacting and enjoy each other, my lovely. I've never wanted a woman as much as you."

Did he say such things to all his conquests? she wondered inanely as his hand continued fondling her breast. She knew she should move, should fight, but his lips touched hers in a soul-searing kiss which left her breathless, stopping all conscious thought. Perhaps she was wanton, a tease, like many of the gentlemen in London had told her. At that moment she'd have gladly stayed in this man's embrace, pirate or not. Had she been fighting him or herself all this time?

His mouth transferred from her lips to the base of her throat to the valley of her breasts. "Come to bed, my sweet, and show me all you've learned in your trade. You'll find me an eager pupil."

His words splashed cold water on her ardor. She froze under his gentle, arousing assault. Couldn't he tell she was inexperienced in such things? Did he truly believe she

12

was here only to pleasure him, receiving nothing in return? The pompous, arrogant boob! Must all men believe women were good for only one thing? If not to browbeat them, to bed them, then to treat them like chattel and desert them. She realized that once this man's lust was satisfied, he'd probably seek out another one of the wenches on board and forget about her. What a love-starved fool I am, she thought, her lips curling in disdain for herself and the man who held her in his grasp. I won't be made a fool again. I won't.

Pushing herself from him, he attempted to grab her anew. "Come here, sweetheart. You've playacted enough for tonight. You've sufficiently aroused me. In fact, your apparent virtue has me more than ready for you. Come."

His tone left no doubt that he was growing weary with her and now demanded she move to the bed. Shaking her long honey-colored hair, she attempted to make her way to the door, forgetting it was locked. Once more, he reached out and ensnared her, pulling her close to him, so close she felt the rapid beating of his heart, could actually feel his hardened manhood against her belly. He wanted her, and no amount of protests would prevent him from having her. She'd have to thwart him herself, and she shook at the thought of what she must steel herself to do if he didn't desist. She'd never killed a man.

"I want you, Beth," he said with a softness which nearly undid her. "Why do you torture me so? Can't you tell that I'm languishing from desire for you?"

Pretty words, but she'd heard them often the last few years from too many men. There had been times she'd have willingly thrown herself into a man's arms, his bed, if he'd promised love, marriage. However, she couldn't marry anyone, since she already had a husband. Though Captain Hawk was more virile than the other men she'd known, he was still a man, and men caused pain to women by deserting them. This was one time she'd be the one to inflict the pain.

"No."

"Come, Beth, my sweet."

"I won't." With a sudden quickness she raised her hand, brandishing the dagger. The steel blade gleamed in the light, and Hawk stiffened.

"Your role as modest maid has gone too far, sweet. Put down the knife."

"Not until you promise to leave me alone."

"As you wish."

He surprised her by letting her go and moving away. "See, I'm standing over here. You've nothing to fear from me, Beth. May I have the knife?"

"No."

"Please."

Her hand wrapped tighter around the dagger until her knuckles turned white. Hawk inclined his head. "You may keep it then, if it gives you a degree of security."

Did he mean that? She didn't know what to think, what to do. It seemed hours passed as she stood there with the upraised dagger, and she guessed that to him she must resemble a madwoman.

She'd never know what might have happened if a knock on the cabin door hadn't startled her. Suddenly Hawk had her wrist in his and attempted to wrest the dagger. But she'd held it so tightly that her fingers wouldn't uncurl, and his profane oaths only served to make her stronger, to survive the attack she'd felt certain would follow.

"Hawk! Captain Hawk! Open the door!" came the cry of the first mate from the other side of the door as he jiggled the locked door to no avail.

"Hand over the blasted thing!" Hawk rasped, but her hand felt frozen to the hilt, unable to bend. Then it happened.

He'd moved too close to her when he pulled down her arm. She didn't mean to do it, really she didn't. The blade contacted with his chest and she felt the dagger push into the sinew and muscle, felt the warmth of his blood rushing onto her hand.

Captain Hawk stood still. His face turned a deathly shade of white before he crumpled to the floor, to fall at her feet.

Gazing in horror at the man, she clutched her throat, unable to scream or move, not having a conscious thought save one.

She'd killed him.

Chapter One

England—The Devon Coast
1771

From high above the clifftop where Lady Bethlyn Talbot sat, a copy of Shakespeare's sonnets resting in the lap of her gown, she had a gull's-eye view of three small fishing boats sailing through the churning waters of Start Bay. Liquid brown eyes in a childlike face, framed by wind-tossed, honey-brown hair, admired the fishermen's skills to neatly maneuver their crafts over the swelling evening tides. A wind from the east had blown in earlier, dispelling the calm of the early fall afternoon, but no one appeared to mind the bad turn in the weather. Everyone who gathered on the pebbly beach laughed and hugged the returning fishermen, oblivious to the strengthening breeze which whipped around them. Women and children gathered to help empty the fishing nets of crabs and to place the hard-shelled creatures into buckets.

Good-natured banter drifted closer to Bethlyn as the men, followed by their family members, strode up the road along the side of the cliff to the safe haven of their homes. Bethlyn could picture in her mind's eye the flickering hearths, the children sitting down to eat with their parents, not the least bit frightened by the approaching storm because love surrounded them.

A surge of longing as strong as the evening tide washed over Bethlyn. Love was a commodity she'd known for a short time, and only from her mother.

The truth was that her father, the Earl of Dunsmoor, didn't seem to care for her. In his presence she'd always felt awkward. The memory of the way he'd gaze down his long, aristocratic nose at her could still chill her. The only time he spoke to her was to criticize her plumpness, her timidity, to warn her not to spend all of her time with her nose in a book or writing sonnets, lest she grow boring like her mother. She hadn't seen her father in over two years, and his admonishments still remained with her. Hadn't he loved her mother?

The first seven years of her life had been spent at Woodsley, her parents' home. She recalled that her father had been absent a great deal of the time, and it was during these long absences that her mother seemed the happiest. The moment her father returned, her mother's whole attitude and bearing changed. One moment she'd be carefree, at play with Bethlyn and feeling seemingly well; the next, upon learning the earl had returned home, she'd take to her room and declare ill health. For as long as her father was home, her mother practically lived in her room, even took her meals there, and Bethlyn was forgotten.

One day her mother truly did become ill, and within a week she was dead. The earl arrived at the country estate from London in time to make funeral arrangements and to engage a governess for his daughter. Then off he went again. The next time Bethlyn saw him a beautiful dark-haired woman clung to his arm. Her father introduced the woman as Jessica, his new wife. Jessica had smiled at the shy child, charming Bethlyn with her beautiful face and even, white teeth. This was all Bethlyn was to know of her stepmother.

The next morning, Bethlyn and her governess, Miss Grosvenor, were dutifully packed off to Hallsands. Her father only nodded woodenly at her when the groomsman settled her in the carriage. Though her father treated her with indifference, she longed to believe he cared for her. She craved his presence, some connection to him because he was her only living relation.

Seven years had passed since that day. Now her life was

16

spent in the company of a poker-faced Miss Grosvenor and Milly, the serving woman who cleaned the cottage and prepared meals, besides looking after Bethlyn. The cottage and the clifftop comprised her life. The cottage had been purchased some years ago by her father to use as a summer place. He'd used it only twice and then stayed for barely three days, declaring that the damp atmosphere wasn't to his liking. Then back he'd gone to the waiting arms of his new wife. As Bethlyn matured, she realized that her father had placed her at Hallsands to keep her out of his way, that for some reason he hated the sight of her.

"If only . . ." she muttered, not quite certain what she'd have wished.

"Bethlyn!"

Bethlyn started at the sound of her name being called. A girl about her own age waved to her and Bethlyn enthusiastically waved back to Mavis Hempstead, Milly's niece. Breaking away from the group of people, loaded down with buckets of crabs, she ran towards Bethlyn. Her dark hair blew wildly in the wind and bright, large blue eyes gleamed warmly at her friend. Pulling her shawl close around her blossoming bosom, she said, "Did you see the catch my papa made today? We'll be swimming in crab stew for the next month."

Bethlyn stood up, laughing and clutching her book to her breasts. Mavis always had a way of brightening her day. Perhaps it was because Mavis's natural ebullience was contagious, or the fact that her friendliness and warmth broke through Bethlyn's natural timidity. Milly had introduced her to Mavis some years ago, and when Miss Grosvenor was occupied elsewhere, Milly would always sneak Bethlyn off to play with Mavis, even for an hour. Without Mavis as a playmate and confidante, Bethlyn's life would have been endless days of studying and appeasing Miss Grosvenor.

"I think I should like to have some of your mother's crab stew. Perhaps she'll consider bringing a pot to Milly for supper tomorrow night."

"Why wait so long? Come join us now, Bethlyn. Mama will have it fixed in no time, long before Miss Grosvenor realizes you're gone. Aunt Milly told me this morning that the old dragon has her monthly malady and went to her room straight after breakfast and hasn't come out all day."

That was true. Miss Grosvenor pleaded ill health after receiving a letter this morning, and Bethlyn kept herself occupied by reading and attempting to write poetry. She knew that if Miss Grosvenor learned she'd been at Mavis's house, she'd be quite displeased. She constantly harped to her that she was above these simple people in station and must never forget she was the daughter of an earl. An earl's daughter didn't cavort with peasants. But Miss Grosvenor would have been shocked to know that Bethlyn would have gladly changed places with Mavis, who had a happy, warm homelife and loving parents.

At first Bethlyn was tempted to refuse Mavis's invitation, but after a few seconds' consideration, she decided she wanted a sample of Mrs. Hempstead's stew and ached to visit Mavis and bask in the warmth of a real family's love. Casting a quick look in the cottage's direction to be certain that Miss Grosvenor didn't watch from the upstairs window, she nodded to Mavis.

Soon both girls were running down the road to Mavis's home, and before either was ready, after much giggling and talking and helping Mrs. Hempstead in the kitchen, the hot-seasoned stew was placed before them.

The meal passed in happy talk, the kitchen bustling with the other members of the Hempstead family. Mr. Hempstead leaned back in his chair and pulled out a pipe and then regaled his brood and Bethlyn with a long-forgotten folk song about the life of a fisherman.

At such times Bethlyn almost believed she was part of the Hempstead family. For years she'd been sneaking away from Miss Grosvenor and partaking of this family's kindness to her, kindnesses she could never repay. For how did one repay others for friendship which was given freely? The only way she knew was to be friendly in return, and with these people her shyness always disappeared and no one treated her as different. She felt free to indulge in conversation, to say whatever popped into her head without thought of chastisement. The younger children

18

climbed onto her lap and snuggled against her, and more than once she prayed that one day she'd have such little ones to love.

Everyone settled by the hearth, warmed by the firelight, forgetting that a storm raged through the night. Mavis was telling a story to the younger children, her face bright and beautiful. A surge of envy for her friend coursed through Bethlyn suddenly. Would she ever be as pretty as Mavis? She sincerely doubted it. More than once Miss Grosvenor told her that plain people couldn't rely on looks to get them through life; they must make their fortunes through ingenuity, their minds. And she told Bethlyn she had a fine mind, which led Bethlyn to believe that Miss Grosvenor and her father, as well, did consider her less than attractive.

A loud rap sounded on the door and was thrown instantly open by a very wet Milly. Her gray hair hung limply about her head and she sneezed in lieu of a greeting before settling her gaze on Bethlyn.

"I thought I'd find you here, my lady. You better be getting on home. The dragon is breathing fire and more upset than normal."

"I'd forgotten the time," Bethlyn said in alarm and grabbed for her cloak off a wall hook. "Miss Grosvenor will probably make me memorize ten Bible verses for morning."

"Then get on with you, miss," Milly said, ushering her through the door before Bethlyn could bid anyone farewell.

The two of them ran through the rain. Bethlyn, being the younger and the faster, reached the cottage first. No sooner was she in the doorway than Miss Grosvenor pulled her into the parlor.

The woman's hands trembled, an unusual occurrence for the normally composed governess, as she helped Bethlyn off with her thin, wet cloak. She ordered Milly to light a candle and the hearth in the damp room. "You'll die of a chill, Lady Bethlyn. How often must I warn you to bundle up properly when you go outdoors? Such a wet and cold night as this will no doubt find you ill on the morrow."

Bethlyn knew that a chill was the ultimate malady to Miss Grosvenor. Bethlyn guessed it wasn't so much that the woman cared about her charge's health, but lived in dread that the earl would dismiss her for negligence. More than once Miss Grosvenor had complained about being forced to take up residence on Hallsands, but she was being paid a more than adequate sum for her services. In that respect, Bethlyn reluctantly credited her father. He did wish her to be well educated.

When the room glowed with dancing flames and the candle had been lighted, Milly departed. Miss Grosvenor beckoned to Bethlyn to take a seat beside a small, round table while she sat across from her. "I doubt your father would be pleased to learn of your associating with those people. You've a position to maintain and I must chide you to remember it. Now more than ever."

Bethlyn dutifully mumbled she would remember, but her ears perked up. What did Miss Grosvenor mean by now more than ever?

Miss Grosvenor settled her spectacles on her nose, and Bethlyn noticed her hand shook. Picking up a book from the table, she withdrew a folded square of paper from it. "As you can undoubtedly see, the seal on the letter is your father's. I received this missive early today." She sounded curt, more so than usual. "The earl writes to say that his wife has died."

"I'm quite sorry," Bethlyn muttered automatically, assuming this was the proper thing to say when one learned that one's stepmother had passed on.

"Be that as it may," Miss Grosvenor continued, not caring for the interruption, "the earl states that he shall send one of his ships for you. Why a man in his position wishes to be involved in commerce is strange to my way of thinking, but the aristocracy's peculiarities are quite beyond me. However, your stepmother left him part of an American shipping company which was bequeathed to her by her father some years ago. The ship will arrive within the next month and you're to go home to Woodsley."

"Woodsley?" Bethlyn's mind whirled. Her father

wanted her to come home! She nearly leapt from the chair, but Miss Grosvenor's next comment left her firmly rooted.

"Your father has arranged a marriage for you with Ian Briston, your stepmother's son by a former marriage. It appears that your days in the schoolroom have ended. As have mine."

Miss Grosvenor rose and folded the letter neatly into fourths before finally tossing the parchment onto the tabletop. "Where will I find a position on this short notice? I ask you that. The earl is unfair, quite unfair to dismiss me in such a fashion. Arranged marriage, indeed! You just turned fourteen and are quite unsuited to become a wife. You're barely old enough to think for yourself much less take marriage vows seriously. What can the earl be thinking?" She rose from the chair and paced the length of the small parlor.

Bethlyn glanced up, startled at this odd display of temperament from the cold Miss Grosvenor. "I don't understand your concern," Bethlyn feebly remarked, somewhat frightened at this sudden eruption of emotion. "I'm quite surprised at this news but excited also. I wish to be married and loved, to start my own family. My father loves me and chose the best possible husband for me. I know he did. He did," Bethlyn finished with emphasis, more to convince herself of that fact than Miss Grosvenor.

Miss Grosvenor pried Bethlyn from the chair and led her to a wall mirror. She positioned the girl in front of it. "Look into the mirror, my lady. See yourself as others see you. You're as plump and colorless as a dove. Who else could he marry you off to but a boorish colonial who lives in the wilds and probably knows nothing of manners and a gentlewoman's feelings? Most men know nothing of a woman's feelings, her thoughts. They care only for how a woman looks, not a ready and quick mind. Your father is no better. He surrounds himself with only the most lovely things, the most beautiful women. Once your mother was buried and you were gone, he no longer had anything to hide. He could open Woodsley to his friends, entertain in grand style with his beautiful new wife."

She caught her breath, her voice filled with heated

emotion. "I was there long enough to realize that the earl adores perfection. He adored your stepmother, and from what I learned from household gossip, he stayed away from home when your mother was alive, hated to look at her, because she was plain and much too plump for his tastes. He prefers stunning women, women without a thought in their pretty heads. Not someone like you or me. Not a homely, spinsterish woman, someone good enough to educate his daughter but unable to catch the eye of a handsome man like the earl."

Dropping her hands from Bethlyn's shoulders, she turned the girl to her. "I doubt he chose a handsome, well-formed man for you, but a man who will dress like a savage and possess the manners of a goat. However, you're an earl's daughter and will tolerate unbecoming behavior in your husband because your father chose him. I hope you do me justice, Lady Bethlyn, and don't forget all I have taught you. Put your good sense to use in this marriage, because I believe that is all you shall have once you realize that fairy-tale endings are found only in books. Cling to any children you have, your poetry, and find pleasure in them. No man will give you happiness. In this life a woman without looks must learn to rely on herself."

Miss Grosvenor was trembling so hard she nearly fell backward and was forced to lean on the table edge for support.

Surprisingly, her cruel words didn't sting Bethlyn. She sensed a deep and bitter pain behind them. Evidently poor Miss Grosvenor fancied herself in love with the earl and knew that love was hopeless. Still, she felt pain and most probably would feel it for the rest of her life. However, Bethlyn was different from Miss Grosvenor. She wouldn't be forced to love from a distance.

Bethlyn touched Miss Grosvenor's arm. "I'm sorry you hurt so much. I won't be hurt by this man my father has chosen. I intend for him to love me, for me to love him. He'll give me the family life I want. You must be happy for me."

Almost as suddenly as the torrential outpouring of emotion had begun, Miss Grosvenor straightened her spine and said quite primly, "Wash up and study for tomorrow's lesson. Until the ship arrives, we continue as before."

She swiftly left the parlor, leaving Bethlyn alone. A flash of lightning nearly blinded her. In that second she caught a glimpse of her reflection in the mirror and saw herself as Miss Grosvenor had. Limp hair framed a full apple-cheeked face, quite pale, and her dark eyes seemed to overpower her features. She thought her nose was too thin, her lips a trifle too thick. Dully, she nodded. Miss Grosvenor was right. She resembled a plain, colorless dove.

Anxiety washed over her. What if Miss Grosvenor's predictions proved correct? Then the homelife she so desperately craved, the love of one man, would not come to pass.

"He'll love me," she found herself saying. "Ian Briston will love me. I'll make him love me."

She left the parlor and found Milly, who helped her clean up. After she'd studied for the morrow's lesson by the candlelight in her room and Milly tucked her into bed, she grabbed Milly's hand.

"Did you hear any of what was said in the parlor?"

"Aye, I did," Milly said truthfully. "You mustn't take Miss Grosvenor seriously. She doesn't mean the things she told you. She's no doubt worried about being dismissed."

Milly started to turn away, but Bethlyn clung tighter to her hand. "Milly, am I so ugly?"

A soft smile curved up the edges of Milly's mouth. "My lady, you're still young and have a great deal of changing to do before you grow to womanhood. But I tell you that I've a good eye and I see that in a few years time, you'll be a most beautiful lady and your husband will be lucky to have you."

"Thank you, Milly." Bethlyn didn't know if Milly was really telling her the truth, but she'd never lied to her and so she took comfort in her words. Before Milly blew out the candle, she asked her if Mavis might consider going to Woodsley with her as a lady's maid. Milly's delighted laugh echoed through the room.

"Indeed, my lady, I've no doubt she would."

After she was left alone in her bed, she watched the play of lightning upon the rain-spotted ceiling. She decided that even if her husband didn't care for her looks, she'd still have Mavis for companionship and then, one day, she'd have children. Perhaps a husband wasn't that important. But she did wish for a husband to love her, to have the family life she so achingly craved. As she drifted off to sleep, Bethlyn hoped she'd prove Miss Grosvenor's less-than-optimistic predictions wrong. She must prove her wrong.

Her future depended upon it.

Philadelphia, Pennsylvania
Two months earlier

"I suppose I shall be forced to marry the little chit."

This comment was uttered dispassionately, almost in a bored tone of voice. Thomas Eversley barely flickered an eyelash at the young man who had just spoken. Though Ian Briston pretended disinterest, Eversley decided that Briston must be quite vexed about the terms of his late mother's will. It wasn't every day that one learned such unusual news. Eversley would have given anything for Briston to rant, to rage, to show some sign of displeasure. Briston had just been told that his mother had left part of Briston Shipping to him on the condition that he marry her stepdaughter. Eversley was one of the few men who knew how much Briston detested the Earl of Dunsmoor. Having acted as the earl's solicitor for the past ten years, Eversley had dealt with young Briston a few times after the death of Briston's father. He'd found the young man to be cool, unusually cool for one so young, and never betrayed by word or deed what he thought.

Secretiveness rankled Thomas Eversley a great deal. He never gave his thoughts away, being of the opinion that if one knew another's thinking, then one had power over that person. At that moment Eversley would have willingly given a year's pay to see anger flash across

24

Briston's darkly handsome face and the fury he knew must be concealed behind those cool green eyes. That pleasure was denied him. Thomas contented himself with the knowledge that Ian Briston had been placed in an untenable situation by his own mother. He'd never liked the young man, finding him to be arrogant and too astute for his own good. Evidently Briston took after his boorish colonial father and not his most charming and gracious mother who'd possessed the good sense to place matters of business in his own most capable hands.

A large part of Eversley's dislike stemmed from the fact that he felt an upstart like Briston would be wasted on the earl's daughter. What did such a man know of the aristocracy? Thomas felt that he himself would have fit quite well into such an enchanted world, if not for his low birth. The son of a tradesman, he'd lifted himself to his exalted position at Briston Shipping on his own, with no mother to leave him a company to run. He felt life was unfair, so it was up to him to even things out in the end, and preferably his end would be a bit fatter than the other.

Eversley leaned back in his chair and calmly folded his arms across his chest. Yes, for the moment, whether the arrogant young pup admitted his true feelings about the will and the arranged marriage, Eversley took delight in knowing the news he'd brought must bother the upstart a great deal.

"Your mother's will was quite specific on that score. Either marry the girl as a way of uniting you with your stepfather, the man your mother loved, and claim your share in the company, or forfeit it all. What is it to be?"

Eversley fixed Briston with a calm stare which he knew must grate upon the younger man's nerves.

Ian Briston grinned a dazzling white smile, seemingly nonplussed by Eversley's placid demeanor. "I won't be used as a pawn in this game, Eversley. Tell your mighty employer that for me. I admit I shall have to marry his daughter, but I will do it on my own terms."

A small ripple of discomfort slid down Thomas's back. He didn't like the sound of that. "What do you plan to do?"

Briston laughed and hauled his imposing six foot frame from a large chair behind his glossy rosewood desk. He went to stand by the second-story window which overlooked Front Street. The roll of carriage and cart wheels over the cobblestones, the raised voices of the dockworkers as goods were loaded onto ships lining the Delaware River, and the hollow clanging of ships' bells drifted up to the two men. A shaft of sunlight shone through the window, enveloping Briston in a hazy sunbeam. The green orbs in his face glowed like fiery emeralds.

Briston stuffed his hands in the pockets of his black trousers, leaning indolently against the windowjamb. The simple black frock coat he wore over a matching waistcoat, reaching to the tops of equally dark knee boots, gave him an austere almost foreboding appearance. Eversley felt a long moment of uneasiness when Briston shot him a penetrating look before speaking. "You don't think that I would tell you, Thomas, now do you. I am entitled to my little secrets, as I'm certain are you."

Thomas straightened in his chair. His face flushed. There was no way Briston could possibly surmise that he'd stolen funds from the London run end of Briston Shipping. Only he and the earl were privy to the books. Nathaniel Talbot, Earl of Dunsmoor, never bothered to check the books, more interested in living the highlife than to be bothered with business. Eversley single-handedly ran the company in England for Lady Jessica, while her son, Ian Briston, took care of mundane matters in the Colonies. As far as Thomas knew, Briston had never had a chance to see the books. In fact, no one ever saw them but himself. He mustn't give Briston pause to think anything was amiss here. He needed the money he pilfered.

How else could he live the luxurious life-style he'd grown accustomed to without stealing? Granted, the earl paid him well for legal advice, but not enough to alleviate his itchy palms. Only money could soothe that affliction.

"I'm certain we all have our secrets, Briston. If you don't snoop into my private affairs, I promise not to dig into yours."

"Agreed," Briston said and barely concealed his disgust for the solicitor who dressed in the most expensive silks and satins, fabrics which Briston surmised he could barely afford without a hand dipped in the till on occasion.

"Then you'll marry the girl?"

"Ah, Thomas, you sound unsure that I'll go through with the wedding. I told you I shall. I'm a man of my word."

Thomas nodded but didn't appear completely satisfied. He stood up and arranged his brown periwig and prepared to take his leave. "We sail in two days. I trust you'll be ready by then."

"Have no doubt, Thomas. I eagerly await the ceremony."

"Good. Until then." Thomas left the office.

Ian went to a small serpentine-fronted Sheraton sideboard behind his desk and opened it to withdraw a bottle of whiskey and a glass. He poured a heaping serving, but instead of drinking it, he lifted the glass and hurled it across the room where it smashed against the wall. The brownish liquid stained the white baseboard and the plush Persian carpet on the floor, but Ian didn't care. At that moment he wished he had the hateful Earl of Dunsmoor's neck between his powerful hands. He'd delight in choking the life out of him. However, his mother was the one who'd listed the terms of the will, and if she'd been alive, he'd have gladly twisted her pretty neck also.

The oak-paneled door to the office opened and Ian's friend and secretary, Jonathan Marcus Gibbons, peered into the room.

"Is it safe for me to come in now?" the young man asked and glanced at the broken glass and whiskey staining the floor. At Ian's brisk nod, he entered.

Marcus closed the door softly behind him. He raked a hand through his curly blond hair. "Eversley delivered some disturbing news?"

"If you call my forthcoming marriage disturbing news!"

27

Marcus looked blank. "Marriage? Are you finally going to marry Lady Cynthia Connors? I know she's a spicy piece, Ian, but to marry a widow with two children . . ."

"Marc, if I were going to wed Cynthia, do you think Thomas would tell me about it?"

"I suppose not," Marcus answered sheepishly. "Was it about your mother's will? I know you told me a few weeks ago that Thomas was to arrive in Philadelphia to go over the details."

"Indeed he did. Here." He picked up a small miniature portrait from his desk and tossed it to Marcus. "My bride, the Earl of Dunsmoor's daughter."

Marcus examined the full, sad face gazing at him. "My God, Ian, she's a child!"

Ian shrugged and poured a new glass of whiskey. "Eversley claims it was painted some years ago. The girl is fourteen now." Ian laughed shortly. "My mother must have been quite desperate to marry her off to me. She probably realized that no man would have the little wren unless there was an added inducement. I never understood until today just how much my mother must have hated me for remaining with Father when she divorced him."

"That's cruel, Ian. I'm not certain why your mother thought you and this girl would make a good match, but I see delicate features in this child's face, the promise of beauty. I predict you'll fall madly in love with your bride."

"You always were a romantic, Marcus," Ian teased.

"I feel that it's best to remain optimistic." Marcus observed his friend and noted how the dark, curly head was bent in thought. "You are going to marry her, aren't you? What is her name, by the way?"

"Bethlyn, and yes, I will marry her. If I want to keep the earl's, and especially Thomas Eversley's, eager paws off Briston Shipping altogether, I must marry her. What a sordid mess! If Father were still alive and knew to what I must resort to keep the company intact, he'd be ill with rage. To think that my own mother would take away my birthright in such a way." He glanced up sadly at Marcus. "I understand why she must have hated me. I flatly refused to leave with her and her 'precious earl' when she divorced

Father. But to abandon Molly, a child who was barely six at the time, for a spoiled jackanape like Nathaniel Talbot is beyond my realm of understanding."

"Love does strange things to people," Marcus philosophically intoned. "Your mother must have loved this man very much to leave her children."

"Then I hope never to be struck by Cupid's arrow."

"The way you're going, my friend, you never will be. Half of the ladies in Philadelphia are eager to have you for a husband."

He raised an eyebrow in amused contempt. "Except for Cynthia. She knows how to please a man and doesn't play games. She is the only woman I know who takes delight in being wealthy and independent and has no use for a man beyond mutual pleasure. The lady will never remarry, and if I weren't in this situation now, I wouldn't marry either. The prospect of such an alliance leaves a sour taste in my mouth. My father suffered untold heartache when my mother left him. She caused his ill health, his early death. I'll never forgive her for hurting him. He loved the blasted woman until the moment he breathed his last. Her name was the last word he spoke."

Ian lifted his glass in a toast to Marcus and before downing it said, "No woman shall ever bring me to heel, because I won't fall in love. Love brings only pain."

Marcus nodded. "If you say so, but I intend to one day fall desperately and madly in love."

"Fool."

"You're the fool."

A merry laugh bubbled up in Ian's throat. "Not any longer. Before I finish, the high and mighty Earl of Dunsmoor will appear foolish."

"Ian . . ."

Ian caught the warning sound in Marcus's voice and grinned, saying nothing further. He left the office and mounted his chestnut-colored roan which waited along the side of the gray stone building. Riding in the direction of home, his heart felt heavy.

The city bustled over with life, and he took a shortcut which led away from the more populated environs of

Philadelphia. He didn't want to chance meeting anyone he knew, and most certainly didn't wish to make polite conversation, especially not this day. Riding hard along the banks of the Schuykill River, he failed to see the incredibly lush beauty of mid-summer, not the least bit interested in the beautiful women who trailed lazily along its banks, umbrellas unfurled to block the sun from soft, ivory skin.

At the moment all he wanted to do was to arrive at Edgecomb and lock himself away. However, he knew he couldn't. He'd never been one to run away from anything in his life. His father, Matthew Briston, had always told him he was a fighter. That when the deck was stacked against him he'd somehow turn out a winner. Ian had endeavored to please his father and his mother when he was young. To his youthful eyes his father was the most intelligent and kindly man, his mother was astonishingly beautiful. He remembered how she'd tuck him in at night when he was a child and plant a loving kiss on his forehead, tell him what a big boy he was and how much she loved him.

Loved him! Her love had turned out to be as thin as gossamer. She'd gone to England to visit a relative and fallen in love with an uppity earl. Never mind that she and the man were both married to other people. Their lust for each other became the driving force in their lives.

Ian recalled that until the day she'd sailed for England, his mother had been a different sort of woman, or he had thought her to be a faithful, loving wife. Her actions always bespoke of love for her husband. To prove her devotion to Matthew she'd turned over the running of the shipping company she'd inherited from her father to him when they married, even insisting the name be changed to Briston Shipping. Though Matthew ran the company, and its sister company in England, Jessica held title to it. As Ian grew older he wondered why she never relinquished control to Matthew since he was the driving force behind it and he felt that his father must feel belittled at times to not own the company he ran.

However, his father appeared happy with things as they

were, and when Jessica sailed to England to visit her old aunt, and to see to the British end of the company, Matthew insisted she go alone. He claimed pressing duties and couldn't break away.

If only he'd gone, Ian found himself thinking for the ten thousandth time in the last eight years. Perhaps then his mother wouldn't have been an easy target for a lecherous nobleman if his father had been by her side. He remembered the day she arrived home with her earl. Ian and Molly had come home from a friend's house, and there the man had sat in the parlor.

He'd never forget the Earl of Dunsmoor rising to his feet, of the way he'd peered down at them, his eyes cold and hard as if they were vermin and he'd delight in brushing them away. His mother came forward to kiss them. "This is a very special friend of mine," she'd said with love in her eyes as she took the earl's hand in hers. Ian discovered sooner than Molly how special this friend was to his mother. Within a month, she begged the fifteen-year-old Ian to leave with her and come to England, that a great fortune and life with Briston Shipping awaited him there. He'd adamantly refused, knowing he hurt her. He expected she'd take Molly, but she didn't, perhaps thinking Molly would be better off with her brother and father. In that regard, his mother was correct. Ian and his father, when he was alive, doted on Molly, spoiling her outrageously. He sincerely doubted the earl would have wanted two strange children underfoot.

Sometimes Ian forgot he ever had a mother, and that was fine with him. He completed his formal education in Italy before returning home to work in the office with his father. Though his parents had divorced, Jessica wished Matthew to still run the colonial end of the company, and because he loved her and still hoped she'd come back to him, he agreed. Such love has no man, Ian thought bitterly. There were moments over the years when Ian wondered why his father never fought for Jessica, why he docilely allowed her to leave and didn't protest the divorce. Had his father been a basically weak, cuckolded man, a man who pretended to adore his wife only for the prosperous company she'd inherited? Was his father, after all, no better than the earl himself? He hated to think so.

When Matthew died five years ago, the doctors said he'd succumbed to heart disease. More like a broken heart, Ian decided. Because of his father's experience, Ian vowed never to fall in love and appear foolish, never to become the discarded object of a woman's whimsy. Never. If anyone would do the discarding, it would be him. He rubbed his chin in thought. He'd do anything to cause the earl as much humiliation as Matthew suffered, to make up for Molly's pain. Growing up without a mother wasn't easy for his sister. Lady Bethlyn Talbot had the privilege of a mother's love these last years, his own mother's love to be exact—something which had been denied him and his sister.

Earlier, he'd hinted to Eversley and Marcus at a way to make the earl appear foolish, not certain at this time how he intended to cause such discomfort. However, as he raced through verdant pastureland towards home a plan formed in his mind.

What better way to wreak vengeance on the hateful man than through his own daughter? He knew he must marry the girl to keep his company. In truth he didn't want to hurt her, but the years of pain had taken their toll upon him, hardening his heart until all he thought of at that moment was the joy he'd receive to see the earl's shocked and surprised face on the day of the wedding ceremony.

A dry, coarse laugh reverberated across the countryside, and Ian realized the sound had come from himself. He'd do what had to be done to assuage his own pain, his sister's, and the betrayal of his father by his unfaithful mother.

His future depended upon it.

Chapter Two

"He's here, milady, and waiting in the chapel for you. I didn't get a good look at him, but I'll tell you that he's taller than an oak."

Tessie Edmonds, housekeeper at Woodsley, bustled around the opulently appointed bedchambers, known as the Queen of Scot's Bedroom because once Mary Queen of Scots had stayed the night in the very bed on which Bethlyn now was seated. The large testered bed rose nearly to the ceiling, and the half-dome at the top was patterned in the same print as the rose, green, and white draperies which surrounded the bed and hung on the two windows. The room was quite feminine and fit for a bride. At that moment, Bethlyn felt less than feminine as she sat in a violet silk gown, trimmed in blue velvet bows at the elbow-length sleeves and the border of the full skirt. She felt ill, unbearably sick to her stomach.

With a face the shade of pea green, she glanced up at Tessie and Mavis, who helped her into a pair of violet satin slippers. "I can't go through with it. I'm afraid I'll disgrace myself by becoming quite ill during the ceremony." She took a deep breath to still the nausea which roiled in her stomach like a simmering stewpot. "How could my father have done this to me? How?"

"Now, Bethlyn," Mavis spoke calmly, referring to her without benefit of title because the earl wasn't there to chastise his daughter for allowing a lowly lady's maid such familiarity. "Before we left Hallsands you were quite happy to be marrying. You've only got a case of wedding jitters. You'll be fine once the ceremony is over."

"Mavis is right," Tessie interjected. "All brides get scared. 'Tis a natural occurrence. By tomorrow, you'll be fit and chipper." She stroked Bethlyn's long hair, the sides held up by two ruby combs.

Bethlyn shook her head and held on to the bedpost for support. She felt weak suddenly. In fact, she'd felt slightly ill for the last two days, having little appetite for food. Her body ached, and right now a horrible pounding started at her temples and slithered to the top of her skull. She successfully swallowed down the sensation that she had to retch, grateful that little was in her stomach. The early November morning held a hint of frost in the air, and the large fireplace in the bedroom now crackled and sizzled, but Bethlyn felt chilly, unbearably cold, and wondered why Tessie's upper lip gleamed with perspiration.

"I don't know this man. I've never laid eyes upon him. Father expects me to marry him within minutes, to sail away to America. I . . . I can't."

Bethlyn's voice sounded low and weak, causing Mavis to glance at her curiously. She seemed to be going to ask her a question when a loud impatient tap was heard on the door. Tessie answered and the Earl of Dunsmoor stood in the doorway, his dark eyes trained on his daughter as she leaned against the bedpost. He frowned and dismissed the two women.

With hands folded behind his back, Nathaniel Talbot entered his daughter's room. At his appearance, Bethlyn stood on slightly unsteady feet. Her stomach turned over at the supreme look of annoyance he shot her. Through his displeasure she envisioned the handsome man he'd been years ago. However, a life of ease and indolence, coupled with much alcohol and rich food, now gave him a rather bloated appearance. His hair, which had once been raven black, gleamed brightly with silver strands.

Bethlyn recalled her last meeting with her father, which had taken place only two weeks ago in this very room. He'd surveyed her in much the same fashion then, too. In fact, she wondered if he donned a mask each time he saw

34

her. His facade always contained a hint of scorn, of disapproval, of a dislike he didn't bother to conceal. He'd inquired as to her health, and before she could even reply, he told her that a dressmaker had been engaged to outfit her in the most fashionable ladies' attire. He hoped all was to her liking, and then he disappeared. This was the first time she'd seen him since that afternoon, and more than anything she wished to please him, to make up for the fact that she felt ill, to somehow believe that if she put a smile on her face, he'd forget he hated her.

Before Bethlyn could utter a word, her father said, "You look ungodly wretched!"

The smile withered and died before it even appeared. "I'm sorry, Father. This is the best that could be done for me"

His eyes narrowed to slits. "Are you ill?"

He asked the question with such disdain that Bethlyn felt unable to admit to her own ill health. "No, sir. I am only nervous." Somehow she managed to smile, though his comment had wounded her deeply.

"The nervousness will pass. I want this wedding to be over with soon. Your bridegroom is eager to set sail for America. His ship leaves London this evening."

Bethlyn hadn't known this, and for a moment the room whirled. "I . . . I . . . I . . ."

"What is it? Don't stammer, girl. You remind me of your mother when you do."

She swallowed. "I won't, I mean, we won't spend the night here at Woodsley?"

"No."

Tears misted her eyes. She'd hoped to stay the night in this bed, to at least have some feeling of security when her bridegroom possessed her. In fact she didn't have a clear idea of what "possessed" meant, but Tessie had told her that would happen on her wedding night and she must endure her husband's possession. Bethlyn recalled that Mavis's cheeks had flared at the term, and she'd asked her if she knew what Tessie meant. Mavis said she had only a vague idea and conveyed to Bethlyn in more concrete language what Tessie had tried to tell her. Bethlyn had been shocked, not able to believe a man would do that to a woman. To her. However, after much thought on the subject, Bethlyn decided that if that's what it took to make a man love her, then she'd willingly allow her husband to possess her. However, now seeing the way her father's eyes raked her in distaste, she was more nervous that Ian Briston might see her in the same way and wouldn't wish to bed her at all.

"Is there a problem with the plan?" her father asked with a bit of challenge in his voice, almost as if he'd dangled a piece of bait at her and expected her to fight for it.

"No, sir." she mumbled. "That is fine."

Talbot sniffed the air. "Certainly you'd say that. You're quite like your mother." He breathed deeply. "Everyone is assembled in the drawing room, but I can't allow you to marry with your face that pitiful shade of green. I swear you look ill, but there's no delaying the ceremony now. Have that maid of yours cover your face with a veil, anything to dispel that tragic look. I'll wait by the stairs for you, and do hurry."

"Father . . ." she cried, wanting to cling to him though he hated her, to ask him to change his mind about the wedding, to do the impossible and love her.

"Yes."

So curt, so cold he looked that she said instead, "I never did express my sympathy to you over your wife's passing. I truly am sorry."

For just a brief moment, the guarded and disdainful expression melted. She detected a softness, almost as if he might give in to the human emotion of grief. He didn't. Nathaniel lifted his shoulders high and inclined his head.

"Thank you for your sympathies. Have your maid cover your face and come downstairs. I want the ceremony finished."

Bethlyn nodded dumbly as his broad shoulders filled the doorway and then he was gone. A sob rose in her throat and she forced it down, knowing that crying would grant her little relief from the burden of her father's disregard for her. Her dream of ever possessing her father's love truly died at that moment. She realized he'd never care for her, coming slowly to the knowledge that it wasn't she he disliked but the memory of her mother whenever he gazed upon her face.

A slight streak of rebellion rose within her. She glanced into the mirror and noticed that her eyes were a blazing amber. "I can't help that I'm my mother's child!" she shrieked and hurled a hairbrush at her own reflection.

The mirror cracked with the force. Bethlyn stood there, heaving her shoulders in outrage when Tessie and Mavis entered the room again. The two exchanged a wary glance as Bethlyn gestured to a lacework veil, resting on a delicately embroidered ottoman.

"Place the veil over my face!" she snapped at Mavis. "I want to get this ceremony over as quickly as possible. And when it is, I'll be glad never to return to this hateful house."

Tessie handed Bethlyn a small violet bouquet on her way out of the door. Bethlyn took a whiff of the lavender blossoms and felt her stomach turn over. I won't be ill, she resolved. Nothing will keep me from marrying Ian Briston and leaving here. Nothing.

Bethlyn had been long away from Woodsley and forgotten the largeness of the house. With her hand fastened on her father's arm, each step along the north corridor to the Painted Hallway and the open colonnade of the entrance hall caused her head to swim. Portraits of her ancestors blurred before her eyes, and the paintings of seventeenth-century masters like Rottenhamer and Berchem which her father had so carefully chosen were gazed at by unappreciative eyes. At one point as she descended the marble staircase, enclosed by gilted ironwork balustrades, she faltered and felt her father's fingers dig into her flesh, pulling her onward.

From the Painted Hall, they entered the Grotto, a small room with only one window to accentuate the splendor of the Diana Fountain in the center. The huntress's stone image was covered with swags of garland and her long, thin arms positioned a bow and arrow in place, an arrow which was pointed straight at Bethlyn's heart. Or so it seemed to her. But Bethlyn felt that the legendary huntress would do far less damage to her heart than the man who now dragged her into the chapel itself.

Once inside, she heard her father breathe a long sigh. Had he thought she'd balk at the last minute? she wondered. For a second she was tempted to do just that, to cause him untold annoyance for the years he'd ignored her. She didn't. Suddenly the urge to be free of him washed over her with new forcefulness. Her stomach and her head hurt, but she ignored the roiling nausea, the ungodly beating at the temples, and glanced around the room.

Of all the rooms in the house, the chapel had changed not at all. Lady Jessica's stamp was on the new furnishings, the draperies. Nothing of Bethlyn's mother's taste remained. However, in the chapel, Bethlyn could still look at the ceiling, painted with scenes from the Life of Christ, the picture by Verrio of Doubting Thomas which hung over the alabaster altar. A tall black marble column stood sentinel at each end of the room. Bethlyn smelled the strong odor of cedar which emanated from the wainscotted walls, elaborately carved in rows of grape motifs.

Seated on tall chairs of needlework seats were Thomas Eversley and some of the staff, Tessie among them, with Mavis sitting nearer the back. When Bethlyn and her father moved toward the altar, Thomas rose and managed a tight smile at her. It was when she moved past him that she saw her bridegroom.

He waited in front of a painting which represented the Marriage in Cana. As a child, this had been Bethlyn's favorite painting. She had sat for hours in the chapel to stare at the figure of Christ as he blessed the wine and the happy young couple, newly married, in the background. The painting had represented all her dreams of marrying and being loved.

Now, as her gaze settled through the lace of her veil on her bridegroom, she suppressed a shudder. The tall, well-formed man who took her hand from her father's wasn't the man of her dreams. No welcoming smile came from him. His face contained a coldness which not even her father's could match. His eyes—were they green or black?

38

At the moment she couldn't tell, because they showed no emotion. They were dull, as dull as the black clothes he wore, the nondescript white periwig on his head. He dressed as if he attended a funeral and not a wedding.

She hadn't known what sort of a man to expect, but Miss Grosvernor's words about "the boorish colonial" came back to her. The woman had been right, and she'd been too dense to admit the truth. Ian Briston was far from a prince on a white charger, come to rescue her from her father and bring her to the fairy-tale land of America across the sea. His hand felt cold, and she shivered, not missing the peculiar arch of his eyebrow as he settled her hand on his arm.

God! she found herself thinking. He's my last hope for happiness and I repulse him, too.

The marriage vows dimmed in her memory. At one point, she heard Briston's voice promising to cherish her, the next her own. Was she really trembling so? An awful chill seized her. In a daze she realized the ceremony had ended and she was being led to the back of the chapel by her new husband. A servant served everyone chilled wine in gold goblets. She watched Ian lift his cup to her in a toast and knew she was supposed to drink from her cup. But the smell of the wine, the taste of it, was too much for her stomach to bear. No sooner had she swallowed than it bolted on her.

Bethlyn made a choking sound and rushed on unsteady legs into the Grotto, clutching at her stomach. Perhaps she could make it to her room before she was sick. Maybe . . .

She fell to the floor, retching, and sobbing for the indignity.

"My God!" she heard her father's voice, coated with disgust. "Someone clean up this mess!"

"Yes, my lord." Mavis ran quickly past, followed by Tessie. Bethlyn knelt on the floor, her dress ruined, the floor spotted. No one made a move to help her. She was seemingly forgotten by all, watched like a freak at a village fair.

She realized that her veil hung limply across her head, having been thrown back by someone when she became

39

ill. Had it been her father? She glanced up, mortification showing in her face. No, not him. He watched her in repulsion. She felt a comforting arm on hers and found Ian Briston beside her. She truly wanted to die.

She sobbed weakly. "I'm . . . I'm . . . sorry. For . . . give me."

The chastisement she expected didn't come, not realizing that her father had been pushed aside and any other comments he'd have uttered had been sufficiently quelled by a sneer thrown his way from Briston. "Don't apologize, my dear. Can you put your arms around my neck? I'll carry you upstairs to your room. Would a servant lead the way?"

Before she knew it, Briston lifted her in his arms and followed a maid to her room. In due time she was laid across the bed and the veil removed from her face by Briston.

He smiled down at her. "I'm certain one of your maids can help you undress. You must rest now and regain your strength."

"I'm very seldom sick," she mouthed, feeling she must reassure him of her good health. Maybe he wouldn't want her if he thought she was sickly.

Tessie appeared then and immediately came to Bethlyn. "Oh, my lady, I knew you were too sick to marry today. Your pretty dress is ruined, too."

"Take extra special care of your charge," Briston said to Tessie and patted Bethlyn's hand. "I'll check on you later," he told Bethlyn.

"Thank you," Bethlyn said, feeling ill again and trying to pretend she felt better. "I look forward to recovering quickly and leaving Woodsley."

He didn't reply to that, just stared at her and smiled benevolently at her like she was a small child.

When he was gone, she said to Tessie, "I think he is a kind man. I will make him a good wife." Then she was sick again.

Ian leaned a black-satin-clad arm against the cool Italian marble mantelpiece in the Oak Drawing Room.

The rich brown carpet at his feet matched the heavy embroidered drapes on the windows, a direct contrast to the light-colored and unadorned furnishings in the room—the sort of no-nonsense furniture on which a man could stretch out, feel comfortable. With the orange-and-blue flames licking at the logs in the fireplace, the room exuded a warmth, an informality Ian found lacking in the museumlike Woodsley.

Swirling the rich Madeira in a wine goblet, he surveyed the bottom of the cup, seeing in the depths things which weren't apparent at first glance. Like this room. He didn't doubt his mother had furnished the Oak Room with the earl in mind. Probably she'd wanted a refuge for her husband, a place where they could be together in loving camaraderie. Somehow Ian couldn't imagine the earl sitting in loving camaraderie with anyone. Not Jessica. Most certainly not with the girl he claimed as his daughter.

The relationship between Talbot and Bethlyn bothered Ian a great deal. Clearly, the man resented her. Upon meeting the earl that morning, Talbot had made no effort to hide his eagerness to have her married and gone from Woodsley. At first Ian believed the man wanted only to marry off an unattractive daughter. Heaven knew the poor girl would have had an awful time finding a man if one hadn't been readily available for her, Ian decided. The memory of her face, deathly pale with red-rimmed eyes was clear in his mind. However, Ian sensed an undercurrent of something else when the earl became angered at the girl becoming ill.

Why did Talbot hate her so?

Shrugging his broad-shouldered frame, Ian glanced out of the long, Palladian-style window at the garden, bereft of blooms. In the distance he spotted a broad walk, flanked by rosebushes and sloping lawns. From his vantage point could be seen the tumbling waters of a cascade and, beyond, a heavily wooded hillside reached skyward. An orangerie and a summerhouse dotted the landscape. Ian couldn't help but be impressed by the beauty and immense size of Woodsley. For all its grandeur, however, he found the place lacking in warmth, in caring. Was that why he detected an eagerness to be gone from here in the voice of the girl he'd just married? Did she realize to what extent her father disliked her? Of course, she must, Ian found himself thinking. Just because the girl was homely didn't make her stupid.

A wave of pity for Bethlyn Talbot, or Bethlyn Briston as she was now known, washed over him. He didn't want to feel anything for the girl. He'd arrived at Woodsley with every intention of marrying her, of turning on his heels and leaving, minus the bride. An ache to see the well-controlled demeanor of the earl crumble with the knowledge that he'd been royally cuckolded by the son of the man whose wife he'd stolen filled him like a poison. During the sea voyage with Eversley that was all he thought about. He'd intended to leave his bride as soon as the marriage ceremony was over, but the girl had fallen ill and spoiled it all for him.

He couldn't forget her pitiful young face, feeling such compassion for her, an emotion he never expected to feel for Talbot's daughter. The sight of her being wretchedly sick before him, her father, the whole household, must have been quite humiliating for her. Yet, she'd been rather dignified about the whole thing. At least she hadn't broken free with a gale of sobs. She'd cried softly to herself, but he could accept that. One thing Ian hated was an hysterical female. Somehow he knew that Bethlyn Talbot very seldom gave vent to her emotions, that she kept herself in check out of self-preservation. Living with a man like Nathaniel Talbot she would be forced to not show weakness. She was so young, so very young.

He shook himself, deciding he was veering from his reason for being here. He mustn't allow the girl to get to him. Guiltily he realized that her future rested in his hands now, and he had no clear idea what he should do beyond following his plan to leave Woodsley and never look back. Briston Shipping, in part, legally belonged to him now. He'd followed the terms of his mother's will and married Lady Bethlyn. No one could deny he'd honored his mother's request. But he didn't want a wife, Bethlyn

Talbot or any woman who'd cling to him, to be dependent upon him for her happiness. The fact of the matter was that he felt unable to love and couldn't set himself up as his father, a man betrayed by the wife he adored.

As Ian poured another helping of wine, Talbot and Eversley entered the room. Eversley stood respectfully at a distance, playing the faithful solicitor to the hilt. Ian wanted to laugh at the man, suspecting that Eversley would knife the earl in the back if the man ever caught on to his pilfering. However, Ian didn't care if Eversley stole from the earl's accounts, as long as he never attempted to steal from Ian's coffers. It was agreed that Briston Shipping would be run like two separate companies, under one name. As long as the British end was run adequately well, Ian didn't worry about Thomas Eversley. In fact, if the crafty Thomas could steal funds from under the earl's nose, Ian wished him luck.

Talbot crossed the room to stand beside Ian. He inclined his head. "A physician has examined your wife. He finds she has caught a malady, peculiar to the servants of late. He feels that within a week she'll be well and able to travel. I trust you'll be comfortable at Woodsley until then."

Ian placed the wine goblet on the mantel and squarely faced his father-in-law. "Thank you for your hospitality. However, I shall be forced to decline."

"I don't understand."

The moment for which Ian had waited was now at hand. His palms perspired with anticipation. He spoke calmly, without emotion, like the earl. "Quite simple. I leave immediately for London to sail home. I've a shipping company to maintain, as you well know. The company was the reason for this unfortunate union between our families."

"You can't leave, man," Eversley broke into the conversation. "The will stated . . ."

"Only that I marry the earl's daughter, which I have dutifully done," Ian spoke sharply to Eversley. "No one can fault me. I lived up to the terms of my mother's will."

Nathaniel's mouth quirked into a scowl. "If you think to pawn the girl off on me after you've made her your wife . . . well, I won't allow it."

"She is your daughter, sir. A fact I think you have conveniently overlooked many times in the past. How can you stand there and see your only child bartered and practically sold to me as a wife? She is barely out of the nursery and not ready for the intimacies of marriage."

"What difference does age make?" Thomas asked. "The girl simply lies there and does her duty by you."

Ian turned on Thomas, a fire in his eyes which belied the calmness of his voice. "You're a crass fellow for all your polished manners, Thomas. She is a human being, not some commodity to be bought and sold. The girl is abed with an illness. How do you expect me to take her to wife now?" His piercing gaze moved towards the Earl. "I wonder, Your Grace, if you have purposely saddled me with an ailing wife."

Nathaniel Talbot surprised Ian then by laughing a deep hearty laugh, his eyes holding a hint of respect for Ian. "I assure you that my daughter will recover in due time. It appears I underestimated Jessica's son."

"It would seem so," Ian said stiffly.

"You've bested me, son. I didn't think you had it in you."

"I'm not *your* son." Ian's voice contained contempt, something which brought the earl up sharply. The man's amusement disappeared.

Ian grabbed for his cloak, eager to be gone from here and to put the whole sordid mess from his mind when Thomas blocked the doorway.

"What about the girl? Some sort of an arrangement for her welfare must be made. As the earl's solicitor, I insist upon it."

Ian glared at Thomas with burning reproachful eyes. There was nothing in Thomas's bearing to cause him to dislike him. Actually, Thomas was well groomed, handsome, and finely dressed for a forty-year-old solicitor. Ian realized money was Thomas's weakness, though the man made a vain attempt to hide it. He couldn't shake the feeling that Thomas would love to see him falter, that perhaps he begrudged him his inherited company while

Thomas had been forced to struggle through years of poverty to become a solicitor. Perhaps even the arranged marriage gnawed at Thomas. Might not a man with high aspirations, a man who loved the feel of gold in his palms, have harbored the desire to marry Talbot's daughter if he'd been rich enough?

The thought flashed through Ian's mind that with Thomas and her father constantly beside her, Bethlyn might need some protection. Until that moment he hadn't known what to do about his bride. The whole ordeal had left him numb. The reaction he'd expected from Talbot about leaving her here wasn't the one he'd gotten, and now he felt responsible for the girl's welfare. His plan for revenge had turned sour and he didn't feel the exhilaration he'd expected.

"Would you like Lady Bethlyn to stay at Woodsley, Thomas?" Ian asked with dispassion.

Thomas was actually salivating. Ian supposed he was thinking about all the money Bethlyn might bestow upon him for legal advice, at empty business ventures in which he'd come away the richer. But being a dutiful solicitor and careful with his words, Thomas cast an eye at the earl, who shook his head in disgust.

"Wherever the lady shall be the happiest is my wish, sir."

"Well spoken!" Ian laughed heartily and slapped Thomas on the back. "When I arrive in London later this afternoon I'll pay a call on my great-aunt Penny." He turned towards Talbot. "You remember her, Your Grace. She is my mother's aunt on her father's side. Mother visited her that time she came to London, the time she met you."

"I remember," Talbot said blandly.

"I've heard through mutual relatives that she is quite lonely in her London townhouse. I believe Bethlyn would brighten her life up a bit if she went to live with Aunt Penny. Of course, I'd dispense a large yearly sum to keep my wife in the style to which she is accustomed. She can take any servants she wishes. I'll incur all her expenses, of course. This agreement is satisfactory with you," Ian said.

Talbot bowed stiffly, but his face barely suppressed his shock, his anger. Ian had finally gotten a rise out of the older man and he'd cherish the memory of it to his dying day. "Another thing," Ian continued. "Both of you must understand that Bethlyn's household is her own. Aunt Penny is there to see to her safety and never doubt that the old woman is quite right in the head and takes no lip service from anyone. At least, that's what I've heard about her. Whatever my wife wants to do is her business. Neither one of you will have a say in her private matters. Have I made myself clear, gentlemen?"

"Certainly," Talbot mumbled, and Thomas nodded, opening the door for Ian.

"See that my wife's things are moved to my aunt's home as soon as is feasible, Thomas. And, please Your Grace, explain to her that I was called suddenly away and wish only for her good health. I shall write her from London and explain the situation as soon as I see Aunt Penny." He bowed and unceremoniously left the room. As Ian climbed into the earl's coach moments later for the journey to London, he knew he left behind two angry men . . . and a young, untried girl who was his wife. But he'd seen to her future and that was something he'd never expected to do.

Under the circumstances, this was the best he could offer her.

Three weeks later the sun shone upon the countryside, dispelling the frost which had fallen during the night. Inside Woodsley the frost of abandonment settled in Bethlyn's heart, hardening it into a rock of ice. In her hand she clutched her husband's letter to her, knowing the contents by heart, having read it one hundred times over the last weeks. In it, he explained the arrangements he'd made with his aunt Penelope Evans and hoped that all would be satisfactory. The last line of the letter requested she understand his decision and not think ill of him, that both of them were aware their marriage was a business arrangement, not a love match. He assured her she'd be well provided for and would never want for anything in

46

her life.

"Except for love," Bethlyn whispered fiercely and thrust the letter into the bedroom fireplace, taking a perverted delight in watching the paper burn.

Mavis glanced up from the bag she packed. "You said something, Bethlyn?"

Bethlyn shook her head and smoothed down her wool traveling skirt and turned away from the fireplace. "I can't wait to be gone from here."

"I feel London will be better for you. Your father won't be there."

"True. At least my marriage has freed me from him. I'm independently wealthy, Mavis. In London I'll possess money and clothes and can have anything my heart desires. However, I'll have no husband, no children to love. In effect, my husband has freed me from one prison to place me in another. All I ever wanted was a family, and it seems that he has unknowingly denied me that wish." She stopped short, feeling a lump form in her throat, but she wouldn't cry. The man had deserted her and wasn't worth her tears.

Within the hour, Mavis waited in the carriage for her while Bethlyn parted from her father. "Your husband has more than adequately provided for you. I demand that you wipe that tragic expression from your face and realize how fortunate you are that he thought of your welfare at all," he stated.

They stood in the entrance hall, her father towering over her. Displeasure shone on his face. His words wounded her, and normally she'd have bowed her head and immediately obeyed. This morning and the last few weeks of her life were far from normal circumstances, though. She'd been wedded and deserted, sent a pithy letter from her bridegroom assuring her that he'd seen to her future, and now her father still felt he could dictate to her, that he could tell her how she should look and feel. The pain of the entire situation took its toll upon her.

With a suddenness which surprised even herself, Bethlyn reared up, and with a controlled but deadly calm, evident in her voice, she faced him squarely. "You can no longer tell me how to keep my countenance, how to feel, or what to do, Your Grace. You abandoned me long before Ian Briston did, and for that I shall never forgive you."

"Why you ungrateful, little—"

Bethlyn continued heedlessly on, not caring any longer. She must go on, as if her father never spoke, as if the anger in the depths of his eyes pushed her to continue. "I've nothing for which to be grateful, sir. You pushed me out of your life, never took an interest in me. I shall never forget your cruelties to me or to my mother. All these years you've expressed your disinterest, dislike, in me. Well, Father, consider that I may feel the same about you."

Talbot grabbed her arm, hurting her with his strength, but Bethlyn didn't show her pain. She was too angry. He bent down, and she caught the trace of whiskey on his breath. "No wonder your husband left you. You'll always be a homely, ordinary little girl. Any man with sense would desert you."

"As you did my mother." She twisted away from him. The thought of the new life which awaited her in London caused her to grow bolder instead of cowering beneath his black, unyielding gaze. In that moment she changed from a shy, obedient child into a willful young woman. "Well, I'm not my mother and will no longer run and hide when you're displeased. You seem to forget that the man I married has truly freed me from your tyranny. I can come and go as I please, do whatever I want with whomever I please. You no longer have a say in my life. For this freedom, I'd gladly be abandoned by Ian Briston again and again. You urged the marriage, because Jessica wanted it. Never forget that, but realize that because of it, I'm my own person. You have no one left to bully now, Father. For the first time in your life, you're very much alone."

Wrenching free her arm, she hurried outside and down the long row of stone steps to the waiting carriage. Instantly the driver urged the horses along, and she didn't take an extra look at the brick-and-flint exterior of Woodsley, didn't notice that her father had come outside and stood on the bottom step, watching after the carriage with arm upraised as if he'd tried to halt the carriage, or see

48

him thrust his hands into his pockets and lower his head in abject misery.

It was just as well that Bethlyn didn't see any of this. Most probably she'd have sobbed and ordered the driver to turn around, eager to know if her father would have embraced her. As it was, she sat stiffly against the leather-and-velvet upholstered cushions, her face a mask of indifference. Mavis sat beside her, having no idea of the scene in the Entrance Hall, not realizing that Bethlyn's face hid a deep pain which welled within her breast.

For Bethlyn, the agony of the final parting with her father tore her in shreds. Somehow, she knew she'd never see him again, and she decided this was just as well. She couldn't stand any more pain from that quarter.

However, a bitterness rose within her for Ian Briston. It seemed that all her pent-up frustration about her father was transferred to him. For his desertion of her, she vowed to make him sorry. Never mind that he'd given her her freedom and money to do as she pleased. None of that meant anything to her since he'd destroyed her dream of ever having a family life. Briston must think he was well rid of her, that she'd never bother him again. He was wrong there.

Turning towards Mavis, she smiled a secretive smile, a suddenly mischievous light coming into her eyes.

"I'm going to make him sorry, make him rue the day he married me and abandoned me. Before I'm finished, he'll be on bended knee, begging me to sail to America."

Chapter Three

"Wild, sir, I tell you the girl is wild. I can't do a thing with her. Between Lady Bethlyn and my grandson, Sir Jeremy Smithers, I'm at my wit's end. I am quite fond of Bethlyn. It's hard not to love someone so sweet and beautiful. And I don't forget how very good she has been to me. Without her, I'd be lost. I tell you I would. She brightens a room just by entering it. But do you think the earl might intervene and speak to his daughter about her unladylike behavior? I'd mark it as a great favor to me.''

Thomas Eversley sipped at his tea, wishing it were laced with something stronger. Seated across from him in a black wrought-iron chair, liberally cushioned with Oriental pillows, was Lady Penelope Evans. A becoming white shawl was thrown over her ample bosom, and the sunlight streaming in through the windows of the garden room highlighted the silver strands of her hair. For a woman past eighty, Penelope Evans was a marvel with her ready wit and quick mind. Eversley had made her acquaintance twice within the last six years. The first time was the day he'd arrived to check on Bethlyn for the earl, to make certain she'd arrived at the St. James's townhouse safely, and now today, because Lady Penelope had sent word to Briston Shipping that she wished to speak to him.

From her comments about Lady Bethlyn, Eversley wondered if he should have kept a closer eye on the girl. Over the last years he'd heard things about her through the London grapevine, the gossip mill. He didn't travel in the same aristocratic circles as an earl's daughter, but he'd been adequately kept up to date about her first ball, the countless rounds of parties—news which surprised Thomas because he'd assumed the chit would rather be cloistered inside with an old woman for company than hobnob with the ton. He'd read about Lady Bethlyn's startling beauty and discounted the reports as a kindness. Now, however, he was intrigued. Could the girl really have blossomed into a beauty?

Placing the fragile china cup on the small wrought-iron table before him, he gently shook his head at the old woman. "I doubt if the earl would care to speak to his daughter, my lady. They haven't spoken since she left Woodsley."

Penelope sighed, her bosom heaving with the effort. "A pity. I had hoped the two of them would work out their differences. I thought the earl would hasten to advise Bethlyn, because I do so hate to have to write to her husband again and inform him about her behavior."

"You've written to Briston about his wife?" Thomas asked with interest. "What does he have to say?"

"He never writes to me, and I'm perturbed at the man. All correspondence is handled through his secretary, and Mr. Gibbons is the one who answers me. Bethlyn is his wife and he takes no interest in her. I thought Jessica brought him up to be more responsible, but I suppose I can't expect miracles, considering his father was a colonial merchant and the boy was raised in the wilds. Have you had correspondence with him?"

"Not directly. We correspond through our secretaries. I haven't seen Briston since he left Woodsley six years ago, on the day of the wedding ceremony." Thomas momentarily glanced out of the window which faced St. James's Park, then back at Penelope. "Just what escapade has Lady Bethlyn been involved in now, my lady?"

"Hmmph! Quite scandalous!" Penelope pulled the shawl closer to her, her eyes growing bright and holding a hint of amusement, though her tone sounded convincingly shocked. "Bethlyn and Jeremy invaded one of the most exclusive men's clubs in London to partake in a game of

51

faro. She dressed in Jeremy's clothes and pretended to be a young gentleman friend of his. It wasn't until they were ready to leave that she pulled off the periwig and waved it in the air like a flag for all to see. Needless to say, everyone was horrified, and I had to smooth things over by contacting an old friend of my late husband's not to cause a scandal. The very idea of a delicately bred young woman being in such a place is terrible to my way of thinking and—"

"You know you'd have done it yourself if you could have gotten away with it, Aunt Penny" came a feminine voice from the doorway.

Thomas and Penelope both turned to see Bethlyn enter the garden room, arm and arm with Jeremy Smithers. Thomas rose, his eyes resting momentarily on the rather plain-looking young man in riding clothes, quickly noting his affable smile. His gaze, however, lingered on the young woman, a young woman with the thickest, honey-brown hair he'd ever seen, whose beautiful heart-shaped face was illumined by eyes so liquid and brown he felt himself unable to stop staring. Was this vision in a green velvet and lace riding suit which emphasized every lush curve of her body really the homely little girl who'd left Woodsley six years ago? He found it hard to believe, but when she extended a hand and said, "Good morning, Mr. Eversley," he knew it was.

With a heart speeded up, and his palms beginning to sweat, he took her hand and kissed it. Somehow he managed not to stare like an idiot at her as he asked her how she fared.

"Quite well." Her eyes contained a teasing light. "However if you listen to Aunt Penny, you'd swear I was going to the devil, and Jeremy along with me." She squeezed Jeremy's arm affectionately.

Thomas cocked an eyebrow, wondering if there was something more to this relationship between Bethlyn and young Smithers other than friendship. He'd make a dutiful report to the earl about his daughter because he felt he must, but he felt a bit of surprise at the stab of jealousy coursing through him at the thought that Bethlyn Briston might be Smithers's mistress. Of course, she was married, but the marriage was in name only. If Briston was fool enough not to care about his wife, Thomas wasn't. This exquisite creature who casually lounged on the settee and picked up a large Persian cat to fondle filled Thomas with lust. And he hadn't felt lust in some time. How propitious for him that his wife had died just six months ago. Maybe, just maybe if he could convince Lady Bethlyn of his worth, he might be able to coerce her into his bed. Just to think such a thought caused him to harden instantly and he retook his seat and placed a napkin over the bulge so no one would notice.

"Our ride this morning was quite invigorating," Jeremy said and kissed Penelope on the forehead. "You really should have Winston bring round the carriage. The days now are quite lovely and warm."

"Posh! I'm an old lady and take delight sitting in my garden. I don't need a jostling carriage ride through the streets of London for amusement. I get enough of that from you two scamps to last me a lifetime."

Bethlyn's mischievous giggle drifted towards them. "You know you love us, Aunt Penny."

The old woman smiled warmly. "I admit it. I do."

Thomas glanced at his watch fob and rose from the chair. "I have to get back to the office. Thank you so much for the tea, Lady Penelope."

Penelope extended a hand for Thomas to kiss. "My pleasure, sir. Bethlyn, see Mr. Eversley to the door."

Moments later, Bethlyn stood by the front door with Thomas. "Has Aunt Penny filled your head with my latest escapade?"

"She has."

"Dear Auntie. She worries so about me." Bethlyn bit at her lower lip. "How is my father?"

"Not well, my lady. He suffers from the cold quite a bit, and stays locked in his room mostly. His health is failing, and I fear that soon . . ."

"He shall die," Bethlyn finished.

"Would you care?"

"I don't know." For a second she lowered her head, and

when she raised it, Thomas noticed an anger in her eyes. "How is my husband?"

"I can't say," Thomas truthfully admitted, finding himself swaying nearer to her, quelling the insane desire to kiss her full, sensual mouth. He coughed. "We don't correspond directly."

"I trust he has heard of my escapades. Aunt Penny, I believe, writes him quite often about me and no doubt begs him to do the right thing by me and take me to wife. But the bounder has never replied to any of her letters. I wonder if he'd reply to me."

"I'm certain he would, my lady. You are his wife."

"I'm not," Bethlyn replied with a hiss in her voice. "And I need your help to rectify a mistake which my father and stepmother made six years ago."

Thomas's blood turned cold, then warmed, instantly realizing the import of her words. "I shall do anything I can, my lady." And he would.

Rearing back on her booted heels, Bethlyn shot him a devastatingly lovely smile. "I wish you to write to my husband in my name and demand that he either agree to have this marriage annulled or live up to becoming my husband in all ways. Every way," she emphasized. "I want children, and without a husband I refuse to bear them in disgrace. He must release me so that I can marry again, and hang any scandal this action may incur. I want my freedom, sir, or I want to be a wife. He must make up his mind. If not, please assure him that my scandalous behavior so far will seem as child's play compared to what I can and will do in the future." Holding out her hand, Thomas took it. "I trust you'll see to this matter immediately."

"I will, my lady."

Without further adieu, Bethlyn turned away, and like a flash of green was up the stairs, disappearing from his sight.

Five months passed. As each autumn day lengthened, Bethlyn waited for word from her husband. Would he fulfill his marital duties by her, or would he opt for an annulment? Bethlyn didn't care either way. She only wanted to end her Limbo-like existence and continue with her life. Perhaps find a man she could love and who'd love her, and hang Ian Briston!

The night of Lord and Lady Stanhope's annual ball had arrived, and Bethlyn found she didn't wish to go. The whirl of parties, soirées, and teas no longer filled her with pleasure. She found the people to be shallow, frittering away their time. Her only consolation was Jeremy, who'd have adored her no matter her looks. The dutiful Jeremy would soon arrive to escort her, to keep the wolves at bay, so to speak. A sad smile played around the edges of Bethlyn's lips as she surveyed her reflection in the gold frame looking glass, decorated with scarlet églomise panels. Dear Jeremy truly believed she needed his protection, and she allowed him to think so, but her anger towards Briston had toughened her. For all the pranks they'd played together, for all the many men who had whispered fervent words of love in her ear, only to be cast aside by her like last year's gown, Bethlyn found no real happiness.

At any time she supposed she could seriously consider bedding one of the men who sought her favor. Everyone knew she was married, but the marriage was more or less ignored by the men who wished to court her, to win a night of love with her. She, however, took her marriage vows quite seriously though no one would have guessed it. Granted, she purposely acted the coquette when it suited her needs, behaved outrageously, and forced dear Aunt Penny to write letters of complaint to Ian Briston, complaints which pleased Bethlyn immensely. She'd hoped that the man would be so riled by her behavior that he'd come for her, beg her to be his wife, or be so scandalized he'd free her from the marriage. None of this happened. He still must view her as the homely child who was wretchedly sick on her wedding day. No doubt Penny had enlightened him that she was now the rage of London, touted as a great beauty—something which had surprised Bethlyn as well as everyone else who'd seen her when she first came to live with Penelope. It was after she'd arrived in London, eager to do her best by behaving scandously, that she took more of an interest in her appearance with Mavis's help and stopped eating so many sweetmeats. Somehow nature lent her a helping hand and smiled kindly upon her in the guise of Jeremy, Penelope's grandson. They rode together every day in St. James's Park, and within six months the plump, homely girl was gone and a beautiful young woman emerged. Briston, the oaf, didn't even have the good sense to answer Aunt Penny's letters. To wonder or care at how much his wife spent on clothes and frivolities. All the bills were paid by the man's secretary, and on each of Bethlyn's birthdays and wedding anniversaries, she received a lovely gift, no doubt sent by the secretary. Briston's silence spoke more eloquently than hundreds of letters. The man hoped to forget she ever existed, that he'd married and deserted her, and he expected that she'd be content to remain in such a stupid and silly arrangement.

"I won't be ignored!" Bethlyn cried, startling Mavis, who entered the room carrying a rose silk gown over her arm. "The horrid man won't ignore me any longer. I'll force him to take note of me."

"Mr. Eversley may hear from your husband within a few days. Please don't do anything rash, Bethlyn. Forget about the man and dress for the ball. Sir Jeremy is in the drawing room with your aunt and ready to leave." Mavis's face had turned white with apprehension that Bethlyn would soon engage in another foolhardy escapade to gain the attention of her absent husband.

Bethlyn threw down a ruby necklace, one of her anniversary presents, like it was a piece of rubbish. "Look at this!" she cried and turned from her dressing table in a huff, the blue satin of her robe swishing in her wake. "Another one of 'my husband's gifts' to me, but where is the wretched man? This trinket can't keep me warm on cold nights or give me the children I long for. He bought me and placed me on a shelf, having found no use for me. I've done practically everything but parade in the buff along the Thames. If I thought that would gain my husband's attentions, I'd gladly disrobe. But I must finally admit that Ian Briston has denied my existence. Well, not any longer, Mavis, do you hear! Not a moment longer."

With her mind made up on that score, Bethlyn rushed from the room and down the white oak staircase and into the drawing room, very much aware of Penny's shocked intake of breath and Jeremy's gale of amused laughter at her state of dishabille.

"Young lady, you're disgraceful!" Penelope rebuked. "Hurry upstairs and dress. Jeremy doesn't wish to see you like this."

"I do, Grandmama," Jeremy said. "I'd wager that I'm the only gentleman in London to see Bethlyn in her robe, and damn if I don't like it!" A suspicious gleam danced in his eyes and he tapped Penelope on the shoulder. "She's up to something."

"Oh, no!" proclaimed Penelope. "What now? I do so dread having to write my nephew another letter."

"Rest assured that this time I shall spare you your letter-writing chore, Aunt Penny," Bethlyn spoke and managed a tight smile. "Since my husband has shown an appalling lack of good manners by ignoring your letters and the letter from Thomas Eversley, I find I have no other choice but to sail to the Colonies and face the man in person. Before this year is over, I shall discover if I'm to be his true wife. The time has arrived for a face-to-face confrontation."

Penelope placed a frail hand on her heart. "Don't do this, child. Accept things for what they are. I fear you'll regret this trip. What if he doesn't want you?"

Bethlyn lifted a silk clad shoulder in a shrug. "I shall order him to release me from the marriage. I believe that when he realizes my situation, he'll agree to an annulment because I'll specify that he can keep control of his company. Fear of losing it might be the reason he hasn't answered any letters. He loves Briston Shipping more than any woman, I think. He married me to retain it. And I feel he is a kind man, considering." Bethlyn was remembering how solicitous he'd been when she became ill, that he was the only one to help her. Still, that one kindness didn't make up for years of neglect.

"You'd do well to consider this some more," Jeremy advised her. "With the American privateers preying on English ships, you might find yourself in a great deal of danger." His caution surprised her. Usually they agreed on everything, and Jeremy could always be counted upon not to put a damper on her plans. How could he not see she was desperate? She'd told him often enough of her desire for a real home, a husband and children, that she wasn't growing any younger. She thought he'd understand.

"I agree." Penelope nodded sagely.

"Well, I don't! I've wasted six years of my life, years when I could have been a wife, a mother. Does the man think he can deny me children? Must I bed someone else and pass the children off as his? Do you think he'd accept them and support them? I sincerely doubt he'd be amenable to such folly." Bethlyn's face flushed, and she turned her impassioned gaze upon Jeremy. "I thought you were my friend. Whether I have your support or not in this makes no difference to me. I am going to the Colonies."

Two hours later Bethlyn and Jeremy danced in the mirrored ballroom, supped with the Stanhopes and the other guests, and she listened to a litany of reasons from Jeremy why she shouldn't make the trip. However, her mind was made up that her future must be settled in a direct confrontation with her husband. "I'm going," she said over and over.

By the time the ball had ended she'd danced with every eligible, handsome man in the room, and some who weren't so eligible or so handsome, fended off at least ten indecent proposals, and convinced Jeremy that if he was worried about her, he should come with her. "You can act as my bodyguard and protect me from those nasty American pirates," she playfully teased him.

"I'll come with you," Jeremy said, and kissed her cheek in a brotherly fashion. "But I don't want to be gone for too long. You know I can't refuse you anything, Bethlyn, but I'm getting older, too, and I think it's time I settled down a bit and looked around for a wife."

"Ah, I knew it! I saw you watching Lady Madeline

Stanhope all evening. She'll make you a perfect wife. I promise you, Jeremy, that we'll be home before the spring. But if you don't wish to go, I'll understand."

"I'm going with you. If anything happened to you, I'd never be able to forgive myself. Since your husband doesn't feel the need to protect you, I will, until he either takes you to wife or annuls the marriage and you find a man worthy of you."

Bethlyn couldn't stop the tears which welled within her eyes. Jeremy was such a dear, sweet man. She'd known him for so long, trusted him, depended upon him, but there was nothing but a deep and abiding friendship between them. Sometimes she thought that if things had been different, they'd have made a perfectly good marriage. However, that would never come to be and she knew now that Jeremy's sights, as well they should be, were centered on Madeline Stanhope. There was no hope for herself as long as Ian Briston kept her trapped in this marriage. She wasn't free to love anyone, not even her own husband.

"I should like to sail as soon as possible," she told Jeremy. "Please contact Thomas Eversley for me. We can sail on one of my father's ships." She smiled ruefully. "One of my ships actually, one of my husband's, since all of them are owned by Briston Shipping."

When she climbed into bed later that night, no thoughts of revenge against Ian Briston filled her mind. She felt that soon everything would be settled one way or another. Soon after she closed her eyes, she fell asleep, not dreaming that all would be decided, but in a way she hadn't fathomed.

Chapter Four

"My lady, please reconsider, Mr. Eversley will be quite displeased. He specifically ordered that you and Sir Jeremy Smithers travel to the Colonies on *Venture* not *Nightingale*. I can't insist, of course, but no one goes against an order of Thomas Eversley." Harold Dempster wiped his perspiring brow with a fine linen kerchief and threw an imploring glance in Jeremy's direction, having already decided that Bethlyn wasn't about to be pacified by such an unusual request. Dempster had been in the employ of Briston Shipping as Thomas's secretary long enough to recognize a stubborn streak a mile away. From the forward thrust of her chin and the nail-hard line of her mouth, Dempster quickly ascertained that he'd lost the battle. And probably his position as well, once Thomas Eversley returned from Woodsley to discover that this stubborn chit of a girl had sailed on *Nightingale* instead of *Venture*. If only young Smithers could dissuade her.

Jeremy, however, appeared to be taking a devilish delight in the war of wills between Bethlyn and Dempster. He offered not a word to persuade her to heed reason and sail on *Venture*. Standing with his arms folded across his frock-coated chest, he leaned against the back of a large, cushioned chair upon which Bethlyn was seated. An amused grin which turned up the corners of his mouth grew larger the more Dempster perspired. But a warning bell went off in Jeremy's head as he realized that something wasn't right about this situation, but he couldn't decide what the problem might be and doubted he'd get a straight answer from Dempster.

Instead of speaking, he remained silent and allowed Bethlyn to have her head. He found he loved watching when Bethlyn was riled. No one possessed more blazing brown eyes than she or had the endearing habit of tilting her head to the side like an inquisitive puppy. To see her rear herself upward, as she did now, her back arching in a suggestive but unwitting way always provoked a naughty laugh from him. She turned and glanced at him for a moment, quelling any further sound with that dazzling and fiery gaze.

"I see no difference as to which ship I choose, Mr. Dempster. I'm certain Thomas had my best interests in mind when he chose *Venture*, but I am eager to sail on the evening tide. The problem with *Venture*'s hull isn't my concern at the moment. Repair it. As I understand, *Nightingale* is set to sail today. Sir Jeremy and I shall be on that ship, sir." Bethlyn's voice was low and steady, but the curtness of her tone left no doubt that she had already made up her mind. No one would dissuade her.

"Your ladyship, allow me to send to Woodsley for Mr. Eversley. I'm certain when he explains the situation to you, you'll be quite amenable to waiting an extra week while *Venture* is repaired. *Nightingale* hasn't the niceties of *Venture*, and for such a lady as yourself . . ."

Bethlyn raised a hand, halting Dempster's further prattle. "Mr. Dempster, I'm not a hothouse flower, I assure you. I shall be pleased with whatever accommodations the *Nightingale*'s captain can make for me." She rose from her seat and, extending her hand to Dempster, she waited while he resignedly took it and placed an obligatory kiss upon it.

Dempster heaved a huge sigh. "As you wish, my lady. I'll speak to Captain Montgomery myself."

Bethlyn nodded her thanks and, taking Jeremy's arm, they left the offices of Briston Shipping.

Ensconced upon velvet cushions in Penelope's cabriolet, Bethlyn noticed Jeremy appeared uneasy. "I did the right thing, Jeremy," she spoke in a rush before he could say anything. "Thomas Eversley is not about to tell me on which ship I may travel. After all, I own Briston Shipping. Thomas Eversley and Harold Dempster are in my employ."

"No doubt Dempster is already penning an urgent message to Woodsley, beseeching Eversley to return to London," Jeremy stated.

"Let him!"

Her quick retort startled Jeremy. Immediately she offered an apology. "Forgive me, dear Jeremy. I'd be lost these past years if not for you. I fear I must learn to control my temper and not allow my nerves to get the best of me. It isn't every day that I sail to America to discover if my 'husband' has a use for his wife."

A ready smile from Jeremy told her that he'd forgiven her. "Grandmama will miss you, as will I."

Touching Jeremy's cheek with her lips, Bethlyn felt on the verge of tears. "I know you want the best for me."

His voice cracked a bit when he spoke. "I hope all works out well for you, Bethlyn. That confounded colonial better learn soon what a treasure you are, otherwise, I might be forced to prove your worth at the point of the rapier!"

"Goodness, Jeremy! I do hope Madeline Stanhope knows what a tiger you are."

"She does," he admitted, and had the good grace to blush.

Later that day, after a teary and warm farewell to Penelope, Bethlyn, Jeremy, and Mavis boarded *Nightingale*. The huge ship sat in London's harbor while the crew mopped the deck and readied the rigging for the evening sail. Harold Dempster personally escorted them aboard and introduced them to Captain Montgomery. The captain seemed courteous but nervous as his eyes darted past them to a door at the starboard end of the ship.

"I have strict rules aboard my ship," Montgomery explained harshly, almost as if he expected one of them to already disobey. "All meals are to be taken in the cabin.

Your ladyship, I've prepared my cabin for you and your maid. Sir Jeremy, you're to bunk with me and the first mate in his cabin. No one ventures out of the cabins except at midday and late evening."

"Why?" Bethlyn interrupted. "We're not ill-mannered children." For a moment she seemed to catch Captain Montgomery off guard with her pointed statement.

She couldn't fail to miss the heated gaze the man threw in Dempster's direction, but when he spoke to her, his voice was laced with respect. "Well, my lady, I must think of your safety. You're quite a beautiful young woman, as is your maid. I wouldn't wish my men to be blinded by such beauty and remiss in their duties." He shot her an ingratiating smile. "And Sir Jeremy, I'm certain, is much too refined to be in the company of unruly sailors."

"Very wise decision, Captain. Now would you please show us to our accommodations. Her ladyship would like to unpack." Jeremy took Bethlyn's elbow and steered her towards a doorway off of the deck before she had ample time to comment further. Taking leave of Harold Dempster, they followed after Captain Montgomery, and when the man stopped to speak to his first mate, Bethlyn whispered to Jeremy, "They're trying to keep something from us."

Jeremy nodded sharply. "Better not to know, I think, Bethlyn. You might be better off for your ignorance."

"Posh! I'm going to discover the secret on *Nightingale*. I swear I will."

Jeremy was afraid she'd say something like that.

A sliver of a moon shone through the porthole and bathed Bethlyn's hair and face with silver fingers. The night felt warm, and she'd opened the window earlier, hoping to catch a breeze. Still, she was unable to sleep and quite restless as the *Nightingale* rode the crest of the waves. Finally she sat up on the bunk and plumped the pillow to lean against the wall and watched moon-kissed clouds skitter across the sky.

It was then she heard the high flutey laughter which drifted from somewhere on the deck above her. She barely gave the sound a thought until she remembered that she

63

and Mavis were the only two females on the ship, and Mavis was sleeping quietly on a cot not two feet from her.

Were there other women on the ship? Could some of the men have brought their wives though Briston Shipping forbade such a policy?

The voices became clearer, the female ones interlaced with male laughter, then they melted away into the night.

"Mavis," Bethlyn whispered and gently shook Mavis, who instantly came awake. "Did you hear women's voices?"

Mavis's sleepy-eyed gaze settled on Bethlyn. "Yes, but I thought I was dreaming. I didn't know there were other women on board ship."

"Neither did I," Bethlyn admitted. Minutes later Mavis was sound asleep again, but Bethlyn was wide-awake. She contemplated the situation minutes longer and finally she made up her mind.

Rising from the bunk as not to disturb Mavis, she reached in the dark for a gray calico gown, the only thing available to her at the moment. She hadn't packed more than a few gowns and the necessities she'd need for the voyage, not certain she'd be welcomed by Ian Briston. If the man did want her as his wife, she could send for her other clothes and personal effects later. For now, ordinary traveling gowns would have to do, and she was glad that the dark-colored gown would blend in with the shadows of the passageways.

She pulled the gown over her chemise-clad figure, then quietly made her way to the door. Easing it open a bit, she involuntarily grimaced at the squeaking noise it made and glanced towards Mavis. Mavis's steady breathing told her that her friend was in deep slumber. A sigh of relief escaped from between Bethlyn's lips. She doubted Mavis would be pleased to know of her midnight jaunt and most probably would inform Jeremy first thing. However, Bethlyn was determined to discover who these women might be, and why Captain Montgomery or none of the crew had mentioned them.

Standing in the passageway, Bethlyn wasn't certain which way to go. Two doorways stood on either side of her, the hall being lighted by the small lantern swaying from a wooden beam. She felt suddenly exposed but confident that no one would see her if she made her way up the short flight of stairs to the upper deck. Somehow she knew she'd find the crew and the mysterious owners of the feminine laughter there and would put to rest the secrets surrounding this voyage.

Moving towards the right doorway, she placed one foot on the stair, bunching the material of her gown in her hand to prevent her tripping on the hem. Bethlyn never got the chance to move further. Glancing up, she saw the imposing figure of Captain Montgomery hovering above her.

"May I be of assistance, my lady?" he inquired in such a silken voice that a chill ran down Bethlyn's spine.

The blood rushed to her face, and Bethlyn wondered if she looked as guilty as she felt. She attempted to hide her discomfiture with a ready smile.

"I was quite warm in the cabin, sir. I thought the night breezes might help lull me to sleep. If you will excuse me . . ."

Making a move to pass him, she found the captain still blocked her way and stood like a sentinel guarding the gates to hell. "I'm sorry, my lady, but I insist you return to your cabin. A storm is brewing, I fear, and you must stay where I can be assured of your safety."

"A storm! How wonderful! I'd love to see a storm at sea. I spent many years at Hallsands and am quite used to vicious winds and rain blowing in unexpectedly." Bethlyn doubted a storm was brewing at all. The moon and clear skies were proof of that. The captain didn't want her above deck.

Montgomery shook his head. "I fear I must refuse your request, Lady Bethlyn. If anything were to happen to you, I'd never be able to forgive myself. Your safety is my first concern. You are the daughter of the Earl of Dunsmoor, and I know you wouldn't wish me to lose my position. Would you?"

He flashed her a disarming smile, but his eyes held a brittle hardness which Bethlyn knew she'd be unable to penetrate. Once again she backed down before this man, realizing that he could very well be dangerous. She knew then that he feared she'd learn his secret.

"I apologize, Captain Montgomery, I had no idea of your concern for my well-being. I'm quite aware of your worth to my father's company." She moved away from the stairs, then suddenly stopped. "I thought I heard women's voices earlier. I assumed my maid and I were the only women on board."

"You are, my lady. I think you must have heard the wind." Montgomery nodded to her, their conversation at a seeming end.

Slipping quickly inside the cabin, she closed the door and leaned against it, unaware of her rapid breathing and the beads of perspiration on her forehead. She'd been so close to the truth! What could be going on above deck to cause Montgomery to be worried she'd discover who these women might be? Not for one minute did she believe she'd heard the wind. She'd heard women's laughter. Mavis had heard them, too. Did the man think she was such a simpleton she'd believe anything?

She undressed and, in a silent rage, she kicked the gown away from her and climbed on the bunk. Once more the sound of voices drew near to her. She strained to listen and clearly heard a man demand, "Kiss me, wench." Then a woman's delighted laugh, followed by a pregnant silence which spoke more eloquently than any words.

True to the captain's word, Bethlyn and Jeremy, with Mavis in tow, weren't allowed outside of their cabins until the appointed time. It seemed to Bethlyn that a sailor was always near the cabin door. Whenever she'd carefully open it to peer into the lantern-lit hallway, a man would suddenly appear and inquire as to her wants. Each morning and evening Captain Montgomery would come and escort them above deck, politely answering their questions concerning the ship as they took the air. At one point, Bethlyn admitted she'd like to see all of *Nightingale*, and she thought the man was going to refuse her, but he escorted her and the others down the long passageways, through the galley and into a small storeroom. However, one door he never went near.

"Where does that door lead, Captain?" Bethlyn inquired despite the warning glance thrown her way by Jeremy.

"To a storeroom, my lady."

"I should like to see it."

"Ah, my lady, I would most like to show it to you, but it is locked at the moment, the key having been lost by a careless fellow."

"Then force the lock, Captain. What do you keep in the room anyway that it should be locked at all?"

"The room is empty, my lady," Captain Montgomery ground out evenly. "There is no reason to open it until we have need. Now, please, come with me above board to catch the last of the evening breezes." He attempted to take her elbow, but Bethlyn pulled away and stared up at the man with large, defiant eyes.

"You're quite aware that I am the owner of this ship, and that you're in my employ, sir."

"Certainly, my lady."

"Then I insist you force open the door."

"The lock would have to be broken."

"Break it, then."

Captain Montgomery's face grew red with rage, not used to being ordered about, especially not by a woman. For an instant, his fist clenched. Jeremy quickly moved forward and propelled Bethlyn away from the man and into the passageway. "Come, Bethlyn, let's not annoy Captain Montgomery with such nonsense. I have no wish to see an empty storeroom anyway. The sunset is much too beautiful to while away the time down here. Do let's watch it set together."

For an instant, Bethlyn nearly balked. She didn't care for Jeremy leading her away like she was a mischievous toddler, and once they were on deck and out of hearing distance from the captain and Mavis was dismissed, she told him so.

"I did it in your best interest, my dear. I told you that you might be better to remain ignorant," Jeremy said, an apology in his voice.

"You know as well as I that the key wasn't lost. The horrid man didn't want us to see what's in the room. Or whom."

"What do you mean?" Jeremy asked.

Bethlyn tossed her honey-brown locks in outrage. "Haven't you heard the laughter each night? Then again, perhaps you're not aware of all the noise since your cabin is on the inside. Well, Captain Montgomery's cabin has a window, and each night since we've been on board, I've heard voices drifting through the window. Female voices," she said with emphasis. "Mavis has heard them also."

"Oh" was Jeremy's only comment.

"Is that all you have to say? Don't you think it odd? Or have you known about this all along?" Bethlyn asked, a growing suspicion inside her that Jeremy couldn't be trusted either.

"Yes, I admit I know about the women."

"How many women, Jeremy? You must tell me. This is my ship. I have a right to know."

Jeremy refused to look at her for a long moment. He concentrated his gaze on the darkening sky and the bluish-purple sea. Finally he turned to her. "*Nightingale* is being used to transport women, about fifty of them, to Philadelphia. These women are being sent there to . . . to . . ." He stopped speaking, and placed his head in his hands. A strong wind blew from the north and ruffled his hair a bit, making Jeremy appear quite vulnerable and very young.

"Bethlyn, why must you constantly question? I wish sometimes you were like other girls, accepting and never asking so many bloody questions. I don't know how to tell you this without offending you."

"For God's sake, get on with it and tell me. *Nightingale is* my ship," she repeated, growing more impatient by the second with Jeremy, not only for his unwillingness to tell her what he knew, but because he knew something which she didn't.

"They're doxies!" he hissed at her. "*Nightingale* is transporting them for the amusement of the soldiers

68

quartered in Philadelphia."

She shook her head almost stupidly. "Amusement of the soldiers?"

"Playthings, Bethlyn. The soldiers need more women for certain base desires." Jeremy swallowed hard. "Things about which a proper lady would know nothing. I wish I didn't have to tell you this."

Bethlyn wouldn't have felt more shocked than if Jeremy had told her she'd suddenly grown two heads. A sudden weakness assailed her, but she fought it down as anger surfaced within her. How dare her father's ship be used for such a purpose!

"Who is behind this outrage?" she whispered in a hoarse voice. "Is it Thomas Eversley? I'd warrant it is. That's why he was so insistent I travel on *Venture*. And that filthy Captain Montgomery is in it also. I shall make both of them rue the day they used one of my ships as a floating brothel. I bet the crewmen have had quite a pleasant voyage this trip."

"Yes, I think so," Jeremy agreed. "But keep this information to yourself, Bethlyn. I fear what might happen if Captain Montgomery realizes you've learned the truth. I stumbled across it from a cabin boy with a ready tongue. We must pretend ignorance for our own safety. When we arrive in Philadelphia, you may do as you like about the situation, but for now, please say nothing."

Jeremy's warning sent a chill through her. She realized that he was undoubtedly right. Everyone had gone to great pains to keep her in the dark. For the first time she wondered if her father knew about this, but she decided he probably didn't, having never taken much interest in Briston Shipping. She vowed that once she was safe in Philadelphia she'd tell her husband and would force Eversley and Captain Montgomery out of the company, but then a thought hit her with such force that she nearly fell. She reached for Jeremy's arm to support her.

"What's wrong?" he asked, seeing her sudden pallor.

"Nothing, nothing. You're right about all of this. We'll keep it a secret. I won't say anything to anyone . . . at least not now."

Jeremy patted her hand and they walked back to their respective cabins. It was only after Bethlyn was settled in bed did she confront the terrifying thought which plagued her.

Suppose Ian Briston knew about the women? What if he'd been the one to engineer the whole scheme? She found she didn't want to think about it, because if she learned he'd known all along, then any hope for a life with him would wither and die within her. Her dream might never come true now.

At Woodsley Thomas Eversley shook his head in dismay and glared at the small bespectacled man before him. Harold Dempster hadn't the decency to come to Woodsley himself but secured his assistant, a nondescript young man named Bartholomew Perkins, to do his dirty work. One thing Thomas disliked was a coward. No matter what he'd ever done in his life, be it good or evil, at least he could claim the credit for himself. Dempster wasn't man enough to face him. The stupid fellow had botched things so!

However, he couldn't pin all the blame on Dempster. He must take a share of the blame himself. Lady Bethlyn was a hardheaded little chit, and he'd left London for Woodsley, confident that Dempster would be able to handle any problems which might arise. Thomas had known Bethlyn was eager to set sail for the Colonies, but he'd had no idea she'd forgo the comforts of *Venture* for *Nightingale*. He'd thought she'd wait for the ship's repair, and by that time he'd have returned to London. Damn Nathaniel Talbot for sending for him now! All of his plans would go up in smoke because of Talbot's health and his blasted daughter's stubbornness.

"I'm sorry to be the bearer of ill tidings, sir." Thomas heard the quiver in Perkins's voice. "Mr. Dempster was quite upset himself, but before he left for the midlands he told me to rush here and explain what happened with her ladyship. He has also entrusted me with handing you his resignation." Perkins dutifully extracted a letter from his vest pocket and proceeded to hand it to Thomas, but Thomas waved it away.

"I have no wish to see his damn resignation. Dempster

better stay as far away from me as possible. The stupid fool! I can't depend on anyone in my employ."

Perkins stood straight, and the quiver in his voice was absent when he spoke. "You may depend upon me, Mr. Eversley. I won't disappoint you."

Thomas glanced from the window which overlooked the garden, and for the first time that he could remember, he carefully perused Perkins. The young man possessed an honest face and an extremely dull facade. He blended in perfectly with the dark woodwork of the room. But Thomas had a critical eye and a way of being able to see beneath the surface. Was Perkins an ambitious man, a man who'd do anything to attain his goals? Could Perkins be a man like himself? If so, then he might be able to salvage something of this fiasco. He wanted to marry Bethlyn Briston. Perhaps she wouldn't discover his secret cargo, but he'd never know this unless he found a way to leave Briston Shipping in competent hands, in the hands of a man like himself.

A small smile played around the edges of Thomas's mouth. "I trust you're aware of *Nightingale*'s cargo."

"Indeed, sir, I am."

"What say you on the matter, Perkins?"

The only hint that Perkins might have been startled by this odd question was the slight arch of a brow. His face remained impassive when he answered. "I think everyone deserves amusement, especially at a nice profit."

Thomas suppressed a snicker of triumph. "Quite right, Perkins. You're an astute fellow. I believe you'll do quite well as my secretary. Return to the offices and assume your new post. I shall brief you after I finish my business here at Woodsley."

Perkins made a deferential bow and immediately left. Thomas went to the sideboard in Nathaniel's study and helped himself to a tall glass of brandy which he aptly deserved. It had been a trying day.

If only Bethlyn Briston could have waited a week. He'd only that morning thought the future looked quite rosy. In his mind he had no doubt that Ian Briston would release his wife from the marriage. Briston hated the earl so much that Thomas reasoned the man would be insane not to annul the marriage and claim his full share of the company without an unwanted wife. Then Bethlyn would return to London and Thomas would begin his pursuit of her in earnest.

Now, however, the situation was more complicated. What if Bethlyn or that milksop, Jeremy, discovered the cargo on *Nightingale*? No doubt they'd be offended. Despite her relationship with the earl, Thomas had no doubt that Bethlyn would make certain her father knew of the secretive business venture. The earl had been cruel to Bethlyn and her mother, and had caused Jessica Briston to leave her husband for him, but the earl would never stand for his ships being used to convey prostitutes to Philadelphia as playthings for the British soldiers quartered in that city . . . no matter the profit involved.

Thomas must do something and do it soon. But what?

He drank deeply of the brandy. Savoring the taste and allowing the amber liquid to soothe him, he began to think that there must be a way out of this dilemma. He'd go to Philadelphia and prevent Bethlyn from returning, but he rejected that idea. He'd indeed appear guilty to her. The best he could do would be to wait until she returned home. He'd somehow convince her of her mistake. Then again, she might never learn about the cargo if Captain Montgomery and his crew were careful, so a voyage to Philadelphia could cause undue suspicion. Especially if Ian Briston took an unwanted interest.

"I'll wait," he spoke aloud. "Sometimes a man must bide his time."

"Bide your time about what, Thomas?"

Thomas jumped from his chair, startled by Nathaniel's voice behind him. He hadn't heard the man enter the room, and he felt surprise that he'd had ample strength to walk down the long flight of stairs unattended. Nathaniel had been ill the last two days, running a slight fever. His skin retained an ashen quality, and he shook as he gestured to Thomas to help him into a high-backed leather chair. When Thomas grabbed his hand to support him, he felt the coolness of the earl's flesh and the tight grip around his fingers.

"Really, Your Grace, you should have rung for a servant to fetch me. I'd have helped you downstairs," Thomas offered and took the seat across from Talbot.

"Bah! I'm not an invalid and I'm tired of being treated as one. The servants tiptoe around me like I'm at death's door. Believe me, Thomas, I'm far from dying. Granted, I've had some bad bouts with sickness lately, but I'm hail and hearty."

Thomas inclined his head. "I'm quite pleased to hear that."

Nathaniel said nothing, seeming to accept Thomas's comment as his due. Thomas saw that the mighty Earl of Dunsmoor seemed to be in good health despite his pallor. When a servant appeared and inquired about supper, Nathaniel surprised Thomas by requesting they be served in the study and then, when the food was placed before them, the man ate with relish and gusto, even refilling his plate a second time with tender roast deer and a more than adequate helping of wild rice, followed by three glasses of port. When the meal was over, Nathaniel's complexion was quite ruddy and one would have been hard pressed to find any indication of an earlier illness.

"Who was that young man here earlier, Thomas? I believe he works for me," Nathaniel commented, his gaze penetrating and astute.

"Bartholomew Perkins," Thomas said smoothly. "He was here to discuss business."

"I trust all is well at the office."

"Most assuredly it is."

"I'm afraid I've been most remiss in my duties as far as Briston Shipping is concerned. My sweet Jessica left me in charge of her company and I run it like an absent landlord. I doubt she wanted this. She thought I might eventually take an interest in the company and unite with her son since he'd be married to my daughter. I promised her I'd see to the business; however, I've never wanted to be involved in it. You know, her family's concern and all that. But Thomas, I'm feeling well lately. The time has come for me to fulfill the promise I made to Jessica. Also, my daughter owns part of Briston Shipping though her husband probably wishes she were never born. Yes," Nathaniel said, and nodded. "The time has come to put old wounds to rest."

Thomas nearly choked on his brandy. Spilling part of it on his silk waistcoat, he quickly forgot to wipe away the spots so involved was he on what the earl had just said. The man couldn't mean what he was implying. He just couldn't!

"What are you saying, Your Grace?"

Nathaniel smiled, something he seldom did. "I'm going to run Briston Shipping from now on. I owe this to Jessica . . . and to my daughter. I wish to see her, Thomas, and tell her what I plan. Perhaps I can make amends to her."

"Your Grace . . . please . . . think of your health. Such an undertaking will put a large strain upon you."

"Don't worry about me. Now send for Bethlyn."

"I . . . I can't, now," Thomas stuttered, an unusual occurrence for him. "She recently sailed for Philadelphia to be with her husband."

"Going to claim the bounder, I'd warrant." Nathaniel laughed heartily.

"I can't say."

"That settles it. As soon as I'm stronger I'll go to London and honor Jessica's wish. I may be a grandfather soon and must make certain that Briston Shipping is in fine shape. I wish to leave a legacy to my grandchildren, something of my own, besides this house and wealth, things I never worked to achieve. Everything was given to me, Thomas. I never had to work at anything. You've no idea how draining such a life of indolence can be."

I should like to know, Thomas resentfully thought. He set his glass on the sideboard, unable to look at the earl. If he did so, he felt certain the man would see the resentment, the panic and fear in his face and ascertain how much he hated him, his dismay that the secretive business venture would be unearthed. God, if Nathaniel Talbot ever got a look at the account books and saw how much he'd pilfered over the years, he'd send for the authorities! What could be worse than for a man like himself to wind up in a debtor's prison as a common thief?

Still, Thomas was curious as to why after all these years, Talbot wanted to run the company and make amends with the daughter he'd sold into marriage. But he didn't ask. After all, he was the man's solicitor and not privy to the aristocracy's penchants. He doubted Talbot would tell him the true reason anyway.

"Thomas, are you bothered by what I plan to do?"

Certainly he was bothered! He hated pretending, detested having to cater to this man's whims, but he didn't have a choice at the moment. He must calm himself and give the matter some more thought.

When Thomas turned away from the sideboard, Nathaniel would never have suspected that this sudden ominous news distressed him. He presented a businesslike demeanor to his employer and appeared convincingly pleased.

"I worry only about your health, Your Grace."

Nathaniel nodded. "I understand, but I assure you that I am much recovered. A new start is what I need, something to occupy my thoughts and my time. Brief me on matters now, Thomas. I'd like to begin taking an active part in the company immediately."

Thomas decided nothing would be gained by refusing him. The man had made up his mind. Gritting his teeth, Thomas sat near the earl and told him only those things he wanted him to know. There were many things, too many nefarious dealings and risky ventures over the years, to confide to him. The earl was better off not knowing anything for now. The clock had long since chimed one in the morning when the two men finally retired for the night. To Thomas's surprise he felt a delicious languor steal across him when he placed his head on his pillow.

He no longer had a worry in the world, his plan to protect himself having been made sometime during the briefing to Nathaniel. He realized he might have to deal with the earl's troublesome daughter should she learn the truth, but he'd handle her. She was only a woman. And the earl himself . . . well, that matter was easily resolved.

He'd simply kill him.

Chapter Five

After a little over a month at sea, Bethlyn increasingly grew bored with the voyage. There was very little for her to do in her cabin except to while away the time with a book or laugh with Mavis over girlhood incidents. The only break in routine came whenever Captain Montgomery escorted them above deck or when Jeremy appeared. Her ire at the absurd situation in which she found herself had peaked, and she found it increasingly difficult to be civil to the captain or his crew. She was the daughter of the owner of this ship, and one day she'd inherit the entire shipping business. Not only did her father own the British end of the company, but she was the wife of the American owner. Didn't that give her enough reasons to vent her frustrations, to tell Captain Montgomery that as soon as she reached Philadelphia, she was going to dismiss him? She'd even started a letter to her father, concerning Thomas Eversley's dismissal.

Jeremy again listened to her rant and rage one night in her cabin. He'd arrived to dine with her, glad to be out of the first mate's cabin, since the man had arranged a visit from one of the prostitutes. More than once Jeremy had been invited to partake of one of these women's charms and always he'd refused, not eager to contract some dread disease just to indulge in a moment of lust. He couldn't wait for the voyage to end, either, and he had already decided that when he came face-to-face with Ian Briston he'd tell him what he thought of him. The man had to

76

know what cargo was being transported on this ship. After all, *Nightingale* would dock in Philadelphia and Briston would, no doubt, be there for the unloading. The thought of human transport sickened Jeremy, but what was worse was the idea that Briston might truly be a monster. Bethlyn wished for a normal married life, yet Jeremy worried just what she might be getting into if Briston decided to fulfill his husbandly rights and keep her for his wife.

Not wishing to upset Bethlyn with his thoughts, Jeremy kept them to himself and listened to her while she voiced her frustration about the whole unseemly mess. "I've penned a message to my father already," Bethlyn said as she spooned a bit of broth into her mouth. "We've had our difficulties, but I sincerely doubt that my father has any knowledge of *Nightingale*'s cargo." She grew silent a moment and peered at Jeremy from under long brownish lashes. "Have you ever seen any of the women close up? How do they look?"

"I've seen one or two at close range," he admitted. "But what do you mean, Bethlyn? I assure you that the women look like any other women. They haven't anything more than any other woman has if that's what's worrying you. Granted, most doxies aren't splendidly attired, but they're human beings, nonetheless. I feel sorry for the poor creatures. It must be an awful way to make a living. You know, selling your body to live."

Bethlyn hadn't thought about that. In her mind any woman who sold herself was a disgusting, lowborn creature. She'd never known poverty or true adversity. Despite her father's hatred of her, he'd provided well for her. She couldn't imagine being poor or resorting to selling herself just to survive. Jeremy's comment took her by surprise, but she felt even more surprise to suddenly feel pity for these women.

"Do you think Captain Montgomery is treating them well?"

Jeremy shrugged. "As well as he can, I suppose."

"Perhaps I should offer them help of some kind."

"What kind of help?"

"The opportunity to make a decent life for themselves. I'm certain that in Philadelphia these women could find gainful employment. There must be some families who need servants or establishments who'll hire them. I might be able to help them."

"God, no!" Jeremy jumped up, sloshing wine on the front of his jacket.

"But, Jeremy, you just said . . ."

"Never mind what I said. I'm sorry now I opened my mouth and said anything. What I hoped to impress upon you, Bethlyn, was that these women are physically like yourself. They don't have horns growing out of their heads. However, ladies don't associate with them."

"You admitted you feel sorry for them," Bethlyn said calmly and took the wet cloth Mavis handed her. She began rubbing the cloth vigorously over the wine stains. "Can't I have the same pity for them?"

Grabbing Bethlyn's hand in his, Jeremy stilled her movements. "Yes, you can, but I don't like that look in your eye. Every time you've ever had it, you've gotten involved in some mess, and pulled me in with you. I'm warning you, Bethlyn . . ."

She gave a high flutey laugh, and her expression was as innocent as a young child's. "I'm not up to anything. I assure you I'm not."

"Fine," Jeremy murmured, not really convinced. "Don't contemplate any of this further."

"Of course not," Bethlyn demurred.

Jeremy continued eating, watching her guileless demeanor, and changed the subject. "Captain Montgomery told me yesterday that we've been quite lucky on this voyage not to have encountered any American privateers. Just last month one of the Briston fleet was captured near the Delaware coast by a notorious blackguard called Hawk who sails a ship called the *Black Falcon*."

"I had no idea our ships were being confiscated. Thomas Eversley never mentioned it to me. Then again, Eversley has forgotten to mention a great deal."

Jeremy nodded. "The *Black Falcon* is painted a deep ebony. Hawk only attacks under the subterfuge of darkness. He seems to materialize from nowhere."

"How very enterprising of him," Bethlyn absently noted, and stirred her peas around her plate. She found she wasn't concentrating on Jeremy's tale about this Captain Hawk. In fact, this news didn't bother her at all. She doubted *Nightingale* would run into the infamous privateer since barely two weeks were left in the crossing. *Nightingale* had made good time, and she expected to see her wayward husband quite soon. The thought still plagued her that he might have engineered the scheme to transport the doxies to Philadelphia, or at the very least was aware of it. For nearly seven years the man had ignored her. She wanted a husband and a normal family life. However, she also wanted to extract a tiny taste of revenge against him for his callous treatment of her. What better way than to foil his scheme before it came to fruition?

Jeremy sensed Bethlyn wasn't listening to him when she yawned widely. "I'm rather tired, dear Jeremy. Please excuse me, but I do so wish to retire for the night."

"Certainly," Jeremy said, an ounce of suspicion in his voice. He kissed her upon her forehead like a dutiful brother and took to his cabin, grateful to find that the first mate and the doxy were gone. He undressed and went to sleep immediately, putting his earlier conversation with Bethlyn from his mind.

However, Bethlyn hadn't forgotten. She sat on the bunk and glanced out at the star-filled sky. "Mavis, what must it be like to be one of those women?"

Mavis glanced up, a strange expression on her face. She pulled Bethlyn's nightrail from a small chest. "I don't think you should be thinking about people like that. You're the daughter of an earl, Bethlyn. You should never forget that you're different."

"You sound exactly like Miss Grosvenor. But sometimes I get tired of being 'different,' as you say. Do you think they enjoy it?"

"Enjoy what?"

"You know, pleasuring a man, having a man touch them. That sort of thing."

"I couldn't say."

"Has a man ever . . . touched you, Mavis? Have you ever let a man make love to you? Is it wonderful?"

Bethlyn watched high spots of color appear on Mavis's pretty face, and she realized that Mavis probably had. Mavis had been in Bethlyn's service for years now, but Bethlyn didn't know what her friend did on her afternoons off, or in whose company she might have been.

Mavis sat next to her on the bunk. Her eyes held a faraway look. When she spoke her voice was shaky and full of wonder. "To have a man love you is the most beautiful thing in the world. I can't explain the feelings to you, Bethlyn." She faced Bethlyn directly. "I really can't tell you how it feels."

"Who was he?" Bethlyn gently probed.

"Dan Cunningham."

"Aunt Penny's groom? But, Mavis, he was killed by a runaway horse. When . . ."

"We fell in love a few months before—the accident—and we were to be married. I loved him a great deal. We'd have been happy together."

"I had no idea. I'm so sorry." Bethlyn embraced her friend, aware that wet tears streamed down Mavis's cheeks. "You should have told me."

Mavis shook her head and wiped away her tears. "You had other matters on your mind."

"Yes, silly and stupid pranks to gain my husband's attention. I feel like I've failed you, my dearest childhood friend."

"Never, Bethlyn. I wish only for you to discover the beauty of love. My time is past now. I must live on my memories."

Bethlyn replied nothing to that. She hoped that Mavis would find true love again and that Mavis's wish would come true for herself as well. However, she couldn't dwell on love now. If her husband was involved with the doxy scheme, then she'd lose her dream of a home and family. She could never love a man who transported women across the sea for soldiers' amusements. Because of him, she might never know how it felt to belong to a man, to melt with desire when a man looked at her, touched her. So, after all these years, the time had come to make Ian Briston pay for what he'd done to her . . . or, to be more exact, for what he hadn't done to her.

The hour was long past one in the morning when Bethlyn quietly left her bunk and reached for her plain gray gown. She dressed in the darkness, and then as she had done weeks before, she opened the cabin door. The squeaking of the hinges practically reverberated through her head, and she waited for the inevitable sailor to appear and caution her to return to bed. No one came.

Mavis's steady breathing was the only sound she heard, other than the gentle swishing noise of the waves against the hull. She opted to go barefoot but disliked the grimy feel of the wood floor. She doubted the interior of the ship had been properly cleaned in years, and this was one other thing she must remember to tell her father in her letter to him. Keeping to the shadows of the walls, she silently made her way to the small storeroom she'd seen during her tour of *Nightingale* with Captain Montgomery. Luckily the door was ajar and allowed her to slip quickly inside when a man's voice came from the other end of the hallway.

A murky darkness enfolded her once she was inside, and a damp chill penetrated her flesh. Adjusting her eyes to the dim light, she saw various-sized crates which contained supplies for the soldiers in Philadelphia. But it was the closed doorway leading to the room where the women stayed which held her interest. She very nearly made a move for the door handle but froze when the door began to open.

Self-preservation propelled her to take refuge behind one of the crates none too soon. The sailor who usually guarded her cabin appeared, and a woman clasped her arms around his neck.

"You were real good tonight, pet," the woman crooned to the burly seaman.

"Aye, me girl, I was. What did you say your name was again?"

"Pearl, I told you," the woman ground out.

"Aye, I had forgotten." He chucked her chin. "Now don't pout because I ain't one with names. Here's a few shillings for you." He reached into his pocket and handed her the money which she took and dropped into the front of her blouse. Bethlyn waited to hear the clink of the money on the floor, but another look at Pearl proved to Bethlyn that the money was quite safe and not about to fall as the woman's bosom was extremely large. "Now how about a farewell kiss?"

Pearl accommodated him, and after he'd playfully smacked her backside and left, another woman, quite young with long dark hair, appeared with a tall sailor. After a few moments of wet kisses, he then paid her and left her standing by the auburn-haired Pearl. The woman looked down at the few coins in her hand. "How much did yours give you, Pearl?"

"Cheap bastard!" Pearl cried. "I've had more sportin' fun with fifteen-year-old lads who paid me better. That's the last time I let that silly fool get a piece of me, Della, I tell you that." The two women disappeared into the room's confines, Pearl slamming the door behind her.

Bethlyn rose from her haunched position, legs straining with the effort. A sickish feeling crept into her stomach at what she'd just witnessed. She'd heard about women like these, but to actually see them accept money, to be willingly pawed by men who didn't remember or wish to know their names, was so debasing. She felt humiliated for them.

Surely these women must want a better and more decent life. She couldn't envision anyone remaining in such an existence if another road opened for them. Perhaps she might be able to help them. Jeremy had told her to stay away from the doxies, but Bethlyn, in all good conscience, felt it was her duty to offer aid. A half-wicked smile curved up the edges of her mouth. By helping them, she would also become a thorn in Ian Briston's side.

Squaring her shoulders, she decided that now was as good a time as any. Not certain at what she would find on the other side of the door, she took deep breaths to calm herself. Finally she opened the door and peered into the storeroom.

Two lanterns gently swayed from the ceiling beams and outlined the sleeping figures of the women as they slept on pallets, covered by coarse woolen blankets. A shudder of distaste ran through Bethlyn to see what little privacy was afforded them for the personal acts they performed. Evidently none of them cared if the others saw them servicing the crew, and apparently the crew members of *Nightingale* didn't mind, either. Outrage washed over Bethlyn to realize once again what one of her father's ships had become.

The creak of the door alerted the woman called Pearl. Before she saw the woman rise from her pallet, Bethlyn heard her voice.

"Bloody hell! Can't a body get some rest without you horny bastards bothering us?"

Pearl moved from the shadows and stopped at the sight of Bethlyn standing demurely in the doorway. Her mouth dropped open, showing two rotten back teeth. "Well, who are you?" Pearl asked, quickly recovering herself. "Ain't never seen you before."

Pearl's statement caused the other women to stir and sit up, then to stand and huddle in a group together.

"My, my, ain't she a fancy-looking trollop," the woman Bethlyn recognized as Della said, an immediate and intense dislike shining in her eyes. "That's the hoity-toity bitch who's been sleeping with the captain. I heard tell of her from one of the sailors."

Bethlyn found her tongue, but stammered at this disgusting assumption. I . . . I have not . . . done any such thing. Captain Montgomery has allowed me to use his cabin for this trip."

"Sure, sure," one of the other women interrupted and snickered. "You may have on a nicer dress than us and may be a bit more expensive, but you're one of us just the same."

"I am not!"

Pearl moved forward, her hands on her hips. "What is it you want?"

Bethlyn licked her lips, not certain that she should even

be here. She felt quite foolish standing before these women in her prim gray gown, but would appear even more so if she didn't state her business. "I'd like to help all of you," she spoke in a rush.

Pearl laughed. "Now how could the likes of you help us, honey? You ain't no better than we are."

"I won't debate that with you," Bethlyn said, not caring for the malevolent way Della eyed her. "I do have a great many connections. Once you're in Philadelphia, I can arrange for you to be decently employed. Many of you can find work as servants, housekeepers, shopgirls. I'll help you in any way I can."

"The woman's daft," one of the women exclaimed, and her comment was followed by a number of high-pitched giggles.

"Aye, that she is," Della readily agreed, shaking her long dark hair. "Who do you think you are to be pretendin' to help us? Why, I bet we've made more money in our time than you'll ever make, even with that stingy Captain Montgomery. You just take your uppity ways back to his cabin. Tell your pretty lies to him."

A murmur of agreement ran through the room. Most of the women laughed openly, but some of them eyed her in speculation. Finally Pearl held up her hand, and instantly everyone grew silent.

"How would you help us?"

Pearl's question was asked out of a sense of curiosity, but Bethlyn sensed that she and the others who didn't laugh were probably the women most anxious to start life anew.

"As I told you, I will make certain that each of you is placed in a well-paying, decent position. I've heard that Philadelphia is a city bursting at the seams with new opportunities. Many families and shopkeepers are looking for hard-working employees. I'll personally see that each of you finds a position best suited to your talents."

"Hmph!" Pearl snorted. "I've been told my only talent is in a reclinin' position."

"That's a good one!" Della shot back. "Tell the fancy trollop to take her tall tales to the captain."

"If you'll listen to me, please," Bethlyn cried above the feminine laughter. "If you're ever in need of help you may ask for Mrs. Briston . . ."

She was cut off by the sudden boom of a cannon slicing through the nighttime stillness and hitting a deck above them. The ship swayed and the women fell to the floor. Their voices and screams, filled with panic, washed over Bethlyn. "We're being attacked!" one of the sprawling women cried when an answering boom sounded from *Nightingale*.

Attacked! *Nightingale*, one of her father's ships, was being attacked and here she was in a den of doxies. There must be something she could do to help. She thought of Jeremy and Mavis and knew they must wonder what had happened to her.

Pearl was beside her, and under her breath she heard the woman whisper, "Blasted privateers! They'll steal all we've got and leave us to starve, if they don't blow us away first."

Making a move to get to her feet and the door, Bethlyn fell again when another resounding boom hit the ship. She had to get to her cabin and assure Mavis she was all right. Perhaps she could do something, anything, to save the ship, but what that might be, she had no idea. From the sounds of running feet on the decks above her, and the outraged voices of *Nightingale*'s crew, she'd be in the way. Still, she found herself clinging to a wooden post and pulling herself up. Finally she moved and grabbed the door handle and pulled with all of her might. She must get to Jeremy and Mavis, must make certain they were all together if anything terrible should happen.

Locked! One of the sailors must have locked the door at the first sign of trouble to keep the women down here and out of danger. But Bethlyn wouldn't believe she couldn't get out. With a sense of desperation, she yanked until the door handle was embedded on her palm with its imprint. Then she banged on the wooden door, yelling to be released, but no one heard her above the din of battle.

"Ain't no use," Pearl muttered and sat up. "We're in here for the duration, whatever that might be."

Pearl was right and Bethlyn knew it. An urge to cry gripped her, but she quelled it. Crying never accomplished a thing, she told herself, not wanting to admit she was as frightened as the other women who clustered together, holding on to one another. But she was more afraid than she'd ever been in her life. She could barely swallow from fear; a cold numbness stole across her. Her mind reeled from the implications of this attack.

If the enemy was a pirate ship, she might make the culprits see reason and release her and everyone unharmed. She'd promise them a large sum of money. From what she'd read on the subject, pirates could be easily bought. But if, as Pearl thought, the attacking ship was an American privateer, she might not be able to bargain. It was a well-known fact that colonials were barbarians and hated the Crown. Her father was an earl, a very wealthy man. She couldn't confess that to a privateer. Perhaps she could tell the wretched colonial captain that she was the wife of a colonial. That might work to her advantage. A colonial privateer would look kindly upon her and somehow she'd gain her release and get to Philadelphia and tell her husband what had happened. Ian Briston might be a recalcitrant husband, but he'd make certain the enemy was apprehended. Yes, she decided, that's what she'd do.

That was what she'd do if she lived through this nightmare.

Chapter Six

After what seemed like an eternity of waiting, of listening to the frightened mutterings and screams of the women, of having her body battered and tossed with each hit from the other ship, silence erupted like a death knell in Bethlyn's ears.

"Is it over?" she wondered aloud when minutes passed and nothing more was heard from above deck.

She lay on the floor, where she had been since the start, fearing to move. Finally, when Pearl and some of the other women rose to their feet, Bethlyn did also.

"Maybe we're goin' to die down here," a small blond-haired girl, who appeared no older than fourteen, worried. "Suppose they forgot about us."

"Tsk, tsk, Annie. You know better than that." Pearl smiled at her and patted the young girl's arm. "How could any man forget about us?"

Despite this confident statement, that seemed to be the situation when the minutes dragged into an hour. Bethlyn had lost track of time, but she guessed it was very late, probably sometime past three in the morning. She bit at her lower lip and prayed that Mavis and Jeremy were safe. She hated herself for having left the cabin, to come down here amid these women and attempt to persuade them that a better life might await them in Philadelphia. Her idea of aggravating her husband with just such a plan didn't offer her comfort any longer. Now she decided that it was an ill-conceived and stupid idea from the beginning. This thought was driven home with a vengeance as Della and some of the other women began straightening their skirts and patting their hair into place when the sound of a key grated in the lock.

"Let's look our best, girls," Della intoned and grinned knowingly. "No matter who might be on the other side of that door, you can bet your blasted bottom that it's a man."

Nervous laughter drifted through the storeroom as each woman trained her eyes on the doorway.

A large lump formed in Bethlyn's throat when the door creaked open. Four men entered the room, and Bethlyn instantly recognized that these men didn't belong on *Nightingale*. None of them wore the dark blue shirts and pants of her father's crewmen. Instead they were dressed in a haphazard fashion of loose-fitting shirts, open to the waist, and tight breeches. Their hair was pulled back in a queue, but each woman in the room stood, partially paralyzed, as all eyes were drawn to masculine faces, hidden behind black masks.

"Lordy!" young Annie breathed and choked back a frightened sob.

Bethlyn placed a comforting arm around her, realizing for the first time that *Nightingale* was truly in enemy hands. No one had to tell her that the masks were a way to conceal identities. Clearly the men didn't want anyone to know who they were, and Bethlyn surmised this meant only one thing. American privateers were now in control. She briefly wondered what had happened to Captain Montgomery and his crew, but she knew she must come forward and speak to these men if she wanted to gain her freedom.

"What a lovely treasure chest," one of the men spoke and smiled approvingly. "It seems that Captain Hawk has finally captured booty worthwhile."

The other men laughed and nudged one another. The first man who spoke made a sweeping bow and waved the women forward.

Della was the first to walk to the door. Her ample hips wiggled suggestively and a large, inviting smile turned up the corners of her mouth. "My, but ain't you a masterly one," she said and winked at the man.

"And you, my pretty, are quite a treat." The man's mouth quirked into a sensual smile. "I'll see you later, my dear."

Della giggled in triumph.

Young Annie stayed close to Bethlyn and Pearl. Her hand clasped around Bethlyn's in a tight hold, and Bethlyn felt her fear. They were the last to leave the storeroom, but Bethlyn hung back a foot and looked directly into the man's face. "Are we to be taken prisoners of this Captain Hawk? Is his ship the *Black Falcon*?"

Only the slight twitch of a muscle around the edge of the man's mouth indicated his surprise that a doxy would know such details. He eyed her suspiciously.

"What concern is it of yours, wench? A woman like yourself has no reason to care on what ship she travels or needs to know anything about its captain."

"I demand to speak with him and discover what is to be done with us."

Bethlyn had lifted herself to her full height and stared haughtily at the man, and for a second utter amazement appeared in his eyes. The man seemed to consider her for a moment, almost as if he were compelled to follow her command. Instead he laughed aloud and grabbed her arm, literally pulling her from the storeroom and up the long flights of stairs to the upper deck.

"You'll discover your purpose soon enough," he proclaimed.

Bethlyn feared this very thing, and she began to yank away from his stong grip. "I shall not be treated in such a fashion! Unhand me at once."

"What did you say?"

"Unhand me!"

Once again, the man perused her, then he let go of her. He pointed to the cluster of women who were being transported to another ship, its black outline barely discernible in the darkness. "Go join your friends," he grumbled.

Opening her mouth to protest, Bethlyn clamped it closed, spying Mavis at the same moment Mavis saw her. The two rushed into each other's arms, Mavis trembling and weeping.

"I was so worried about you." Mavis's voice quivered with emotion and a bit of admonishment. "I woke and you were nowhere to be found. I called for Sir Jeremy, and the poor man was beside himself with worry. Where did you go? Why did you leave?"

"A fool's errand, I'm afraid. Where is Jeremy? I don't see him." Bethlyn peered in the gloomy night for some sign of Jeremy, but he was nowhere to be seen. She also discovered that none of *Nightingale*'s crew seemed to be present. All she noticed were the privateers as they hauled cargo from the hold of *Nightingale*, and the women.

Mavis held a kerchief to her mouth in seeming distress. "Sir Jeremy has been placed in a longboat, along with Captain Montgomery and the others who survived the attack. They've been set adrift."

A wave of horror swept over Bethlyn and she felt about to faint. "Not Jeremy. They couldn't have done that to him. He . . . might not survive."

"I know." Mavis began to cry in earnest. Huge tears fell from her eyes. Bethlyn felt helpless to console her friend, and more helpless because she couldn't take control of this situation as she thought she might.

"Perhaps if I'd been with you both at the start of the attack, I might have been able to prevent this." Bethlyn's voice drifted away into nothingness as Mavis placed a hand in hers.

"Don't blame yourself, Bethlyn. There was nothing anyone could do. We should be thankful we survived. Just look around you."

For the first time Bethlyn grew aware of her surroundings. *Nightingale*'s sails were no more; the deck flooring lay splintered and a huge hole gaped at her from the center. Wooden beams leaned in all directions or were twisted into grotesque shapes. Bodies of her father's crewmen littered the deck, and she recognized the man who'd been given orders to watch her only by the large, silver buckles on his shoes. His face bore no semblance to a human being.

She wanted to retch. Such chaos, destruction, and death

weren't to be believed. Mavis tightened her hold on her hand. "Don't become ill, not with these horrible men watching. Keep your chin high. Remember, you're the daughter of the Earl of Dunsmoor."

Bethlyn took deep breaths of the night air and steadied herself. "That would make no difference to these men," she said after she composed herself. "I can't very well march up to their captain and tell him I'm the daughter of this ship's owner. But I can insist upon seeing him and inform him that my husband is a colonial. Perhaps that would gain our freedom. I don't relish spending all my time with these women."

"Do you think it would help?" Mavis asked, hope in her voice.

Bethlyn placed a hand to her head, her mind unable to seize upon some sort of a plan. Even now, poor, dear Jeremy was adrift in a longboat with no indication where he might end up. Responsibility for his dilemma rested upon her shoulders like a heavy sack. She'd been the one to insist they sail on *Nightingale*. If not for her, they'd be safe on *Venture*, and Jeremy— She didn't want to think about Jeremy at this moment. She had to keep her wits about her.

"I don't know," she truthfully admitted to Mavis. "I've never dealt with renegades before. But if I could only speak to this Captain Hawk and convince him he has made a terrible mistake."

During the time Bethlyn and Mavis spoke to each other, the women were being transferrd from *Nightingale* to the *Black Falcon* by way of a wide gangplank which bridged the two ships. With wide eyes, they managed to make it safely across, not realizing how much the dark of night disguised how high up they were. However, they both heard the churning of the sea beneath them, and more than one woman clung to a stalwart privateer who seemed only too happy to carry across a frightened woman.

"I see you made it," the man to whom Bethlyn spoke earlier stated. "I congratulate you and your friend on your courage." His eyes settled on Mavis and lingered much too long. He took her hand, and Mavis jumped backward.

"Please, no," she began.

91

"I won't bite you, my dear. Now what is your name?"

"Ma-Mavis," she stammered, and even in the darkness two red splotches were visible on her cheeks.

"A lovely name for a lovely lady," he intoned and drew her closer against him. "I'm known as Crane. I promise I won't hurt you. I could never hurt anyone as beautiful as you. I really don't like hurting anyone at all, please don't turn away from me."

In all the years she'd known Mavis, Bethlyn had never seen her truly afraid. Mavis had been the person to give her courage, to offer her friendship. Now, Bethlyn perceived panic in her friend's eyes. Mavis's two small fists bunched together and pushed in vain against the man's chest.

"Leave her alone!" Bethlyn ranted, not realizing she screamed to the top of her voice. This time Bethlyn's fists made contact with the man's back. The adrenaline pumping through her caused her to deliver more than one hearty wallop. She'd never have known if she would have actually harmed the man. One moment she was pummeling his back and the next she found herself spinning like a top in midair, only to land in the arms of the man who broke her contact with Crane.

Long strands of honey-brown hair covered her eyes, blocking her view of the man who towered over her. With an urgent motion she pushed her hair from her face and saw him clearly for the first time. No one had to tell her his name; she knew she was staring into the masked visage of Captain Hawk.

All of Hawk's men wore masks to cover the upper portion of their face. Hawk's mask, formed in the shape of his namesake, covered his eyes and ended at the bridge of his nose. A black scarf, tied in a queue, hid his hair from sight. Even in the dim glow of the lanternlight, she discerned the broad shoulders which strained against the white shirt, open to his navel. He stood with one arm on his slender hip, which was covered by black breeches. His other arm held her wrist in a grip as solid as iron.

"What's the problem here, Crane? Are you going to allow this slip of a girl to undo you?"

Even his voice sounded disguised, almost as if he feared

to speak in his own natural voice.

Crane instantly released Mavis, causing her to falter a bit. He reached out and kept her from falling, then quickly let her go again. "I was taking liberties with the young lady." Crane nodded to Mavis, then formally bowed before her. "Please accept my apologies, miss."

Mavis seemed at a loss. One moment the man was pawing her outrageously, like she was a common tart, and the next, she felt as if she could be in a fashionable drawing room, accepting the highest compliments from a gentleman suitor. She didn't know what to say, but Bethlyn did.

"A feeble apology, sir." Bethlyn sounded huffy and indignant. "How dare that man treat my friend like a doxy."

"He treats her like that, because she is one, as are you. Now what is *your* name?"

Bethlyn winced. This arrogant man assumed she and Mavis were prostitutes. She wondered how the man could think such a thing. Couldn't he tell from her clothes and bearing that she wasn't? Suddenly Bethlyn looked down at her plain gray gown, and she realized she was shoeless. With the wind whipping her hair around her face, she most assuredly didn't resemble the Earl of Dunsmoor's daughter or the wife of a wealthy colonial. Her gown and her face were dirty from lying on the floor in the storeroom for so long. Indeed, she looked most wretched. She took a long, shuddering breath. She did look like one of those women. Oh, why couldn't she have been captured in one of her better gowns?

"I'm not what you think I am!"

"Then what are you?" he countered, seemingly amused by this haughty version of a lady.

"I'm the Ear—" She stopped speaking. She couldn't tell him who she was. He might harm her, or Mavis, if he knew Nathaniel Talbot was her father.

"Yes?"

She wet her lips, her gaze settling on Mavis, and saw the girl shake her head in a warning gesture. The look clearly said not to tell Captain Hawk anything. Until this moment Bethlyn had decided to admit she was the wife of

93

Ian Briston. Now, however, she couldn't bring herself to tell him about her husband. Ian Briston owned part of this ship, too. Suppose this arrogant Captain Hawk decided to hold her for ransom? She wondered if Ian would pay it, but more importantly she didn't want her husband to know she'd been captured by the notorious Captain Hawk . . . not until she could tell him herself. News of such a humiliating experience might cause Ian to question their marriage and end it before giving it a chance. She wouldn't allow Captain Hawk to ruin her hope of finally winning her husband's affections and the children she might one day have by him. Perhaps it was better for her if the man standing before her thought she was a prostitute for the time being. Nothing would be gained by revealing the truth to him. Somehow she'd blend in with the other women, having already decided that she and Mavis would hide if any of the men approached the others. Or fight, if cornered themselves.

Her hair blew in the brisk sea air and framed her face with brown wisps. Bethlyn straightened her spine and stared at the masked rebel. She barely perceived any eyes behind that mask. But she did notice a smoldering flame in the depths of the black orbs and wasn't certain she liked it. "My, my . . . name is . . . Beth, sir. My friend is called Mavis. We admit we're your prisoners, but we are quite tired and would like to go to bed. Could you please show us where the other women have been taken?"

Hawk inclined his head and glanced towards Crane. "Take Miss Mavis to where the others reside. And don't attempt to steal a kiss," he warned good-naturedly.

"Aye, Captain." Crane grinned, and he held out his arm like a grand gentleman to Mavis, who at first didn't know whether to take it or not. Finally, after giving Crane a long, searching look, she lifted her hand and placed it on his elbow. He led her away like a duke leading a duchess from a ballroom.

"Hmm," Hawk said, considering. "That little doxy has captured Crane's heart."

"Please, sir, you're speaking about my friend."

"Ah, of course. I had forgotten that you're both grand ladies. Pardon me. Now, my dear. You said something about bed, I believe."

"Yes, I wish to go to bed."

"My sentiments exactly."

Captain Hawk took her by the arm and led her away from the direction in which Mavis and Crane had gone. "Where are we going?" she asked, her voice catching as he led her past the galley room where she saw many of the men, relaxing with some of the women on their laps; past dark corners where heavy breathing and moaning sounds emanated.

"Why, to bed."

They stopped before a cabin door and Hawk opened it. Immediately she sensed that this was his cabin, and the bed he led her to was his own. She held onto the door when he attempted to bring her inside.

"No! I won't. You horrible beast of a man. I won't sleep in here."

"I don't care where you sleep, wench. Sleep wasn't what I had in mind."

"I won't go in here. Let me go," Bethlyn cried and tried to force her way past him, but Hawk was stronger than the finest stallion ever housed in the Woodsley stable.

"Calm yourself, wench." His breath fanned her cheek and he held her easily in the crook of his arm. "I'm not going to do anything to you which hasn't already been done. I like fight in a woman, but I'd rather you be a bit more docile. I've had a long night. Now, go on inside like a good girl."

"No!"

"You're trying my patience. Go inside now and wait for me. I have things to clear up first before I join you." For an instant his lips nuzzled her neck, sending an electric current through her. She bolted again and pushed at him with her hands, but Hawk thrust her inside the room and quickly locked the door.

"I won't be long, my tigress," she heard him rasp on the other side of the door.

She clawed at the heavy wood, demanding her release, but she heard nothing. The man was gone.

*   *   *

95

Hawk watched the dawn-kissed horizon, feeling more than weary. He longed to go to his cabin and sleep but remembered the beautiful woman who waited there. A small grin split his lips. Not only was she beautiful but spirited too. Hawk liked that in a woman. He'd found most women to be simpering fools, only too eager to come to his bed, to please him. Most men, he knew, would have killed for the chance to bed willing women, but Hawk was different than most men. More than anything, he appreciated a challenge, and he instinctively knew that the honey-haired doxy wouldn't disappoint him.

On this particular morning, he breathed deeply of the salt air and admired the rainbow of colors in the water's surface as the sun rose. One moment, a soft shade of brown covered the liquid surface, a color not unlike the woman's eyes. The next minute, a pale rose blended into the water and reminded him of the bloom on her cheeks, and when a vibrant red enveloped the undulating waves, he thought of her soft, yielding lips beneath his. For a moment he felt himself lost and mesmerized by this woman's image, and finally he shook himself.

"Lord!" he muttered aloud. "I've been too long without a woman."

"Haven't we all" came Crane's voice behind him.

Hawk turned and laughed. "Neither of us are destined for a monastery, my friend."

The edges of Crane's eyes crinkled into a smile beneath his mask. "How is your prisoner faring?"

"Fine, I suppose. I haven't heard a sound out of her for a few hours. I imagine she must be asleep. Could you arrange some breakfast to be taken to her, Crane? She'll probably be quite hungry, and I doubt I shall see her until tonight. There are some things I have to do before I can join her."

"I'll attend to her, but tell me. Will you be able to please such a spunky wench tonight? You haven't slept for twenty-four hours."

Placing a booted foot on an overturned barrel, Hawk managed a brilliant smile which looked far from tired. "With a wench as beautiful and fiery as that one, I think sleep will be the last thing on my mind." Crane nodded his agreement, but he shrugged his shoulders.

"This girl, Mavis, she's different. I can't explain it, Hawk, but she isn't like any other doxy I've ever met. When I look into those wide blue eyes, I see a person who has known great sadness, but for the life of me, I don't see a woman who holds herself cheaply."

"Perhaps she just charges more than other doxies," Hawk said, sounding heartless.

Crane took offense. "No, and you shouldn't say such an awful thing about her. She isn't like the others, I tell you."

"A romantic at heart, I fear."

"Stop it, Hawk. I'd rather have some feelings left than to be like you, hardened and cynical where women are concerned."

Hawk felt unable to reply to that, because Crane was correct. He was a hardened skeptic about the opposite sex. No woman could hold his attention for long. He thought all women were flighty and faithless, and he'd vowed long ago never to fall in love. So far he hadn't and doubted he ever would. But a part of him did wish to be more like Crane and lose his heart. Maybe then he'd find life worth living.

"I take it that your Mavis has met all of your expectations to have cast such an enchanted spell over you." Hawk's tone sounded gentle, and he hid his envy from his friend.

Crane shifted his weight, a bit embarrassed to face Hawk directly, so he kept his eyes on the changing sea. "That's just it. I didn't touch her." His gaze drifted back to the hawklike demeanor before him. "I wanted to make love to her. She even *allowed* me to kiss her, and I think if I'd been a bit more forceful she'd have come willingly to me, but I couldn't do it, Hawk. She likes me, I can sense she does. But Mavis isn't like those other women." Crane scratched his wind-tousled blond locks. "She's not a whore. Damn if I don't know what to do with her."

Hawk almost made a lewd comment about his knowing what he'd do with the wench, but he realized that Crane was far more than just smitten with a pretty face. Had his friend found his true love at last? Hawk ached to warn him away from this Mavis, to remind him she was a doxy, a woman who was captured off of a ship and destined for British soldiers' amusements, that she could be discarded at will, but Crane already knew this. What magic had this woman woven over him? Again, envy pricked at Hawk for an emotion he'd never experienced.

Hawk could think of nothing else to say and was grateful when his quartermaster called him to check into the crates which had been confiscated off *Nightingale*. As he thought he would, he found muskets, bayonets, and medical supplies. A fruitful night's work, he decided. Anything to put a crimp in the British might was fine with him. He hated the British, one British man in particular. Hawk found he couldn't help scowling. Supplies for the soldiers stationed in Philadelphia were one thing, but to supply them with women was quite despicable. Suddenly his scowl disappeared, and he found himself smiling.

Because of him the soldiers would spend some very lonely and cold nights. But he wouldn't. As soon as he was finished with his duties, he'd bathe before going to his cabin to claim the most beautiful treasure he'd ever captured.

The moon had long since risen when Hawk stopped before a water barrel and, removing his shirt, splashed the liquid across his muscular arms and chest. He'd have liked to bathe fully, but fresh water at sea was scarce and needed for drinking and meal preparation, rather than indulging in a tepid bath. Another week and the *Black Falcon* would land at Windhaven, an island off the Delaware coast which he used as a refuge from British ships patrolling the area. His ship would fit snugly into an isolated cove, protecting it from view. Hawk couldn't suppress a smug smile. He'd outwitted the English frigates so many times that the game of privateering had become somewhat boring.

Nightingale, though not a frigate but a merchant ship, had fallen easily into his hands. Of course, the ship's crew had made a vain but valiant attempt to outmanuever the *Black Falcon.* In fact, Hawk had possessed no knowledge of *Nightingale's* ownership until he noticed a flag atop its mast, flying the Earl of Dunsmoor's coat of arms. He'd laughed aloud at the sight.

He had expected to find supplies for the British in the storeroom, however, the women did surprise him—especially the honey-haired vixen who now waited in his cabin. Unwillingly his loins tightened to think about her. In his life he'd known and possessed many beautiful women, but this woman appeared refined and like no doxy he'd ever seen. Probably, he decided and splashed water over the portion of his face which wasn't covered by the mask, that was her attraction for him. She was an oddity in a sea of predictable females, but once he'd taken her to bed a few times, he figured he'd grow tired of her. All women bored him after he'd amply tasted their charms, and he expected this woman to be no different.

Suddenly Hawk's train of thought was broken and he spun around, his hand on the dagger at his waistband, to feel someone run a jagged fingernail familiarly down his back.

"What the hell do you want?" he hissed at the dark-haired woman standing before him. Her eyes were wide with fright, and she jumped backward.

"No harm done, Captain. It's just me, Della. You remember me, don't you? I know you do. Your eyes never left me face when I came aboard."

Hawk gave a sullen nod. He did remember the wench. Of all the doxies this one seemed to be the most self-assured, and he'd have thought her the most beautiful except for the woman his mind had dwelled upon all day long. "You shouldn't sneak up on me like that," he said reproachfully. "I might have hurt you."

"Oh, Captain," Della whispered, her fear gone. She moved towards him until her breasts touched his bare chest. "Sometimes a little pain can feel real good, if it's done right."

The moonlight emphasized the lust in her eyes. One of her hands pressed intimately against the bulge in his trousers. Standing on tiptoes, she stretched to reach his mouth, and her small teeth nipped at his lips. The sting of pain caused him to flinch, but he didn't find the experience totally unpleasant. He suspected Della was quite proficient in her trade, and he'd have gladly taken her up on her offer but for the woman in his cabin.

Della smiled her triumph, thinking the telltale bulge was because of her. "Come on, Captain. Della here can give you what you want. I know how to please a man like you." Lifting her arms, she curled them around his neck, but Hawk firmly disengaged them and pushed her gently away.

"Thank you, but I must refuse your most gracious offer."

"Why?" she wailed. "Ain't I good enough for the likes of you? That mask on your face don't fool me. You want me, I can tell."

"Not tonight."

Della's eyes narrowed wickedly. She licked her full lips. "It's her, ain't it? That other one."

"What other one do you mean?"

"The haughty bitch who shared Captain Montgomery's cabin, that's who. Ah, I can see you didn't know about her and the *Nightingale*'s captain. But it's true. Just ask her. Montgomery kept her almost a prisoner, he was so besotted with the likes of her. Heaven only knows why. She ain't as pretty as me," Della declared with more than a hint of envy in her voice.

She's more beautiful than you could ever hope to be, Hawk thought, overcome by a sensation of jealousy which felt foreign to him. The image of the woman called Beth, entwined in Captain Montgomery's arms, rose unbidden in his mind and he forced it down. He knew what she was, but he hated to think of her with any other man but himself . . . which was absurd. Beth was a doxy.

"You better run along now, Della. I imagine someone on my crew is just pining after you, and would love a sample of your distinctive style of kissing."

"You're damn right," she cried. "I ain't going to stand here and be thrown over for the likes of an uppity bitch by

100

you or any man. Not when there are men aboard this ship who'll gladly pay me price for some special fun." Della began to turn away in a huff, but she suddenly turned back again and grinned at Hawk. "But if you ever change your mind . . ."

Leaving the rest of her sentence unfinished, she hurried away.

By the time Hawk left the upper deck and went down the stairs which led to his cabin, he had forgotten Della. His concentration centered on Beth. Physically he felt a bit tired, not having slept in over thirty-six hours. Yet the thought of the beautiful body he knew must exist beneath the plain gray gown chased away his exhaustion. Even now, he could hear the sound of muffled laughter and the cries of ecstasy which emanated from behind some of the hallway doors and the dark corners of the galley. Indeed, this voyage would be a memorable experience for his men. Hawk's own loins tightened and bulged anew.

"This night will be memorable for me also," he muttered aloud, and unsheathed the latch on the cabin door.

Hawk wasn't prepared for the vision before him when he entered the cabin. He hadn't known what to expect, but the sight of this doxy, standing proudly before him, her hair fanning across her shoulders and catching the candlelight, inflamed his passion further. A mental image of him burying his face within those thick, sweet-smelling tresses increased his desire for her. Yet, from the contemptuous way she eyed him, he knew she intended to play the game of outraged maiden a bit longer, and this was fine with him. Any woman who came too easily to his bed wasn't worth having, in his estimation.

Placing his hands on his hips, he said, "Have you finished your tantrum, wench? It isn't every day I have to imprison a woman in my cabin. Usually my bed companions come quite willingly, even gladly."

He noticed her stiffen, and she moved towards him a bit. "You're an arrogant, conceited man. I assure you that I'm not like your other women and won't become a mewling kitten for your pleasure."

101

A deep laugh escaped him. Hawk found her amusing, a beautiful and headstrong young woman despite her station. But he sobered a bit and felt the hot blood singing through his veins to see her heaving breasts and to crave the nectar which he'd suckle from them. "I have no wish for a kitten, my sweet, but a wildcat. You seem to be of the latter persuasion, and my blood grows warm at the sight of you. I do admit that you're the most comely doxy I've ever seen and quite refined, too." In fact, it was this refinement which compelled him to stalk towards her. He longed to break down her resistance. However, the wench skittered away from him and found refuge on the opposite side of a table from him. He laughed again, but this time the tone was melodious and filled with his desire.

"Ah, so you wish to play the reluctant maid, I see. Fine with me if playacting pleases you . . . Beth. That is your name, I believe. So, shall I play the lecherous duke and you the beautiful but virtuous serving girl? Or perhaps you'd like to be . . ."

She cut his words off with her own heated rantings. Why, the little chit even screamed she'd kill him if he came closer to her. Hawk admitted inwardly that this woman was very good at pretending to be a reluctant virgin. Apparently she'd played this part many times in her profession and had it down to an art. To cajole her further, he undid his belt and threw it to the floor, applauding her on her creativity to spice thing up. Yes, this was one wench who'd make this a memorable voyage.

Flashing her a smile, he grabbed for her, and again she eluded him, but not for long. In a second he held her firmly in his embrace, catching the female scent of her and longing to bury his face within that golden sheath of hair. Reaching into her bodice, his hand captured one of her breasts and he felt it swell and fill his palm. She stopped fighting him and her body rested familiarly against his, almost as if they were made for each other.

"God, you're beautiful," he whispered, overcome by the desire which rushed through him. "Let's quit this playacting and enjoy each other, my lovely. I've never wanted a woman as much as you."

This was true. For the first time he could remember, Hawk let his guard fall with a woman and found he seemed unble to control the raging desire which soared through him. He kissed her then, tasting of the soft sweetness of her lips, feeling her grow more pliant against him. His tongue moved from her lips to trail the line of her slender neckline and rest within the lush valley of her breasts.

"Come to bed, my sweet, and show me all you've learned in your trade. You'll find me an eager pupil." More than eager, he thought to himself. He intended to lift her in his arms and carry her to the bunk, but Beth surprised him by going stiff in his arms and pushed away from him. He grabbed for her, but she managed to shake her long hair and try for the door, which was locked.

Hawk was unbearably weary of this stupid game now. He'd played along to amuse her and to arouse himself, and aroused he was. He wasn't about to wait a moment longer to possess her.

"I want you, Beth. Why do you torture me so? Can't you tell that I'm languishing from desire for you?" For you, only for you, he found himself thinking.

For a moment, he saw her face soften and thought she was about to relent. Instead, she muttered a harsh, "No."

"Come, Beth, my sweet," he cajoled. He'd never cajoled any woman into his bed, and he detested himself for doing it now. But he wanted this woman, wanted her willing and hot for him.

He saw the flash of the blade when she raised her hand. The jeweled dagger shot silver fire his way, and he silently cursed himself for leaving the thing on the tabletop before the confrontation with *Nightingale*. This turn of events angered him. Who did this doxy think she was? How far was she going to go to fight for her "honor"? he wondered.

"Your role as modest maid has gone too far, sweet. Put down the knife." He managed to speak calmly.

"Not until you promise to leave me alone."

Bowing, he moved away from her, telling her that she had nothing to fear from him. He asked for the knife and she refused. God, he even pleaded with the wench, only to have her brandish it at him again. Then he did the only thing he could do. He told her she could keep it.

Watching her face, he discerned suspicion there within those hauntingly beautiful brown eyes. He wondered if she might be a bit mad, but decided that somehow he'd blundered. The young woman before him wasn't insane, but frightened, truly afraid of him. But why? Certainly she'd been with too many men to count.

Both of them faced each other. He had the advantage of reading her thoughts, but she didn't. His face was masked and, at that moment, he was glad of it. The wench had nearly made a complete fool of him. To think that he thought all of this was a game, a very deadly game, he reminded himself. The silly woman could have stabbed him to death at any time; in fact, she might be a danger to herself. He had no idea how long they'd have stood staring at each other, she poised to descend the knife if he moved closer.

It was the harsh sound of the knock on the door, of Crane's upraised voice which startled her. Hawk used this moment to lunge for her.

He felt her resistance when he grabbed her arm. "Hand over the blasted thing!" he cried, and attempted to wrest the knife from her. He managed to pull down her arm, but her hand refused to break free, and it was at that moment he felt the blade's icy tip tearing through his shirt to enter his chest.

The stinging sensation caused him to stiffen, and he realized she'd stabbed him. He could see her eyes widen in mute horror. He wanted to reach for her, to touch that glorious mane of hair, but he couldn't will himself to do that. Weakness assailed him, and he toppled, falling into a dark pit. His last conscious thought was that he'd never get to bury his face within the soft fullness of honey-colored hair.

Chapter Seven

"What am I going to do? What is to become of me?"

Bethlyn wrung her hands together and paced the confines of the small room she'd been placed in earlier by the man called Crane. This room wasn't as nice as Hawk's cabin. The floor felt damp to her bare feet, and in the light of the dawn from the small cabin window, she saw that there wasn't even a bunk. A small pallet rested near the wall, but no blanket offered any warmth. The room was as bare and lonely as she felt.

Each time she heard footsteps outside the door, she stiffened, waiting for someone to come in and drag her outside, to cast her overboard for killing Captain Hawk. The whole incident blurred in her memory. All she could remember was her fear of the man, of his searing kiss, which turned her legs to jelly, and how she'd very nearly succumbed to him before sanity returned. Then his tenderness vanished and he would probably have forced her into his bed, except for the knife. She shook her head, wanting to drive away the image of the man's masked face from her mind. She had been unable to see his eyes, but she knew that surprise and shock must have mingled within them. As long as she lived she'd recall the sensation of cutting into him, the warmth of his blood upon her hand.

"God help me, I'm going insane," she muttered aloud, and took a deep, controlling breath to steady herself. She longed to cry but wouldn't give into tears. Keep your wits about yourself, her mind repeated over and over.

But it was hard not to be frightened. When Crane broke open the cabin door to find Hawk lying by her feet, the dagger protruding from his chest and her hand and gown covered in the man's blood, she thought she was as good as dead. Crane had roughly pushed her aside and called for help. Instantly the cabin was overrun with Hawk's men, and Crane issued orders to one of them to take her away to this small cold room.

Crane never glanced in her direction, but she sensed his recrimination of her. The privateer who herded her away from the cabin didn't speak to her, only shoved her inside and locked the door as if she were a criminal. A murderess.

"I didn't mean to kill him. It was an accident," she had stated, but no one listened to her, no one believed her.

Sinking to the pallet in abject despair, she wondered how soon it would be until someone came for her. Her mind reeled with thoughts of Jeremy, Mavis, even her father. Would he miss her? She doubted it. Certainly, her errant husband wouldn't care that she'd been killed by privateers when he learned of her demise. The circumstances surrounding her death would mean nothing to him. She'd ably defended her honor, and for what? All she'd succeeded in doing was killing the debaucher who'd have raped her and getting herself hung or thrown overboard for the deed. A shiver wracked her to contemplate her own end.

She knew it was late afternoon because the sun was sinking behind the horizon when the waiting became almost more than she could bear. The sound of the key grating in the latch catapulted her to her feet. Breathing hard, Bethlyn watched as the man who'd brought her there entered the cabin, a tray balanced in one hand and a nasty-looking knife in the other.

"Don't be gettin' any ideas about runnin', missy. I don't want to hurt you, but I seen what you did to Captain Hawk, and I ain't about to be one of your victims."

Another man eyed her cautiously from the doorway as the first man placed the tray on the floor beside the pallet. "Best eat up," he said. "If word leaks out that I'm feedin' you, me and my friend here will be taken to task by the others. You ain't a very popular lady today."

Bethlyn noticed the way he sneered the word "lady," and she couldn't help but wince.

"I won't apologize for what I did," she said almost haughtily. "Your precious captain would have raped me. I was defending myself—but I didn't mean to kill him."

Through the mask, the man's eyes shifted, and he appraised her, unable to look away from her. "You're a peculiar one, I give you that. I ain't never met a doxy like you. It's clear you ain't like those others, but give it up, miss. All Hawk wanted was some fun with you. You had no need to hurt him like you did. I mean, you weren't givin' nothin' to him that you ain't already gave to other fellows."

"That's not true! Please, tell me what is to be done with me, I didn't mean to kill the horrid man!"

A huge grin split the man's lips. "Hawk ain't dead, miss. But I will tell you that you did a nice job of almost sendin' him to the beyond. Any other man would most like have died, but Hawk is stronger than most men. I taught him everything I know about the sea," he said with pride and a hint of sorrow in his voice. "I wouldn't want to hate you for what you did, but I'd have no choice if you'd killed him. Hawk's like the son I never had."

"He isn't dead?" Bethlyn sounded unbelieving.

"Nay, but, mind you, he almost died. He'll pull through, and I'm glad for your sake."

Bethlyn didn't care for the warning in those words. The man moved towards the doorway, and Bethlyn said, "I'm grateful for the food. Thank you, Mr. . . ."

"Sparrow."

"I should have known. Everyone on board has a bird's name. Why is that?" she asked, thinking that a sparrow suited this plain-speaking and nondescript-looking man.

"Birds like freedom, miss, and also birds are hard to catch."

"Yes, and Captain Hawk is the most high-flying bird of all of you."

Despite the fact that Sparrow probably didn't like her a great deal, he managed to smile warmly. "Aye, he is, and

107

don't you forget that."

"I won't."

After he'd gone, she realized she was terribly hungry and gulped down the bowl of broth, which was cold, but she didn't care. She felt that a burden had been lifted from her shoulders. Captain Hawk wasn't dead, and now she had no fear she'd be killed by his men. Though a lethargy stole across her and she'd have liked to sleep, Bethlyn found she couldn't.

Captain Hawk had survived, and now for the first time, she wondered just exactly what that would mean for her.

Two days later Mavis visited her. Her friend sat next to her and the two embraced, Mavis fighting back tears.

"I'm so happy you're all right, Bethlyn. Crane told me you were placed here. I've wanted to see you, but it wasn't until last night I convinced Crane to allow it. Since Captain Hawk is recovering, Crane is in charge."

Mavis mentioned that fact almost proudly, and Bethlyn sensed a change in her friend concerning this privateer named Crane.

"Mavis, you may tell me that its none of my concern, but how did you convince this Crane fellow to allow you to see me? Please tell me you didn't do what I think you did."

Mavis blushed, but she smiled such a brilliant smile at Bethlyn that Bethlyn gasped. "You did!"

"I love him, Bethlyn. Be happy for me. From the moment I met him I knew Crane was special. Last night was the happiest night of my life. Crane asked to marry me, and I agreed."

"You know nothing about him. For heaven's sake, Mavis, the man is a privateer. He and his captain confiscated my father's ship," Bethlyn reminded her.

Mavis nodded sheepishly. "I know that, but Crane is a good, decent man. He feels it's his duty to anger the British."

"You're British. How can you marry such a man, knowing how he feels?"

"I love him, he loves me. That's all I need to know. One

108

day you'll fall in love, too, and will understand. Be happy for me, I beg of you to understand."

Bethlyn hugged Mavis and assured her that she did understand, but she didn't. She felt betrayed by Mavis, the one person besides Jeremy she thought she could count upon. It seemed that she was now truly alone. Before Mavis left her, Mavis said, "I haven't told Crane about who you are. As much as I love him and believe him to be a good man, I'm not certain he'd keep this information about your identity from Hawk."

"I'm grateful to you for that. How is Captain Hawk's recovery progressing?"

Mavis hesitated. "He's better, but . . ."

Bethlyn cocked an eyebrow. "What?"

"He plans to send for you soon."

Cold fear clutched at Bethlyn's heart, but she managed a brave facade. "Good, I hope he does. I have a great deal to say to the hateful man."

"Be wary of him, Bethlyn. Hawk isn't a puppet like Jeremy, or uncaring like your husband. You injured him, and I doubt he'll soon forget that."

"I hope he's scarred for life and every time he sees it, he'll think of me."

Mavis sighed. "Believe me, Bethlyn, Captain Hawk will never forget *you*."

Bethlyn feared as much.

The summons came three days later.

After having spent a total of five days in confinement and without benefit of bathing, Bethlyn gladly followed Crane when he ushered her from the small room. A sense of fear filled her with each step she took, and when Crane pushed her into Hawk's cabin, her legs shook and nearly gave way. She'd had adequate time to think about what she'd done and to be sorry for hurting the man, but she wouldn't cower before Hawk like a frightened sheep and refused to apologize to him, no matter what punishment he decided to mete out to her. She'd had enough bullying from her father to last a lifetime, but not once had her father physically harmed her. She doubted she'd be able to say the same for Hawk.

No matter what she'd done, she didn't deserve to be punished any further, and she'd already decided that she wouldn't allow the hateful privateer to sense her fear of him and worry as to what he'd do to gain his revenge upon her. However, no matter what he decided to do to her, she resolved to make it as difficult as possible for him to get any satisfaction from her punishment. She'd scream and kick and bite if necessary, but she'd be damned if she'd allow him to harm her without putting up a fight.

Hawk's raspy-sounding voice broke into her thoughts when she heard him say, "Come in, Beth."

No sooner was she inside than the door closed behind her, but she guessed that Crane was on the other side, ready to defend his captain if she took it into her head to do away with the man again.

Twilight started to descend, and without the lantern-light the cabin retained an eerie glow. At first she didn't see Hawk, but she felt his gaze upon her and, glancing towards the bunk, she made out his silhouette as he rested against a number of pillows.

"I won't bite," he assured her.

"I'm not afraid of you," she snapped back, instantly on the defensive.

"Good. I like a woman with spirit, even if she's fool enough not to be afraid. Or *are* you so foolish as not to be afraid of me, Beth?"

Her mouth suddenly dried up. Was there a hint of menace in his voice, or did she imagine it? Perhaps he wanted her to be afraid, and, God, she truly was, for at that moment she realized that he still wore the hawk mask over his face. If he wished to intimidate her, he was doing a good job of it. Even in his invalid state, the man caused her limbs to quiver. She might stiffen her spine and pretend not to fear him, but when she spoke her stammer betrayed her.

"I don't know . . . what you—you—mean."

"Of course you do. Your voice is filled with fear, though I do admire you for not wanting to admit it. Please, could

110

you light the lantern for me? I wish to see you."

"I shall not be made an insect for your perusal, sir," she said, and lighted the lantern which hung on the wall.

Soft candlelight filtered through the room, and when Bethlyn turned, she couldn't help but wince at Hawk. In the semi-darkness, she'd been afraid of him. In the light she noticed how pale he appeared against the darkness of the mask on his face. His shoulders were still broad, his arms powerful looking, but the white linen wrapped around his chest was proof of his vulnerability. The great Captain Hawk, the man who inspired fear in the British and other privateers alike, was still only a man. His men knew this now with no uncertainty. Bethlyn sensed Hawk was a proud man, and heaven knew how much he must hate her for what she'd done to him. She'd managed to reduce him to an invalid.

She made a move towards him, no longer afraid.

"Are you in much pain?" she asked, biting at her lower lip.

"Do you care?"

"Not really," she admitted. "You deserve my hatred of you. If you recall, you attempted to force yourself on me."

"Perhaps you're right, but I do seem to remember that for a moment or two you didn't mind."

The hateful wretch was throwing up her weakness in her face. How dare he allude to a moment of folly at a time like this! She wasn't the one who'd kissed him until her head spun, until she couldn't think clearly. "You're a horrible man! I hate you!" she ranted.

"I'm well aware of that."

"Then toss me overboard and be done with it! I can't abide one moment longer in that little hole I've been put into. Any punishment is better than being forced to endure such an existence."

It seemed that for the first time he truly noticed her. His eyes behind the mask scanned her thoroughly until she couldn't help but blush. She knew she must look a sight with her hair all atumble, not having brushed it in days, and the dried blood on her gown. Admittedly, she'd nearly killed him, but any punishment would be better than

111

being confined.

"You're quite a stalwart soul, Beth. What makes you think I intend to punish you?"

She nearly laughed. "Well, of course you shall. You're a pirate, a rebel who lives by thievery. You have no heart, none at all. But mind you, Captain Hawk, I won't take to torture easily. I'll fight to the death if need be. You won't find me a docile puppy under the whip."

"Oh, God, this is too rich!" Hawk did laugh, a sound which was filled with amusement and possessed of a delightful timbre. She found herself hating him all the more for laughing at her.

"What is the matter with you?" she cried, thinking he might be a bit demented.

He pointed a tanned finger at her. "You're a delight! What sordid pieces of literature have you been reading? At least I assume you can read to make such an idiotic and totally false assumption."

"Yes, I can read," she muttered. "I've read a great deal about pirates and privateers. The whole bunch of you are a scurvy lot."

Hawk bowed his head. "My thanks, madam. I should rather be considered a scurvy knave than a slave to a foreign power."

He'd grown serious, and Bethlyn decided that he had no intention of punishing her, but the next words out of his mouth dispelled that notion.

"I believe your punishment must fit the crime."

Her eyes grew large and the pupils shone like two amber-colored lights. Once more she felt fear and pushed it down. "I shall fight," she whispered.

"I leave that choice entirely up to you, my dear. Crane!" he called, and instantly the cabin door opened to reveal Hawk's first mate. Crane turned icy eyes upon Bethlyn. "You know what to do," Hawk told him.

"Aye, sir."

Crane hurriedly left, leaving Bethlyn standing in the center of the room, her limbs quaking and a burning lump in her throat. From the bunk, Hawk glanced casually at her, infuriating her and frightening her all the more.

112

Bethlyn jumped when the door was thrown open again and Crane and Sparrow entered the room, carrying a tub of water between them. Placing it by her feet, they then left, leaving Bethlyn totally baffled.

"Am I to drown myself in two feet of water?" she asked Hawk.

"The thought is appealing, but no, sweet. I told you that your punishment must fit the crime, and that is your punishment, or let's say the beginning of your atonement." He gestured towards the water. "I am in sore need of a bath, and since you're the reason I can't bathe myself, weak as a kitten that I am, then you shall do the honors for me."

"No."

"I fear my hearing must have dimmed. What was that you said?"

"I said no. I won't bathe you." Her face was entirely consumed in scarlet. She'd never seen a man naked before. The thought frightened her, yet excited her since the man was Hawk, and this was more frightening to her than his nudity.

"Ah, I had forgotten," he mused, and placed a finger on his full, sensual lips. "You said you'd fight."

To her surprise, he got off of the bunk, a bit unsteady at first, but in a second, his hand grabbed her wrist, belying any lack of strength on his part. "Fight me then, wench. But I believe you'll lose."

"I hate you!" she spat, already sensing her defeat.

"Don't become repetitive, Beth. I know how much you hate me, and I could say the same to you, but I won't. Believe it or not, I fancy myself a gentleman at times. I need and want a bath and I aim to have one, and you're the one who is going to wash me and tend to my wound. Also, unless you want to go back to that little prison you were in the last few days, you'll do as I say, everything I say."

"I won't be your whore," she nearly choked on the word.

His breath fanned her cheek, and his lips were dangerously close to hers. For an insane moment she thought he was going to kiss her, and for an insaner one she felt her traitorous body responding to his, but he

113

sneered at her, dispelling the notion.

"I don't want you for my whore, as you call it. I don't need you. There are fifty willing women on this ship, one of which you aren't. However, you can't get away with nearly murdering me and think you'll not pay the piper, love. I promise I won't touch you. All I ask is restitution for what you've done by caring for me as a human being. I can't rely on my men. All hands are needed on deck. You will help me, Beth, until I am well enough to take command. There is nothing worse than a man who can't captain his own ship. The men will sense weakness, and I won't allow that. You don't want to be responsible for a mutiny."

"Suppose I don't care if your men mutiny."

His hand stroked her cheek, and his voice contained a sadness and a warning. "I should hate your lovely body to fall into less gentle hands than mine."

An urge to scream gripped her. She felt she was living a nightmare, and all because she'd taken the wrong ship. Thomas Eversley was to blame for her misfortune, and she vowed that when she met that man again, if she met him again, for the chance of surviving appeared dim, she'd tie his blasted hide to the back of a horse and drag him through the streets of London like a sack of meal.

"It appears I have no other choice in the matter," she said at last.

Hawk managed a smile. "I'm pleased you're a reasonable woman."

He let her wrist go and waited expectantly in front of her. "You may proceed."

"With what?"

"Undoing my breeches, of course. I can't bathe with them on."

Her face paled, then turned so hot she felt as if she were on fire. She was about to protest anew, but Hawk cocked his head a bit, warning her. Steeling herself with a shuddering breath, she reached for the cord at his waist, fumbling with the knot.

"What sort of a doxy are you?" he asked, and grinned. "How could you have gotten so far in your trade and be so clumsy when it comes to undressing a man?"

"I don't have to explain anything to you," she ground out, too aware of her face near his chest, of her fingers brushing against the pelt of hair by his navel when the cord finally broke free. "I'm acting as your nurse until you're well, that's all."

"I've never had a nurse as pretty as you. What's wrong? Why did you stop?"

"Your breeches are ready to be taken off now."

"Then take them off."

"Me? I . . . can't . . . I've never . . ."

"Do it."

His voice was whispery soft but left no doubt in Bethlyn's mind that he intended for her to obey him. With trembling hands, she grabbed the top portion of his breeches and began to pull them down. This time her flesh encountered more than the soft hairs by his navel. The pants fit tight on his legs, and there was no way she could avoid touching his hard, lean thighs though she closed her eyes, willing herself not to open them and see that portion of him which in all sensibilities she knew she shouldn't want to see, but couldn't resist.

"Beth, look," she heard him say and, like a moth to a flame, she opened her eyes and saw his manhood, rock-hard and surrounded by a dark bush of hair. She swallowed hard, unable to believe how huge this man was, aching to touch him, and hating herself for the thought. With a gentle hand, he lifted her face upward, and she saw that his expression held some tenderness.

"I've stepped out of the breeches. You can move now so that I can step into the tub.'"

"Oh, yes!" she cried, and scampered away. She turned her back to him and placed her hands on her face to cool herself, but her hands practically scorched her cheeks. What's wrong with me? she wondered, as if in a daze. Never in her life had she seen a naked man, and her reaction to this one puzzled and unnerved her. Had her time with the doxies caused her to think like one, to act like one? But she wasn't one of those women, she told herself, and she refused to be made into one of them because of Captain Hawk.

When she heard him say she could start washing him, she very nearly refused, but thought better of it. Somehow she felt that Hawk wanted to humiliate her by serving him, and she was determined to turn the tables on him. He'd told her he wouldn't touch her, and now she decided to put him to the test.

"Of course," she said, much too docilely, not missing the way he raised an eyebrow when she took a soft linen rag and began lathering it with soap.

Though the tub was large, Hawk appeared ridiculously huge in it. He'd drawn up his legs, extending them over the sides, and the water barely covered his waistline. The bandage around his middle would need to changed, but for now it wasn't his wound which intrigued her. It was the man.

"Do you never remove your mask?" she asked, and knelt beside the tub with rag upraised.

"Never."

"I don't believe you. There must be times you do. What about when you sleep?"

"Depends on whom I'm sleeping with."

Bethlyn couldn't help but blush at such a forthright reply. As she began washing his back, the thought streaked across her brain that Hawk was quite vulnerable to her at that moment. She could pull away his mask and inform the authorities of his identity whenever she reached port. But a large, restraining hand clamped down upon hers when her fingers came into contact with the back of the mask. "I warn you, Beth, that I'm not a fool."

"I didn't think you were, sir."

"Just so you know that."

Arrogant, pompous boob! she silently fumed. He released her, and she washed the muscular and hard lines of his neck and back, aware of his every breath. Gulping, she found the courage to lightly skirt the rag across his pectoral muscles, very much aware of the steellike quality against the softness of her fingers.

From behind the mask, he watched her and she sensed his perusal. Though she wished to keep her face composed, she couldn't help but bite her lower lip, her eyes growing huge when she stopped washing only to have him gently move her hand down the length of one thigh.

"I need to be washed everywhere, Beth."

His voice sounded husky but detached, as if he took great delight in humiliating her but didn't wish her to know it. A part of her recognized that touching him so intimately was causing a part of her own body to throb, and never had she experienced any such feeling in the center of her womanhood. She wasn't quite certain how to stop the sensations, but she did know that this man was causing them and she'd prove to him that she could resist him.

Clearing her throat, and setting her face into a more than passive expression, she nodded and proceeded to move the washcloth along the length of one thigh, lightly trailing across his manhood and washing the other thigh. The water barely covered his shaft, and Bethlyn couldn't believe her eyes when it began to grow. Somehow she knew that her ministrations were the reason for this phenomenon, and a sense of power filled her.

Hawk might believe he had her at his mercy, but she'd prove to him just who possessed the upper hand, and if he touched her, she'd declare him less than a gentleman and the scurvy rogue she thought him to be. And maybe this time, she'd finish off the bounder.

With a sensual movement, she dangled the washcloth above his manhood, then casually she combed it through the dark bush of hair before finally locating her target. Beneath the cloth, she clearly felt the pulsating heat of him, the hugeness of him. She'd never touched a man in any way except for a few brief kisses, never had any indication of how a man looked when aroused, but realizing Hawk's arousal was for her, she didn't seem to mind. He was a fine specimen of a man, and Bethlyn slowly discovered that she enjoyed touching him.

"Am I doing a good job, Captain?" she asked, feigning innocence.

"Ah, what did you say?" His voice sounded unusually thick.

"I want to know that I'm not remiss in my punishment."

"You know you're not. Beth?"

"Yes?"

"I want something from you."

She stifled a smile. This was the moment he'd command her to come to his bed, and she'd refuse, forcing him to live up to their agreement. "What is it, Captain?" she practically purred.

"Hand me the towel. I'm finished my bath."

She blinked in disbelief, watching his lips turn upward in wry amusement. Plunking down the washcloth, she stood up and grabbed the towel from the back of a chair and handed it to him. The hateful man had somehow guessed what she was about, and fresh fury rose within her. Somehow she'd best this man!

Rising from the tub, he resembled an Adonis. Rivulets of water dripped down the hard length of him, and that strange sensation tightened and coiled within her womanhood at the mere sight of him. He handed the towel out to her.

"Your duties aren't finished, Beth. Dry me."

Words of rebuke rushed to her lips, but Bethlyn didn't utter them. What good would it do to call the man names? He knew what he was and knew how much she hated him. Matters would only be made worse if she filled his ears with vituperations.

Smiling a dangerously sweet smile, she took the towel and in a most brusque manner, she dried him.

When finished, he put on a clean pair of breeches and got onto the bunk, leaning weakly against the pillows.

"My wound needs tending."

Pointing to clean linen, he explained how she was to undo the old bandage, wash the wound, then wind the new cloth around his chest. The procedure seemed simple to Bethlyn, and she dutifully unwrapped the linen, but couldn't suppress a dismayed moan to see the damage she'd done.

The wound was an ugly red line, about half an inch wide, halfway between his navel and rib cage. She realized

118

fully how lucky Hawk was not to have died. How lucky she was not to have incurred his entire wrath.

"It's quite ugly, isn't it?" he said without emotion. "Old Bluebelly, the man who acts as surgeon and physician on board, did an adequate job of stitching me up. He said I'll be as good as new in another week or two. But I will be scarred."

"I'm . . . sorry," Bethlyn said, and meant it.

Hawk shrugged. "Goes with the life I lead. Now, please clean it and cover the blasted thing."

Immediately Bethlyn took a clean washcloth and dipped it into a bowl on the table beside the bunk. The bowl contained healing herbs which Bluebelly deemed would heal the cut more quickly. After she'd applied the sticky salve, Bethlyn managed to wind the linen around Hawk's chest. When she finished, she stood back and noticed that Hawk appeared pleased with her.

"Thank you, Beth."

He didn't need to express his gratitude as she felt quite rotten for what she'd done. She hadn't meant to stab him and she told him so.

"I still won't ask your forgiveness," she contended with a bit of defiance in her voice. "You acted like an animal that day."

"Then perhaps I should ask your forgiveness."

Had she heard him correctly? "You're apologizing to me?"

"Yes. I'm sorry for frightening you. I'm not sorry for wanting you. Before this trip is over, you'll want me, too, Beth. You'll beg for me."

"Never," she shot back.

He laughed and wagged a finger at her. "Never say never, my sweet."

Suddenly he lunged off of the bunk, looking less than weak, and began pulling at her dress. She tried to back away, but in one swift rip, he tore the gown in half, leaving her clutching at her scanty chemise. Breathing hard, her eyes filled with hatred which quickly dissolved into disbelief when he pushed her near the tub.

"I think you need a good washing. You're a mess, a

fetching mess, but a mess nevertheless. That gown is ruined. Here." With a purposeful stride, he crossed the cabin and went to a trunk against the wall and withdrew a pretty violet-and-pink-print gown. He tossed it on the bunk. "You should look very nice in this dress. Take your bath and put it on."

"But . . . but . . ."

"Do as I say, Beth. I shall leave you to your privacy. And don't ask me where I got the gown." Hawk left the room.

Bethlyn's mouth dropped open in complete bafflement, not having expected this turn of events. Could the man have a heart after all? When Mavis entered unexpectedly, she almost thought he did.

"Captain Hawk wants me to help you bathe," Mavis informed her.

"I don't understand him at all." Bethlyn cast aside her torn gown and pulled off the chemise to delight in the feel of the cleansing water when she sat in the tub. Her body flowed with heat to think that Hawk had sat in this same water only minutes earlier. Somehow the situation struck her as obscenely intimate, and somehow she didn't mind.

"Hmm," Mavis muttered, and helped Bethlyn wash her thick mane of hair. "I understand the man only too well. He said that if you're not squeaking clean and presentable, he'll wash you himself."

Bethlyn pulled her dripping wet head out of the water. "That bully of a man said that?"

"He did." Mavis nodded.

"Good Lord! I wouldn't put anything past that bounder."

Though Bethlyn pretended to be outraged by such a statement, she did feel that perhaps Hawk's strong hands moving across her body wouldn't be such an awful thing.

Chapter Eight

Bethlyn snuggled deeper within the feather mattress of the bunk, pulling the soft blanket about her shoulders. For the first time in a week she felt quite contented and imagined herself in her room at Aunt Penny's. It was only when she heard the loud, insistent ringing of a bell that she fully woke, startled and then angry.

"Aggravating man!" she muttered and rose from the bunk to quickly don the gown Hawk had given to her. Running slender fingers through her hair, she swiftly arranged the long tresses into some semblance of order. When finished, she spun around and pulled open the heavy door of the cabin which adjoined Hawk's.

"What is it now?" she asked him, and set her hands on her hips in a gesture of defiance.

"What a testy wench you are this morning," Hawk said from his spot on his own bunk.

"It took me quite a long time to fall asleep last night," Bethlyn admitted and stifled a yawn.

"Come now. Don't tell me that you haven't enough to do. If that's the case, I can think of a few more chores for you."

"No! I mean, I have quite enough to occupy myself." If he gave her anything more to do, Bethlyn felt she'd be too tired to move a muscle. For the last two days she'd waited on this man hand and foot. Each time he wanted a drink of water, food, or a cover, she fetched them. She was growing to feel more and more like an obedient dog than a human

121

being. Though Hawk hadn't informed her how much longer this voyage would take, Mavis had told her that Crane mentioned they'd be landing within the next three days. Then she'd be free of her servile existence, and, more importantly, free of Captain Hawk.

"Consider yourself lucky that I don't force you to sleep in here with me each night and play my attentive servant. I didn't have to supply you with accommodations any woman on this ship would kill for." Flashing her a dazzling white smile, Hawk folded his arms across his chest. His subtle threat found its mark. She'd rather die than sleep in here with him and didn't want to go back to that sorry room in which she'd been imprisoned.

"Thank, you, Captain. You've been most kind." She hid a sneer and smiled at him. "What can I do for you?"

Did she imagine that his eyes blazed beneath that mask? At first she'd thought his eyes were black, but now she knew they were green, a beautiful, translucent green, filled with dancing sparks of fire. She hated when he looked at her like that, as if he were mentally taking inventory of her and undressing her. Yet she shivered with some perverted sense of anticipation when he did.

"I'd like my pillows puffed."

"You woke me for that?"

"I require your expert puffing, my sweet."

"There's nothing wrong with you."

"Not any longer. I just like getting a rise out of you." Hawk inclined his head towards the two pillows behind his back.

Gritting her teeth and holding back the less than kind comments she wished to hurl at him, Bethlyn moved forward and rearranged the pillows, patting them in place. When one of her hands brushed against the thick pelt of fur on his chest, Hawk grabbed it and placed a warm, sweet, and totally endearing kiss upon her silken flesh. "Thank you for taking such good care of me, Beth."

Bethlyn's face flushed a deep shade of scarlet. She felt at a loss as to what to say to him, and a part of her softened. She'd thought Captain Hawk was a man with no heart, but she was fast finding that he could be kind and a man of his word. He could have whipped her, or worse, for what she'd done to him, no matter how justified. Instead, each evening he left the cabin so she could bathe and had provided her with a cozy cabin next to his. She knew that he was regaining his strength quickly, and at any moment he could attack her. So far, he hadn't. Hawk was proving to her that he was a gentleman.

Was that why she sometimes wished he'd take her in his arms and kiss her? Perhaps the trauma of the whole voyage was taking its toll upon her and she was losing her mind to even think such an absurd thing. She very nearly killed the man to keep him from touching her. Taking back her hand, she turned slightly away from him, not wanting him to see the play of thoughts upon her face. She felt certain that if he knew she might be weakening where he was concerned, he'd somehow use her weakness to his advantage.

"Hand me my shirt," she heard him say. "I believe it's time that I take over running my ship."

"Do you feel up to it?" Bethlyn reached for the shirt and watched him fill the silky material with his massive shoulders.

"I'm quite well today."

"I think you've been quite well the last few days and enjoy having me wait upon you."

"Would I be so heartless as to do that?" he asked in such a wounded, innocent tone of voice that she nearly laughed.

She breathed a sigh of relief. Since he was well now, she decided she wouldn't have to wait upon him any longer. "Yes, you would."

Walking towards the door, Hawk stopped and waited for her. "Come along, Beth. Your punishment has not ended."

"But I thought when you were well again and could captain your ship . . ."

"You know, Beth, that's your problem. You think too much for a woman and assume things you shouldn't. I said I was better today, but I'm far from recovered." He bowed and held the door for her. "Shall we go?"

Her eyes flared into beams of killing light. If she had a knife in her hands at that moment, she'd have gladly run him through again. "Everyone will assume I'm your—

woman," she stammered, unaware that her flushed face looked becomingly pretty.

"Don't worry about such trivialities, my sweet. My men have enough to think on but you. Besides, they already believe you belong to me, and you're old gossip now."

From the murderous look she shot him, Hawk threw back his head and laughed, seemingly very much aware of how much she hated him and would love to finish him off.

A cool, pleasant morning greeted them. Able-bodied seamen diligently tended to their duties. To Bethlyn's surprise, not one of them lecherously eyed her or made a ribald comment. For the whole morning she followed behind Hawk as Crane and Sparrow briefed him about what had happened during the time he was ill. All of the men spoke warmly to him, and Hawk took an interest in each of them and their jobs, asking questions, giving suggestions. Bethlyn almost forgot she was aboard a privateer ship, and not one of the first-class ships of Briston Shipping. She sincerely doubted that any of her father's captains possessed the same trust and confidence of their men.

It was this blind obedience and respect for Hawk which led Bethlyn to believe that the *Black Falcon* was never in any danger of mutiny. No doubt the man had lied to her to gain her compliance in acting as a servant to him. He probably knew she'd never be able to live with herself if the crew mutinied and feared she'd be turned over to the men for their less than honorable use of her body.

Rage washed over her. From Hawk's vantage point in the crow's nest, she made certain he noticed her withering, hate-filled gaze. When he scurried down a half hour later, he stopped before her and pointed to a cup which rested on a barrel of water.

"I'd like a drink, Beth."

"Get it yourself."

"What did you say?"

"You heard me, Captain." Tossing her hair in a gesture of defiance, she stared him down. "I don't care what you do with me, but I won't be your slave any longer. You lied about a possible mutiny only to keep me in line. You wanted to humiliate me for what I'd done to you, to cause me to suffer indignities. Then I suppose you'd have expected me to crawl into your bed out of a sense of guilt or shame. Well, I won't do anything else for you . . . ever again." She clenched her fists by her sides. "Go on. Lock me in that little room again. I don't care. I don't feel guilty for . . . hurting you."

Hawk stepped closer to her, his breath on her cheek, and she shivered. The eyes which had filled with passion earlier that morning were now frozen and contained not a hint of warmth. "Never be it said that I forced you to wait on me, to atone for your crime, Beth. So you won't believe that I'm an ogre, I release you from your punishment. To prove that I'm sincere, I shall allow you to remain in the cabin next to mine. Is this fair to you?"

She didn't know what to think about this man. He could banish her to the bowels of the ship; instead, he was allowing her to remain where she was. But at what cost?

"I . . . don't want you to touch me, or any of your men to touch me."

"I give you my word as a gentleman that no one will touch you without your say-so."

This was all so confusing to her, and she didn't know whether to believe him, but the man was giving her what she wanted. So why didn't she feel pleased about this turn of events?

He formally bowed and, with a turn of his heels, he stalked away from her.

That evening Bethlyn possessed little appetite for food. Sparrow appeared in her cabin, standing just inside the doorway which separated hers from Hawk's. She didn't care for the fact that there was only one door to this cabin, and the only way out was through Hawk's room. She'd have liked to wander on deck, but she remembered the raised eyebrows of the crew that afternoon during her altercation with Hawk. Apparently, everyone had heard them.

"You ain't ate nothin'," Sparrow chided and shook his head. "That fish was the best I ever fixed. I don't take lightly to havin' my food left uneaten."

Bethlyn offered an apology for her lack of appetite. "I promise to eat tomorrow. I've lost my appetite today."

"More than likely you're upset 'cause you lost Captain Hawk."

"How dare you say such a thing to me! I thought you were my friend. I can see you're no better than that arrogant, pompous captain you serve. I never *had* Captain Hawk, and I never wanted him. I hate him."

"Sure, miss," he agreed, a pleasant but unconvinced smile on his face. "Still, I think you're clever enough to find a way to hold his interest. But be warned that Hawk likes women willing . . . real willing, if you understand my meaning." Sparrow picked up her tray and closed the door behind him.

"Willing, is it? Bethlyn muttered aloud. "I'll never come willingly to that bounder. I detest him, abhor him."

Finished with her verbal tirade, she flung herself onto the bunk. The sun had just set, and the cabin was bathed in a pale light. She realized that this was the first time in three days she'd gotten to bed before midnight. A small smile of satisfaction played about her lips. This was one night she'd be able to sleep and not have to play the docile servant for Hawk. Before long, she fell asleep, but was roused from slumber by a woman's high, flutey laugh.

Opening her eyes, Bethlyn realized that the hour was late. The moon outside her tiny window was perched high in the sky. For a moment, she wondered if she'd been dreaming, but when she heard the woman's laugh again, this time mingling with the masculine timbre of a man's, the sudden jump of her heart told her she was wide-awake. The voices came from Hawk's cabin, and without a doubt she recognized Hawk's laugh.

I don't care who he has in his cabin, she staunchly told herself and chewed on her lower lip. She wanted to fall back to sleep, but she found she couldn't. Their laughter was filled with something other than mirth, and she recognized the huskiness in Hawk's voice as low conversation drifted through the wall.

"Damn him to hell!" she declared softly and placed her hands over her ears. She didn't wish to hear him and his lady love, not certain who the woman with Hawk might be until she heard the woman's voice again and knew he was with the doxy called Della.

An emotion, not unlike jealousy, ate away at her to imagine Hawk with Della. However, she convinced herself she didn't care that he entertained the woman. She forced down the envy, reminding herself how much she hated the man, and therefore, she didn't care what he did or with whom he did it.

It was the sudden silence which undid her. Sitting up, her long hair streaming down her back, she found herself listening, scarcely breathing. Nothing.

Getting off the bunk, on silent feet she made her way to the heavy, planked door and put her ear against the wood. Still, she heard nothing. A blush consumed her entire body to suddenly wonder at what might be happening in that room. Images of Della in Hawk's arms, of their kissing each other, of the way he'd lower himself upon her, burying his face within those dark tresses and then his manhood into Della's eager body, brought unexpected and unwanted tears of pain and humiliation to her eyes.

Never in her life would she forget how Hawk looked when undressed. Over the past days she'd nursed him, cared for him, bathed him. Of course she knew he was most capable of performing these tasks for himself and she told herself he took delight in his punishment of her. Yet, she didn't want to admit how much she enjoyed tending to him—touching him. Oh, she was most careful not to touch that part of him, but, nevertheless, she had wanted to discover how he'd feel within her palm. Now she'd never know. Della knew. And for the first time in her life, Bethlyn cradled her head in her arms and sobbed her disappointment.

"Another night," Hawk told Della and kissed her on the lips.

Della sighed, not hiding her aggravation. "You didn't put me out because of that 'other one,' did you? I don't take lightly to being sent on my way after I done got you lathered up for me. If you think I'm one to be tossed aside after I've got you bothered so you can spill yourself within that haughty bitch . . ."

Hawk laughed and playfully patted her on her rounded bottom. The crisp sea air stirred the dark wisps of Della's hair, and the moonlight accentuated the beauty of her face. Only minutes ago, they'd been on the bunk in his cabin while Della ably handled his flesh and excited him. Truly, Della was well versed in her trade. He'd have turned her on her back and entered her willing, moist body, but a slight sound from the cabin next to his had caught his attention. He remembered Beth, and a bittersweet feeling rushed over him, compounded by anger. The little bitch once again had invaded his thoughts.

He'd looked at Della, lying on top of him, and he realized that the dark hair spilling across his chest wasn't honey colored, that the lustful blue eyes smiling into his weren't a soft shade of brown. Though Beth was in his mind, her image was suddenly displaced by the faded memory of another face altogether, a child's sick face, and he found he couldn't go on.

So now he stood on deck with Della, and reaching into the pocket of his linen shirt, he handed her a guinea.

"This should compensate you for your time, Della."

Della's eyes grew round and bright, her anger dying away. "But I didn't finish with you."

"As I told you, I have some duties which must be performed. But, my voluptuous wench, expect that you shall indeed 'finish with me' soon." Hawk winked at her.

"Oh, Captain, I can't wait," she whispered and suggestively rubbed her breasts against him. "I ain't never pleasured a man with a mask before."

"There's a first time for everything," he told her and hoped that this would be the first and last time he put a willing woman from his bed.

"He treats her shabbily," Mavis complained to Crane that same night. She sat in his bunk, the sheet pulled up to her breasts, and her long dark hair cascaded around her shoulders like a waterfall. Her face was flushed with their recent lovemaking and she made a fetching and most provocative sight. "All day long he forces her to trail after

128

him like a puppy and at night to sleep with him."

"She isn't sleeping with him," Crane reminded her. "Beth sleeps in the cabin next to his."

"It's almost the same thing."

Crane leaned over and kissed her on her ruby-colored mouth. "My love, you know it isn't."

Mavis grinned up at him and placed her arms around his neck. She sighed her contentment and returned the kiss. "I know what you mean, but, darling, you must see it from Beth's point of view. She isn't used to this sort of treatment."

A frown furrowed his brow and he stood up, handsome in his nakedness, and pulled on a robe. "Mavis, I don't understand this whole situation between you and Beth. If you two girls aren't doxies, then why were you both on *Nightingale*?"

Mavis shook her head. "I can't tell you that. Don't ask me again."

"You still don't trust me, even after I've removed my mask when we're alone."

Crane sounded hurt, and Mavis instantly got up and went to him, tenderly touching his face and gazing into warm, loving eyes. "You're loyal to Hawk. I can't tell you, because we may all be better off if you don't pursue the matter. Please trust me, Crane. For now. After all, you've never told me who you truly are. I'm not certain you don't intend to cast me aside when we land."

Uncertainty filled her eyes, and Crane pulled her close against him and nuzzled her neck. "I love you, Mavis. We're going to be married. Trust me."

"I love you, too."

He tipped her face up to his. "After we reach Philadelphia, and I settle you there, I'll tell you everything about me. But that's all I can tell you. There's nothing I can tell you about Hawk at the present time."

"I understand, darling."

He felt comforted that she did understand, and he watched as she crawled back into bed. Crane smiled at the modest vision she presented with the cover pulled up to her chin and those long raven tresses fanning his pillow. He loved Mavis so much that sometimes he actually felt a physical pain to imagine that she might be lying to him, that she really had sold herself for money. Still, he believed her. Though Mavis hadn't been a virgin and had told him she'd given herself to a man she'd intended to marry, he found he couldn't doubt her story. Something kept her from telling him the complete truth, and he realized Beth was most probably the reason for her reticence.

Sitting in a large chair, Crane sorted through the papers he'd taken from Captain Montgomery's cabin the night the ship was confiscated. Even now, *Nightingale* limped far behind the *Black Falcon*, under the control of some of Hawk's crew. Once they reached Windhaven the ship would be repaired and repainted, and no one would ever guess it had belonged to Briston Shipping.

Most of the paperwork consisted of bills of lading, invoices, and correspondence between Montgomery and one Thomas Eversley. Nothing of importance, and he almost placed the paperwork back into the brown box he used for storage, eager to join Mavis in bed. However, Crane's expert eyes noticed a piece of cream-colored parchment bearing a most interesting name.

It was a letter to Nathaniel Talbot, Earl of Dunsmoor, from his most obedient daughter. The girl's name leaped from the page at him. She'd signed her name with a flourish, causing Crane's hearty laugh of amused disbelief to waken Mavis as it resounded in the cabin.

Mavis sat up and gazed sleepily at him. "What's so amusing?" His eyes were filled with merriment now that the whole situation was so clear to him. Putting the letter away, he then disrobed and went to Mavis, pulling her warm and beautiful body next to his.

"My love, don't worry about your friend Beth any longer. Believe me, she'll come to no danger with Hawk. Allow them to find one another, because I believe that before this voyage is over, they will."

"How can you be so certain?" she asked suspiciously.

Crane pulled the sheet from her, and before he began to kiss her breasts, he said, "Because Hawk has at last found his match."

Chapter Nine

The next morning Bethlyn opened the door a crack and breathed a relieved sigh to find Hawk's cabin empty. She didn't relish the thought of being imprisoned in her tiny cabin until the bosomy Della left the privateer's bed. Bethlyn couldn't help but to sniff the air disdainfully. It reeked with Della's scent.

To rid the room of the smell, she pulled open one of the smaller windows and breathed in the fresh salty air.

Her gaze trained upon the bunk, and she noticed with a start that the covers were smoothly in place. Apparently Hawk and Della had finished their business quite early for the bed to be already made. Recalling the moaning sounds she'd heard the night before, the images which ran rampant through her mind, Bethlyn clenched her fists at her side and shook her head to dispel what she'd heard and imagined happened on that very bunk. The very idea that she'd given way to tears over the horrid incident caused a hard naillike line to replace the soft curves of her mouth

"Better Della than me," she muttered, but a niggling twinge of jealousy told her that she didn't truly mean that sentiment, and to combat what she felt, she straightened her back ramrod straight. What Hawk did with Della was none of her concern, she convinced herself, and left his cabin to seek out Mavis.

Moments later, when Bethlyn hesitantly knocked on Crane's cabin door and Mavis had bade her entrance into

131

the room, she discovered that Mavis was still in bed. Bethlyn's breath caught in her throat at the sight of her friend. With the sheet wrapped around Mavis's ample breasts, the long dark hair falling wild to her waist, and those incredibly blue eyes shining brightly in her glowing face, Bethlyn realized that never had Mavis looked more beautiful. Could love really transform a person? Bethlyn wondered. Would such a love ever happen to her?

At that moment, Bethlyn envied Mavis, the daughter of a poor fisherman, and ached to know how Mavis felt.

Bethlyn cleared her throat. "Perhaps I should return later."

Mavis shook her head and got off of the bunk, clutching the sheet and bringing it with her. "No need, Bethlyn. Crane is on duty. Would you like some tea?"

"Yes, thank you."

After Mavis poured the tea and handed Bethlyn the cup, she watched while she drank it.

"You look wretched," Mavis noticed. "You have dark circles under your eyes. Didn't you sleep well last night?"

Bethlyn grimaced. "How is a person expected to sleep when the occupants of the next room are rutting?"

"No!"

"Yes."

"Who was Hawk with?"

"Della, I think. It doesn't really matter."

Mavis gently touched Bethlyn's hand. "It matters to you, a great deal more than you're letting on. Are you in love with Hawk?"

"Are you crazy?" Bethlyn leaped to her feet and dropped the cup on the floor, spilling the tea on a small Persian rug by the bunk. "You're insane to even suggest such a preposterous thing to me, Mavis. I loathe the man, despise the bounder."

Calmly, Mavis took a linen towel and dabbed at the tea stain and placed the cup on a round oaken table. "Don't act so hotheaded, Bethlyn. I only asked you a question. However, you don't have to answer me."

"I did answer you!" Bethlyn retorted, her brown eyes shooting amber fire at her friend.

Mavis laughed softly. "You told me I was insane, that you loathed and despised Captain Hawk. Not that you didn't love him. To quote one of your favorite writers, 'I think the lady doth protest too much.'"

"I can't love him." Bethlyn grew weak-kneed and sank onto a chair. "The man is an arrogant, pompous beast, and if that isn't enough, he's an enemy of the Crown. Mavis, he destroyed one of my father's ships."

"But do you love him?"

Every instinct within Bethlyn told her that no, she could never love Hawk. Her mind reeled with all the reasons she shouldn't love him, but her heart beat out the message that she might care for him more than she realized. She'd been jealous of his night with Della, her flesh had burned when she imagined that she, not Della, could be lying beneath his searching hands, enjoying his kisses. But she'd never know such pleasure, would never be happy and contented like Mavis in her newfound love.

"I have a husband," she said lamely.

"Yes, you have a husband who has ignored you for seven years, who sends you baubles and trinkets. But those gifts don't warm you at night, Bethlyn. Take my word on that. I'd never give up one moment of my time with Crane for a ruby necklace or anything else. I love him more than my own life, and treasure each and every kiss and touch. I want you to feel for Hawk what I feel for Crane."

Love shone in Mavis's eyes for Crane, and Bethlyn experienced that stab of envy once more.

"I'm happy for you and your privateer, but Hawk detests me as much as I detest him. There's no hope for either of us, I'm afraid. Besides, I must worry about what I'll do once I'm off this ship and in Philadelphia. I can't come to my husband as spoiled goods."

"Do you think Ian Briston will care?" Mavis asked her gently. "Perhaps you should seize the moment, for no one knows what tomorrow may bring."

Bethlyn gulped and managed a smile. "I hope it brings my freedom of this ship and Captain Hawk." Quickly Bethlyn kissed her friend's cheek and left the cabin, too overwhelmed to say anything more.

She hated to admit that Mavis might be correct. Maybe she did love Hawk, but she doubted it. For years she'd buried any true emotions, knowing the pain of loving when that emotion wasn't returned. She'd loved her father until she sensed his hatred of her, and she could have loved Ian Briston, if only he'd have taken her with him to America. She was certain she'd have loved him. Beneath his disregard for her, she thought he was a kind man who'd come to care for her. Not like the arrogant Captain Hawk.

The object of her musings suddenly appeared on deck beside her. His masked face leaned down until he was but two inches from her lips.

"What a sour expression, Beth. You look like you didn't sleep at all well last night."

"I slept quite soundly," she said, emphasizing each word.

Hawk backed away a bit and flashed her a wide grin.

"Good. Glad to hear it. I've a job for you to perform."

Bethlyn fairly groaned. What now? she wondered. Before she could utter a word, he grabbed her arm and steered her in the direction of his cabin. When she started to protest, he threw open the door and, before her startled eyes, she noticed that the table he used for going over his paperwork had been transformed into a breakfast setting for two. She blinked her astonishment, not quite believing that fine, gold-edged china and Bavarian crystal sat upon a snowy white tablecloth. In the center of the table was a large gold candlestick, and the flickering candlelight melded into the warm sunshine which streamed into the cabin from a wall of windows.

Beside the table stood a masked sailor who politely bowed and helped her into her chair.

"What is all this?" she asked Hawk, her bafflement plain to see.

"Breakfast."

"But . . . but, I don't understand."

Hawk shrugged his massive shoulders and took his place across from her. "Nothing to understand, Beth. You must eat, and I must eat. I decided we should eat together.

You don't object, do you?"

Was he giving her a choice? Bethlyn couldn't believe that he would, but from the hopeful way he leaned forward, she sensed that he was.

"No, I don't object at all."

He motioned to the sailor to serve them, and after they'd eaten a breakfast of warm biscuits and oatmeal, which Bethlyn realized had tasted better than the eggs and sausages at Aunt Penny's, topping it off with, of all things, a spicy-tasting liquor at eight in the morning, she couldn't help but grin.

"What's so amusing?" Hawk asked, and it seemed that he watched her closely, much too closely.

"I was thinking that you might be attempting to seduce me."

"Do you find the idea of that so terrible?"

Bethlyn ran her fingernail around the rim of her glass. "You assured me that you would act like a gentleman."

"I have, Beth."

"Yes, you have," she agreed, trying to cast out the image of Della in his bed and being unsuccessful. Did the man think that a breakfast and liquor would make him more appealing to her? If so, then he didn't know her very well.

"I'm not so easily swayed by the trappings of seduction," she said.

Sitting further back in his chair, he said, "Your words wound me. I didn't intend for our breakfast to be taken that way."

"Then just how am I supposed to take this?" she snapped. "For days you treat me wretchedly, and then to take that horrid woman to b—." She stopped herself and felt the furious red flush devour her face.

"I see." He stood up and towered over her, appearing awesome and somehow more frightening in the clear light of day than on any night she could remember. Behind his mask she saw the pain in his eyes and knew that she was the cause of it. Bowing stiffly to her, she heard no trace of emotion in his voice. "I'm sorry to have offended you. Good day, Beth."

He left her, sitting speechless and staring stupidly at the

door he'd just closed quietly behind him.

For the remainder of the day Bethlyn didn't speak to Hawk. A number of times she saw him, working on the rigging, issuing orders to his men, and more than once their eyes met. However, he never acknowledged her presence, and not only did she feel a strange sense of hurt by this slight, but guilt to realize that the cozy breakfast in his cabin was most probably his way of making amends for his treatment of her. She silently cursed herself and her snippish tongue.

After a lonely supper in her cabin, she walked on deck. The night breeze slid sensuously through her hair and gently molded the skirt of her gown to her body. Bethlyn had no idea of the pretty picture she made as she leaned against the railing, her face lifted towards the heavens.

"Look! A shooting star," she cried and earned Sparrow's attention as he stood behind the large ship's wheel.

"Aye, miss. I've seen quite a number of 'em in my time."

Bethlyn turned to him. "Do you believe the legend that when you see a shooting star it means someone has died and gone to heaven?"

Sparrow considered her for a long moment and smiled. "Nay, I'd like to think that it means someone has lost his heart to a lover. Or her heart. Whatever the case may be. I wrote a poem years back on just that thing."

This romantic side to Sparrow surprised Bethlyn. She'd never have thought this thin, dull-appearing man possessed the soul of a poet.

"I write poetry, too. Would you recite your poem for me?" she asked and feared he might protest, but Sparrow only nodded and began in a hesitant voice.

> "A shooting star I did see
> Up above the stormy sea
> Silver fire streaked the sky
> And fell to earth with a sigh
> My lady love now owns my heart
> Never, never shall we part."

Sparrow finished, and he bowed his head shyly.

"That was lovely," Bethlyn told him, quite impressed, and touched the sleeve of his shirt. "What happened to your lady love?"

For a second she felt a tremor rush through him, but Sparrow composed himself. "She was much too grand for the likes of me, miss. She was a grand lady on Jamaica, a relative of the royal governor. I knew she'd never marry me, and I didn't ask her. Things just don't work out the way you want sometimes."

"I'm sorry," Bethlyn mumbled, sorry for his pain.

Sparrow glanced down at her. "Ain't no reason why you can't have things work out for you. I saw the way you been eyein' Hawk all day, and he's been lookin' at you. Missy, if looks could melt, we'd all be swimming in the sea to cool off."

"I don't understand what you mean." Purposely she used her haughty, icy lady's voice which had worked so well in London whenever anyone broached the subject of her husband. Those people had been put off by it, but Sparrow wasn't.

"Don't play games with me or with Hawk. You'll lose him for certain."

"Perhaps I don't want him at all."

In the moonlight Sparrow's teeth gleamed brightly. "Aye, you want him all right."

The confounded blush rose to her cheeks again and she felt unbearably warm. Must she always blush so hard and give away her thoughts?

Choosing to ignore him and not wanting to speak further about Hawk, she ran her hand along the circular wheel. "Is it very difficult to guide a ship?"

"Nay, not if you learn how."

"Could I try?"

"If you want." Sparrow moved and allowed Bethlyn to stand between him and the wheel. He placed her hands on the smooth wood and guided her, explaining certain navigational laws to her. Nodding her understanding, she didn't realize when he suddenly withdrew his thin hands from atop hers. Her gaze was fixed straight ahead, her hair blowing gently in the wind, and she barely registered the

137

fact that strong, powerful bronzed hands now guided her.

"Leeway is measured by the angle of the course steered and the direction through the water. If the wind hits from the left, the ship will move to the right of the course and vice versa. Understand?"

Hawk's voice was so gentle, so heart-stopping, that she found herself mesmerized, and she lifted her face to his. "Yes," she whispered, but she had no idea what he'd just told her and felt no surprise to find him behind her. His presence struck her as quite natural.

He smiled at her. "You're an apt pupil."

His body leaned into hers, and against her own better judgment, she molded her buttocks against his thighs and listened while he rambled on about navigation and the sea. Bethlyn heard not a word, but she didn't want him to stop speaking. She trained her eyes on his lips, aching to touch them, wanting him to kiss her. Minutes passed and still he droned on. She felt he wanted to kiss her, knew that he wanted to do more than that by the hard bulge pressed against her buttocks. Sweat must have broken out on his forehead, for she noticed some droplets running down the length of his face, not concealed by the mask.

A musky male scent enveloped her, the scent a man gives out when he wants to love the woman in his arms. Bethlyn found her body ached in the strangest place, a place she barely thought about. However, since being in Hawk's presence the last few weeks, she found it throbbed more often. Pressing himself against her, she nearly moaned his name, so certain was she that finally he'd kiss her. The kiss didn't come. He continued talking, but now his voice contained a husky quality, as if he ached for her, too.

Kiss me! her mind screamed, and wondered why he didn't. Suddenly, with clarity, she knew. She'd forced him to promise not to touch her, to act the gentleman. Apparently Hawk intended to keep that promise, no matter the discomfort to himself or to her.

"The drift of any current is uncertain, at best," she heard him saying. "A navigator must take special precautions to prevent . . ."

"You horrid, aggravating man, do be quiet and release

my hands."

"Why?" Hawk asked, growing peeved she knew by the tensing of his jawline, but he let her hands go.

Turning to face him, she lifted her arms and wrapped them around his neck. "So I can do this," she said in a silky, seductive whisper against his ear. Her lips touched his in a sweet kiss which shortly filled with fire when Hawk's mouth responded. His arms tightened around her, pulling her against him with such ferocity she thought she'd break in two, but she didn't mind. All conscious thought stopped for her. Bethlyn became a creature of delightful sensations, enjoying the heat of desire which coursed through her.

She knew when he picked her up, only breaking their kiss to carry her the distance to his cabin. Placing her gently on the bed, she eagerly reached for him, their only light the shimmering silver orb in the sky.

Hawk threw off his shirt, his muscles straining and bunching together when he reached for her and drew her against the hard expanse of his chest. Timidly Bethlyn ran her fingers through the springy pelt of chest hair, growing a bit bolder when she heard him groan.

He caught her hand in his, stopping her. "Are you certain about this, Beth? If not, I'll leave you alone. I promised to act a gentleman with you."

She thought she heard a bit of a smile in his voice, and she shook her head. "The last thing I want is a gentleman."

"Oh, Beth, Beth, that's the last thing I want to be with you right now."

Expecting him to kiss her, she was a bit surprised when he bounded from the bunk and strode to the windows. She watched him pull the heavy drapes, blocking out the moonlight and encasing the room in total darkness. The reason was obvious when he joined her again and brought her hand to his face. His mask was gone.

A small sensation of hurt that he didn't entirely trust her to keep his identity was healed when his lips captured hers. She forgot everything but the growing fire within her. With expert hands he peeled away her dress and his

139

mouth, warm and filled with heat, moved across her shoulders to find the sensitive tip of one of her breasts.

Slowly, he suckled but his mouth grew greedy and soon devoured as much as could fill the cavity. Bethlyn moaned as a strange churning began in her loins and beat out a pulsating cadence between her thighs. Then he shifted his interest to her other breast, inflicting upon it the same sweet, mind-drugging torture as its twin. Her arms stroked his broad back, her flesh very much aware of the powerful man who pleasured her. Tiny, moaning sounds came from her throat, and she heard Hawk give a low, husky laugh before removing his mouth from her.

In the darkness he moved his face even with hers. "You liked that, didn't you, Beth?"

"Yes."

"I bet most men don't pleasure you too often. But I'm going to be the one to make you moan with ecstasy."

In a haze of growing passion, Bethlyn wondered what could be more wonderful than Hawk suckling her breasts, and though she found his statement odd, too overcome to realize he still thought her a prostitute, she wanted to know how he could make her feel any more wonderful than she did already.

"Please do," she whispered when his lips trailed across her naked flesh to kiss and nip at her breasts, her navel, and down the flat plane of her abdomen. Heedless of his tongue's destination, she allowed him to part her legs, in fact, she willingly parted them for him.

His breath warmed the spot between her naked thighs, and for a split second she nearly closed her legs, but Hawk's hands gently kept them at bay.

"What . . . what are you doing?" she panted, wondering if this was what all men did to women when they made love.

"Let me love you, Beth," he breathed against her silken down. "I want to love you as no man ever has."

Before she could speak again, he buried his face into the velvet folds of her body, and he speared her with his tongue. She arched away from him in a panic, but his hands stroked her inner thighs, gentling her, and then his hands settled on her buttocks and pulled her closer while he feasted upon her sweetness.

Bethlyn's mind screamed for him to stop, to never stop. Never in her life had she known such a gathering of violent, and infinitely delicious feelings in one part of her being. Her body writhed and wriggled, unable to discover what to do with the building force of heat within her. She felt as if she'd been thrown into a storm of white heat, so scalding, that she only knew something horrible or wonderful was destined to happen. Before she was prepared for it, her body exploded in a tempest of silver sparks, so fantastic and intense in feeling that she cried out Hawk's name.

When her body felt fully satiated, she realized that Hawk held her against him and he'd removed all of his clothes. She buried her face in the hair on his chest, her face burning with embarrassment and glad of the darkness. Hawk kissed the top of her head.

"I told you I'm a man of my word."

"You are so smug," she said, but her words were spoken with tenderness for this man who could give such pleasure to her. She lay within his arms for some moments, her eyes growing heavy with sleep.

"Beth?"

"Hmm?"

"We're not finished yet."

Coming awake, Bethlyn wondered what he meant. What was there to finish? she wondered. She realized how naive she must seem to him when he took her hand and guided it to his hard shaft. Suddenly what Mavis had told her about mating all of those years ago registered in her brain and finally made sense.

"What do you want me to do?" she innocently asked.

"Oh, Beth, you are so very good that I almost believe you're a true innocent. But, sweetheart, the time for playacting is long since over. I want you, I ache to fill you with me. Open your legs for me, open them now."

Instinctively Bethlyn opened herself to him, wanting more of the pleasure she'd recently experienced. She was a true innocent, but she wouldn't tell him she'd never been

141

with a man before. Probably he wouldn't believe her and, more than anything, she wanted him with a fierceness which undid all of her staid and proper upbringing. She couldn't bear for him to seek out someone like Della or stand for him to pleasure another woman in the same way. He'd have to discover her virginity for himself.

Leveling himself atop her, Bethlyn felt him guide his manhood into the folds of her flesh. She clasped him to her, urging him to enter her more deeply, which Hawk was only too glad to do, but a quick, sharp ache took her breath away and she bucked.

If she'd seen his face she'd have been quite aware of his shock.

"You're a virgin." He sounded hoarse.

"Y-yes."

"Why didn't you tell me?"

"Does it matter now?"

"Do you want me to stop?"

Just having his length fill her now stirred up the desire and heat within her. She gave an involuntary wiggle which seemed to nearly drive Hawk out of his mind when he issued a lusty groan.

"No," she told him, but her answer would have made no difference, for his shaft drove fully and deeply within her. Pulling him closer against her with her slender legs, she reveled in their complete, mindless joining. All she could feel was the heat of him as he took her to a new level of desire, and finally when he gave a particularly lusty thrust, her cries of ecstasy tumbled from her mouth. An instant later Hawk grew still and cried aloud as his seed filled her.

Hawk's lips caressed the top of Bethlyn's head, which rested against his chest. He knew she was asleep by her soft, easy breaths, and for a moment he longed to wake her and take them both to paradise again. Hawk resisted for two reasons. Her body would, no doubt, be sore from his lovemaking. He'd give her a day or so to recuperate before he loved her again. However, never one to take a girl's virginity lightly, he felt moments of qualm about this turn of events. He'd have sworn she was a seasoned prostitute and much too beautiful not to have remained virginal for long. She looked about twenty to Hawk's trained eye, and he couldn't help but wonder why no man had seduced her before now.

She'd given herself freely, willingly, to him. Why?

This question led him to the second reason for not waking her and loving her. He needed time to think. Questions rolled around his head like the ship's wheel. Why was Beth on a ship filled with doxies, why had she allowed him to believe she was one of them? Granted, she had fought him and practically killed him to defend her honor. His chest still ached at times from the cut she'd inflicted. Beth had told him he wouldn't have believed she wasn't one of the women, and he grudgingly admitted to himself that she was right. He wouldn't have believed her.

And Mavis, Beth's friend and the woman Crane loved, was she one of those women? Apparently not. If neither of them was being sent to Philadelphia for the British soldiers' amusements, then why were they on *Nightingale* in the first place?

Only one answer made sense, and though he longed to push the thought out of his mind, he couldn't. Too much was at stake; his work could be endangered if what he thought turned out to be true. He decided to bide his time and watch this sleeping tigress well. But until she made her move, he'd find pleasure in the taking of her lovely body.

Beth stirred and stretched a bit, then growing aware that Hawk held her in his arms, she stiffened but relaxed to recall the memory of the wondrous love they'd recently shared. With feather-soft touches, her fingers traced the angled lines of his face, and in the darkness she smiled.

"Have I been sleeping long?" she asked.

Hawk's hand traced the soft curves of her backside. "No, but you deserved a nap, little tigress."

Bethlyn giggled and planted a kiss onto one of his nipples. She sighed, much contented and extremely pleased with herself. She belonged to Hawk now, body and soul. The faded memory of her husband prodded her conscience some, but she'd deal with Ian Briston later. For the moment, her world was Hawk.

143

Lovingly, she stroked his face, delighting in the feel of his stubbled chin against her palm. Then she traced the outline of his lips, his nose, his eyes, and finally buried her fingers within the fullness of his hair.

"I'm pleased you aren't bald," she told him.

"Why would you have thought that?" Hawk gathered her more closely against him.

"I've never seen you without your head covered. I'd like to see your face."

She felt him stiffen. "I don't show anyone my face."

"You've never shown Crane, any of your men? They have no idea what you look like?"

"Barely a handful of my men have ever seen me, and these men I trust with my life."

"You don't trust me."

"No."

"Not even after what just happened between us?"

"No."

His voice was curt, much too cool and sounded strangely suspicious to Bethlyn. "I'd never turn you in, Hawk. Not now."

"At least I know you think me a good lover. Thank you for small favors, Beth."

He started to push her away and get up, but she clung to him. "Tell me why you hate the Crown. You're an Englishman."

Hawk said nothing at first, and she thought he was going to leave her. Instead, he settled back against the pillows. "I'm an American, not an Englishman. There's a difference which only those people born on American soil can feel. We've come into our own, and as soon as the king realizes this, the better off everyone will be."

"Then if you hate the British, you hate me also."

In the darkness she heard a ragged sigh. "Again, Beth, you don't understand. I can't explain my purpose to you, because you've closed your mind to liberty and equality. I'd think that you, a girl from humble origins would understand. The king and the aristocracy can't fathom what people like myself want. We want to be self-governing, and we are. A Declaration of Independence was signed only one year ago, and as far as I'm concerned, America is free of British tyranny. I won't rest until the British are driven from our shores."

She wondered how he'd truly regard her if he knew that she was the Earl of Dunsmoor's daughter and the rightful owner of the ship he'd captured, but she weighed his words and found some substance to them. However, she was a loyal subject of the king who couldn't change her allegiance any more than he could change his.

"We've reached a stalemate," she murmured and felt him heave up and leave the bunk.

"It appears we have, but I doubt our political opinions will keep us apart." He kissed the top of her nose, and she heard him dressing in the darkness.

"Where are you going, Hawk?"

"I must tend matters on deck. Go back to sleep." He pulled open the drapes, and moonlight filtered into the cabin.

Bethlyn saw that he was fully dressed and he wore his mask. Before he left she asked him what color was his hair, but gained no response.

Later that morning, a gentle tapping on the cabin door woke Bethlyn, and she opened her eyes to find Pearl peering thoughtfully at her.

"Sorry to be waking you," Pearl apologized and eased herself into the room, carrying three gowns with her and two pairs of shoes. "Captain Hawk said I was to tend to you this morning."

Bethlyn sat up and pulled the sheet about her, not able to still the blush which rose to her cheeks to be found in Hawk's bed.

"Thank you, Pearl, but I can manage on my own."

Pearl grinned. "I wonder about that. You and that friend of yours ain't like the rest of us." Bethlyn rose from the bed, not aware that Pearl had suddenly stopped speaking or that the woman's eyes had grown wide when her gaze settled on the bed sheet, still on the bunk. "You *ain't* like the rest of us," she said with finality.

145

Bethlyn turned at the disbelieving tone in the woman's voice and saw why Pearl sounded so convinced. The crimson color which rose to Bethlyn's face matched the bright stains of blood on the sheet. Bethlyn looked away, and Pearl industriously went about changing the bed linen. When a knock sounded on the door, Della and the young girl Bethlyn remembered as Annie stood there with a large bucket of water held between them. Pearl ushered them into the room to dump the warm water in the tub, and Bethlyn didn't miss the hatred festering in Della's eyes.

Seconds later, the two were gone and Bethlyn stepped into the bath. She fleetingly wondered why Hawk had commissioned Pearl to wait on her, but the bath relieved the tensions which had built inside her after Hawk had left her during the night. She sensed she'd displeased him by her questions and also felt a bit used by him to so cavalierly dress and take his leave. A part of her wondered, now that he'd finally gotten her into his bed, if he'd seek out another woman. Such an easy mark she'd been, throwing herself at him like she'd done. More than once, during the hours alone, she'd asked herself what had gotten into her to act so wantonly.

Pearl handed her a clean towel when she'd finished bathing, and after Bethlyn dried off, she reached for one of the gowns she'd laid on a chair when she'd entered the room. Bethlyn suddenly recognized this and the other two gowns as those she'd packed for her voyage on *Nightingale*. The gown wasn't one of the most elaborate she owned, those still being at Aunt Penny's. In fact it was rather plain, but a becoming deep shade of violet with fine cream-colored lace on the cuffs and rounded neckline. Pearl pulled it over Bethlyn's head and stepped back to admire her charge.

"You are a pretty one, miss, with your beautiful thick hair. An unusual color it is, too, almost like a daffodil, but a deeper shade. No wonder Captain Hawk prefers you over that Della."

"How do you know that?" Bethlyn dared to ask.

"Well, look at yourself in a mirror sometimes. You're

beautiful and refined. Not like that common Della, not like me. Besides, I was on deck when that Crane fellow was carrying a few of your pretty gowns from *Nightingale*. I guess he'd taken the trunk off the ship, and he came right up to Captain Hawk, Mavis was with him, and told Captain Hawk that you might like your pretties with you. Well, that Della was standing there and she reached out to take one of your dresses, but the captain took her arm and gave her a look that could kill. That was when he motioned to me to bring your clothes to you and told me to tend to you. I think Captain Hawk is right smitten with you, miss." Pearl smiled a toothy smile and picked up the soiled bed linen.

Bethlyn remembered how he'd left her when he finished making love to her and she disagreed. "I doubt Captain Hawk cares anything for me. I can't wait until I'm free of the man."

"Shouldn't be too long," Pearl informed her and made for the door. "I heard that Crane fellow tell Mavis that we'll be reaching shore soon. The voyage is near over."

A sinking sensation in the pit of Bethlyn's stomach caused her to sit down. If the voyage was almost over, then they'd probably be set ashore soon. She'd never see Hawk again. Granted, he'd made love to her and left her, and she knew she should be more than glad to be free of him, but a part of her couldn't bear to be pushed out of his life, never to see him again.

"Did you happen to hear how much longer until we land?"

"No, maybe Mavis or Crane can tell you. Ask Captain Hawk." Pearl left the cabin.

She wouldn't ask Hawk anything, somehow afraid he'd assume she might care for him, which she did. The memory of his voice, filled with suspicion the night before, came back to her. For some reason, he didn't entirely trust her, and if he knew she dreaded the moment when she'd leave him, he might not want to love her again. She sensed he hated clinging women, and in his line of work, he didn't need entanglements.

Besides, she had a husband in Philadelphia. She'd

147

forgotten him during the last hours and her reason for taking the voyage in the first place. Now, however, Ian Briston didn't matter. No self-respecting husband would want her, not after he learned she'd been a conquest of the notorious privateer, Hawk. *A willing conquest,* she reminded herself. Any hope of salvaging her marriage died within her. She'd never have the homelife and children she so desperately wanted. No doubt, she could convince Briston to quietly annul their marriage now. She'd simply have to tell him the truth when she saw him. The solution to ending her marriage appeared so simple to her that she shivered.

With her mind made up about her status as Briston's wife, Bethlyn turned her thoughts upon Hawk. She knew nothing about him, except that he was a wonderful lover, an expert captain, and she felt a gentle person, but a man who'd been hurt and disillusioned by life too many times. His shell was hard, but his heart was soft. She understood that he had no place in his life for her, but whatever time they had left together, she wanted to fill that time with passion, to savor the memory of his kisses, his embraces, and the fiery need of his body for her.

She'd fill up her heart with memories of Hawk to sustain her for the rest of her life.

Chapter Ten

In the wavering candlelight the high sheen of perspiration glistened on the naked bodies, entwined together. Twin sighs of completion echoed within the cabin, and soon Bethlyn felt the touch of Hawk's lips upon her forehead. Despite her sexual satisfaction with this man, a feeling of desolation welled within her. She sensed this would be their last night together, though Hawk hadn't mentioned anything about landing in the morning. When he'd entered the cabin an hour earlier, he'd scooped her up into his strong arms and undressed her in a lazy fashion, almost as if fate had promised them forever.

Bethlyn knew differently.

In the morning he'd bid her farewell, and her heart would break. She vowed she wouldn't cry. She doubted that tears would move a man like Hawk, but she'd smile bravely and somehow, someway, continue with her life. First off, she'd find Ian Briston and free herself from his shadowy memory. She found she couldn't remember his face any longer, which was just as well, she told herself. Their marriage was a sham, and she'd be glad to be free.

To be free of Hawk—well, it would take a very long time to be free of his burning kisses, the intimacy of his warm hands on her skin. She lifted herself up on an elbow and gazed down at him, noting that the usually wakeful Hawk slept soundly, something he never did after making love to her. The previous night he'd loved her until dawn crested the horizon and then loved her again after the sun had colored the sky with golden streaks. Hawk was an insatiable lover, and she the willing participant, but he never slept, always leaving her to fall asleep alone.

Now, she noticed that his mouth had grown slack with sleep, and his wonderful, male body fit snugly against hers in a trusting, relaxed state. The only thing which obscured her view of his face was the mask, and the dark scarf which covered his head hid the color of his hair.

She'd never see him after tomorrow, and Bethlyn ached to know what Hawk looked like. Would he be handsome? She didn't care if he were ugly and bald. This man had given her hours of intense pleasure, had awakened her to the hidden delights of her own body. Somehow, seeing his face would dispel the feeling that she'd dreamt all of this when on land again. She wanted to see his face.

With tentative, shaking fingers she reached for the string at the back of his head and worked it loose. Hawk uttered a sound in his sleep, and she stiffened a moment, but with a careful hand, she grabbed the mask and gently began to remove it from his face. Swallowing hard, her whole body trembling, she gazed upon the face of her lover.

Inhaling slightly, she knew that she'd never seen a more perfect-looking man. Hawk's eyes were closed, and long lashes rested on bronzed cheeks. An aquiline nose completed the portion of his face she'd never seen, and a thrill of excitement coursed through her at his rugged handsomeness. She even thought that his ears were wonderful looking. With an urge to see more, she pushed back the ebony scarf to discover that Hawk's hair was the same deep black shade as the scarf.

"Oh, Hawk," she breathed, shameless in her renewed desire for him and strangely close to tears. She wanted him to wake and make love to her again; she wanted to see his passion for her on his face when he filled her with his love.

As she watched him, Hawk's eyes opened, and she knew without a doubt that they were a bright, gleaming green. He watched her, not with unveiled desire, but contempt.

She mouthed his name again, but this time her voice shook with fear, and suddenly she wished she'd never removed the hated mask.

"Memorize my face well, sweetheart," she heard him say. "It shall be the last familiar one you see for quite a while."

"Hawk, please."

He grabbed her wrist, and jerked her along his naked length. "Please what? Am I hurting you? Sorry, sweet." He didn't sound sorry at all, but very, very angry. "You know, Beth, I would have loved to have trusted you, but I learned long ago that women are a sorry lot to trust. No man is safe from any female. But I admit, I nearly gave you the benefit of the doubt, your being a virgin and all. However, it was your virginal state which led me to think that you were less trustworthy than the others. I mean, you were so interested in seeing my face, knowing the color of my hair."

Hawk reached out and stroked her cheek, but she felt no warmth in his touch. "Instead, my conniving little virgin, I decided that you should see my face. You're the first captive I've allowed to see the great Captain Hawk. Regard yourself as highly honored." His eyes traced the features of her face, seeming to memorize each pore.

"I wanted . . . wanted to see you, to know how you look. Why are you so angry?" Bethlyn whispered, finding her voice at last.

Hawk laughed and pushed her away from him. Standing up, he loomed over her prone figure on the bed. "You're a damned good actress, Beth. I give you that. Even your stammer is adorably authentic. Your teacher is to be congratulated on a job well done."

"What do you mean, 'my teacher'?"

"Just the right amount of confusion, too. But I'm not stupid. Someone put you up to traveling on *Nightingale*, perhaps someone expected me to confiscate the ship, and you'd conveniently be aboard to gain knowledge about my dealings . . . and me."

"No, that isn't true." Scrambling off the bunk, unaware of her nakedness, Bethlyn reached for Hawk only to be rebuffed when he turned away to dress. "How was I to know *Nightingale* would be attacked? What are you

151

accusing me of?"

Hawk finished tucking his shirt into his breeches and swung around. His face appeared cold and the finger he snaked across her breasts felt like ice. "You're a spy for the Crown, and a damned able one at that. The doxy act was quite convincing, except we both know you aren't one of those women. However, don't feel too proud of yourself for discovering how I look. I pretended to be asleep to see if you'd fall for the bait. You did. I knew that if you were a spy, you'd take off the mask. My suspicions about you are proved correct."

For a second Bethlyn felt as if he'd slapped her. So, he thought the only reason she'd wanted to see his face was to turn him in to the authorities. If this had been two weeks earlier, she would have relished the chance. However, now things had changed. She'd given her heart to this blackguard, and he was too caught up in his masquerade as the fearsome Captain Hawk to realize the truth.

"You're wrong, Hawk. I'm not a spy. I wanted to see your face because I think I might be in love with you. Under the circumstances it's only natural."

She noticed him wince, almost as if he might be weighing her words. "If that's the truth, and you aren't a spy, why were you on *Nightingale*, pretending to be a prostitute? Tell me who you are, Beth."

Bethlyn stifled a groan. He *would* demand an explanation, and one which she found impossible to give. She was the Earl of Dunsmoor's daughter and the wife of Ian Briston, a noted loyalist. Hawk was an American privateer. As much as she cared for him, she considered that he might use her position against her, entangling her future, and she'd never be free of Ian Briston. He might hold her for ransom, thus confusing an already unusual situation with her husband. She couldn't risk telling him the truth.

"I won't tell you anything about myself, but I'm not a spy. I'd never turn you into the British. Not now."

"Ah, but you did consider that very thing. Because of your blunder with the mask, Beth, I must rethink my plans about you."

"What are you going to do with me?"

"Imprison you."

Shaking her head, her tousled locks streamed across her breasts and her large brown eyes filled with fear. Her usually pink lips grew paler than sand. "Please don't lock me up again. I swear I'm not a spy. I want to go to Philadelphia with the other women. I can't bear being cooped up in some tiny room again. Please, Hawk!"

He didn't seem to hear her, but threw her gown at her. It landed by her feet in a crumpled heap. "Get dressed and be quick about it. We're due to go ashore at first light."

"Where are you taking me?"

A sneer turned up the edge of his mouth before he retrieved the mask and covered his face. "Prisoners don't ask questions, my love, no matter how fetching they are. Just be forewarned that you're not going to Phildelphia with the others. I have my own private prison in mind for you, and I doubt you're going to like it very much."

Hawk's orders to transfer all of the women, save Beth, to *Nightingale* took Crane unaware. One moment he slept peacefully with Mavis in his arms, and the next, a loud pounding on his door woke him. Half asleep he remembered the fierce, furious tone of Hawk's voice as he issued the command that Crane take charge of the confiscated ship and see that somehow the women reached Philadelphia safely. Crane was too confused by this strange turn of events to argue with Hawk. Never had he seen the man this riled, and Crane, who had been with Hawk through years of turmoil, realized that only one person could get Hawk this bothered. Bethlyn.

Now, as he stood in the center of his cabin, a shiver shook him. He noticed that Mavis's large blue eyes appeared even larger in her small face.

"Why isn't Hawk allowing Bethlyn, I mean Beth, to go to Philadelphia?" Mavis asked in a worried voice.

Crane turned to her, and hurriedly he reached for his clothes. "I don't know, but I have to stop him. Hawk looked ready enough to kill."

153

"Crane, don't let him hurt her. I don't know what she may have done to upset him, but please— You must have guessed by now that she isn't like these other women."

Crane nodded. "I know that, Mavis. I also know that her name isn't just Beth. She's Bethlyn Briston, the daughter of Nathaniel Talbot, Earl of Dunsmoor, and wife of the Philadelphia ship owner, Ian Briston."

"Yes, but how do you know about that? Bethlyn tried to keep her identity a secret. She was on her way to Philadelphia to ask her husband to annul their marriage or to make her his wife. I suppose I should have told you sooner, but I didn't want to betray Bethlyn's confidence. She's been like a sister to me, Crane. Don't allow this fearsome Captain Hawk to harm her."

Crane finished dressing, all too aware that he might have done Bethlyn Briston a great disservice himself. He'd known for quite some time who she was, and he thought that things would progress nicely between Bethlyn and Hawk. He'd been wrong. "I promise I'll do my best to calm down Hawk," he promised Mavis before he left the cabin.

However, once on deck Crane realized with a sinking feeling of dread in his stomach that he was too late. The early morning sun emphasized the outline of the island known as Windhaven, an island off of the New Jersey shoreline, where the *Black Falcon* would be tucked away in a remote bay, hidden from view by huge sand dunes. However, Hawk didn't wait for the ship to anchor. Crane spotted his formidable figure in a longboat with Bethlyn by his side, and Sparrow rowed in the direction of the shoreline.

Crane suppressed the urge to yell and halt them. He couldn't very well scream the news about their relationship to Hawk. Too many ears and eyes even now watched them. Somehow he'd have to trust the fates to keep Bethlyn safe.

He must perform his duty as he'd been ordered. Time was precious, and the women must be transferred to *Nightingale* for the trip down the coastline where Crane would drop them off and see that each woman was given

154

enough money to find her way to Phildelphia. Then he'd oversee the refurbishing of the confiscated ship. By the time he and the men finished the repainting and overhauling, no one would recognize *Nightingale* or would be able to point blame at any of them.

No one except Bethlyn Briston.

Crane decided he'd tell Mavis that Bethlyn was safe, because no matter how fierce and forbidding Hawk could be, he knew the man would never really do her bodily harm. Besides, who knew how close these two people would grow, once alone together on Windhaven? The longer Hawk kept Bethlyn sequestered on Windhaven, the safer they'd all be. The question which concerned Crane most was what would the impetuous miss do when released.

Soft ocean breezes blew through the window of the small wooden house where Hawk had brought Bethlyn earlier that morning. Bethlyn sat on a small stool by the open window and watched the ocean surf swell and retreat against the sandy beach. By the sun and the growling of her stomach, she gauged that it was early afternoon. She wondered if Hawk intended to feed her or let her starve to death. She knew she could easily mastermind an escape. After all, the windows were all open, the door to the house, unlocked. But where would she go? The beach appeared deserted, not one rickety boat could she see. In fact, she hadn't laid eyes on a living soul. The perfect place for a notorious man like Hawk, she found herself thinking. Deserted and much too warm for her liking, having grown used to England's damp and chilly weather, she wondered if Hawk had purposely placed her in a living hell.

"How could I have thought I cared about him?" she groused aloud. "He's an arrogant, pompous idiot. What do I care how he looks? In fact, he isn't even that handsome."

As she mumbled these words, she saw Hawk meandering through the sand towards the house. His face was unmasked, and the breeze tousled his dark hair. Without a doubt she knew she hadn't meant what she'd just said. No man could possibly be more handsome than Hawk. The breath caught in her throat to see that he'd removed his shirt, revealing his powerful, bronzed chest. Images of the times she'd kissed his chest, buried her face against him, rose up and taunted her. Just to know she'd reveled in this man's lovemaking caused her face to grow heated, and when he entered the house, she flushed anew, hoping he couldn't read her thoughts or see the flare of desire in her eyes for him. No matter who he was or how he'd treated her, he could still make her legs go wobbly with passion for him.

"I trust you've familiarized yourself with the house," he said, sitting on a chair and pulling off his boots.

She had, but she pretended disinterest. The house possessed three rooms: a sitting room where they now sat, a kitchen, and a bedroom upstairs with a glorious view of the ocean. She recalled the feather bed, even having sat upon it and finding it quite comfortable. A colorful quilt covered the linen-clad sheets, and though the room was simple in style and furnishings, she found it most enchanting.

"It's very rustic" was all she said.

"Be that as it may, you better get used to it, Beth. You'll be here for quite some time to come."

"I won't stay here. You can't make me stay here!" She rose from her stool and clenched her fists. "I'll escape."

Hawk shrugged. "Try it. I doubt you'll get very far." He rubbed his hands together. "Now, what about lunch? I'm starved."

"I was about to ask you the same thing. I'm quite hungry."

"Well, fix us something, Beth. You did notice the kitchen."

"Of course I noticed it, but you can't expect me to cook."

"I can, and I do."

Bethlyn blinked in astonishment. "I don't know how to cook." Infuriating man, she thought, and a bit of anger rose in her. He had the nerve to imprison her on this godforsaken island and then expect her to cook for him.

156

She placed her hands on her hips. "And even if I could cook, what makes you think I'd cook anything for you?"

Hawk rose to his feet, and without warning, he pulled her into his arms. His lips were inches from hers. "You'll do what I say. Believe me, Beth, if not for your pulling off my mask, I'd have gladly shipped you off to Philadelphia with the other women. Women are a great bother, and good for only one use. The only reason I haven't killed you for being a spy is because you're so damned beautiful, and I want you for one reason and one reason alone." With a lowering of his head he touched her lips and bestowed such a long and lingering kiss upon her that she felt like a mass of jelly. Despite the circumstances, her body melted against his and she'd have given in to the pleasant ache in her womanhood except Hawk broke away from her. His next words threw freezing water upon her ardor.

"I think you know now what reason that might be."

He left her so abruptly that she found support by leaning against a chair. "I'm to be your whore while I'm here."

"Yes."

"I won't."

"You will. Whenever I want you, you'll come to me. When we met, you wanted me to think you were a doxy, so now you shall be."

"I see that I'm being punished because you believe I'm a spy."

Hawk sighed and walked into the kitchen. She heard his voice. "What I believe isn't important any longer. You present a danger to my operation and must remain here. While here, you shall avail me of your body. I think, under the circumstances, you owe that much to me."

Suddenly she almost hated him. "When will you free me?"

Hawk reentered the room, munching on an apple. "That depends on how well you behave."

She knew what that meant, and she winced, hating to have to bury her pride. Once again, as on the ship, she'd become his virtual slave and do his bidding. She'd come to his bed when he wanted her, whereas on the ship, she had wished to make love to him and came willingly to his bed. Tears stung her eyes to think that he now regarded her no better than Della or a common trollop.

"I hate you for this, Hawk."

"I know, sweetheart, but you'll love the nights." He sounded unbelievably conceited. "Since you can't cook," Bethlyn heard him say, "I'll arrange for a local woman to help you in the kitchen and give you cooking lessons."

"Someone else is on the island other than Sparrow and us?"

Hawk laughed. "Yes, but don't get your hopes up that anyone in the village will help you escape from me. The *Black Falcon* is moored near here, and my men have families on this island. Without their masks, you won't know who is who. I wouldn't recommend trying to enlist help from anyone, not even a woman. She might be a wife, a daughter, of one of my faithful crewmen. No one will risk my fury, Beth."

"You're so certain of yourself that you make me ill."

"I have to be sure of myself," Hawk said, and moved close to her. His voice was whispery soft against her cheek. "I'm so certain of my power over you, love, that I know for a fact that when I touch you, when I make love to you tonight, you won't pull away. You'll eagerly open your arms and legs to me."

The crudity of his words stung, excited, and mortified her, because she feared he was correct.

Chapter Eleven

True to his word, Hawk sent for a woman to help Bethlyn in the kitchen, and by late that afternoon, Bethlyn had helped prepare a seafood stew under the guidance of Mrs. Tansy Tolliver. The hardest part for Bethlyn was the actual cleaning of the fish, but with an expert hand, Mrs. Tolliver instructed her how to do it properly and also told her which spices would give the mackerel a delicious and pungent flavor.

After simmering the stew for over half an hour, Bethlyn carried the bubbling brew in a white soup tureen and placed it on the table in front of Hawk. He motioned for her to spoon the stew into a bowl for him, and Bethlyn very nearly refused, but she stifled her impulse to hurl a nasty remark at him because the kindly and grandmotherly Mrs. Tolliver stood beside her. The old woman's face beamed with delight as she urged Bethlyn to serve Hawk the stew. "I just know you'll find it quite tasty, sir," Mrs. Tolliver said to Hawk. "Beth is a very good cook."

"Is she now? Well, I can hardly wait," he said in a tender voice to Mrs. Tolliver while Bethlyn dutifully served him.

When Hawk shoved the first spoonful into his mouth, Bethlyn didn't realize she waited with baited breath for his approval. It was only when he nodded and continued eating that she breathed a relieved sigh. "I told you he'd like it, Beth." Mrs. Tolliver winked at her and Bethlyn followed her to the door, thanking her for the help in the kitchen. "Don't worry, dear. I'll come back in the morning to help you with breakfast, but not too early." The kindly woman patted her on the arm and whispered, "I remember how it was when I married my Jack. Newly married people like to sleep late."

Too stunned to say anything, Bethlyn watched the old woman hobble through the sand to her home on the other side of the island. A warmth suffused Bethlyn's whole body to realize that Mrs. Tolliver thought she and Hawk were married. She felt she should have told Mrs. Tolliver the truth, but a part of her hated to admit that Hawk wanted her for only one thing, and apparently he didn't care what people thought about her virtue. But she did, and she found she didn't want anyone to know she was Hawk's whore.

Going inside, Hawk waved her to a chair. "Eat some soup, Beth. You've done a more than adequate job for your first cooking effort."

Was he being kind to her, or belittling her cooking? Sometimes she couldn't tell when Hawk meant what he said. He had a habit of disguising the tone of his voice and of making his eyes look inexpressive. Probably because of that damned mask he wore he could manage to hide his emotions, she thought in disgust. Suddenly she wasn't hungry and told him so just as Sparrow knocked and entered the kitchen. With barely a nod in Sparrow's direction, she lifted the hem of her gown and took herself upstairs to the bedroom.

"What's the matter with her?" she heard Sparrow ask Hawk.

"Must be her time of the month" was Hawk's reply.

Even from upstairs color suffused Bethlyn's face that Hawk would be so crude as to say such a thing about her to another person. However, what could she expect from such a blackguard, a man who'd keep her prisoner here and expect her to enjoy it? Yet she mentally calculated the number of days since her last flux and realized, so far, she wasn't late. She gave a relieved sigh. Nothing could be worse than to find herself pregnant by Captain Hawk. Most probably the bounder wouldn't take responsibility for the child if she did conceive.

Hawk's comment caused her to laugh to herself. So, he thought he would come up here later tonight and claim her again, that he'd be able to make her purr for him like a kitten. Well, she wouldn't. She'd tell him she was ill, and if he had the audacity to ask her what ailed her, then she'd recant word for word what he'd told Sparrow.

This was exactly what she did some two hours later. Hawk stood looking at her from the doorway, but instead of inquiring further, he left the house. A sense of elation filled her. He wouldn't treat her like a whore, she told herself, but she did feel a bit lost without him beside her in the soft feather bed. She also couldn't help wondering where he'd gone, and if he'd spent the night alone.

Lulled by the sounds of the surf outside the window, she drifted off to sleep. She dreamed that she came to the door of a small house on the island. In her arms she carried Hawk's child. When she knocked on the door, Hawk opened it, and a beautiful woman stood beside him. Through tears of shame, Bethlyn pleaded with him to do the right thing and marry her, but Hawk threw back his head and laughed unpleasantly. "Silly wench," he told her. "You're already married. Take yourself and the brat off to your husband." Then he kissed the woman and slammed the door in her face.

With a start, Bethlyn woke to discover that tears streamed down her cheeks, and though she attempted to control herself, she couldn't stop crying. Finally she managed to halt her tears and climbed out of bed, only to discover that her flux had started. She began to cry anew, feeling like a helpless, spoiled child, and berated herself for her silliness. Over and over she told herself that she should be relieved she wasn't pregnant.

However, another part of her wouldn't admit that she felt disappointment not to be carrying Hawk's baby.

For the next few days Bethlyn contented herself in the kitchen. Each morning Mrs. Tolliver appeared with the necessary foodstuffs and instructed her how to bake breads, muffins, cook fish and soups. One evening she served Hawk wine-berry soup and felt quite gratified when he asked for seconds.

One morning Mrs. Tolliver appeared with her grandson, a sturdy-looking boy of about twelve, named Nate. Nate watched attentively while his grandmother instructed Bethlyn until he grew bored and sauntered onto the beach.

Mrs. Tolliver shook her head in dismay. "That Nate is a problem child, I tell you. My husband and I don't know what to do about him since his parents died. My son was his father, you know. He and my daughter-in-law were killed in a sailing accident two years ago." Her eyes misted over with tears for a moment. "Nate is all we have left of them, but he wants to go to sea, and I fear one day he will. He's much too young to think of such a thing, and with the unrest on the seas right now, I hate to dwell on what might happen to him if he decides to take off on his own in a year or so."

Having seen the outside world, Bethlyn realized that Nate probably hungered for more than this tiny island. She didn't blame him in that respect. The island, she found, was quite nice, or that portion of what she'd seen of it. However, she knew a larger and more exciting world awaited Nate than Windhaven. Yet she also knew how important a family could be to a growing youngster, never having had the opportunity to win her father's love and admiration.

"Does Nate have any chores to occupy himself?" Bethlyn asked.

Mrs. Tolliver nodded, but added, "Only the usual things. He helps my husband catch cod and mackerel, but he stays at home when Jack brings the catch to Philadelphia."

A warning bell went off in Bethlyn's head. "How far is Windhaven from Philadelphia?" she asked offhandedly while she pared a potato, hoping that Mrs. Tolliver didn't hear the anticipation in her voice.

"Hmm, I'm not certain. It takes Jack only three days to take the catch to the market there and return home. Windhaven is quite near the Delaware and New Jersey shorelines, so Jack sails up the Delaware River."

This geographical information meant very little to Bethlyn, who was unschooled in the area, but she did guess that Philadelphia was about a day's sail from the island. She stored all she'd heard in the back of her mind, keeping it for future use.

"Perhaps Nate might like to accompany his grandfather on his trips to the city. I've heard Philadelphia is an exciting place and might allay his wanderlust."

"Yes, Beth, you might be right. I'll speak to Jack about taking Nate with him on his next trip."

Mrs. Tolliver smiled warmly at Bethlyn, and she smiled back. Perhaps she'd get away from Hawk and Windhaven yet, she found herself thinking. Then Mrs. Tolliver kindly invited Bethlyn and Hawk to supper that night, and Bethlyn found she couldn't refuse the woman's polite invitation. However, she wasn't certain Hawk would be there since he hadn't slept at home the last few days. Later, after Mrs. Tolliver had left, she finished baking a batch of cookies and called to Nate, who waited on the beach.

Eagerly he munched on two cookies at once when Bethlyn offered them to him. She sat beside him on the beach and delighted in the warm sun on her face and the incredible blue of the sky. Windhaven was a place of enchantment, but to her it seemed a prison.

"Do you have a boat?" Bethlyn asked Nate.

Nate shook his head. "Naw, but my grandpa does."

"Is it a large boat?"

"Sort of."

"Your grandmother told me that he usually goes to Philadelphia to sell his catch. How often does he go?"

Nate considered for a moment. "Two more weeks, I think. He came back a few days ago, and he goes about twice a month. Why are you so interested?" He reached for another cookie on the plate which rested on the sand between them.

"Just curious about everyone on the island," Bethlyn told him and changed the subject to the beautiful weather. She doubted the child would become curious as to why she pumped him for information, but she didn't want to take the chance that he might very well mention to Hawk or someone else about her interest in his grandfather's schedule and boat.

Two more weeks before Mr. Tolliver left for Philadelphia. She hated herself for making friends with Nate only to use him later, but her hands perspired in anticipation of escaping Hawk.

That same afternoon Nate escorted her to the village. Bethlyn found the village of Windhaven to be quite small. About fifteen wooden houses dotted the landscape, and huge sand dunes rose like pyramids in the distance. Small boats bobbed by a dock, and Nate introduced her to one of the fishermen who sat on his boat as his grandfather. Jack Tolliver was as friendly and kind as his wife, and he regaled her and Nate with tales of the sea for an hour. Bethlyn listened with interest, but her eyes rested covetously on the boat. *Two more weeks, two more weeks,* her mind repeated over and over.

Her ears perked up at the man's mention of Hawk, and she gave her full attention to Mr. Tolliver. "Should be a grand party, I hear," he said. "Everyone likes Mr. Hawk."

She'd missed something. "What party is that, Mr. Tolliver?"

"Why, your wedding party, missus." Jack Tolliver clamped a hand over his mouth. "I'm sorry, it was to be a surprise. My Tansy's been planning it for days now. Don't say a word to her about me telling you. Promise me? She'd be awful upset that I let the cat out of the bag. And you, too, young Nate. Don't you be telling your grandma how I can't keep me mouth closed."

Both of them promised to keep the party a secret, but Bethlyn felt a sickening sensation in the pit of her stomach. A wedding party. Good God!

That evening Hawk returned. Upon entering the house, he nodded at her, his arms loaded down with clothes she recognized as her own.

"I thought you might need your dresses," he told her and smiled, a tone of apology in his voice. "I slept on the *Black Falcon* the last few nights and realized you didn't have a change of clothes when I saw your things in the cabin."

"That was kind of you," Bethlyn said, and took the clothes from Hawk. It seemed that the moment he stepped into the house, she grew alert and unable to tear her gaze from his. She hadn't seen him in a few days, and Hawk seemed to have grown more handsome if that was possible. She hadn't realized until this moment how lonely she'd been without him, having accustomed herself to falling asleep in his strong arms each night. Worst of all, a sense of jealousy ate away at her and she couldn't stop herself from asking her next question. "Did you sleep alone?"

A blush like a tidal wave consumed her face when he started to laugh. "Beth, you little minx, you're jealous!"

"I am not! I only wondered . . . Oh, never mind!"

She started to flounce away, hating the way this man could rankle her and cause her not to think straight. Hawk, however, grabbed her arm and spun her around to face him. His voice sounded low and husky when he said, "I like you to be jealous."

For a moment his eyes darkened to a deep forest green, and she waited for the inevitable kiss. In fact, she moistened her lips in anticipation of one, but Hawk only released her arm and smiled. "I understand Mrs. Tolliver is giving us a party tonight."

For a few seconds she felt like the worst fool, hated the way her face blazed like a furnace, but she took a deep breath and pretended she'd never longed for his kiss. "How do you know about the party? I thought it was going to be a surprise."

"Everyone on the island knows about it. No one can keep a secret for long here. The party is one of the reasons I brought you the clothes. I want you to look your best tonight." He reached out and fingered a green gown with beige lace on the elbow-length sleeves and low neckline. "Wear this one. The color brings out the gold of your hair."

"I presume you're aware that this party is in honor of our marriage."

"Yes."

"Hawk, we're not married. The men on your ship know we were never married. This situation is humiliating to me. Mrs. Tolliver has been very kind to me. I can't deceive her into believing something which isn't true."

"Why? You deceived me into thinking you were a prostitute and denied being a spy for the Crown. How am I supposed to believe you? I advise you to get dressed, and don't dawdle. What other people think isn't my concern, but you are—that is, until I decide what to do with you."

"You can be a very hard man."

"True," he agreed, nonplussed by the coldness of her tone.

Bethlyn saw she was getting nowhere with Hawk. She wanted to experience his warmth, the caring he'd shown her before she'd removed his mask. Apparently, he felt free to walk about Windhaven without the mask's protection, knowing that the people on the island were loyal to him. It seemed that the only person he didn't trust was her. For a second she almost blurted out again that she wasn't a spy and wouldn't turn him in, but she didn't. Once more, it appeared they were at an impasse, and she refused to humble herself to him by declaring her innocence. She did have some pride.

Saying nothing further, Bethlyn started up the stairs, but heard him say, "I want you to know I slept alone." Her heart soared at his words, but she said nothing to him, feeling a bit triumphant that he hadn't found the need to seek out another woman. Still, their situation was intolerable to her, and she cursed under her breath at her own folly to think Hawk cared about her.

When Bethlyn and Hawk arrived at the Tolliver's small wooden house half an hour later, they found the party had started without them. Strange faces, people Bethlyn had never seen, smiled or peered intently at her when Tansy Tolliver made the introductions. Bethlyn fought not to grimace when Tansy introduced her as "Mrs. Hawk." Catching a quick glimpse of Hawk's face, she noticed a glint of amused delight in his eyes, almost as if he enjoyed her humiliation. She wondered how many of the men who now watched her were members of Hawk's crew and thought her to be a whore. Despite the warmth of the evening air, Bethlyn shivered and silently vowed that in two weeks time she'd escape to Philadelphia. She doubted the arrogant Captain Hawk would be smiling then!

The party spilled out of the house and onto the moon-drenched beach. A fire had been lit earlier, and islanders sat in easy companionship while the children rushed hither and yon with small buckets in their hands and dug for clams in the soft, cool sand.

A sweet-tasting ale was offered to Bethlyn by a gracious Jack Tolliver, and everyone stood to toast the bride and groom. This was the hardest moment of Bethlyn's life. She stood stiffly by Hawk's side and mouthed an acknowledgment to the toast, the whole time bristling with indignation that Hawk thought nothing of duping these people, and worst of all, he appeared relaxed and nonchalant.

However, by the time Bethlyn had imbibed three more cups of the delicious brew, she barely realized she leaned her head against Hawk's broad shoulder and listened in rapt appreciation to a lovely melody one of the men played on a harmonica. A wonderful lethargy stole across her, allowing her to forget how much she should hate Hawk. Instead, she found a comfortable place within the crook of his arm and closed her eyes, delighting in the caressing breeze upon her cheeks.

Finally a soft butterfly kiss landed on her lips and, opening her eyes, she saw Hawk's dark face.

"Time to go home, sleepyhead."

She nodded and allowed him to help her up from the sand, and they bade everyone a good night. Tansy and Jack Tolliver hugged her and wished them well with their marriage. Guilt washed over Bethlyn to think that she was going to use these kind people, take advantage of their friendship, for her own end. As she and Hawk sauntered leisurely along the beach on the return trip to the house, she mulled over the events of the last few weeks, but her brain was so fuzzy from the ale and her step rather uncertain that she found she didn't want to dwell upon her future escape. If not for Hawk's arm, secure about her waist, she would have fallen at one point.

"I can tell you're not much of a drinker."

"I never acquired the taste for alcohol," she admitted, "but Mr. Tolliver's concoction was quite tasty. I wonder if Mrs. Tolliver might give me the recipe."

"You have become a domestic little mouse."

Bethlyn started to take offense, but his tone was light and bantering. "There's nothing else for me to do here but keep house and cook."

"Perhaps it's time to find another way to spend your time, Beth." Hawk stopped walking, and with the moonlight spilling across his darkly handsome face, he leaned down and kissed her on the lips. She moaned at the desire which erupted within her. It had been so long since Hawk had held her like this or kissed her in this way that no matter their differences, she found she wanted him to make love to her. In fact, she ached for his possession and her complete surrender to him.

Wrapping her arms around his neck, Bethlyn arched against him, delighting when their tongues met in a riotous assault upon her senses. She was lost and didn't care.

"Easy, sweetheart. We still have a distance to walk to the house. Kiss me like that again, and I might be tempted to love you right here on the beach."

"Please do," she murmured, overwhelmed by passion's flames which seemed to scorch her insides. "I can't wait that long for you, Hawk. I want you now." Her hand made contact with the obvious bulge in his trousers. She smiled up at him. "You can't wait, either."

Hawk groaned into her hair, and suddenly he scooped her up into his arms and walked the short distance from the shoreline and crossed a sand dune. On the other side of the dune, Bethlyn couldn't see the ocean, but she heard its gentle roar. At least she thought it was the ocean she heard. It might have been the rapid beating of her heart. But the dune protected them from view, and this was all Bethlyn cared about at the moment.

She still felt deliciously groggy from the ale and she leaned into Hawk, her hands pulling his head down to her mouth. She kissed him with such fervor that she caused them both to fall to their knees. The sand cushioned the fall, and she found herself laughing as their arms and legs became helplessly entwined.

"I think I like this," she said.

"I know I like this." That was Hawk's comment, and she shivered, knowing that she'd like to see much more of him. With trembling fingers, she began to take off his shirt until he took the lead and pulled the soft linen shirt over his head to reveal his well-muscled chest to her. Bethlyn buried her face within the springy cushion of chest hair and kissed him. Her hands massaged the hard pectoral wall.

"I adore how you look," she told him, a husky catch in her voice.

"Even without the mask?"

"Hmm. That's a hard question to answer," she teased, and giggled to see him glower. No man could possibly be more handsome than Hawk, she thought. But when she helped him pull off his trousers and held his stiff member in the curl of her palm, she said, "I know I adore this." And she wasn't teasing.

"Taunting vixen. Let's see how well you take sweet torture."

Hawk started to pull at the lacings on the bodice of the green gown, but Bethlyn stopped him with a gentle hand on his chest. She had a captive audience when she gently began to untie the lacings on the front of the gown. Like a seasoned temptress she slowly undid each one until her breasts strained to be free. As she did this she watched the play of passion upon Hawk's face and saw his eyes turn a smoky green. This is how she'd imagined he'd looked at her all those nights he wore the mask. She had ached to see the desire on his handsome face for her, and now she did. Delightful shivers shook her when he'd had enough of her teasing and pulled the bodice apart to allow her breasts to spill into his hands.

Lifting them to his lips, he took the tip of one into his

mouth and gently circled the throbbing peak with his tongue. Then he worked the same magic on Bethlyn's other nipple. Moans of ecstasy spilled forth from Bethlyn; but she wanted him to suckle her more deeply, and the way she arched toward him indicated her desire. Hawk opened his mouth wide and freely laved one breast and then the other, driving Bethlyn wild with need.

His hand found its way under the material of her gown and snaked upward to the throbbing peak of her womanhood. He touched her and she heard him mumble, "So warm, so wet."

Bethlyn was more than ready for Hawk. A part of her wondered if he intended to torture her endlessly with his lips, his fingers as they stroked her and filled her.

"Undress me, Hawk. I can't . . . stand any more." Her voice sounded thick.

Apparently Hawk couldn't take any more either when her hand flew to his aroused manhood. With a surprisingly steady hand, Hawk ripped the bodice from her and pulled her skirt off. He laid her clothes on the sand, then pulled her on top of them. He straddled her and, instinctively, Bethlyn wrapped her silken legs around his back. For a second she felt his warm, pulsating shaft against her thigh before he plunged into her moist softness, taking the breath from her.

Hawk's hands tangled in the honeyed depths of her hair. Her body arched upward to his, following his rhythm to the age old tune of love.

"Beth, Beth, I love to feel myself inside you. I . . . love . . ."

His voice drifted away. She could barely hear him with the sound of the surf, her own heartbeat pounding in her ears. Nothing mattered at this moment but the incredible pleasure, so intoxicating with its sweetness that when their bodies crested in a climax, Bethlyn and Hawk cried out their ecstasy in unison.

Hawk kissed her and his lips tasted tears. "Why are you crying?" he gently asked and wrapped her in his embrace.

Some seconds passed before Bethlyn was able to speak. "It's so incredibly wonderful, Hawk. Nothing ever can feel as wonderful as when we make love."

"Yes, Beth, lovemaking is wonderful."

She couldn't help but to bite her lower lip to keep from crying anew. His statement sounded so generalized to her ears. Bethlyn had meant that their lovemaking was special and sometimes it seemed as if they had been destined for each other. Evidently, since Hawk was a worldly man who no doubt had loved many women, he didn't see her as special. A feeling of dread rose within her to wonder how long he'd keep her on Windhaven before he was finished with her. She'd feel like a discarded pair of boots when that day came. She must guard her heart or lose it entirely. She could play the same game as Hawk. As long as she was on the island she'd find rapture in Hawk's lovemaking, but when the day dawned to escape, she'd leave and never look back.

However, when Hawk kissed her again and she opened her legs to him willingly and without reserve, her mind didn't dwell on her departure and the world which awaited her away from Windhaven.

At the moment, Hawk *was* her world.

Chapter Twelve

The longer Bethlyn stayed with Hawk, the harder it would be for her when she left him. During the week following the party, Hawk barely left her side. Their mornings and nights were filled with unbridled passion, and in the afternoons they walked the beach and played in the ocean. Bethlyn's fair complexion turned a becoming shade of peach and her hair's natural highlights gleamed, courtesy of the sun. Never in her entire life had she been this happy, this contented. Being with Hawk added a dimension to her life she'd never dreamed existed. During the long stretch of lazy days, she forgot she ever dreamed of escaping him and didn't think about the future.

However, her idyllic existence dissolved one rainy afternoon. She and Hawk had finished making love when a loud knock at the door startled them. Hawk dressed quickly and went downstairs. As she pulled on her gown she heard Crane's voice, and Bethlyn's heart jumped with joy. Perhaps Mavis was with him!

Running headlong down the stairs, she suddenly stopped short. Crane stood, maskless, in the parlor, and for the first time Bethlyn got a good look at his face. Crane was as fair as Hawk was dark, and almost as handsome. She could see why Mavis had fallen in love with this privateer. If she would be honest with herself, she'd admit to Hawk that she loved him, and at that moment she vowed she eventually would. But she wanted Hawk to love her, too. However, Hawk turned and glared at her when she entered the room. What had she done wrong?

"Hawk, what's the matter?" she asked, and gingerly moved towards him.

"You're the matter."

"I don't understand."

He distractedly raked his dark hair with a bronzed hand, then told Crane he'd meet him at the ship within the hour. "Let me make this clear to you, Beth," he said after Crane had left and Bethlyn noticed that he seemed to be having a hard time controlling himself. "While I've been forced to hide away on this island, purposely to baby-sit you and keep you in line, Crane arrives and tells me that an American frigate was destroyed by the British and all hands who survived the attack were taken prisoner."

"I'm sorry," she broke in.

"Are you?" His voice sounded harsh, quite unlike the ardent lover who'd taken her to paradise only minutes ago.

"I hate for anyone to be killed or imprisoned." Bethlyn felt bewilderment. "Why are you angry with me?"

Hawk pulled her close against him, his fingers curling around her upper arm and digging into her flesh. "Because I believe you might be a better spy than I thought. At first, I wondered about the reason you pretended to be a doxy, a reason you've never answered for me anyway, because God knows no doxy is a virgin. Then your clothes for instance. Granted, your gowns are rather plain, but they're made from the finest materials. I don't know how you came upon them, if you stole them or what, or . . ." Here he broke off and fingered the unadorned bodice of her yellow gown before tapping her lips with his index finger. ". . . If someone financed your venture in the hope that my ship might happen to come into contact with *Nightingale*. You've been less than honest with me, Beth, and I can't help but wonder if you purposely used your innocence to seduce me and pulled off my mask in the hope that I'd be forced to bring you here, that I would have to take charge of you personally. I'd be out of the way for a while, and the seas would be free of the *Black Falcon* while the British did their dirty work."

Bethlyn's mouth fell open, and it was some seconds

173

before she could even speak. "You're wrong. I never . . ."

"Quiet! I'm through with your lies." Dropping his hold on her, he reached for a frighteningly long pistol which rested on the table beside a piece of parchment and placed it in the waistband of his trousers. Then he grabbed the parchment and began folding it into fourths before tearing it into pieces and allowing them to fall to the floor. He speared her with his gaze. "This is correspondence from General Washington. He advises to beware of a very beautiful enemy spy who gives the impression of being an innocent, but in reality she is one of the most capable British spies. No one knows her name. However, she is a well-trained actress, proficient with disguises. Thus, she is quite difficult to catch." Hawk smiled, but his eyes held frosty condemnation. "I believe I have easily accomplished such a feat."

Shaking her head in numb disbelief, Bethlyn reached for him. "You're wrong, Hawk! I'm not a spy."

"Then why were you on *Nightingale*?"

"I . . . can't tell you that."

"I didn't think you would." Shrugging off her hand, he went to the window and called to Sparrow who waited on the beach. "Sparrow, take care of this young lady while I'm gone. In fact, guard her every hour of each day. I don't want her taking it into her head to escape."

Bethlyn heard Sparrow's "Aye, aye, Captain," and she watched in disbelief as Hawk moved menacingly toward her and pulled her against him.

With a groan, he swooped down like the bird of prey he emulated and greedily kissed her. She pushed against him, unable to breathe, barely able to think. She only knew that he wanted to humiliate her for something she hadn't done. "Stop it!" she ground out from between clenched teeth. "You won't treat me like a whore!"

Suddenly he laughed, a very harsh and grating sound to her ears, and pushed her away from him. "I treat you like a whore, because that is exactly what you are, sweetheart. You're my whore. Hawk's whore."

She actually winced, and he laughed again before leaving her trembling figure in the center of the room.

Within the hour all of Hawk's men assembled on the

Black Falcon. Soon the ship slipped from its hideout and once again took to the sea. Hawk stood on deck without his mask, but he knew that as soon as the English warship, *Jersey*, was sighted, he'd once more don his disguise. The truth of the matter was that he'd grown weary of being Captain Hawk. The last few days with Beth had been some of the best of his life, and now he felt lonely and empty without her beside him. Gritting his teeth, he placed his hands on his hips and surveyed the horizon. He didn't want to think about the deceitful little tart. But he couldn't seem to help himself.

Beth stayed on his mind constantly. What was he going to do with her? he asked himself for the twentieth time. He hated turning her over to the Americans. She'd be hung as a spy, and he couldn't bear the image of her beautiful, swanlike neck dangling from a rope. His only alternative was to keep her sequestered on Windhaven, but how long could he expect her to stay? How long did he want her to stay now that he was almost certain she was the spy mentioned in Washington's correspondence? He hated to think that his beautiful honey-haired Beth had deceived him.

Hawk had almost begun to believe her denials, and he found himself unwillingly drawn to her, hoping that somehow things would work out between them. But he was an American privateer and she might be a British spy. What hope of a life could they share under such circumstances?

Perspiration broke out upon his forehead at such a foolhardy thought. Share a life? What was wrong with him? He'd never loved any woman, and now here he was entertaining thoughts of spending the rest of his life with a woman who'd sooner turn him over to the king's men. Perhaps when he finished this mission, when he rescued the impressed American seamen from the British frigate *Jersey*, he'd return home for a while. Maybe he needed a change.

"Hawk."

Hawk turned at Crane's voice. "The storm is over," Hawk said, silently noting that the gray clouds skittered away and a pale shade of blue lightened the sky. "Smooth sailing ahead."

Crane agreed, but he looked far from agreeable. "We have a real problem with . . . Beth."

"Probably she's the spy Washington mentioned."

"I don't know. I only know that if we'd been patrolling the ocean, we might not have lost one of our ships. Captain Kelley was a friend of mine, and now he's dead. I feel awful about all of this."

Hawk felt awful, too. "I'm heading for Philadelphia after we capture *Jersey*."

"That's a good idea," Crane agreed. "I hated leaving Mavis alone."

"How is Mavis?"

Crane blushed. "We were married two days ago."

Hawk didn't know whether to be happy or sad for his friend. Mavis was an Englishwoman, but he remembered that she seemed to adore Crane. He wished them every happiness, but he felt far from happy himself.

"Business as usual when we get to Philadelphia?" Crane asked.

Hawk nodded. "Aye, but a sideline for pleasure, I think, with a fetching widow."

Crane grinned and watched Hawk's back as the man walked toward the quarterdeck. He suppressed a sigh, wondering if he'd ever be able to tell him what he knew about Bethlyn Briston. He doubted it. Though Crane had Mavis's word that Bethlyn wasn't a spy, Crane couldn't be certain of that fact. Mavis was her servant, and servants were not always privy to the aristocracy's secrets, no matter how close. He wondered why after all of these years would the silly chit decide to cross the Atlantic and claim a wayward spouse. Crane figured it would be better not to tell Hawk the truth and to keep Bethlyn on Windhaven for Hawk's safety as well as her own. Somehow Hawk would learn the truth about Bethlyn in his own good time.

Contenting himself with the knowledge that things were well as they stood, Crane joined Hawk in his vigil for *Jersey*.

*   *   *

Sparrow barely left Bethlyn's side. She had hoped that after a few days he'd end his watchdog tactics, but she was wrong. The man's loyalties belonged to Hawk, and though he might be a kind and friendly man, she soon realized that he'd never disobey his captain. So much for her plan to try to escape. She never had a moment alone with Nate, because Sparrow was always within hearing distance. She had hoped that she could somehow speak to Nate alone, to persuade him to help her hide on Mr. Tolliver's boat. But two more days were left until Mr. Tolliver sailed for Philadelphia, and so far, she didn't know how to shake Sparrow's shadow.

On the morning before Mr. Tolliver's departure, Tansy Tolliver paid Bethlyn an unexpected visit. She arrived with a large straw basket under her arm which contained jars of preserves and herbs.

Tansy handed Bethlyn one of the jars. "If I do say so, I make the most delicious preserves from wild strawberries which grow on the island. Perhaps one day you can come pick some with me, when the berries are in season again."

"I'd like that." Bethlyn graciously took the jar, feeling guilty because she hoped she wouldn't be around when the next crop of berries bloomed and all too aware of Sparrow as he sat on the beach outside of the house.

Tansy's gaze followed Bethlyn's. "Mr. Sparrow is a nice gentleman."

Bethlyn agreed that he was, but said nothing else and the two women sat on chairs by the kitchen table. Finally Tansy broke the silence. "I can help you escape."

Bethlyn blinked in astonishment. "What do you mean?" She felt as if she couldn't breathe because of the hope rising in her chest.

Tansy patted Bethlyn's hand which rested on the table. "I'm quite fond of Mr. Hawk, but I'm not blind, my dear. Or deaf. I've heard some things about . . . your relationship with Mr. Hawk."

"More likely that I'm not Mrs. Hawk," Bethlyn said bitingly.

"I don't judge you or what is in your heart for the man. But for some reason he has made you into a prisoner, with

Sparrow's help. Or perhaps I'm wrong." Tansy leaned back and surveyed Bethlyn, who quickly nodded her head.

"You aren't wrong, Tansy. Hawk believes I'm guilty of something I didn't do. I need to get to Philadelphia as soon as possible. Can you help me? I'd be ever so much in your debt."

"I don't want you to feel that you're in my debt, child, but I do want to help you. Sometimes men can be such fools." Tansy smiled and looked quite young despite her sixty years. "Jack leaves tomorrow for Philadelphia. I know I can persuade him to take you on the boat. Nate's going along, too, and he's so excited and pleased that you're the one who suggested Jack take him on the next trip that he'll never breathe a word to Hawk or anyone about how you left the island. Of course, Hawk isn't a stupid man and will probably realize it was Jack, but once you're gone, you're gone. The deed is done."

Bethlyn smiled and embraced Tansy. "I'll never be able to repay you for this. Thank you so much."

"That's quite all right, dear, but we may have a problem with Mr. Sparrow."

Bethlyn's hopes plummeted for the moment. She'd forgotten about him, already mentally sailing away from Windhaven. Sparrow was as tenacious as a bulldog. Tansy, however, smiled in reassurance. "You leave all to me. I know how to get Mr. Sparrow's mind off you for a while. I've never known him yet to turn down my elderberry wine, and with a smidgen of sleeping powder in it, I think Mr. Sparrow won't notice for a number of hours that you've left."

"Aw, Tansy, I don't feel right about this," Jack Tolliver told his wife, who waved farewell to him from the dock. "It ain't right to interfere in another man's business."

"Get on with you now, Jack, and be quiet." Tansy's bright smile could be seen as the boat skimmed away, and she called to Bethlyn, "Have a fine life, dear. And you, Nate, stop bobbing around and sit down or you'll be swimming to Philadelphia."

178

"Aye, aye, Grandma." Nate made a mock salute and sat obediently beside Bethlyn.

Jack heaved a sigh, causing Bethlyn to feel more than guilty. She watched as he maneuvered the boat away from the island and listened to Nate's happy chirping for the rest of the morning. By noon, she wondered if Sparrow had wakened yet from the effects of Tansy's elderberry wine, and again she felt a sense of guilt. But she buried the feeling, deciding that she was right to escape Hawk. The man had had no business accusing her of being a spy, of keeping her a prisoner. As much as she craved the hateful man's hands on her and knew her wanton heart would belong to him always, she had to escape. No future awaited her with Hawk.

A pleasant breeze scurried the boat along, and by nightfall Jack spoke kindly to her, apparently realizing that he must make the best of the situation. They stopped by a small grassy bank somewhere on the Delaware River near a settlement which Jack told her had been founded by Swedes over a hundred years ago. Here they opened a basket packed by Tansy, filled with smoked salmon, topped off by biscuits and sweet-tasting strawberry jam. Then they fell asleep to the gentle sway of the river beneath them.

Before dawn the next morning, they were off again, the water fanned by a gentle breeze from the east. It was nearly noon when the day turned very warm and the bright blue sky disappeared behind large, purple-black clouds.

"Damn!" groaned Jack. "We're gonna be wetter than three mackerel in this downpour. I was hoping to make Philadelphia early this afternoon."

Jack's prophecy proved true. Large drops of rain pummeled the boat and the occupants. Bethlyn and Nate took refuge beneath a large blanket while Jack made certain the boat stayed on course. The rainstorm turned out to be short in duration, but when it was over, the blanket lay in a sodden heap in a corner of the boat. Bethlyn, Nate, and Jack didn't look much better.

Bethlyn's hair lay plastered to her head and water dripped down her face. The green gown with the beige lace, the one she thought was her prettiest, now lay wetly

179

against her skin. Two of her gowns, which she had packed within some brown paper and tied with a string, were now equally as wet. The silk shoes on her feet, green to match her gown, bore large water stains. Bethlyn doubted the shoes would last much longer, the fragile things having been made purposely for sweeping turns around a dance floor. Pushing her drooping strands of hair away from her face, she sighed and wished that Hawk had brought all of her shoes from the ship instead of only one pair. But if she must make do in her wet gown and shoes, she would, though she had anticipated making a grand and elegant entrance into the offices of Briston Shipping. Yet it didn't matter any longer how she looked when her husband saw her again. Most certainly she didn't wish to stay married to him, not after having belonged to Hawk.

Hawk. His face and figure rose up before her eyes, and she closed them tightly, not wanting to see him or think about him. But no matter, his image floated behind her eyelids and she opened them again to find Nate smiling sadly at her. "I'll miss your cookies," he told her.

Bethlyn stifled a sob. Suddenly she knew she'd miss Nate and their talks, she'd especially miss Tansy, and the way the setting sun bathed the island in a peach tint every day. With each watery mile, Windhaven became more and more a memory. But for some odd reason, Hawk seemed closer and closer to her.

Three hours later, she kissed Jack and Nate farewell. She assured Jack she'd be perfectly fine, and he told her that if she changed her mind and decided to return to Windhaven she could find him at the High Street Market until dawn the next morning. Bethlyn knew she wouldn't seek out the Tollivers again, as much as she'd miss them. The Tollivers reminded her of Windhaven and Hawk, and she didn't want to think about Hawk anymore. She had to live her own life now, even if it meant confessing to Ian Briston about her involvement with the infamous privateer, Hawk. Her husband certainly wouldn't want her for a wife then, and she'd be blissfully free of Briston, free to return

180

home to England and start a new life. Perhaps she'd even marry again, but that idea held no appeal at the moment.

She couldn't imagine being intimate again with anyone but Hawk.

After gaining directions to the offices of Briston Shipping from a street vendor, Bethlyn clutched the soggy package which contained her two gowns and headed south on Front Street. The cobblestones dug through her thin slippers with each step, and she hoped her destination wasn't too far off. The bustling activity of the town caused her to feel qualms of discomfort. Never had she been out alone in the midst of so many people, usually sequestered within the confines of Aunt Penny's phaeton, with Jeremy beside her. People hurried past, some carrying baskets of produce, while wagonloads of squawking poultry rolled in the general direction of the market. Children raced by her, the adults seemed to trot at a quick pace. She wondered if no one walked leisurely here. A wave of homesickness for Jeremy and Aunt Penny washed over her. She felt so alone and more than a bit frightened, but she wouldn't allow Philadelphia to intimidate her. She had lived through too much with her father all of those years ago to cower like a timid child now. Besides, within the past month she'd become a woman at Hawk's hands. That knowledge was enough to push her onward.

She began to wonder how much longer to Briston Shipping when her attention was diverted by a number of British soldiers, attired in traditional scarlet uniforms, milling about the sidewalk in front of a tavern.

They hovered around a tall, olive-complexioned young man, dressed in a red coat with two gold epaulettes. He wore a white wig, the queue held in place by a jaunty scarlet ribbon. The young man held up a sketch pad for their inspection and some of the officers burst out in laughter.

"John, you've captured that American dog's profile perfectly. I wonder what General Washington would say if he could see your sketch of him. Bet he wouldn't be too pleased with that long nose you've given him," one of the junior officers observed. The rest of the men agreed just as

181

Bethlyn brushed past.

"Now who is that haughty vixen?" she heard someone say.

"I haven't a clue," the officer named John responded, "but I'd love to sketch her."

"Heavens, John, look at her. She looks like something fished out of the river. Must be a fishmonger's daughter who fancies herself a lady."

Bethlyn couldn't help but blush to hear the man speak so disdainfully about her. Her hair had dried out by now, but she suddenly realized that her silk gown was covered in dried water spots, as were her shoes. She looked a mess, but she'd never allow anyone to believe she thought so. Instead, she squared her shoulders and turned her head back toward the soldiers in a defiant gesture and said in her best modulated tones, "Good afternoon, gentlemen."

Some of the officers stood with their mouths open, but others, like the young officer named John, bowed gallantly.

Barely two minutes later she came to a gray building which consisted of three floors. The shingle on the front proclaimed it as Briston Enterprises. Bethlyn's heart beat loudly and for a second her knees quaked. This wasn't how she imagined meeting her husband after all these years. She'd wanted to impress him, to allow him to see that the shy, plump child he'd married was gone and a beautiful, self-assured woman had taken her place. But at the moment, she looked neither beautiful nor self-assured. In fact, she most closely resembled a dried-out water rat, but she couldn't help her appearance. Ian Briston would have to accept her wretched, now that she'd come all of this way. Or not accept her at all, which was quite fine with her. However, the man did owe her a warm bath, dry clothes and a roof over her head. She *was* his wife.

Entering the cool interior of the foyer, she was amazed at the beautiful but practical furnishings. Persian rugs dotted the oak floors, and industrious heads bent over Sheraton desks. At her approach one of these heads glanced up at her. A pudgy little man eyed her curiously over the horn-rimmed glasses perched on his long, thin nose.

"May I be of assistance?" he offered in a curt, businesslike tone.

"I should like to see Mr. Briston."

His watery eyes raked her from head to foot and he sniffed. "Mr. Briston isn't in."

"Then may I speak to Mr. Gibbons?" she said, remembering the name of her husband's secretary, the man who always chose her birthday, Christmas, and wedding anniversary gifts.

"He's not in today."

"I see. Do you know when Mr. Briston shall return?"

"I can't say, miss."

"It's Mrs.—Mrs. Ian Briston."

The man cocked an eyebrow at her. "What did you say?"

"I said my name is Mrs. Ian Briston. I wish to speak to my husband upon his return. I don't mind waiting in his office."

"I just bet you won't mind waiting." The little man stood up, his pale face turned red. "I don't know what sort of game you're playing, but I want you out of here now, otherwise, I'll call in the law."

Bethlyn was so stunned for this hireling to speak to her in such a fashion that all she could do was stare with an open mouth. Finally she turned cool eyes upon him. "I assure you, sir . . . What is your name?"

"Mr. Eakins."

"Mr. Eakins, sir, I am Bethlyn Briston, wife of your employer. I advise you to please treat me courteously."

"You are an audacious strumpet!" Eakins intoned and gestured to a large, brawny man who sat by a corner desk. "Escort this young woman out of here, Demming."

Demming firmly placed a large hand around Bethlyn's upper arm and pushed her to the door. "You're making a mistake, Mr. Eakins!" she cried and would have fought, but she didn't dare, for the cold-eyed Demming was more than twice her size and three times her weight. "I'm Ian Briston's wife!"

"Bah! If you knew anything about Ian Briston, woman, you'd know that he isn't married and never has been. Away with you now!" Mr. Eakins returned to his desk and his work while Demming shoved Bethlyn bodily out of the door and forced her to stumble onto the street. The door was slammed tightly closed.

Never had she been so humiliated. She found herself kneeling on the cobblestoned street, the object of curious glances by the passersby. If she wouldn't have been so stunned by being thrown out of her husband's business, a business which she herself partly owned, she'd have risen to her feet and angrily entered the office again to rebuke that horrid little man with such scathing language that he'd be unable to speak.

However, her circumstances of the last few weeks, the sense of loss she felt over Hawk, and the sudden knowledge that her husband must never have mentioned his marital state, caused her to nearly weep right there on the street.

"Get out of the way, you stupid wench!" the driver of a large carriage screeched to her. She barely had time to glance up to see the large coach thundering toward her, her first inclination was that the horse and the turning wheels would soon splatter her body upon the cobblestones. She froze, but in an instant she found herself on the sidewalk, pressed against a red-coated chest as the coach flew past her.

"Have a care!" her rescuer screamed to the fleeing coachman. "Are you all right? Please, miss, tell me you're not hurt. You're so still I can scarcely feel you breathing."

Through a fog Bethlyn realized that the man who held her in his arms spoke to her. His hand smoothed back her tousled hair from her eyes while a comforting and strong arm held her securely around the waist. Her heart beat so hard that she could hear the deafening beats within her ears. Even her mouth had grown dry from fear. However, she slowly grew aware of the man and the fact that more curious faces stared at her.

"I should like to sit down somewhere," she mumbled weakly.

"Certainly, miss. Come this way. Are you able to walk?"

Bethlyn nodded, but her legs almost gave way when they started off, growing a bit stronger under the man's guiding hand.

184

Minutes later they stopped at the tavern she'd passed earlier. This time none of the soldiers was about, and the man lowered her to a sitting position on a bench outside. Suddenly a cup of water was pressed into her hand, and she drank it down, feeling better after a minute or so. At least she wasn't frightened any longer, only terribly weary. Glancing up at the young man, she recognized him as the soldier with the sketch pad. In fact, now that she could see him up close and saw the insignia on his uniform, she realized he was a captain. He sat beside her, an attentive arm placed around her waist.

"Are you feeling better? You'd have been killed by that bloody colonial and he probably wouldn't have stopped."

Bethlyn managed a smile of gratitude to the handsome young man. "I owe you my life. If not for you, I'd be dead now, I suppose."

"Don't even think such a thing, miss. I'm glad to have been there to help you."

"May I have the pleasure of your name, Captain?"

Instantly he rose to attention and bowed to her, taking her still trembling hand in his. "Captain John André at your beck and call, miss." He planted a warm, sweet kiss on her hand.

"Well, Captain John André, I'm most pleased to meet you. I'm Bethlyn Briston."

"Are you related to Ian and Molly Briston?"

"Yes, I'm Ian Briston's wife."

A look of complete surprise passed across his face. "I had no idea Ian was married. I'm acquainted with both Ian and his sister, Molly. Many nights have I spent at Edgecomb and delighted in their company."

Bethlyn didn't bite back the sarcastic retort which rose to her lips. "It seems you're not the only one who didn't know of my husband's marital status. That beetle-faced little man at the office didn't know, either." She sighed tiredly. "I would love a nice bath and clean sheets to sleep in. I've traveled a long way to find my husband." She startled and glanced around. "My package . . ."

"You mean that brown sack? I'm afraid the carriage claimed it. I noticed it was torn and trampled. If you wish I'll go back and retrieve it for you."

185

Bethlyn shook her head; nothing was going right for her today. She'd just lost her two best gowns and nearly been crushed to death. What other unforeseen tragedy could happen?

"I wish I could find my husband," she muttered.

"Then find him you shall," André said in a rush, and rose to his feet. "I'll get a carriage for us and before you can say Jack Rabbit, you'll be at Edgecomb, safe within the loving bosom of your family."

Bethlyn wasn't certain how loving and safe she'd be, but tears misted her eyes at John André's kindness to her. Once again he came to her rescue. "I do appreciate your help, Captain André."

White teeth flashed in his olive-complexioned face. "Call me John. All of the fair ladies in Philadelphia do, and you, Mrs. Briston, are the fairest of the fair."

"Ah, I believe you have the soul of a poet."

André made a slight bow. "Among other things, dear lady."

"A wife? I don't believe it!" Molly Briston sat in the parlor of Edgecomb with Bethlyn and John André. An amused smile lit up her pretty face, which was framed by dark wispy curls. Her eyes, the color of hazelnuts, filled with curiosity at the disheveled young woman who claimed to be her sister-in-law.

Bethlyn sipped her tea slowly. A large lump lodged in her throat. God, Briston hadn't told his own sister he'd been married seven years ago! She felt so humiliated she wished to find a hole in the floor and sink fast away. However, she hid her emotions as she'd done all those years ago with her father when she'd been hurt. "You're quite shocked, Molly," she said kindly. "But it's true. The marriage took place shortly after my stepmother died."

A shadow of sadness passed quickly across Molly's pretty face. "She was my mother. I still miss her and remember her. However, Ian commands that I never mention her name in this house. That's a very hard thing to do." Molly suddenly brightened and embraced Bethlyn.

186

"I've always wanted a sister, and now I've got one. How delicious! And how thrilling it will be when Ian sees you again."

"Yes," Bethlyn commented, pleased that Molly accepted her, but she didn't believe for one moment that Ian Briston would be so glad to see her again.

After bidding a fond farewell to John André, Molly showed Bethlyn to her room on the second floor of the large and luxuriously furnished mansion. Bethlyn had been able to see very little of the outside of the house, since she and John had arrived after dusk had fallen. She had seen that it was a grand, elegant-appearing structure. Two massive chimneys stood on either side of the three-storied mansion. The third floor contained two dormer windows while the other windows were in the Palladian style.

A newel staircase led up to the second-floor landing, and Molly opened the arched doorway of a room at the end of the hall. "I hope you like this bedroom. It's the prettiest guest bedroom in the—" Molly halted, and two red splotches marred the perfection of her face. "But you aren't really a guest now, are you? Perhaps you'd care to stay in the bedroom next to Ian's, the one which was my mother's?"

"This is fine," Bethlyn assured her, and smiled. She didn't feel as if she were the wife of Edgecomb's master, and she doubted she'd be staying long anyway. The guest bedroom was fine with her. Molly left her to get acquainted with the room. The walls were painted a buff color and the ceilings were pearly white, while the paneling was a warm brown. She especially liked the green-and-yellow-print counterpane and the lime-green drapes on the double windows which flanked a large marble fireplace.

On one side of the room stood a hand-painted silk screen which depicted delicate-looking birds, perched on thin vines with a volcano in the background. Moving the screen aside she found a white porcelain bathing tub with brass-clawed feet. Moments later, Molly came back, followed by two servant girls who carried buckets of warm water which they promptly poured into the tub. Under Molly's arm was a fine lace nightdress.

"I'll loan you one of my nightgowns and I'll have Sally alter one of my dresses for you until we can go shopping tomorrow. I know of the sweetest little dressmaker. She makes absolutely wonderful clothes. I do look forward to shopping with you, Bethlyn. You've just arrived from abroad and must be up on all the latest fashions. Oh, how lovely it will be to have a woman to shop with, to share secrets!"

Molly's gushings caused Bethlyn to feel extremely guilty. The dear girl never questioned her as to how she'd come to Edgecomb with nothing, not even a decent pair of shoes. She was so trusting and kind that Bethlyn embraced her and assured her they'd be the best of friends.

She sincerely hoped this would prove true, but she doubted it would come to pass. Not if Ian Briston had a say in the matter.

Chapter Thirteen

Weariness propelled Ian Briston from the foyer and up the flight of stairs to his room. He was even too tired to eat and had never been so aggravated in all the years he'd run Briston Shipping. Couldn't anyone do anything correctly? he wondered. Must he personally oversee every small problem? He and Marc had returned earlier that evening after a day spent seeing to the outfitting of a new ship. No sooner were they in his office than Eakins had barged in, intent upon telling him about an incident which had happened during the day, but Ian had waved the man away; in fact, he actually almost growled to silence him. He'd felt unable to concentrate on trivialities and informed Eakins he'd have to brief him in the morning. Leaving the office, he headed for home, a sticky feeling clinging to his clothes despite a sudden cooling of the warm Philadelphia temperature. The mid-November heat was unusual, and he hoped that fall would soon arrive. Ian had grown tired of the city already and longed to feel his feet on the deck of a ship once more.

He wanted something else, too, or rather someone, but he didn't dare think about her.

So, climbing the stairs, he resolved to wash away the accumulated sweat and grime of the day, then crawl into bed and sleep—and forget. Removing his frock coat, he moved soundlessly along the carpeted corridor, stopping abruptly by one of the guest bedrooms. He noticed that the door was ajar.

A flickering candle, burned down to the nub, barely illuminated the covered figure sleeping on the large bed. But from the shapely contours and curves of the person, Ian discerned that a woman rested beneath the thin coverlet. Strands of light hair fanned the pillow and hid the profile of the woman, but Ian couldn't help but smile. A surge of desire and amusement rushed through him. Suddenly he no longer felt tired, because he knew that the woman who slept so peacefully wouldn't be sleepy for long. The moment he'd kiss her, she'd awaken and open herself to him like a dewy flower.

Hadn't that always been the way with Cynthia? The many nights she'd visited Edgecomb, on the pretext of seeing to Molly so she'd be forced to spend the night in this room, had always ended in the same fashion. He'd come to her after Molly was asleep, and they'd made passionate love until both of them were spent. No woman in Philadelphia could match Cynthia's beauty and, he doubted, her insatiable appetite for lovemaking. Ian knew she had other lovers and he didn't mind. Cynthia, long a widow, professed no interest in marrying again. Why not take advantage of what she offered? Perhaps her soft, pliant body would erase another woman from his thoughts for a while. At the moment he didn't want to think, only feel.

Entering the room, he found it stuffy and opened the window. A sudden fresh, cool breeze floated into the bedroom and caused the candle to sputter and die. In the darkness Ian quickly shucked his clothes and joined the woman he believed to be Cynthia in the bed.

His long, well-muscled body fit snugly against the curve of her derriere when he pulled her against him. What was this? A nightgown. He wondered when the lusty Cynthia had started to wear nightgowns. Enfolding her in his arms, he breathed in the intoxicating scent of her hair. She smelled wonderful, like satin in his arms. His hand trailed lazily across a full breast, instantly feeling the nipple harden beneath the thin nightdress. He smiled because even in sleep Cynthia's body responded to his touch.

His lips kissed the nape of her neck and his tongue

followed the curve to the valley between her breasts. A trickle of perspiration met his lips and he licked it away, breathing her name against the silken flesh.

The woman moaned and slowly turned her face. He felt her lips meet his, and her kiss was gentle but laced with the promise of passion. Ian's loins felt on fire. Never before in all his couplings with Cynthia had he felt so protective of her or kissed her so tenderly as he did at that moment. Only one woman had ever stirred such feelings within him, and he didn't want to think about her.

He positioned the woman so that her body was beneath him and felt her arms embrace his neck. She kissed him sweetly and slowly, almost as if she were half awake. Ian wanted her fiercely, and his hands stroked the satiny softness of her lower body, finding the pulsing center of her womanhood beneath the nightgown which rode above her thighs. His desire was quite evident and pulsing to enter her, and at that moment he would have thrust inside her except the woman moaned.

"Oh, Hawk," she whispered in a sleepy, husky voice.

Ian's head shot up. Blood pounded through his veins. Cynthia had never called him Hawk; she didn't know anything about Hawk. Who was this woman who responded to his kisses?

"Who are you, madam?" His voice sounded vicious to his own ears, so it was no wonder that he felt the woman stiffen, and though he couldn't see her eyes in the darkness, he guessed sleep fled and that they were round and full of shock. He didn't expect the frightened and bloodcurdling scream which followed.

"Help! Someone help!" She clawed and pushed at Ian, knocking his body from her when she kicked out at him and attacked his bulging manhood with her foot.

Ian groaned and doubled over on the floor. He saw shooting stars for a moment and didn't realize that Molly had entered the room and held a candle aloft until he heard her voice cutting through the air.

"Whatever is the matter?" Molly cried and placed the candle on the bedside table.

From his vantage place on the floor Ian couldn't see the

woman on the high rice bed, but he knew she had scrambled off the mattress and stood beside Molly from the two pairs of feet he saw on the other side.

"A man is in here," the woman said in a breathy voice. "Call the constable."

"A man?" asked Molly, and a hint of panic could be heard in her tone.

"I kicked him. He's on the floor—over there on the other side of the bed."

Ian sensed her apparent fear and indecision and didn't relish his sister running off, screaming for help. He didn't want the servants to see him in such a state. He called out her name and saw Molly's nightgown-clad legs moving toward him. Glancing up, he saw her face bending over him. Her hands came up to her mouth in a gesture of shock. Pulling the bed sheet off of the bed she managed to cover him. "Are you hurt, Ian?"

Ian grunted. "How do you think I feel after being kicked in the . . ." He broke off, seeing that Molly appeared flustered. "I'm sorry," he said, and meant it. "Who is that woman?" he whispered.

"Don't you know?" she whispered back, perplexity in her eyes. "Why are you undressed if . . ." Suddenly she reddened. "You thought Cynthia was sleeping in here." She sounded disapproving.

Ian nodded curtly, suddenly aware that Molly must have known what happened in this room whenever Cynthia visited. Now he had the good grace to blush and pulled the sheet around his torso. Thank God the pain was abating. He wondered if he'd be incapacitated for life because of Molly's houseguest.

"Who is she?" he asked again, and wondered how he'd apologize to the woman.

Molly grinned and stifled a laugh. "I think you should find out for yourself."

She stood up, leaving him dumbfounded and in a haunched position on the floor. He heard her say to the woman, "It's only Ian. You have nothing to fear from him. I find the whole incident rather amusing, and I guess in the morning that you will, too. Good night to both of you."

Then she was gone, and he felt so utterly stupid and baffled. Why had Molly gone and left him alone in the room with this strange woman? What could have gotten into his sweet, innocent sister to do such a thing?

He couldn't stay in this position for the rest of the night. He must get up and face the woman, whoever she was, and apologize to her. Peering under the bed, he saw that she hadn't moved one bit. Her feet peeked out of the gown, and a handful of material was bunched in one of her fists, showing off more than an ample amount of a shapely calf. She was as nervous as he was. Taking a big sigh, he pulled himself to his feet, and wished this accursed day was over. Nothing this embarrassing had ever happened to him, and he couldn't wait to get the damn apology over with so he could get some sleep.

Bothersome woman, he found himself thinking. If she hadn't been such a warm, responsive bundle in his arms none of this would have happened.

Grabbing the sheet firmly around himself, he rose upward, all six feet of him. The woman stood on the opposite side of the bed, and he found himself unable to focus on her at first, but noticed the long honey-brown hair which hung in graceful tendrils to her waist. He almost mumbled the beginnings of his apology, but stopped himself and blinked in disbelief. She made a raspy sound of dismay, her hands clutching at her throat.

For a second Ian felt unable to speak because he couldn't concentrate on the words. But finally after what seemed like eons had passed, the gift of speech returned.

"So, you found me out, you conniving wench!"

"Hawk . . . Hawk."

"Is that all you have to say? Just what do you think you're doing here in my house? How did you get off the island? I'll wring that Sparrow's neck for this."

He wanted to say so much more. In fact, he wanted to wring *her* neck. God, she must be a damn good spy to have tracked him here. But how? If Beth could ascertain his true identity, then who else might discover that Ian Briston, noted loyalist and faithful servant of the king, was in actuality the notorious American privateer, Captain Hawk? No one knew except for Marc, his secretary, otherwise known as Crane when they took to the seas, and Sparrow.

Stalking over to her, he grabbed her by the arm and shook her, all too aware of the deathly pallor on her face. "How did you find me?"

She glanced at him as if in a daze. "Hawk, it is you. It is. I can't believe it's you."

"Silly wench. You know who I am so stop the play-acting."

For a moment she gazed at him long and hard, then before his startled eyes, she began to laugh and couldn't seem to stop. Tears streamed down her cheeks, and she threw herself on the bed, seemingly devoured by gales of laughter.

"Too . . . funny . . . Hawk . . . Ian . . ." she practically squealed with delight.

Ian loomed over her, his face gone red with fury and indignation, not aware that he looked lost and baffled as he clutched the sheet around his imposing torso. Finally he'd had enough and, tossing the sheet aside, he joined her on the bed. His large hands pinned her arms to the mattress, and for just an instant he felt her legs rise.

"Push at me again, Beth, and I'll whack your bottom so hard you won't be able to sit down for a month."

Apparently she thought better of launching another attack. She stopped laughing and a deep, resigned sigh shook her.

"Don't you know who I am?" she said.

"I know you're a damned good actress and a better spy. No one but Crane and Sparrow know who I really am. I congratulate you, Beth."

"My name is—Bethlyn. I'm your wife." Her voice shook, and her brown eyes were as large as serving platters.

Ian studied her for a moment, his own eyes impaling hers. "You're more clever than I thought to come up with such a ruse. I don't know how you learned about my marriage, but no wonder Molly took you in."

"Why do you think I'm lying?" She began to struggle,

but he held her down. "It's true. I'm Bethlyn Briston, the daughter of the Earl of Dunsmoor and the wife of Ian Briston, a noted loyalist." She sneered the last word. "You're loyal to no one but yourself, I find. You prance and preen around Philadelphia and all the time you're robbing British ships. And you have the nerve to accuse *me* of playacting. No one is better than you, Ian Briston, or, let me say, Captain Hawk."

"I don't believe anything you say." This time uncertainty tinged his voice.

She lifted her face upward so he'd be forced to look at her. "I speak the truth. Open your eyes, dear husband. Remember the day of our wedding, recall how you barely glanced at your plump, plain little bride. Remember how I vomited all over the floor of the Grotto and how you carried me upstairs. So kind you were, so solicitous of me. I thought you'd be the answer to my prayers, that I could find some happiness in life and not in a book or penning poetry to while away the time.

"And then what do you do, kind, concerned husband? You send me to Aunt Penny's to live out my years, bereft of a husband, of the children I wished to conceive. I hated you and all the gifts Mr. Gibbons sent to me on my birthdays and wedding anniversaries. I doubt you even know the month I was born, or remember the date we were married. I behaved scandalously in London to gain your attention. I gained nothing but your apathy. In your eyes, I didn't exist. But I exist to you now, I warrant. You won't forget me now, Ian Briston. Captain Hawk. And all because I took the wrong ship."

The words which spilled so easily from her mouth were now silenced. Bethlyn took great breaths of air, her full breasts straining against the thin gown. Ian let her go, but didn't take his gaze from her. He took the candle and held it to her face, a face he'd seen so often in his mind lately. But another face superimposed itself upon the one which he now saw. A child's face, streaked with tears, but one which had looked at him with hope in those large brown eyes.

His wife's face. The face of the woman he'd captured off

Nightingale. How hadn't he seen the resemblance? But he admitted any resemblance was remote at best. The child he'd married had blossomed into a beautiful woman over the years. The time he'd spent with her at Woodsley on their wedding day was barely fifteen minutes in length. How was he to realize that the passionate woman he'd held in his arms all of those nights on *Black Falcon* was his own wife?

Ian felt extremely tired.

He sat beside her on the bed. "I believe you."

Bethlyn sat up, moving away from him until she positioned herself at the bottom of the bed, almost as if she might flee from him. Long tousled curls streamed across her shoulders and down her back. "Then free me."

"What?"

"I want my freedom. I want an annulment of our marriage. I came to Philadelphia to rid myself of you, and now that I know who you really are, I insist on ending our farce of a marriage."

"Suppose I decline?"

"You must do as I want. I refuse to be tied to a man who is an enemy of the Crown, a man who confiscated my father's ship. You may retain control of Briston Shipping for all I care; I give you your share of the company. But I want to be free of you. I insist upon an annulment!"

Ian watched as Bethlyn defiantly thrust herself forward, almost as if she expected him to deny her. She was right to think he would deny her request. He had no intention of freeing her.

"My sweet wife, I beg to differ. I cannot grant you an annulment."

"Whyever not?" She arched forward, a warning fire in her dark eyes, and he had the insane urge to kiss her. She'd never looked more lovely to him than at this moment.

"I might not be a barrister," he began, and grinned, "but I know that annulments are granted only if the marriage has never been consummated, and if my memory serves me well, and it does, I can recall countless nights— and days—when we didn't leave my cabin." A bronzed finger snaked out and traced the outline of her lips. "I

196

doubt you have much of a case, Bethlyn."

"Oh, no."

"Oh, yes."

"Then I want a divorce."

"On what grounds, my love?"

Bethlyn nearly sputtered. "For God's sake! You're Captain Hawk, a man wanted by the Crown for piracy . . ."

"Privateering, sweet," he interrupted.

"The devil take you, Ian Briston. Piracy, and you know it. If you don't agree to a divorce, I'll turn you in to the authorities." She sat back, seemingly pleased with herself by the Cheshire-cat grin on her face. The chit thought she had him cornered, but Ian refused to rise to the bait.

He rubbed his chin in thought. "According to you, I confiscated one of your father's ships, and for that so-called crime, you will turn me in if I don't agree to a divorce."

"Yes."

"You have no grounds."

"But I do . . ."

"No," he corrected her. "*Nightingale* belongs to Briston Shipping, and as part owner of Briston Shipping, then the ship was mine to do with as I wanted. I can't be arrested for confiscating my own ship."

"But there were other ships."

"Do you have personal knowledge of them, dear wife?"

He saw that he had her there. She shook her head in dismay and for a moment he thought he saw a glistening tear in one of her eyes.

"I can still turn you in and tell what I do know about you," she said softly.

Ian didn't doubt for a moment that she might do that very thing. He couldn't allow that to happen. Too much depended on his privateering.

"You can do what you like," he told her. "However, if you do turn me in, then I think you'll be sorry. You might be arrested for consorting with the enemy. I doubt you'd like to spend time in prison."

"None of that is true. I'll make someone believe me."

She sounded unconvinced now.

This time he did see tears sparkling in her eyes, and he felt immense guilt for what he'd put her through the last month, in fact for what she'd gone through since he married her. He'd thought he'd seen to her wants all of these years, but he hadn't done a very good job. Though Bethlyn might be beautiful and grown up now, a tigress when they made love, he still discerned the lonely child within her.

He must make everything up to her. He didn't want or need a wife. Heaven knew he felt something for her, something he couldn't name, and shrunk from admitting what it might be, but she deserved some happiness. All she wanted was a husband, and he couldn't be that to her. With her as his wife, he might fall in love and he didn't want the pain love could bring. He'd seen how his father had fared after loving too deeply. Her request was so simple that he felt taken aback. However, he could give her her freedom and send her on her way eventually. She wanted a divorce; then he'd see she got one.

But a part of him dreaded the day he freed her.

Ian stood up, unaware of his nudity, and cupped her chin.

"If you want the divorce then I'll see that you get your wish."

Surprise and shock mingled on her beautiful face. "Should I say thank you?"

He shrugged, dropping his hand. "I don't care. There's a catch to all of this, however."

Bethlyn groaned. "I knew there would be."

He couldn't suppress the smile which rose to his mouth at the defiant way her eyes snapped at him. He admired her spunk. "I've heard a rumor that I might be under suspicion. These are only rumors, mind you, but I must protect myself. I request that you remain as my wife until I know I'm safe. You must admit that my marriage to the Earl of Dunsmoor's daughter will protect my image as the faithful follower of the king. Then when I feel that suspicion has turned away from me, you can quietly divorce me. However, Molly mustn't learn about any of this. I don't want her involved. Have we a pact?"

"This is the only way you'll free me?"

"Yes."

She searched his face for a long moment, then gave a trembling sigh. "I agree."

"Fine. I think it best that you move into the bedroom next to mine so it will appear that we are truly husband and wife."

"This room is more than adequate . . ."

He shot her a warning glance, and Bethlyn gave in.

"Whatever you say, my dear husband."

Ian left the room, not caring for the sound of that.

Chapter Fourteen

For the next few days Bethlyn's time passed in a whirl of shopping trips with Molly, during which she was fitted with the most fashionable gowns and accessories. When the purchases later arrived at Edgecomb, Bethlyn's bedroom was strewn with undergarments of the finest lace, nightrails of whisper-thin material, silk shoes, and hats in every style and color to match the satin, silk, and velvet dresses which the servant girls dutifully hung in the wardrobe.

"Goodness, Bethlyn, there's hardly any more room to hang up your dresses," Molly commented, and draped a long strand of pearls around her pretty neck, observing herself in the pier mirror. "I've never seen so many clothes at one time."

Bethlyn finished slipping into a lavender gown with a pointed bodice, trimmed in alabaster-colored ruching which matched the lace on the elbow-length sleeves. A middle-aged servant named Sally closed the many hooks on the back of the gown, and Bethlyn broke away to peer in the same mirror as Molly. She smiled, pleased with her appearance. It had been a long while since she had worn anything comparable to this satin gown, which had been made especially for her by a well-known Philadelphia dressmaker. For the first time since leaving London she felt she looked quite pretty. Her eyes sparkled with an amber twinkle within their depths, and she allowed Sally to pull her hair atop her head with soft curls framing her face and baby-fine wisps at the nape of her neck.

The gown was possessed of a low neckline which Bethlyn realized showed too much décolletage, but she genuinely liked this dress and hated to take it off. So, she reached for an ivory lace kerchief and placed it within the valley of her breasts. She twirled around the large bedroom, instantly coming to a dizzy standstill when she heard Ian's voice from the open doorway.

"So this is what you ladies do all day while I slave away at the office."

Molly giggled and rushed to him, kissing him on his cheek. "You're home early. How wonderful. You're going to dine with us tonight?"

Ian inclined his head, his green eyes bright. "Yes, Captain André will join us."

"Oh, I better tell Cook. Come, Sally, we must see to the preparations." Taking off the pearl necklace, she placed it on the dressing table, then Molly and Sally withdrew from the room.

Ian leaned against the doorjamb with folded arms, and his gaze raked over Bethlyn, causing an all-too-familiar blush to consume her face, her whole body. She hated when he looked at her in such a possessive, scrutinizing fashion. It was almost as if he remembered their nights together . . . nights which would never happen again. She silently reminded herself that she was his wife, but a wife in name only now that she knew the truth about him. Whatever had happened between them on the *Black Falcon* and Windhaven was over. Yet how was she going to convince her traitorous body of that fact? Whenever she saw him, and thankfully she didn't see him very often, her legs always managed to go weak and she felt breathless. Like now.

She mustn't let Ian know how much she still wanted him. Their love was doomed from the start. No two people could be so ill-suited to each other. Molly had made mention of a certain Lady Cynthia Connors, and it was from what Molly hadn't said that caused Bethlyn to infer that Lady Cynthia and Ian had been more than passing acquaintances. Perhaps they still saw each other. Her heart hurt to think about Ian and this other woman. But, once again, she reminded herself that Ian had never wanted a wife, especially not her for a wife. She meant nothing to him except as a means to an end. They had made a pact: her freedom from him in exchange for her silence about Captain Hawk.

She'd honor their agreement, but she didn't have to allow the overbearing, pompous man to know this. She enjoyed keeping him off guard.

"Shame on you, Ian."

Ian cocked his head. "What have I done?"

She turned away and straightened her hem. "You invited John André for supper. Do you hope to get information about British activity from him? I like him and I don't approve of your using him." Tilting her head in his direction, she flashed him an impish smile. "I think he might be quite interested in my tale about the infamous Captain Hawk."

Ian entered the room, and in an instant he had whirled her about. His large hands imprisoned her elbows. "Bethlyn, don't taunt me. I hate game-playing, and you know this. Mention anything about what you know, and I can't vouch for your safety."

"Or your own."

"I'd be lying if I said I cared nothing for my safety. I do. I also have an innocent sister to protect and don't want her dragged into any of this because of your rebelliousness. I know you'd love to get even with me for the way I left you on our wedding day—for everything. I can't change the past, and I'm trying to atone for my treatment of you."

Bethlyn shrugged off his hold; her eyes now blazed with a challenging light. "Yes, I can see you are. All of these clothes, the jewelry. But I've received trinkets and baubles from you for years, Ian. Of course you don't remember what you sent to me, because you never picked any of them. However, I will tell you that your secretary, Mr. Gibbons, has marvelous and expensive taste. I see now that all of this," and she gestured around the clothing-strewn room with her hands, "is meant to buy my silence. You don't trust me to keep my word to you, so you treat me like the child you married and deserted.

"Instead of a pat on the head, you indulge me with fripperies, hoping that I'll keep your secret for a handful of trinkets." Bethlyn grabbed the pearl necklace from the top of the dressing table and flung it at him, hitting him in the center of his chest before it clattered to the floor. The strand broke, causing seed pearls to roll across the room.

"That is what I think of your gifts to me! Not once have you given me anything chosen with your own hands, and I no longer care. Yet I gave you my word I would keep my silence about Captain Hawk, and I shall. Never fear, Ian. I promise you I won't tell. And that is more than you've ever given to me."

Her breasts heaved with her fury. Her face was flushed, and her eyes incredibly bright. She saw a muscle twitch in his cheek, and she guessed she'd made him angry, but she didn't care. She'd gladly ride out the brunt of his anger to gain some response from him. Since he discovered she was his wife, he'd kept his distance and been coolly polite. At night she could hear him moving around his room and then he'd leave and wouldn't return home until quite late. She figured he saw Lady Cynthia. He probably didn't need his secretary to choose gifts for his mistress, and this was the main reason she unleashed her temper.

She was jealous of a woman she'd never met.

He waited before her in silence, and this rankled her further.

"Have you nothing to say?" she demanded.

"I believe you've said it all quite well, my dear."

She nearly gave in to the inclination to stomp her foot in outrage. "Pompous, arrogant . . ."

"I know, Bethlyn. No need to finish your sentence. I need a bath before John arrives. Finish dressing and meet us downstairs in the dining room. And be on your best behavior." He winked at her and grinned before he left the room.

"Boob!" she finished the remark she'd have made earlier, and in a huff she threw her gold-plated hairbrush at the door.

The evening passed in quite a pleasant fashion.

John André praised the food, the company, and his compliments to Molly and Bethlyn warmed Bethlyn's heart. She'd missed the compliments from the gentlemen she'd known in London, and André with his good-natured warmth caused her very much to want to be viewed as pretty again. She found herself flirting outrageously with him, not because she was interested in him romantically, but because she sensed that Ian was quite peeved over her actions. A sly smile curved her pretty mouth whenever Ian glared at her from across the dining table.

After supper the four of them sat in the parlor. From his pocket, John withdrew the small sketchbook she'd noticed the day she first met him. Holding it out to her, she saw a charcoal drawing of herself.

"How very talented you are!" she gushed. "May I keep it?"

John beamed, his excitement at pleasing her evident in his eyes. Tearing off the sheet, he handed it to her.

"To the most beautiful lady I've ever met," he said grandly and stood up to bow before kissing her hand.

Bethlyn curtseyed. "You, sir, are a true gentleman."

Molly giggled and tapped Ian's arm with her fan. "I think Bethlyn has an admirer, dear brother."

Ian remained silent, pretending to be engrossed in a card game with his sister, but his gaze constantly wandered towards his wife and André. Moments later, Bethlyn gave André her arm and requested they stroll around the estate. When the parlor doors shut on the lavender-and-scarlet-clad figures, Ian threw down his cards.

"I'm tired of this game."

"I believe you're agitated over John's attentions towards Bethlyn," Molly said with a knowing gleam in her eyes.

"Molly, sweet, I've never been jealous of anyone in my life."

"Did I say jealous? That's your word, not mine."

"You think that, however."

Molly gathered the cards together and couldn't suppress the pleased smile which curved up the edges of her lips. "I admit that I do. You know, Ian, I don't understand why you never told me you had married Bethlyn. Really, seven years is quite a long time to keep it a secret. Frankly, I don't want to know your reasoning. I probably wouldn't like what I hear. Whether you believe it or not, I'm not a child." She noticed his indulgent smile and reared upward. "I'm fully grown. I am, and I can tell when a man is in love with a woman. And, my dear brother, you're in love with your wife."

"Molly, this is none of your—"

"Concern? Yes, it is. I want you to be happy; I've prayed for you to find a woman who can touch that hardened heart of yours with love. Ever since Mother left—and I will say this, so get that scowl off of your face—you've changed from a loving person into a piece of ice. Mother left not only you, Ian, but me as well. I hope not to become hard like you."

"Thank you ever so much," he said with a sarcastic lilt to his voice.

Molly sighed and reached over and took his hand. "You're not Father. Remember that. I think that our parents never truly loved each other. If they had, then Mother wouldn't have left him for—that man. They must have married for the company's sake. But you have a chance to change things and not repeat their mistakes. Don't lose your wife. I can see by the way she looks at you that she loves you."

What a romantic Molly was, Ian thought, and felt a surge of tenderness for his sister. Yet he couldn't discount her words, because they held many truths. When had his dark-haired moppet of a sister grown up to be so wise? However, he sincerely doubted that Bethlyn loved him. She detested him now that she knew the truth about him.

And love her? No, he didn't love her. He might desire her, but not love, never love. He wouldn't love any woman and risk the pain his own father had suffered. Still, he ached to have Bethlyn in his bed, to hold her in his arms, but he couldn't touch her, wouldn't risk her rejection of him.

As far as he was concerned, nothing had changed. Bethlyn was still his wife until the day he freed her . . . but love? Never love.

Ian cleared his throat and sent a slicing glance at the open doorway, framed by a pediment, from which his wife and André now entered. Her usually pale cheeks were flushed from the chilly night air, and Ian noted that she must have thrown John's coat over her shoulders to protect her from the cold. Had John André's arms warmed her, also? He couldn't help but wonder, and felt rather surprised at the jealous feeling which stung him.

They laughed together, and Bethlyn handed back the coat to John. "Thank you for a lovely time in the garden. I hope I didn't bore you with my prattle about my childhood."

John slipped into his coat. "Never, dear Bethlyn. I enjoyed hearing about Hallsands and that prude of a governess. What was her name again?"

"Miss Grosvenor."

"Exactly." André's eyes slid to Ian. "I never did learn about how you and Ian met."

Bethlyn shrugged, her happy smile dissolving. "I'm certain the story would bore you, John, dear. In fact, come to think on it, the whole meeting and our marriage has been rather a large bore."

Bethlyn didn't miss the scowl which crossed Ian's face as she sat down and poured a cup of tea, holding it out to John, who dutifully took it and lowered his eyes in seeming embarrassment at Bethlyn's forthrightness. It was only when Molly engaged him in conversation that the atmosphere lightened. Half an hour later, John stood to leave and invited the three of them to the opening of the Southwark Theater, an endeavor dear to his heart, since he had been instrumental in painting the colorful backdrops and was the producer of the light comedy to be presented.

"We call ourselves Howe's Thespians, in honor of General Howe, of course," he explained. "I can't believe Philadelphia has been without a theater for so long."

"If I recall," Ian said, "Congress closed it because the theater was thought to be extravagant and dissipative during a time of war."

"Tsk, tsk, man. Even brash colonials deserve some amusement. I expect to see you on Sunday night." His words were meant for all of them, but his gaze centered on Bethlyn when he spoke.

Bethlyn extended her hand after Molly, and her palm was rewarded with a gallant kiss. "We shall be there," Bethlyn promised.

Moments later, the door was shut against the cold night air and Molly excused herself to hurry upstairs to bed. Bethlyn started to follow, but Ian grabbed her arm and stalled her.

"Kindly explain why you thought it necessary to flirt with John André, a captain in the British Army and an aide to General Howe. You know he is an enemy."

"Your enemy, not mine," she reminded him. "You forget that I'm a loyal British subject while you only pretend to be one. Are you riled because I flirted with a British captain, or that I flirted with a man?"

"I'm not jealous," Ian lied, all too aware that he couldn't stand the thought that Bethlyn might prefer the gallant André to himself.

"How very pleased I am for you. I must remind you of our agreement that I pretend to be your dutiful wife; however, with whom I flirt is my own concern. I am rather adept at it, you know."

An unreasonable fear of losing her surged through him. He now recalled all of the letters from Aunt Penny, declaring his wife a notorious flirt. He'd discounted his aunt's claims, remembering a plain, plump, and sick child. But the woman who now gazed at him with amber eyes, flecked with gold within the centers, was breathtakingly beautiful. And she was his lawful wife. He could make love to her whenever he wished, and he wanted her now. No matter their differences, he couldn't get her out of his mind, his blood.

He softened at the thought of winning her affection once more, and his fingers on her arm grew gentle and warm. "I would like to hear about your childhood, too."

"What sort of ploy is this?" she asked suspiciously. "You wish to know about my childhood, yet you left your childbride behind and sailed away, without a further thought about my welfare."

"I left you with Aunt Penny," he reminded her, her frosty, self-righteous attitude dispelling his desire. "I knew you'd be safe with her, and, never forget, it was my money which supported you for the last seven years."

She pulled her arm away from his grasp. "I can't forget. I was bought like so much chattel but denied the husband and children I desperately wanted. Can you be a true husband to me, Ian? Can you give me a home life and children?"

He'd like to do just that. He couldn't. Too much stood in their way for any true happiness. Her father for one. He'd never be able to forgive her father for taking his mother away. The wound ran deeper than a valley, destroying his ability to feel love for any woman, especially *this* woman. He wanted her in his bed, but each time he looked at her, he remembered his father's torment. At quite a young age he'd vowed never to fall in love. The pain if the woman rejected him would be too great for him to bear. And if he gave his heart to Bethlyn, the daughter of the man who'd destroyed his father, she might trounce upon it. She was a loyalist, he reminded himself, and an aristocrat. Something he wasn't.

Too much kept them apart. He couldn't risk the pain. "Whatever is mine is yours until the moment the marriage ends. That is all I can give to you."

Without a further word, Ian left her and headed up the stairs to seek his solitary bed.

She was getting nowhere with Ian.

In fact, he barely spared time to speak with her, much less dine with her in the evenings. Molly was her only company, and sometimes Molly mysteriously disappeared. Like today when she'd promised they'd go shopping together. However, Molly claimed a previous engagement with an old school friend and left the house shortly after Ian did that morning. So Bethlyn was alone and feeling unaccountably sorry for herself.

The beauty of Edgecomb in the winter couldn't keep her interest. Soft flurries had fallen the previous night, and when she woke, the landscape was covered in a fine layer of snow. However, the sun now peeped from behind a cloud and the snow was melting. But she found the weather too cold to ramble about the garden, and, inside, Bethlyn grew tired of counting stitches, embroidering a scene which depicted a waterfall and a young deer. She could see to the household tasks, but laying aside her hoop, she knew that Molly did a capable job, having run the house with the housekeeper's help since the departure of Ian and Molly's mother years ago.

What to do?

Inspiration came to her in a flash.

Running out of the parlor and up the stairs to her room, she rang for Sally, who helped her change into a velvet blue gown whose elbow-length sleeves had a row of tiny white bows around the edge and two large matching bows to hold up the overskirt, beneath which was a white lace underskirt. The neckline was rounded and just an inch under her collarbone.

Sally piled her hair atop her head, and then she stepped into matching slippers and threw on a deep blue cape, fur-lined with a matching hood.

"My, but you look nice, Mrs. Briston. Where are you off to this morning?" Sally asked, her eyes lighting with pleasure at the picture Bethlyn presented.

"Someplace I should have returned days ago." Bethlyn pulled on a pair of black kid gloves and shot Sally an engaging smile. "And I doubt I'll be welcome."

Like a whirlwind, Bethlyn left the room and, before settling in Ian's carriage, she gave directions to the driver.

Ignore her, will he! she silently fumed to herself as the carriage rolled along the frost-slicked streets. Ian Briston would rue the day he thought he could gain the upper hand with her. She knew him well enough to realize that he wanted to be rid of her, and would gladly do so when he was free of suspicion. But in the meantime, he expected her to sit at Edgecomb and act the docile wife.

Well, she wasn't docile any longer. She'd never let anyone tell her what she could and couldn't do. She'd gone through that with her father years ago, having seen the fear on her mother's face whenever the earl was in residence, forcing her to tiptoe around Woodsley like a timid mouse.

Granted, Ian hadn't told her she had to stay at home. She could come and go as she pleased on shopping excursions or visits to people's homes as she'd done just the other day with Molly. Ian hadn't been with her for these visits. He allowed Molly to introduce her to his friends instead of doing it himself, and it was this slight which irritated Bethlyn more than his highhandedness or the fact that he expected her to do whatever must be done to save his colonial hide.

She'd felt quite embarrassed for Molly and humiliated for herself at the surprise she'd seen on people's faces to learn that Ian Briston had a wife . . . a wife he'd never claimed for seven years.

"He might wish to keep me locked at Edgecomb, but I refuse to allow him a moment more as indisputable head of Briston Shipping," she spoke aloud in the carriage. And she meant every word of this.

Ten minutes later when she flounced into Briston Shipping, closing the door loudly behind her, Mr. Eakins glanced up sharply from his perch behind his desk. She expected him to rear up like a rooster and order her out. She even prepared herself for the large man named Demming to come forward with brawny arms and attempt to lift her from her feet and throw her onto her backside on the street. Her pride still smarted from that incident.

However, Mr. Eakins came forward with an apologetic smile on his face and bowed.

"My most humble apology to you, Mrs. Briston. Please excuse me for my behavior to you that day you were looking for your husband. I had no idea who you were."

Bethlyn felt taken aback for a moment. "I told you who I was that day, sir."

"Again, forgive me. I didn't know Mr. Briston was married. He informed me the next day about my . . . treatment . . . of you. Forgive me, ma'am."

Bethlyn didn't care for Mr. Eakins, but she could see he was sorry for what he'd done and he called to Demming, who apologized in turn. She was surprised by this turn of events, but even more surprised that Ian had actually informed his employees that she was his wife.

"I accept your apologies," she told the two men. "But never treat anyone who enters this office again in such a fashion. Do I make myself clear?"

"Yes, Mrs. Briston," they mumbled in unison, and both of them looked sheepish.

"I should like to see my husband," Bethlyn said.

Mr. Eakins squinted. "Mr. Briston isn't in this morning, ma'am. Would you care to speak to Mr. Gibbons instead?"

"Yes, my husband's secretary will do for now."

Following behind Mr. Eakins, he led her upstairs through a carpeted hallway and knocked on an oak door. At the words "Enter," Mr. Eakins opened the door and stood aside for Bethlyn.

"Mr. Gibbons," he spoke to the curly blond-headed man whose head was bent over a large ledger book which rested on a large desk, "Mrs. Briston wishes to speak with you." Eakins departed.

Jonathan Marcus Gibbons lifted his head, a startled look in his blue eyes to find Bethlyn standing before him, and she appeared just as unsettled.

"Crane," she mumbled as the shock caused her to sink into a leather upholstered chair. "I should have known you were Mr. Gibbons."

He flushed and closed the ledger book.

"Yes, well, now you know my identity. I presume you won't mention anything about me to your friend, Captain André."

"I give you my word that I won't, and only for one reason. Mavis. How is she? Tell me where I may find her?"

Marc laughed. "Hold on, Bethlyn . . . er, Mrs. Briston. Mavis is fine. We were married shortly after arriving in Philadelphia. Didn't Ian mention that?"

She shook her head. "Ian mentions very little."

"I'm certain Mavis would love to see you again. We have a house in Elfreths Alley. I'd bring you there, but with Ian out of the office, I can't leave at the moment."

"I'm sure my driver can find the house," Bethlyn started

211

to rise when Marc glanced curiously at her.

"What did you want here today, Mrs. Briston?"

She'd momentarily forgotten her reason for coming here in her excitement to see Mavis again. She settled a level gaze on Marc. "Most probably I won't see my husband tonight. No doubt he'll be occupied elsewhere." Probably with Lady Cynthia Connors, she thought. "You may inform him that I stopped by to see him and tell him that I shall come again tomorrow. I believe the time is ripe for me to take an interest in the running of Briston Shipping."

Marc flashed her an encouraging smile. "I shall be happy to relay the message, Mrs. Briston."

"Call me Bethlyn, and I shall call you by your first name."

"Marc."

"Marc. I like that." She offered him her hand in parting. "And, Marc, you have exquisite taste in jewelry. I'm certain my husband would have been unable to choose lovelier birthday and anniversary gifts than you."

Marc appeared uncomfortable. "Yes, thank you, but, Bethlyn, I warrant that this anniversary your husband shall choose the gift for you."

"I doubt he'll remember it, and please don't mention that our anniversary is but a week away. Under the circumstances I don't wish him to feel obligated."

"I won't."

Smiling her thanks, she left Marc's office and brushed past Mr. Eakins downstairs with a slight nod of her head. Soon she found herself in a quaint, cobblestone older section of the city, sitting beside Mavis in her kitchen, which smelled of beef stew and freshly baked pumpkin pie.

Mavis poured tea for them, her eyes alight with gladness to see Bethlyn again.

"You'll never know how worried I was that day when Hawk, I mean your husband, took you to Windhaven. I thought never to see you again and feared what he might do to you."

"He's a big, arrogant bully, Mavis. But I can say that to

212

you because I've known you so long. I could never tell Molly such a thing about her beloved brother. As far as Molly's concerned, Ian can do no wrong." Bethlyn sipped her tea and then smiled at her friend. "You seem very happy with Marc."

"I am!" Mavis gushed, not hiding her happiness. "I love Marc so very much."

"And you were the one who thought she'd never find love again," Bethlyn reminded her, a prickle of envy in her voice.

"That's true, but if I recall, I wished you good fortune, too. Have you discovered love with your Captain Hawk?"

Bethlyn laughed. "That's another thing. You're the only one other than Marc and Ian himself who knows about Captain Hawk."

"You didn't answer my question."

Bethlyn stirred uneasily in her chair. "I don't know. As much as I disliked being abandoned by Ian all those years ago, my situation was easier. I could hate him, because I didn't really know him—didn't know about . . . Well, you know what I mean."

"Lovemaking."

"Yes."

"And now?"

"That's what has me confused, Mavis. I should hate the bounder and turn him into the authorities. I can't, however, and not because of the agreement I made with Ian to free me when suspicion turns away from him. I remember how it felt to be held by him, to be kissed, loved by him. I can't forget so many things. If I could forget I'd be better off. I could leave Philadelphia and go home again, start life anew. But for some stupid reason, I'd feel so empty without him, so alone. As it is now, he barely speaks to me. I don't think he trusts me."

"Do you want him to trust you?"

"Yes."

"Bethlyn, do you want Ian Briston to love you?"

A shaky sigh escaped Bethlyn. "That seems to be all I've ever wanted."

Mavis sat back, seemingly satisfied with Bethlyn's

answer. "Then if you want your husband, you know what you must do."

Mavis made everything sound so simple, but it wasn't. Nothing in her life had ever been simple. Ian Briston was the most complex man she'd ever known, save for her father, and maybe besides his physical attractiveness, that was why she felt drawn to him. Their physical attraction wasn't enough, she mused. Their backgrounds were different, and most definitely their political loyalties would keep them apart.

Ian had made it quite clear that he didn't want her for his wife. No matter the stirrings within her breast for the man, for the pulsating desire she felt when he was near. Passion wasn't enough and she'd never humble herself to beg for his love, not certain she loved him either.

Mavis stirred her tea, and her words brought Bethlyn out of her reverie. "I'm expecting a child next June."

Bethlyn hugged her friend. "How happy I am for you and Marc! A baby. I should love to have my own child one day."

Mavis winked at her. "Well, you know what you have to do to get one."

When the carriage pulled up to the house an hour later, Bethlyn went inside and pulled off her cape in the foyer. Going into the parlor, she stood at the window which faced the garden and quickly backed away, peering through the web of lace on the curtains. A tall man, dressed in the green uniform of a Hessian soldier, held the cloaked figure of a woman in his arms, whom Bethlyn readily identified as Molly.

The girl's head was tilted upward, and even at a distance Bethlyn discerned love on both of their faces for each other. She clung to the man as if she feared to release him, and finally after a tender kiss, the soldier left. Bethlyn noticed Molly lift a hand and wipe away a tear from her eye before hurrying to the front of the house.

Soon Bethlyn heard the front door close. Molly, carrying some boxes, smiled at her. "I went Christmas shopping with my friend," she told Bethlyn before heading upstairs. Bethlyn didn't question her about the Hessian soldier. Somehow she knew Ian wouldn't approve of the man, and she saw no harm in allowing Molly to claim some happiness.

For the second time that day, Bethlyn envied lovers.

The evening of the play arrived. A bone-chilling cold settled over Philadelphia in early December, and the hint of snow was evident in the air. At Edgecomb, however, as Bethlyn dressed, the warmth from the blazing fireplace in her room kept the cold at bay.

As her chemise and a layer of petticoats were pulled over her head with Sally's help, and Molly flitted in and out of the room to borrow a hair ribbon or a pair of Bethlyn's new slippers, Bethlyn wondered about the wisdom of sleeping in the room next to Ian's. Granted, the room was larger and much more beautiful than the guest room. It had belonged to Jessica Briston, and though the room no longer reflected the woman's personal tastes, Bethlyn could almost imagine her as she sat before the ornately carved dressing table, brushing her thick mane of dark hair.

Was it because of Jessica that Ian felt unable to love her? Was it because of who her father was? More important, did she want to love Ian? The memories of their nights together still haunted her. She'd never thought lovemaking could be so wonderful, or that she'd crave the man's hands upon her after what she'd learned about him. But she did, and she almost hated herself for wanting him.

"Which pair should I wear, Bethlyn?"

Molly's voice broke into her thoughts and Bethlyn noticed that she had a red satin slipper on her right foot and a green one on her left.

"I'd say you look very Christmasy."

"Which one goes with this dress?" Molly asked, and giggled at Bethlyn's remark. She turned and the berry-colored satin swished about her legs.

"The red ones."

"I think so, too." Molly took off the green shoe and replaced it with a red one. "I do so love your gown. The color suits you so very well."

Bethlyn glanced at her reflection in the mirror, somewhat unconcerned with her appearance. The forest green of the very low-neck gown livened her eyes and caused the unusual color of her hair to be more noticeable. With the large pendant at her neck, set with emeralds and pearls, and the companion ear bobs, she looked extremely elegant. However, her appearance was of little concern to her since Ian barely seemed to acknowledge her existence anyway.

"I trust I shall do," Bethlyn mumbled, and grabbed for a velvet black cape with hood.

Moments later, Bethlyn and Molly sauntered into the parlor where Ian rose from a large, overstuffed chair. In a brown velvet jacket with black trousers and high knee boots, he looked so handsome that Bethlyn felt a catch in her throat.

"We're ready to leave for the play," she told him, and couldn't keep the appreciative gleam out of her eyes.

"So, I see," he said, and took in both their appearances, not bothering to hide the lustful gleam in his eyes as his gaze speared Bethlyn's.

Bethlyn felt somewhat flustered and started to turn away when she felt Ian's hand on her arm. "I have something for you. Perhaps you might indulge me by wearing it tonight."

From inside his breast pocket, he withdrew a gaily wrapped tiny package and placed it into her hand. "Happy wedding anniversary."

Bethlyn's fingers curled around the gift. She felt stunned that he'd remembered. Or had Marc reminded him?

"A present!" Molly cried. "Do open it, Bethlyn, or I shall die of suspense this very moment."

Slowly she opened the package and then the satin-lined box. Inside was a delicately wrought spray brooch in a gold and enameled-silver setting, garnished with rubies and diamonds.

"How lovely," she breathed, and allowed Ian to take it from her and pin it on the front of her gown. His fingers brushed the tender flesh above her breasts, and a hot, surging heat rushed through her.

"Thank you for the gift," she told him, sounding wooden.

"Goodness, Bethlyn. Aren't you going to show your appreciation by giving Ian a kiss?" Molly asked, a mischievous grin on her pretty face.

Bethlyn felt herself coloring at the request, but she lifted her head and kissed Ian's cheek.

"You can do better than that," he mumbled, and his arms locked around her waist, pulling her against his hard frame. His moist, warm lips devoured hers, and when he drew away, her mouth burned with fire.

Extending an arm to her and Molly, he smiled. "Shall we go?"

The play proved to be a delightful comedy, and afterward everyone milled about the theater. Colorful silks and satins mingled with the scarlet-coated soldiers. Bethlyn, Ian, and Molly left their box and wandered among the crème de la crème of Philadelphia society.

To Bethlyn's surprise, Ian kept her at his side and introduced her to his acquaintances, many of whom she'd already met with Molly. His hand constantly stayed at her elbow, guiding her through the crowd and whispering choice pieces of gossip to her about each of the people she met.

"Lord Montague is a senile old man, but he keeps a beautiful young woman as his mistress. However, his mistress doesn't care that he's addled in the head, only that he's wealthy," he told her before the man and woman in question made their way to them.

And so it went for the next hour. Ian never left her side except to fetch her a cup of punch. She felt comfortable with him, almost as if she truly belonged to him. She might be his wife, but no one would guess they led separate lives and would soon divorce. Bethlyn didn't wish to contemplate the end of her marriage at that moment. The brooch he'd given to her earlier was a reminder of his thoughtfulness. Perhaps, just perhaps, there might be a chance for them. His gift had touched her in a way she couldn't fathom, because somehow she knew that Marc had kept his word and hadn't reminded Ian of their wedding anniversary. She knew without a doubt that Ian had chosen the brooch for her, and the realization that he'd taken the time out of his day to shop for her meant more than the actual gift to her.

From the kiss he'd bestowed upon her earlier, and the solicitous way he hovered around her, she wondered if his attitude towards her had changed. Might he also want their marriage to last? She didn't dare hope such a thing. Not yet. But the thought intrigued her immensely.

John André broke into her thoughts when he approached them with a very pretty young blonde beside him. He introduced the young lady as Peggy Shippen, proclaiming her as one of the loveliest Philadelphia belles.

"Oh, John, what a flatterer you are," Peggy crooned up to John, but she didn't dispute his remark. She turned her attention on Ian and Bethlyn, who were joined by Molly at that moment. "My parents are giving a soirée next Saturday evening. I wish to take this opportunity to invite all of you in my parents' absence tonight. Please say you'll come."

Ian bowed to her. "We'd be most pleased to attend."

"How divine. I shall inform my parents." She shot them a dazzling smile and presented her hand to André, who placed it on his arm. "I see some other acquaintances and must speak to them. Adieu until Saturday."

Peggy Shippen and John André breezed through the crowd in a montage of a lavender lace and crimson cloth.

"Such a flighty creature," Molly noted, her nose wrinkling in disdain. "I don't know what John sees in her."

"Miss Shippen is a pretty young lady, and we know how John adores attractive women. It seems Peggy has earned a place in John's heart, Bethlyn," Ian said, not hiding his complacent grin.

"John is my friend," Bethlyn countered, not really minding if John André squired Peggy Shippen around.

Molly asked Ian to fetch her a cup of punch, and as Ian walked away, Bethlyn kept her gaze trained on him. Clearly, she found him to be the most handsome man in the room. The British officers in their colorful uniforms couldn't compete with Ian's good looks. Just watching him caused her silly heart to pound harder, and for the first time in weeks she entertained the idea of going to his bed that night. To think about being in his arms again caused thrills of excitement down to her very toes.

"My, but you have a sly look on your face," Molly commented.

Bethlyn turned her attention to her sister-in-law. "Do I? I hadn't realized."

"It's quite easy to see how much you love my brother."

"Molly, please. Let's not discuss such a private matter here. But if you're wont to discuss being in love, then let me ask you a question. Who was the Hessian officer I saw you with a few days ago?"

Molly attempted to look blank, but the high spots of color on her cheeks belied the look. "I—don't—know what you mean."

"Certainly you do, or did my eyes deceive me and that wasn't you I saw in the arms of a German officer in the garden?"

"Oh, Bethlyn, please don't mention that to Ian. I admit you saw me, but I don't want Ian to know about Hans. My brother still believes me to be a child, and if he knew I wanted to marry Hans, he'd try and stop me. I do so want him to approve."

"I understand. What is your young man's full name and how did you come to meet him?"

Molly moved closer to Bethlyn and whispered to her. Her eyes now contained an animated gleam just to speak about her beloved. "He is Captain Hans Gruber, a Hessian soldier. I met him over a month ago at the home of a friend. Ian couldn't accompany me that night, so he has no idea that Hans exists. We love each other so much and plan to

219

marry just as soon as I can gather the nerve to bring him home to meet Ian. Please don't tell Ian anything until I feel the time is right."

Molly's pleading and the lovestruck look in her eyes caused Bethlyn to give her her word. She envied Molly her German officer, just as she envied Mavis and Marc. How wonderful it must be to love someone and to have that love reciprocated. Could there be a chance for herself and Ian?

The bit of hope she felt about keeping her marriage together faded the moment she went in search of Ian. She saw him with a beautiful and voluptuous auburn-haired woman, standing in a secluded corner behind the stage. The woman leaned near to him, her nearly naked ivory bosom resting against the front of his jacket. His arms were twined around her waist, and Bethlyn didn't miss the way his lips touched hers in a kiss so intimate that Bethlyn blushed.

She wanted to rush past the potted palm which hid her from view and do what? Attack them, pull out the hussy's hair? Never had she been so jealous of another human being, not even that loathsome Della on board ship. But then Della had never truly posed a threat, because the woman was a common trollop. The woman in Ian's arms was not common. Her very being oozed wealth and status, and Bethlyn suddenly realized that this woman just might be Lady Cynthia Connors.

Feeling tired and drained, she turned away from the sight of Ian and the woman she thought was Cynthia and returned to Molly.

"Have you seen Ian?" Molly asked. "I would like some punch, and he's taking so long that I could have gotten it myself."

"I didn't see him. Molly, I feel quite ill and would like to go home. I'll send the carriage back for you and Ian later."

"You do look quite pale," Molly noticed, concerned. "I'll accompany you home. I see Captain André. I'll tell him to relay the message to Ian."

Bethlyn nodded, and she headed for the carriage and was soon joined by Molly. "I do hope Ian isn't so worried about you that he braves this cold night to walk the distance home before the carriage returns for him," Molly commented, and patted Bethlyn's hand in a comforting gesture.

"I doubt he shall miss me," Bethlyn said bitingly. "He's in good company and even warmer hands."

Molly lifted an eyebrow in puzzlement, but said nothing. Bethlyn closed her eyes and leaned her head against the cushioned seat. She was so angry and hurt, emotions she hated to admit she felt. She wouldn't allow Ian Briston to hurt her again, refused to give him the satisfaction of knowing she knew about him and Lady Cynthia.

Her eyes smarted, but she refused to believe she wanted to cry.

Chapter Fifteen

Bethlyn felt like a ninny for running away.

The next morning she cursed herself for her foolishness, convincing herself that she felt nothing for her womanizing husband. Even when she joined Ian and Molly in the dining room for breakfast, she felt thoroughly certain that Ian's dalliance with Lady Cynthia didn't bother her a bit.

She flashed both of them a charming smile and looked quite pretty in a dark blue velvet gown with tightly laced bodice. A spray of pink silk roses at the neckline added a very feminine appearance.

"How do you feel today?" Molly's concern was evident on her sweet face.

"Much better," Bethlyn responded, and laid her napkin on her lap, not missing her husband's scrutinizing gaze.

Ian poured coffee from a silver urn, the strong aroma wafting through the room. Sipping the brew, he leveled Bethlyn with a steady look. "You seem in the best of health to me. I had no idea you were ill last night. Why didn't you say something? I'd have escorted you home."

Bethlyn's brow rose up a fraction of an inch. "You were occupied elsewhere, and I didn't wish to intrude upon your conversation."

"Next time, come fetch me when you're ill."

"I shall," she replied sweetly like a dutiful wife, but she wished to slice his hypocritical face with the butter knife.

Molly pushed her plate aside. "Shall we go shopping today, Bethlyn? I saw the most adorable hat in a shop window and simply must have it."

Cutting into a sausage, Bethlyn shook her head. "I'm sorry, but I have other plans. I'm going to the office today with Ian."

"You are?" both Ian and Molly chorused.

Bethlyn smiled an innocent and demure smile. "Yes. I was there a few days ago and saw Mr. Gibbons. I'm surprised that he didn't mention my visit to you. I'd like to see the books, to know all there is to know about Briston Shipping. Unless there's something about the company which you don't want me to know." Her eyes were on Ian, pleased to note by his sudden speechlessness she had flustered him.

"I have no secrets from you," he said at length, throwing down his napkin and standing up. She expected him to balk, waiting for him to warn her away from the office, but in truth she could discern nothing which might indicate any upset that she wished to peruse the books. "When you've finished your breakfast we can leave. I'll be in the library waiting for you." His voice held a tone of bored indifference, and that was one thing Bethlyn wouldn't accept from Ian any longer. He might not want her as his wife, but she'd be damned if he intended to ignore her, or worse yet, mollify her by seeming to go along with her request to see the books and brief her on her father's company.

Well, Ian Briston was in for a surprise, she thought, and hurried her breakfast along. Before the day was over he would discover that his wife had a head for business matters.

When the late-afternoon sun streamed into Ian's office, and Mr. Eakins tiptoed into the room to inquire if Bethlyn needed any other account books before he left for the day, Ian answered she had all she needed and sent Mr. Eakins on his way.

Bethlyn had been so involved in the books that she barely heard the door close behind Mr. Eakins. It was only when Ian stood and closed the book before her did she glance up.

"Closing time," he told her and smiled. "You've gone

223

over so many figures that it's a wonder your eyes aren't crossed. I must compliment you on your diligence. I had expected that you'd have gone home long ago."

"I know you did," Bethlyn confessed. "And I would have except I feel I should take an interest in Briston Shipping." She leaned back in her chair, feeling bone-weary. "I must pay you a compliment. Your books are in impeccable order."

"Ah, so now you're convinced that I'm not absconding with company funds."

"Quite satisfied and convinced."

Golden sunlight spilled onto his handsome face, and Bethlyn caught her breath. She'd been so engrossed in the account books all afternoon that she'd barely paid any attention to Ian, who had sat beside her, explaining any questions she might have. That morning he'd escorted her to the docks to see to the building of a new ship, and Bethlyn had been suitably impressed with the ship itself and Ian's knowledge of shipbuilding. Their jaunt and subsequent luncheon had passed in pleasant camaraderie. Now, she was all too aware of him as a man, her husband, and she hated feeling this way. Too many delicious memories surfaced. Memories better left forgotten, considering that Lady Cynthia was the woman who possessed his black heart.

"Time to be getting home," she said curtly and began to rise, but a crick in her neck caused her to moan in pain.

"That's what happens when you keep your head bent in the same position all day," Ian rebuked her when he realized her problem. "Sit back down. I have just the cure."

He pushed her back into the chair before she had time to protest, and his warm, sure hands clamped behind her neck.

"What are you doing, Ian?" She wasn't certain she wanted his hands upon her, but they felt so wonderful.

"I gather you've never been massaged before. You're in knots, just relax."

It seemed she had no other alternative. Ian took control of her, and his fingers seemed to drain the day's tension

224

from her. Her head lolled to the side, and she'd have gladly stayed in that position forever. When she felt Ian place a kiss on the side of her neck exposed to him, her eyes flew open and widened. Without realizing, she bolted from the chair and stared him down.

"How dare you take liberties with me! I'm not a whore—or, or—your mistress." She thought of Cynthia Connors in Ian's embrace and sneered.

"And you aren't a very pretty sight with such a look on your face," he countered. "I kissed you. So? I've done more than that to you in the past, and you never seemed to mind."

Bethlyn flushed and brushed past him, pulling her cloak from the hook on the wall. "I was stupid, that's my only defense. But I'm not a silly little girl any longer."

"No, you're not. You're a hardheaded female. You know, I think I miss that innocent child you used to be."

"Hah! You were never around when I was a child, and thanks to you I lost my innocence. I can do very well without you, thank you. And don't forget, Ian, we made a bargain."

He appeared nonplussed by her outrage, yet a flicker of bafflement crossed his face. "I don't know what's gotten into you, but I refuse to be screamed at. All I did was kiss you."

Reaching for his cloak, he then threw it over his broad shoulders and opened the door for her. "The carriage awaits outside."

In a huff she sailed out of the room, but once she settled herself in the carriage, she wasn't even certain why she'd exploded like that. She felt unaccountably foolish. The words of apology sprang to her lips, but were left unsaid when Ian closed the carriage door, not bothering to get inside. He stood by the window and spoke to her.

"Tell Molly that I won't be home for supper. And, Bethlyn, don't start playing the part of an outraged wife by waiting up for me. I doubt I'll be home until quite late."

Then he turned and walked away, and the driver spurred the horses into action. Huge tears gathered in her eyes, but she refused to shed them. It seemed that all she wanted to do lately was cry, and she wouldn't cry over Ian Briston.

But she couldn't suppress the stray tear which coursed down her cheek at what Ian had said. Or rather, what he had left unspoken.

He might not return home at all that night, and she knew who he'd be with until dawn colored the sky.

Ian finished the sumptuous meal and, following Cynthia into the parlor, he smiled at her as she poured him a whiskey.

"You look like you need to drink something strong tonight, Ian."

"Let it never be said that you don't cater to my moods, love."

Cynthia took a place beside him on the Chippendale-style sofa and placed the decanter on the tea table beside it. A long russet curl draped provocatively across one of her lush breasts to rest against the peach satin bodice of her gown.

"Quite true, Ian. We know each other very well. Tell me what's troubling you, or need I ask? I'd say your problem is your beautiful young wife."

"When is a wife not a problem? My father seemed to always have problems with my mother, and now I am cursed as well. I never wanted to marry her, you know."

Cynthia's clear blue eyes took in the handsome and fashionably dressed man she'd known so well the last ten years. They'd been lovers for nine of those ten years, but Ian hadn't approached her since before leaving Phila-delphia on a business excursion some months ago. She'd gotten used to his mysterious disappearances, but she had never gotten used to sleeping alone. Her dear husband had died a decade earlier, and she'd vowed never to marry again, though taking lovers had come quite naturally. She often wondered what her answer would have been had Ian Briston offered to make an honest woman of her.

Now, she'd never know, and not only because a wife had unexpectedly turned up. Ian, she deduced, had never loved her enough to marry her and never had she seen him quite so upset over a woman. Her woman's intuition told her that Ian Briston was in love with his wife but wouldn't admit it—not as long as he could bend her ready ear with his tales of marital woe. That was one situation she decided to remedy.

Ian reached out to her and pulled Cynthia into his arms. "Do you love the girl?" she asked and let him cushion her against his chest.

He groaned. "Don't you women ever think of anything else but love? I'm surprised at you, of all people, for asking such a question." Tilting her chin, he gazed down into her pert and pretty face. "Let's forget all of this nonsense and retire to the bedroom. I want to make love to you. I fear I've neglected you these last months."

Cynthia sighed and extricated herself from his arms. "You haven't been the most arduous suitor, Ian. However, I don't want to fall into bed with you, not now. Your lovemaking wouldn't be for me. Granted, I'd have your body but not your heart. You don't love me and never have. You're such a large, wonderful idiot and don't even realize the truth. You're in love with your wife."

She pirouetted and sat on a sofa opposite from him. "Besides, you won't have me to come to in the future with your marital problems, or for anything else. I'm to be married next month."

"You? Married?" Ian sounded so disbelieving that Cynthia laughed.

"Yes, do wish me well. Did you truly think that I'd never marry again? Perhaps I did give that impression over the years. But, my darling, you never wanted to marry me and deep down I knew you didn't love me, that we'd never be entirely happy together. I've met and fallen in love with the most divine man. Have you met Major Benjamin Fallows?" At Ian's nod, she continued. "Then you know how handsome he is and how very gallant. He recently arrived from England, and we met at Lord Montague's birthday celebration last month.

"Not to be unkind to you, but from the moment I saw Benjamin I knew I wanted to marry him. We loved each other instantly. Please, Ian, wish me every happiness. I want so much for our parting to be amicable."

Ian stood and went to Cynthia. He kissed the top of her golden-red head and smiled. "I hope you shall be the happiest of women, and that your Benjamin makes you a fine husband and good father to your children."

Cynthia took his hand and squeezed it. Her eyes held a gentleness. "Thank you, my love. I wish the same happiness for you. Go home to your wife, tell her you love her."

"I never admitted to love, Cynthia."

"Certainly you have, but you just don't realize it."

Standing up, Cynthia escorted Ian to the door. "I shall never forget you," she declared, and pushed the buttons on his cloak through the loops. "But return to your Bethlyn and the warmth of her love. The nights can be so lonely and bitterly cold without love."

"You're an unusual woman." His compliment was laced with respect.

"I'm glad you think so. Shall I meet your wife at the Shippens's soirée on Saturday? I do look forward to it."

"Perhaps," he said noncommittally.

With a sweet, lingering kiss from Cynthia, he then departed into the cold night air.

Ian walked back to the office and let himself in, determined to get some work done which he hadn't been able to do because he'd spent the day with Bethlyn and had to explain every time she asked a question about an entry in the account books. He hadn't minded answering her questions at all, having found her to be highly intelligent, possessing a ready and keen mind. This was one aspect of her personality which had gone unnoticed by him to some degree. Her beauty was unmistakable and her body held untold delights. But the fact that she had brains and beauty only fueled his desire to win her love.

However, once in his office, he found he couldn't concentrate and left to walk the docks. The mournful clanging of a ship's bell reverberated through the silence and he noticed the silhouette of a gull circling overhead. The bitter cold didn't bother him at all, he was so deep in thought.

Bethlyn. Love.

What an absurd notion, he thought as he looked at the watery expanse before him. Cynthia must truly be in love with her soldier to even suggest such a thing to him. He couldn't be in love with Bethlyn. She was the daughter of the Earl of Dunsmoor, the man who'd forced his poor father into an early grave and ruined his own life and Molly's by taking away their mother. Love had destroyed his father, and he'd never become besotted by a woman like him. However, wasn't he already besotted by Bethlyn?

Ian, ever honest with himself, hated to think on that question, posed by his own inner self. But the answer was so clear it leaped into his brain. The woman was all he ever thought about. Even now, her image invaded his thoughts, clouding his judgment.

Her face shimmered before him in the moonlight, and he recalled the feel of her hair within his fingers, the sweet warmth of her lips beneath his own, and the way her body moved when he made love to her. He hardened at the memory. It had been so long since they'd made love that he had the urge to bound home and claim her as his at that very moment.

He didn't, because his legs felt unable to move, his whole being waited in stunned disbelief at the realization that Bethlyn intended to leave him once suspicion passed from him. He'd truly lose her, and at that moment, he knew he couldn't let her leave him. He also knew something else, and this knowledge was so shattering that he felt something cold within the center of his heart explode inside him, leaving him with an incredible feeling of warmth and passion, of tenderness and gentleness.

A soft whistle of disbelief through his lips caused him to move and walk as if in a trance. Ian saw no one as he meandered along the side streets though people passed him, and an occasional carriage thundered past. He wasn't certain where he was going until he found himself at Marc's door, waiting impatiently for Marc to open it and let him inside.

When Marc opened the door, Mavis stood alongside of him.

"I love her," Ian told them before either one of them could utter a sound. "I love Bethlyn."

Marc and Mavis both laughed, and Marc pulled Ian inside while Mavis served up plates of pie for all of them. However, Ian couldn't eat, because his whole being was satisfied.

He'd already feasted on love.

Chapter Sixteen

Ian baffled Bethlyn.

For the last few days he'd been more than solicitous of her, even seeming not to mind her days spent at the office. Whenever he wasn't busy with outside appointments, he managed to be in his office with her to answer her questions. Questions she decided that Marc or Mr. Eakins could have answered equally as well.

In fact Ian was so amenable, so kind to her, that if she wasn't careful she might mistake this concern for love. But that was one emotion Ian Briston seemed incapable of feeling. Still, he had treated her like his equal, almost like his true wife. He managed to inquire if her room and the meals at Edgecomb were to her liking, and she had no doubt that if she didn't care for something, he'd immediately substitute something which pleased her.

He constantly kept her off balance, and she had no idea what she should think. Sometimes she very nearly allowed herself to imagine that they might have a future together. But she didn't. He hadn't touched her since before he learned her identity. She wondered if he regretted that Cynthia Connors wasn't his wife. Bethlyn couldn't forget seeing Cynthia cuddled in Ian's embrace the night of the play, and his kindnesses to her the last few days made the memory all the more painful—and Bethlyn all the more spiteful to prove to him that he meant nothing to her.

The night of the Shippens's soirée would more than convince her husband how little she thought about him.

For the past week she'd dwelled on Ian and Cynthia, hating herself for caring so much, but aching to cause him as much pain as she felt. He thought he could marry her and keep her cloistered in England while he dallied in America with his mistress. No more, she decided, as she dressed for the soirée.

On this night Ian would free her from this disastrous marriage. She wasn't even certain that the British suspected he was Captain Hawk. She had only his word on that, and what good was the word of a man who married a young, unsuspecting girl and left her to her own devices? She'd get on with her life and somehow forget Ian—a hard thing to do when even her dreams betrayed her by desiring her husband.

She'd chosen her gown with special care. Molly hadn't seen it yet, but she didn't wish to impress Molly. She dressed to enrage her husband. All of the times she'd flirted in London with men about whom she didn't care a fig, the slightly scandalous activities in which she'd engaged with Jeremy to catch his attention, had all been for naught. The bounder hadn't cared, but if there was one thing she had learned about Ian Briston was that he was a prideful man.

He hadn't taken her earlier escapades seriously because of the distance involved. Tonight she'd put his pride to the test and force his hand by giving him a taste of all he'd missed in London.

Smiling like a sly cat as the carriage pulled up to the Shippen House, Bethlyn held her cloak securely about her, preventing anyone from seeing the gown, and her hood hid a great portion of her hair. Molly, with Ian's help, emerged from the carriage first, and then he held out his hand to her.

Her hand touched his, and for a second an electrical shock jolted her. He hadn't touched her since the night in the office when he'd massaged her neck. She barely glanced at him, but she felt shaken by the contact.

When they entered the house, Peggy Shippen, with John André beside her, greeted them in the foyer. After Peggy made introductions to her parents and her sisters,

Ian escorted his wife and sister into the parlor, which was ablaze with lights. Holly and red berries, in celebration of the coming holidays, were wrapped around the marble columns which separated the foyer from the large parlor.

A servant dutifully helped Molly off with her cape, and Bethlyn couldn't help thinking how sweet and pretty her sister-in-law looked in a deeply flounced pink gown. She'd miss Molly when she left, and a bittersweet sadness filled Bethlyn to realize she might never see Molly again after her return to England.

Ian pulled off his own dark cape to reveal his ebony attire of velvet jacket and trousers, the black boots which rose up to his well-proportioned thighs, and a white, ruffled shirt which contrasted with the bronze coloring of his neck and face. A handsome face, Bethlyn thought, and hated herself for that melting sensation which invaded her legs.

"May I?" he invited, and his hands moved to the neckline of her cloak despite the hovering servant.

"Of course," Bethlyn replied demurely, but her heart thudded and her palms sweated. Her bid to escape Ian Briston was now to begin in earnest.

Her cloak fell away, and it seemed that all the people in the room turned in unison to look her way. A gasp could be heard throughout the room, and in that second Bethlyn knew the gown had produced the effect she'd planned. Until that moment all of her gowns had concealed her attributes, and she'd made certain that if a gown was too low, a bunch of flowers or a kerchief in the neckline would prevail.

This gown was different.

The ruby satin of the décolleté neckline barely covered her full breasts, the tight-fitting bodice descending into a point and accentuating her tiny waist. She wore the elbow-length sleeves, which dripped in a double cascade of gold lace, off her milky white shoulders. Her full, draped skirt was ruffled in golden lace and festooned with small red roses which were repeated on the ruby slippers. On her neck she wore a garnet-and-gold necklace, and at her ears the matching earbobs set off the beauty of her porcelain complexion.

Her honey-brown hair was a tower of puffs and curls with shimmering rubies and gold dust scattered through the thick tresses. Never had she looked more beautiful, and Ian's face when he bent near to her was wreathed in unmistakable desire.

"My dear," he said, and she heard a husky quiver in his voice as he presented his arm to her.

It took all of her courage not to melt at the passion in his eyes, not to give in to her own desire for her husband. But Bethlyn quickly flapped open her fan and refused to take his arm. Snubbing Ian, she walked past him and headed for Captain André where she was summarily introduced to the young swains who materialized around them like ants at a picnic.

She flirted outrageously and drank far too many glasses of champagne until her head swam. From the corner of her eye, she noticed Ian standing sullenly by the fireplace, and a certain smugness filled her. The feeling of power which claimed her soon evaporated when she again turned her attention to Ian after a few minutes and noticed he was in earnest conversation with Lady Cynthia.

Her blood boiled, all too aware of the curious stares from the people in the room. Everyone knew about Ian and Cynthia's past history and watched to see her reaction to the twosome. Well, she decided then and there, she'd give no one, not even Ian, the satisfaction of knowing she was hurt.

Placing a hand on the arm of a young officer—Lieutenant Holmes, she believed was his name but she couldn't be certain since her attention had been riveted on Ian earlier—she laughed and pretended to be engrossed in an inane joke he'd just told.

"Dance with me, please," she breathed, and the lieutenant was only too glad to whirl her about the Shippens's parlor.

When the dance ended, numerous young men came forward to claim her for a partner, and for the next few hours her feet moved in rhythm to the music. She was the belle of the party, and not the least bit happy about it. Her stupid game seemed to have no effect on Ian. In fact he and Lady Cynthia had disappeared, and any sense of triumph had long since faded.

Begging a reprieve from her latest conquest, Bethlyn went to a bedroom which had been set aside for the needs of the ladies present. She didn't feel the least bit like talking to anyone, and luckily the room was empty except for an old serving woman who dozed in a chair near the window. Bethlyn availed herself of a chamber pot which was positioned behind a large silk screen and, afterward, as she adjusted her voluminous skirts, she heard the door open and the voices of two women as they entered the room.

"I tell you, Cynthia, the woman is the most outrageous flirt" came a high, nasal voice. "In fact, she's outdone me on the best of my days before Lord Montague took a fancy to me. I don't know how Ian can stand being married to such a light skirt."

"Now, now, Letice, you mustn't be so harsh on the girl. She is very young."

"Young is one thing. The behavior of a strumpet is something else again. She's making a huge fool of herself."

Cynthia Connors laughed. "You're just jealous because old Montague would throw you out if you even gave an indication that you were flirting. You're acting like a gossiping dowager. Leave young Mrs. Briston alone."

On the two women prattled, but Bethlyn had ceased to hear them. Her cheeks burned with humiliation for her name to be bandied about. What was worse to her was that Lady Cynthia had the nerve to defend her to the gossiping mistress of Lord Montague. God, how awful fate was that Ian's mistress defended her actions, and here she stood behind a folding screen with a chamber pot for company!

She wanted to rush from the room and go home, never to show her face again.

The door closed. The room fell silent except for the gentle snores of the old servant woman. Bethlyn gave a relieved sigh and came from behind the screen only to stop dead-still when Lady Cynthia turned to face her.

Cynthia looked as surprised as Bethlyn.

Finally Cynthia smiled, and the smile caused the woman's beauty to overwhelm Bethlyn. No wonder Ian loved her, she found herself thinking grudgingly.

"I don't believe we've met," Cynthia said. "I'm Lady Cynthia Connors."

"I know who you are." The words came out through gritted teeth.

"Ah, I see. I suppose you also heard what was said in here."

"I did."

"Don't take Letice seriously, my dear. She's a cat with very long claws."

"And you aren't, I take it. How magnanimous of you to defend my actions, but I don't need you or anyone else to speak up for me. Especially not you, Lady Connors. Good evening."

Bethlyn made an attempt to brush past Cynthia, but the woman had the audacity to block her path.

"We need to talk, Mrs. Briston."

"I have nothing to say to you."

"I have something to say to you, however." Her voice sounded gentle. "Your performance tonight in the parlor was for your husband's benefit, I think."

"I don't know what you're—"

"Yes, you do. You wanted to make him jealous or force his hand for some reason, but he ignored you and now you're peeved. And well you should be. If I had exerted so much energy in capturing all those men's hearts, I'd be peeved, too, if my husband ignored me."

"He didn't ignore *you*." The obvious contempt in Bethlyn's eyes caused Cynthia to flinch.

Cynthia placed a gentle hand on Bethlyn's wrist. "I should like to be your friend, Mrs. Briston. I'm not your enemy."

"You're the woman my husband loves!" Bethlyn felt her composure crumbling, and she wrenched her hand away. She wanted to weep again, but she'd never give Cynthia Connors the satisfaction.

"Oh, my dear, you're quite mistaken in that. Ian loves

236

you, not me. I told him that a few nights ago when he came to see me. I won't lie and tell you that Ian and I were less than friends, because it isn't true. We cared a great deal for each other and still do. Our relationship, however, has changed. Ian is married to you, and I'm going to marry a man I adore. You must believe me when I tell you that Ian loves you."

Bethlyn's mouth dropped open and she sank onto a large divan. Her mind whirled with Cynthia's words, but she didn't doubt the woman's sincerity. However, could she believe her?

"Do you love your husband?" Cynthia asked gently.

Bethlyn nodded, somehow wanting to confide in the woman. "More than I ever thought possible."

"Then there is no problem. Tell Ian how you feel."

Cynthia made it all sound so simple. She couldn't tell Ian she loved him, because she doubted that he loved her in return, no matter what Cynthia thought. Bethlyn gave a shaky laugh.

"There's a large problem, Lady Connors. Ian doesn't love me."

"I tell you he does," Cynthia persisted. "Use some of your feminine wiles on him instead of those prancing jackanapes outside and discover this for yourself. You have nothing to lose."

The truth of Cynthia's words hit her like a horse at full gallop. She didn't have anything to lose now, but much to gain if Cynthia proved correct.

Standing up, she and Cynthia hitched their arms together and giggled at the absurdity of the situation. Here she was, the wife of this woman's former paramour, gaining advice from the woman and suddenly discovering that she genuinely liked her.

"I believe we make very odd companions," Cynthia said as they left the bedroom and made their way to the parlor. Bethlyn couldn't agree more.

Ian was nowhere to be found.

Bethlyn searched through the rooms, filled with people,

and Lieutenant Holmes arrived to help her but it seemed Ian had disappeared. The words to tell him that she loved him burned her lips, and if she didn't find him soon to tell him how she felt, she feared she might lose her courage.

"Perhaps your husband is in the garden," Holmes suggested.

Bethlyn peered through the frosty windowpane. "I doubt it. The weather is much too cold."

"Shall we look anyway. He might very well be there. It is stuffy in here."

The room did feel close with all of the people milling about. Bethlyn searched for Molly, and she saw her in a dimly lit corner in conversation with the man Bethlyn recognized as the soldier she'd seen her sister-in-law with that day in the garden and decided that Molly was in capable hands.

"Let me get my cloak," she told Lieutenant Holmes, not quite certain she wanted the man's company in the event she found Ian, but not wanting to wander around the garden alone either.

Moments later, they were outside. The bitter cold stung Bethlyn's cheeks, and she suddenly couldn't help but to wonder how many of the soldiers, American and British, fared on nights such as these. Would this war ever end?

She shivered and Lieutenant Holmes noticed. "You're cold, Mrs. Briston, er, Bethlyn," he said, his teeth flashing in the moonlight like a hungry wolf's.

She hadn't given him permission to call her by her first name, but she didn't rebuke him. She needed to find Ian and somehow set things right between them. Nearing a hedgerow, Bethlyn stopped, deciding that Ian wasn't in the garden. They should go back inside.

"We'd best go in," said Bethlyn, and began to turn back towards the house, but she met with the arms of Lieutenant Holmes. The man pulled her against him, kissing her in a way which hurt her mouth, and his hand groped inside her cloak until it made contact with her breasts.

"Stop, let me go!" She attempted to wriggle free, but Holmes only laughed and held her tighter. His long, lean

238

face leered at her.

"You're no lady, so stop pretending to be one. No lady flirts as you do and then expects a gentleman not to take her invitation seriously. Kiss me, you beautiful wench."

His lips descended once more against hers, and she found she was powerless against Holmes, who was a large man. Her game-playing had gone awry, and she didn't know how to stop this man from pushing her onto the grass and raping her.

She felt unable to breathe and grew dizzy. The blood pounded so hard in her ears that when she heard the words she wasn't certain she hadn't imagined them.

"Let her go."

The deadly intent of the voice caused Holmes to instantly loosen his hold. He backed off, all too aware of the larger man who waited behind him in the darkness. Bethlyn fairly staggered when Holmes turned around to face Ian.

Making a military bow, Holmes said, "Sir," and started to pass Ian, but Ian's hand shot out and rooted Holmes to the spot. "Come near my wife again, and I'll make certain that your face matches the color of your uniform."

"Yes, sir, I'll remember that," Holmes declared, but a taunting quality tinged his tone, almost as if he thought Ian to be a coward. Bethlyn wondered just how brave Holmes would be if he knew that the man whose wife he'd just manhandled was the notorious and feared Captain Hawk.

"And, Holmes," Ian warned the young man who prepared to walk away. "Don't be so cocky. General Howe is a personal friend of mine. I just might decide to tell him what happened tonight. I sincerely doubt that you'd like to lose your rank."

Holmes's shoulders sagged in defeat, and he hurried inside the house.

Bethlyn let out a ragged sigh, and rushed to Ian, expecting him to enfold her in his arms. "Thank God you got here when you did. I dread to think what would have happened."

A muscle twitched in his cheek. "Do you? I think you

239

might have enjoyed whatever the lieutenant might have had in store for you."

"Ian!"

"You know damned well you acted like a hussy tonight, so wipe that outraged look off of your face."

"I refuse to be insulted like this. I'm going home!"

His hand snaked out and grabbed her wrist in a steellike vise. "You're damned well going home—with me."

She began to protest, not caring for the menacing gleam in his eyes, so like Captain Hawk when in combat with an enemy. Pulling from him to break free, her wrist hurt, not fully aware that he nearly dragged her into the house and through a sea of staring, stunned people.

Molly came forward, shock on her face. "Ian, what are you doing?"

"Bringing my rebellious wife to task," he shouted. "Find your own way home tonight, Molly. I have my hands full with this—this wench."

Loud guffaws and titters followed them when Ian pulled open the front door to practically throw her into the waiting carriage at the curb. She landed unceremoniously on her backside on the seat and, though she attempted to sit up, his body landed on top of her, keeping her pinned beneath him.

"Let me up, you scoundrel," she ranted at him, and would have clawed at him except he held her hands above her head.

"I like you best in this position, love. Lying on your pretty derriere somehow suits you. After all, why shouldn't I get some use out of you while I have you for my wife? You were more than eager to accommodate Holmes and the others tonight. Why not your more than willing husband?"

"It was all a game, Ian. I was playing a horrible game to get your attention, and I'm sorry. You know, I was a notorious flirt in London, and I thank God for Jeremy who always got me out of my scrapes in time. I thank you for coming to my rescue tonight. So you realize now that it was a childish game. I admit that. Now let me up."

His green eyes bored into her brown ones, and she felt

240

unable to look away, but a chill raced down her spinal column when he spoke.

"I think your game-playing has truly ended, love. Jeremy might have saved you from a fate worse than death just as I saved you from Holmes. But who will save you from me?"

"But I don't want to be saved from you!" she cried without thinking. "I love you and want to be your wife."

He drew away from her for a second, apparently stunned by her confession of love. The movement of the carriage caused passing lights and shadows to flicker across his face, and she noticed a bewildered expression clouding his eyes. Her own face burned with humiliation at having admitted her love to him. Had Cynthia been wrong about Ian's feelings for her? If so, then she felt like the biggest fool.

His silence was oppressive, and Bethlyn felt unable to breathe.

Ian lightened his weight, and in the darkness his fingers traced the softness of her lips. "I love you, too, Bethlyn. I want to be a husband to you. God knows I can't live without your love."

Suddenly she could breathe again. "Do you really mean you love me? Please don't tell me something which isn't true. I couldn't stand the pain."

His lips found hers and chased away any misgivings she felt. His voice was a husky whisper. "I love you, love you."

Clasping him to her, her heart nearly exploded with joy.

Ian kissed her lips, her eyes, her throat. The same longing to give herself fully to him swept over her like a sudden summer storm. Her body ached for his possession, and by the time the carriage wound its way up the drive of Edgecomb, halting at the front door, both of them were more than ready for each other.

With a swift movement, he lifted her out of the carriage, and held her in his arms, pushing open the door and kissing her the whole while he mounted the stairs to his room.

Neither one of them was aware of the few servants who

241

watched in stunned disbelief at the antics of the master and the mistress, only to turn away with a slight shake of their heads and go about their business.

In his room Ian set Bethlyn gently to her feet, then closed and locked his door. A candle had already been lighted by a dutiful servant earlier that evening, and now a soft, translucent gold suffused the room.

Bethlyn barely realized she stood in Ian's room for the first time, not interested in the furnishings at all. All she saw was Ian's face near hers, felt his wonderful, warm hands pull the cloak from her shoulders. Then his lips, eager and filled with heat, kissed her. She thought she'd drown in her desire for him and shook from passion so intense that Ian noticed.

"I feel a bit shaky myself," he whispered.

"I've never felt like this before," she told him, and nearly melted when his lips trailed to the lush valley between her breasts.

"That's because we both love each other, sweetheart, and this time we know we're husband and wife."

Her hands clung to the thickness of hair at the back of his head. "Will it always be so for us?" she asked.

"No, darling, it will be better as time goes on."

Bethlyn didn't believe anything could ever feel as wonderful to her. For the first time since she'd known Ian as himself or Captain Hawk, she experienced a complete sense of abandon. Ian was her husband, the man destined to be hers from the day she was born. Nothing and no one would take him from her now.

They belonged together.

Agile fingers pushed the scarlet gown from her shoulders until she waited before him in her many-layered petticoats. Swiftly, Ian removed them and pulled her naked body against his clothed one.

"I prefer you so much more without clothes on," he said, and brought one of her nipples to his mouth to feast on the creamy peak.

Waves of intense pleasure washed over her, and she arched towards his mouth, giving a mewllike whimper when he turned his attention to her other breast. Her

242

hands began to remove his jacket. "I feel the same way."

With that remark she helped him undress until he stood before her more handsome and manly than she remembered. Leading her to the large bed, he lifted her up and sat beside her, cradling her in his arms. With tender ministrations he removed the ornaments from her hair until the honey-colored tresses fell across her shoulders and down her back, gleaming like molten gold in the sunshine.

"Do you know that it was your hair I fell in love with first?" he asked her, burying his hands within the exquisitely soft and verbena-scented locks.

"I presume it wasn't the day we married," she said, growing breathless when a hand slipped to her breasts and fondled their ripe fullness.

"It was the night I attacked *Nightingale.* However, if I'd known what I do now about you, I'd have paid more attention to the child I married."

Her arms wrapped around his neck, and she straddled his thighs, pulling herself closer to him until she felt the tip of his probing manhood. "It wouldn't have mattered, Ian, because I wouldn't have been ready for you then. I was much too young to know about love."

"And now?" His voice was coated in desire so thick she barely heard him.

"I want you so much that I ache."

"Oh, Bethlyn, my sweet wife, I'll gladly ease your pain."

The kiss he then bestowed upon her lips caused her to cling wantonly to him. Her fingers explored the muscular broadness of his shoulders, feeling the muscles bunching beneath them as he gathered her to him. In their sitting positions his lips never left hers, scorching her mouth with smoldering heat. She trembled in his arms from fiery emotions she'd suppressed for weeks, wanting him so fiercely that her body literally knew an emptiness only Ian could fill.

She broke away from his mouth's possession momentarily. "I want you so much, Ian, that I can't wait a moment longer. Please, please . . ."

His lips slanted across hers, and he plunged deeply into her, taking the breath from her. Never before had she known such exquisite sensations, reveling in the driving force of his manhood within her. They clung to each other like two people on a high precipice, knowing that at any moment they'd fall to earth but delighting in the spiraling descent.

Whimpers of ecstasy and husky groans sliced through the room, growing more intense with each mating thrust. Bethlyn imagined herself flying through the air as the pleasure grew and grew, then burned through her very being. When the moment Ian tensed and released himself into her with one final, heart-stopping thrust, she felt that her body exploded into multicolored flames.

"Oh, God" came Ian's voice beside her ear, and she realized his voice shook with emotion.

He pulled her down with him upon the mattress, their bodies still entwined. They lay like this for some minutes, listening to their mingled breathing and the beating of their hearts. Suddenly Bethlyn began to weep.

"What's wrong?" Ian asked in alarm.

For a second she could barely speak, but she managed to gulp back her tears. "I'm so—very—happy. My dream came true."

He stroked her hair, her cheek. "What dream is that, my darling?"

"The dream of being loved by my husband."

Ian kissed her. "Never doubt that you're loved by me."

Pure love shone in Bethlyn's eyes when she smiled at him.

"I know you love me, but only part of my dream has come true. There's still one other thing I want to make all of my dreams a reality."

"What's that?"

Bethlyn colored, suddenly shy to say it, not certain how Ian would feel. "I want to have our child, Ian. I want a baby."

"Hmm," he said, considering her with passion-laced green eyes while his hands began a renewed exploration of her body. "That's a tall order, but I think I'm up to making all of your dreams come true."

"Oh, Ian, do you really want a child?"

"Let me show you how much, Bethlyn. Your dreams are now mine."

When his lips teased at her nipples, causing the flame to ignite within her once again, he loved her leisurely and with so much passion that Bethlyn had no doubt all of her dreams would come to pass.

Nathaniel Talbot felt unbearably weak, but he refused to give in to the sickness which plagued him. Even now, as he penned the note to his daughter, he could hardly gather the strength to move the quill across the parchment. But he must warn her, must do the only noble thing he'd ever done for the girl.

His penmanship was ungodly awful, and he wondered if he were fortunate enough to find a loyal servant to send the note to Bethlyn would she be able to decipher his handwriting. He prayed so, prayed she'd realize the seriousness of the situation.

Thomas Eversley was slowly killing him.

Nathaniel knew this and could do nothing to stop the man. It was now too late to save himself. He hadn't realized that the acute stomach pains, the loss of his hair, and the weakness he'd suffered over the last two months were due to arsenic poisoning. He'd trusted Eversley to care for him when he first started with what he thought was the grippe. Nathaniel nearly laughed, but he was so weak he couldn't summon the strength. All of his energy was in moving the quill across the paper.

"Bastard," he mumbled, and leaned against his pillow for a moment as a wave of nausea rolled over him. He'd thought Thomas was his friend, at the very least a trusted employee. His condition proved the opposite. All of those evenings he'd sat discussing business with Thomas, drinking the wine the man offered to him, wine from his own stock which he realized now had been doctored with arsenic. He'd been a trusting, blind fool, imagining himself to be invincible. But Thomas wanted him dead,

245

and by the time Nathaniel realized he was being poisoned, it was too late.

The door to his room was locked. He, the powerful Earl of Dunsmoor, was a virtual prisoner in his own house. A house which Thomas now used as his own, and Nathaniel didn't doubt that the papers he'd been forced to sign, giving Thomas control of Briston Shipping, were the two reasons Thomas wanted him dead. But he'd only signed the documents because he felt too ill to run the company himself, having no idea at the time that Thomas was slowly killing him.

With heavy lids, the earl forced himself to keep his eyes open, watching the sunshine stream through the windows. He'd thought a great deal about death lately and wondered if when he died would his soul meld with the sun. He wanted to think he'd see Jessica again, but she was no doubt an angel and he'd be . . . Well, he didn't wish to think about what private hell awaited him. He'd taken Jessica from her husband, seduced her actually, until she was so besotted with him and the passion he introduced her to that she couldn't be blamed for their sin. Matthew Briston had been a less than passionate man, from what he remembered about the man. If Matthew had truly loved her, he wouldn't have let her leave with her seducer.

"Jessica, I hope you're waiting for me," Nathaniel whispered softly, a painful ache in his stomach.

But he couldn't dwell on what awaited him in death. He had to concentrate on finishing this letter and try to find a servant to smuggle it out. That, however, would present a problem. Thomas had hired people he'd never seen before, and he knew they were loyal to Thomas. Somehow he must find a way to get this note to his daughter.

Bethlyn. His mind wandered. He remembered her as a plump, white-faced little girl, who was so frightened of him that whenever he looked at her she'd tremble.

He hadn't wanted to frighten his own child, but she resembled his first wife so much that he couldn't bear to gaze upon the girl without thinking of the hatred between him and the woman who was her mother. He'd never wanted to marry Bethlyn's mother, a rich heiress whose parents were dead and with no living relatives. His own parents had arranged the match to unite two wealthy families, and he'd probably have continued in that existence, but then Jessica entered his life; he didn't care about his family or morals. All he wanted was her, greatly relieved when his wife suddenly died because he wouldn't be forced to suffer a scandal.

But Bethlyn intruded upon his life, and he'd sent her away, too caught up in his passion for Jessica to care about the girl. He'd pay for that, probably was paying for his neglect now with his life.

Nathaniel contented himself with the knowledge that Bethlyn was safe with her husband. But she must be warned about Thomas. Somehow he knew that since Thomas lusted after Woodsley and the company, he would also lust after Bethlyn, for without her he'd never be accepted into polite society, and Thomas needed to forget his low birth.

"Write," he commanded, and he did. However, all he could muster the strength to do was pen, "Thomas poisoned me. Beware, daughter."

He'd done it.

Feeling incredibly tired, Nathaniel placed the quill on the bedside table and the letter beneath his pillow. Somehow he'd find someone to send it to his daughter, but first, he must sleep. His eyes felt so heavy he couldn't keep them open a moment longer.

He dreamed that Jessica waited by the foot of his bed, looking lovelier than he remembered. She held out her hand to him, and taking a deep breath, he took it. He felt himself rising up to meet her.

Feeling strong and youthful, they embraced, and as one, they walked into the sunshine.

Two hours later, one of the servants Thomas had hired unlocked the door of Nathaniel's room and discovered that the Earl of Dunsmoor was dead. Thomas was swiftly informed.

Thomas, never one to take things on faith, hurried up the stairs to convince himself that Talbot was dead. One look at the earl's ashen face and the feel of his cold flesh convinced Thomas.

"Bury the body in the family cemetery, and say nothing about the earl's death to anyone. As far as the world is concerned, Talbot still lives, but is ill and has put all business matters into my hands," he informed two of the male servants. "See that the linen is changed and lock the door. No one is to ever enter this room again."

The servants nodded, and within the hour the earl was buried in an unmarked grave, and a pretty servant girl began to change the sheets. When she took the pillow from the bed, her attention was diverted by the appearance of one of the men who'd buried Talbot.

"Now, what would you be wanting, Ned?" she asked slyly, licking her lips because she knew very well what he wanted.

Ned leered at her partially clad bosom and closed the door to the room. "I've been thinking that I've never had the use of such a bed as this one. Would be a shame to close up the room before I had a chance to mate with you on the earl's bed." A second later, he'd pushed the willing girl onto the bed and quickly unbuttoned his pants while she raised her skirts. In their passion and the heated movements of their flesh, they weren't aware that a letter slipped from the mattress to land on the floor between the bed and the night table.

And there it would remain until the person for whom it was written discovered it.

Chapter Seventeen

Never had Bethlyn been so happy.

Each morning she awoke beside Ian, her lips aching for his kiss which he was only to glad to bestow upon her. And then she'd arch towards him, oblivious to everything but her husband and the wonders of her own body.

More than anything she longed to give Ian a child, a tangible proof that she loved him and would be true to him, but her flux began earlier than expected that month, disappointing her. Yet she felt confident that soon she'd become pregnant, and perhaps the child would cause Ian to see the folly of continuing his masquerade as the nefarious Captain Hawk. She hoped so, because whenever she mentioned to him about giving up his privateering, he'd retreat into stony silence after telling her to drop the matter.

Still, she worried he'd be found out and arrested. What would happen to him? To her? She dreaded thinking about the consequences. However, Ian came home one afternoon and told her they no longer had to worry. He'd had it from good authority that no one could prove Hawk's identity, and since he hadn't taken out the *Black Falcon* after capturing the British frigate *Jersey* some weeks ago, the British had grown lax in their investigation.

One sunny but bitterly cold day, some two days before Christmas, Bethlyn decided not to go to the office that morning. She'd been given some other account books by

Ian to mull over during the week, and now she decided to stay home and oversee the cooking and decorations for the holidays. She'd been remiss in her duties as mistress of Edgecomb, but now that she felt secure in her role as Ian's wife, she determined to look after things.

Besides, Molly, who was regarded as mistress by the household staff, had been more than willing to turn over the running of the house to Bethlyn. And Bethlyn knew the reason for that was a handsome German soldier who Molly arranged to meet in secrecy once or twice a week. When she didn't see Hans Gruber, she walked around like a lovesick calf, barely hearing anything anyone said and showing no interest at all in the holidays. The girl was clearly in love, and she had confided to Bethlyn that Hans wanted to marry her, but she feared Ian would claim she was too young to wed and wouldn't approve.

Bethlyn knew Ian wouldn't approve of Hans and not because of Molly's age. The man was a mercenary Hessian soldier in the employ of the British government to subdue the Philadelphia citizens and quell their need for liberty. No, Ian would definitely disapprove, but Bethlyn didn't know what to do about Molly's dilemma.

As Bethlyn sat sipping her tea in the dining room, a servant appeared to inform her that she had a guest, waiting rather impatiently in the parlor.

"Who is it?" she asked.

"Sir Jeremy Smithers, ma'am," the servant replied.

"Jeremy!" Bethlyn couldn't believe her ears. In a flash she rushed from the dining room and into the parlor to be quickly ensnared into Jeremy's embrace.

"It really is you!" Bethlyn cried, tears of joy running down her cheeks.

"Yes, and no worse for wear," he told her, his own eyes expressing his pleasure at seeing her again.

Bethlyn held him at arm's length. Jeremy had lost some weight over the last two months, but the loss only sharpened his features and made him look rather handsome, something which Jeremy had never been. A qualm of conscience stung her to realize that whatever trials he'd been through were because of Ian and his fight for liberty.

"Tell me what happened to you after the ship was attacked." Bethlyn sat beside him on the sofa, her hands in his, afraid he'd dissolve into thin air if she let him go.

Jeremy's soft expression hardened. "I'll never forget that horrible night or forgive that infamous Captain Hawk for what he did. I feel lucky to have survived that attack, but I doubt the privateer ship would have attacked at all if *Nightingale* hadn't fired the first volley."

This was a revelation to Bethlyn. She'd assumed Ian's ship had instigated the battle, but she listened as Jeremy continued.

"I believe Captain Montgomery was to blame, arrogant bastard. I was put in a longboat with him after the battle, and all he could do was bemoan his fate, that Thomas Eversley would have his hide."

"What happened to him?" Bethlyn broke in.

"A British ship picked us up two days later. We arrived in Charlestown, South Carolina, after a week, and I didn't see Montgomery again. Perhaps he turned tail and ran, fearful to go back to London and have to report his failure to Eversley. Anyway, it no longer matters. I stayed at the home of a wonderful family in Charlestown, and left just two weeks ago to seek you out."

Jeremy gazed deeply into her eyes, his hands tightening around hers. "Did any harm come to you, Bethlyn? I mean—did that blackguard Hawk hurt you?"

Jeremy wanted to know if Hawk had touched her, but she couldn't confide to him that Hawk was her own husband. She decided it was better to lie about everything than to enrage Jeremy with the truth.

Shaking her head, she smiled tenderly at him. "I wasn't molested in any way."

"Thank God! I've been beside myself with worry since that night." He kissed her on the cheek. "I should have protected you, but Mavis and I couldn't find you."

"I sneaked away to the room where the doxies were kept."

He groaned. "I should have known."

Bethlyn laughed at his harried look. "I was perfectly

safe." She rang for tea, and a servant hastily arrived with the tray and teapot in hand. Settling back on the sofa, they couldn't stop smiling at each other. It was so wonderful to be with Jeremy again.

"Mavis is married," she informed him.

"To whom?"

"Believe it or not, she married Mr. Gibbons, my husband's secretary."

"Ah, the gentleman who has such superb taste in jewelry. I wish her well." A pregnant pause followed. "How is your husband?"

Placing her teacup on the table beside the sofa, she shot Jeremy a brilliant smile and clapped her hands in delight. "He is so wonderful to me, so kind and considerate. You must stay and dine with us this evening. Please say that you will. I want you to meet Ian."

"Goodness! When did all of this adoration come about? If I recall it was only two months ago you declared you hated the bounder and wanted your freedom."

Her face glowed and her eyes shone brightly. "I didn't love him then, Jeremy, but I do now. More than anything in the world."

"I believe you," he remarked, and gathered her to him in a brotherly embrace.

The evening passed in good cheer. Bethlyn and Ian sat at each end of the long mahogany table, casting lingering looks at each other. Molly and Jeremy carried the conversation until supper was finished. Afterward, Bethlyn, followed by Molly, went into the parlor and embroidered initials on handkerchiefs to be given as Christmas gifts to the servants.

In the library Ian poured Jeremy a snifter of brandy and sat beside the roaring fireplace in a wingback chair, his long legs stretched out in front of him. Jeremy was seated in a companion chair.

"Fine brandy," Jeremy complimented his host.

Ian inclined his head. "The best of my stock, but I think you have something on your mind other than my brandy."

All through supper I noticed your eyes darting between Bethlyn and myself, weighing the situation, I gather."

"You're quite astute, Mr. Briston, so it should come as no surprise to you that I care deeply for Bethlyn and worry about her future."

"Her future with me is secure, I assure you." A frown marred Ian's brow. "Do you think I will treat her in a poor fashion?"

"If by 'poor fashion' you mean material things, no, I find Bethlyn more than adequately cared for. I'm worried that you might abandon her again, and I doubt she'd be able to stand another rejection from you."

"Ah, so it's my past mistakes which color your opinion of me. I should like to be able to defend myself, but in all good conscience I can't. I admit I was a poor husband to her."

"And now?"

Ian's expression gentled. "I love her more than my very life."

Jeremy sipped his brandy, seemingly weighing Ian's words. "I trust you mean that sentiment. When I return to England I should like to think that Bethlyn is happy and will never be mistreated."

"You have my word as a gentleman."

"Glad to hear that, sir. But I wonder if Bethlyn can ever come to love this country of yours. Some of it, from what I've seen, is quite lovely, but a great deal of it is most savage and wild. Bethlyn is a rare and beautiful creature, quite delicate beneath that rebellious streak of hers. She was intended to rule over a manor house as a nobleman's wife, but—"

"Was forced to marry a lowly colonial instead," Ian interjected, not hiding a smile.

"No disrespect on your person," Jeremy quickly assured Ian, "however, that is the truth of the matter. Will Bethlyn feel safe in her love for you once the novelty of romance wears thin? You must admit that the two of you are ill-suited in a great many ways. Your roots are here, hers are in England, and I fear that one day she may pine for her homeland. If so, would you let her return?"

We're more ill-suited than you know, Ian thought, and gulped down his brandy before pouring another one. It seemed that he'd underestimated Sir Jeremy Smithers, having decided before meeting him that he'd be a simpleton despite his wealth and status. The young man was quite intuitive and truly concerned about Bethlyn's welfare. Until that moment Ian hadn't worried about losing her, now that they'd truly found each other and loved each other. But the problem Jeremy posed might just arise one day. He didn't want to lose Bethlyn, never having figured she might grow discontented with his homeland.

More than once she'd badgered him about giving up the identity of Captain Hawk, he not taking her plea seriously. But he knew this would always be a source of contention between them. Bethlyn was British by birth, loyal to her king. He wasn't. Would she ever feel about liberty the way he did? He knew without a doubt that he'd never rest until the British were driven from America's shores.

Had his foolish heart, the heart he had protected for so many years, fallen so desperately in love with his wife that he'd lost perspective? Would his love of liberty be the reason if she ever left him?

A shudder slid through him, but when he turned to Jeremy, his eyes held assurance and he smiled with confidence.

"I'm not Bethlyn's lord and master. She's free to do whatever she wants."

Jeremy nodded and stood up, extending his hand to Ian.

"You're a good man, Mr. Briston. Bethlyn is safe with you. I shall take my leave now, and bid Bethlyn and your sister farewell. No need to see me to the door."

Jeremy exited the library, and Ian stared at the flickering flames in the fireplace, a feeling of dread settling over him to think that his politics might be the ruination of his marriage.

A number of men, many of them posing as loyalists and some of Philadelphia's true patriots, met once a week to rally together, to plan and scheme. Patriotism was at an all-time low since General Washington and his ragtag group of soldiers had taken up winter quarters at Valley Forge only a week past. It was rumored that conditions were exceedingly bad due to the intense cold. There was a shortage of adequate warm clothing, and food was hard to come by.

Ian gritted his teeth to think of Americans being forced to endure under such deprived circumstances while the British wined and dined in warm comfort in his own city.

No, he decided, he couldn't give up the cause of liberty, not for anything—not even for Bethlyn.

Yet he'd never give her up and must turn her mind away from his nefarious dealings as Captain Hawk, from the nights he returned home quite late after a meeting. Lately she hadn't mentioned her dislike of the whole situation, and he hoped this meant she was growing contented as his wife and with her new homeland. Still, her wifely duties didn't take up all of her time. She needed something else on which to concentrate.

The answer to his problem was Briston Shipping. He'd allowed her to come to the office whenever she liked to look over the books, and he admitted that she had a good head for business. Why not openly encourage her interest in running the company? Marc would be there to supervise on those days when his identity took him away as Captain Hawk or on those nights when he attended the secret meetings. Bethlyn would be so busy with the office and so tired in the evenings that she'd barely have the time or energy to spend wondering where he was or what he might be doing.

As soon as the holidays were over, he'd spark her interest in the company. Now, having decided he'd found the solution to his problem, he left the library in time to see Bethlyn closing the front door behind a departing Jeremy.

"I shall miss him," she told Ian with tears in her eyes.

Holding out his arms, he immediately wrapped her in a tender and passionate embrace. He tilted her chin and looked into her eyes.

"Perhaps I know a way to make you forget your sorrow

255

for a while," he whispered in a husky, suggestive whisper.

His kiss held tenderness but also something wild and unquenchable. Desire thrummed through them, and without any further words, Ian lifted Bethlyn from her feet and brought her to his bed, where he more than adequately showed her the intensity of his love.

Despite the freezing temperatures, Bethlyn enjoyed visiting the marketplace. The bustling activity always filled her with awe, especially this day before Christmas when a festive feeling hung in the air.

People seemed somehow more polite, more eager to be friendly. Walking among the crowded stalls, she chose the vegetables and fruits for the holiday meal, stopping before a butcher's stall to choose the hens. A servant from Edgecomb waited dutifully beside her, holding a basket in which to place her purchases. She'd never had reason to patronize a market before, but now that she was truly mistress of Ian's home and his heart, she wanted to please him and be the perfect wife.

Loud squawking noises were heard when the butcher grabbed a plump hen, and to her surprised eyes, he twisted the creature's neck, then took a sharp knife and beheaded the animal while she watched.

"Oh, my," she moaned, feeling sick, and turned away before issuing orders over her back for the servant to carry home the produce and the Christmas hens later.

She'd never seen an animal slaughtered, and she doubted that she'd be able to eat the trussed-up Christmas bird when placed before her at mealtime. But after her stomach settled into place, she silently scolded herself for being squeamish. If she wanted to be the perfect housekeeper and wife, she'd have to become used to such things.

Passing a fish vendor, she searched for some sign of Mr. Tolliver and Nate, but didn't see them. She'd have walked by, but a small voice calling to her from behind the counter stopped her.

She turned around and saw Annie, the young girl who'd

256

been on *Nightingale*. Annie smiled shyly at her and curtsied. Bethlyn immediately discerned that the girl's thin cloak, out of which peeked wool-gloved hands with holes in the fingertips, wasn't warm enough for such bitterly cold weather. Bethlyn felt guilty for her fox-lined cloak and expensive kid gloves.

"How are you, Miss Beth?" Annie asked.

"I'm so pleased to see you again. Do you work here?"

"Yes." For a second Annie's smile faded as she glanced down at the dead fish, packed in ice on the counter, but then she brightened. "At least I ain't whoring now."

"Annie, shush," Bethlyn warned, and hoped that no one had heard the girl. "Are you well cared for? Where are you living?"

"I've a room near the market. I'm eating fine, I suppose, but the money from selling fish ain't as good as the money I made before—but I never liked that other life."

Poor child, Bethlyn thought, to be so young and having to make her way alone in the world like this. Perhaps there was something she could do for her.

"Can I get anything for you, Annie? Do you need some money?"

Annie became thoughtful. "I could always use some money, Miss Beth, because then I could pay the leech and get some medicine for Pearl."

"You still keep in touch with Pearl?"

"We been staying together, trying to make a new life. She had a job at a pub, but she got awful sick last week and ain't been able to work. We ain't got enough money to buy the medicine." Annie lifted her hands in a gesture of helplessness, and her voice quivered. "I'm feared Pearl's going to die and leave me alone, Miss Beth."

Pity clutched at Bethlyn's heartstrings for this child and her valiant attempt to put her past behind her and care for her friend. "Take me to Pearl."

"Oh, I can't. I'd lose my job here if I leave," Annie protested, her strawberry locks bouncing around her red and chapped cheeks.

"From what I can see, this isn't much of a job. Don't worry, Annie, I'll make certain you get a much better

257

position. Now, come along. I want to see Pearl."

Annie looked disbelieving, but she left her job, much to the aggravation of her employer, and got into the carriage with Bethlyn.

"My, but this is grand," Annie exclaimed with wide eyes. "Are you able to afford this by whoring?" she whispered to Bethlyn.

Bethlyn laughed, not offended by Annie's remark. "No, dear, I'm married to a wealthy man. My husband's name is Ian Briston, and I no longer call myself Beth, but Bethlyn. In fact, I was never a doxy."

"Pearl told me she didn't think you were. You weren't like the rest of us. That nasty Della didn't like you too much. I've seen Della parading down the street once with a British soldier. She had on real silk and the prettiest pair of shoes I ever did see. Her hair was all done up, too. I told her hello, but she pretended not to see me." Annie sniffed the air disdainfully. "I guess she's too grand now for the likes of me, but even in her pretty clothes, Della will always be a doxy."

"You know, Annie, I believe you're right."

The two of them dissolved into giggles. When the carriage halted at Annie's boardinghouse, Bethlyn immediately noticed it was in a rough section of town. Seedy-looking characters and heavily rouged women lined the streets and alleyways. Some of the people stared at her like she was a leper, and more than one pair of shifty eyes took a more than passing interest in her purse.

The stench inside the boardinghouse nearly choked Bethlyn as they made their way up a flight of stairs to a doorway which led to a small alcove-type room. On a cot Bethlyn discerned the figure of Pearl, covered by a thin, moth-eaten blanket, a vain attempt to ward off the cold.

"Look who I brought," Annie said, and went to Pearl's side.

Pearl lifted sick eyes to Bethlyn, and it took some seconds before recognition dawned.

"Well, my goodness, what a fine lady you are, miss." Pearl tried to rise, but Bethlyn moved to her side and gently pushed her back on the cot.

"I met Annie at the market, and she told me you were ill. I'd like to help you if I may."

"Aw now, ain't that kind of you, miss, but we can manage somehow. No needs to bother a lady like yourself."

"I insist on helping you," Bethlyn said, a note of persistence in her tone. She glanced around the small, poorly furnished room. "First thing to do is move you to better surroundings." Turning to Annie, she ordered her to fetch the driver and to then gather their things.

"Where are we going, miss?" Annie asked, biting at her lower lip, seeming almost a bit puzzled and frightened by this sudden change in her life.

"We're going to Edgecomb."

After settling Pearl and Annie in the servants' wing and sending for a physician to care for Pearl, Bethlyn joined Molly in the parlor for a cup of tea. She knew this respite would be short-lived, because she must oversee the preparations in the kitchen and still dress before guests began arriving for the Christmas Eve party that night. Sipping her tea she watched as some of the servants dusted the furniture and tied red ribbons around the marbled pillars in the foyer while others bustled in and out of the dining room and parlor.

"Sally told me we have new servants," Molly said.

"Yes, I've decided that Sally needs some help with the washing and the pressing. Annie can help with that, and Pearl, when she's well, can help cook."

Molly nodded in an absent fashion, and Bethlyn realized that she probably hadn't even heard her.

"You seem rather glum considering that in a few hours this house will be filled with guests." Bethlyn reached for Molly's hand. "Is something wrong?" she asked in concern.

Molly's eyes clouded with tears. "I'm so unhappy, and I don't know what to do. Hans may be transferred to New York, and I'll never seem him again. I couldn't bear to be separated from him." Her voice caught, and she gave a

259

tiny sob.

Bethlyn didn't know what to say. She'd never met Hans, but somehow she knew he was a decent man despite his German mercenary status. Molly loved him and that was reason enough to believe the man was honorable. However, she thought his transfer might be the best for all of them. Ian would never accept Hans as Molly's choice. Perhaps the separation would be a blessing for Molly. Her face always possessed a faraway look, her eyes dreamy with thoughts of Hans. Luckily Ian had been too busy with business matters lately to notice his sister's preoccupation. Once Hans departed Philadelphia then Molly would be forced to socialize more and maybe she'd meet someone else.

"Molly, you're very young. I know this hurts you, and I feel for you, truly I do, but you've hardly had the chance to try your wings with other young men, to flirt. I can tell you from experience that flirting can be very nice." Bethlyn smiled at her.

Molly shook her head in disgust. "I'm not a flirt like that horrid Peggy Shippen, nor do I want to be. And as far as being young, I'm almost twenty and considered an old spinster by some of my acquaintances. I want to marry Hans and have his children. I . . . want . . . to be a wife. Can you understand?"

Bethlyn understood very well, and her heart went out to Molly. "Yes, I know how you feel."

Molly nodded, her curls bouncing atop her head. "Good, so you can smooth things over tonight with Ian before the guests begin to arrive. I've invited Hans to the party to meet him. Once Ian sees how much we love each other, he'll approve of Hans and not believe me to be a child who needs coddling."

Bethlyn suppressed a groan at this news and gave Molly a considering look. "I hope you don't intend to do anything ill advised if Ian and Hans don't get along."

"Whatever do you mean?" Molly asked innocently.

Bethlyn meant an elopement, but since Molly apparently hadn't thought of the idea, she wouldn't mention it, either. "Never mind," she said, and stood up. "I'm certain

Ian and Hans will like each other very much."

Heading towards the kitchen, Bethlyn didn't think they would.

Shortly before the guests arrived, Bethlyn was already dressed in a royal blue velvet gown, her hair atop her head, and a long, swirling curl hung enticingly over her milky white shoulders. She quickly informed Ian about Molly and Hans while he dressed, not missing the arch of his brow or the subsequent frown which followed. He didn't say a word to her when she'd finished; he *couldn't*, in fact, because the first of their guests began arriving. But she could tell he was displeased and a bit uneasy at the idea that his sister wanted to marry a Hessian officer, and she knew the reasons why. Politics and Captain Hawk.

Splendidly attired people milled about the festively decorated rooms, laughing and talking. The scarlet uniforms of many British soldiers were very visible in the throng, and soon General Howe arrived with John André by his side. The general made glowing comments about Bethlyn's loveliness, and André was only too quick to agree. Ian stood beside her, the polite host, the seemingly loyal subject of the king, as Howe commented on the sudden inactivity of Captain Hawk.

"The bounder must have come to his senses and realized he'll never win, just as Washington will after this winter is over and his ragtag band is reduced from the cold and starvation," Howe commented and proposed a toast to a British victory.

Ian agreed and lifted his glass with what Bethlyn perceived as perverted pleasure in his eyes.

Soon Peggy Shippen swept Bethlyn away to discuss the latest fashions, to play the coquette with John André. The whole time, Bethlyn watched the doorway for Molly's beloved, sensing Molly's impatience. The girl was so much in love that Bethlyn hurt for her, fearing the outcome of the meeting between Ian and Hans.

Her thoughts didn't dwell on this much longer when Marc and Mavis arrived. She delighted in seeing her childhood friend, not having seen her in weeks, surprised at how fast she progressed in her pregnancy. Envy pricked

261

at Bethlyn. She wanted a child so much, but again this month she'd been disappointed. Ian had been so gentle and understanding when a tear slipped from her eye as she told him that this month she again hadn't conceived. "Next month," he had said, and she wanted desperately to believe him.

Cynthia, however, arrived in a swath of silk and lace, her British officer, who was now her husband, by her side. Her face glowed with love and true happiness, and Bethlyn decided that she was glad Ian had had Cynthia's companionship, no longer jealous of a woman she considered her friend.

Still, Hans hadn't arrived. Molly paced the foyer, forgetting everyone else. Bethlyn tried to persuade her to give up her vigil and join the party, but Molly refused. As she was about to rejoin her guests in the parlor, a knock sounded on the door. Molly waited expectantly as a servant opened it, but her face fell in disappointment while Bethlyn's mouth dropped open when Della entered her home.

Into the foyer stepped Lieutenant Holmes, the rake who'd attacked her in the garden at the Shippen House, and on his arm hung Della, attired in a flowing black velvet cape trimmed in red fox, which she removed to expose her ample bosom, covered by her fashionable red satin gown. She fingered the double strand of expensive pearls at her neck, exceedingly pleased at Bethlyn's reaction to see her again.

Holmes had the grace to flush as he introduced his companion to Bethlyn and Molly, the humiliating incident with Ian in the garden still vivid in his memory.

Bethlyn composed herself and gritted her teeth. She and Ian had invited Holmes, as much as they disliked him, and all the staff, to bring an escort. But Della?

"How do you do?" Bethlyn inquired in cold civility.

"I do very well, thank you. Now, don't pretend you don't recognize me, Mrs. Briston."

"I didn't know you and Mrs. Briston were acquainted," Holmes said.

"We met a while ago," Della told him, a malicious smile splitting her lips.

Retaining her composure, Bethlyn managed to tell them to enjoy themselves, making her way into the parlor on unsteady feet. Della in her house! Dear God! She searched for Ian, finding him standing by the fireplace with General Howe, and she smothered a groan. What if the woman mentioned that Ian Briston's wife had been on *Nightingale* as Hawk's lover. Heaven help all of them if she did.

Bethlyn rushed to Ian's side, hoping to warn him of the potential danger that Della posed. Her eyes implored him. "I should like to speak with you alone," she whispered when Howe turned to take a glass of champagne from a servant.

Ian started to excuse himself from the general, but suddenly Lieutenant Holmes and Della approached them. The only indication Bethlyn had that Ian might be concerned by the woman's presence was the slight arch of an eyebrow.

Holmes introduced Della to Howe and then to Ian. Bethlyn held her breath as Ian took her hand and inquired how she fared. Did she recognize his voice? Bethlyn decided that she didn't, the soft gravelly voice of Captain Hawk quite unlike the melodious, deep tones of Ian Briston.

"Trammel," Howe said to Della. "Did Holmes say your last name was Trammel?"

"Yes, sir."

"Could you be related to the Trammels from Bath? Sir Nigel Trammel? A fine fellow, has a huge house there with indoor plumbing."

"No—no, sir."

"Then you must be related to Lord Pinckney Trammel from Manchester."

High spots of color suffused Della's cheeks. "I ain't, I mean I'm not a relation."

Bethlyn almost felt sorry for Della's discomfort. She wondered if Della even knew who her own father had been, much less if she might be related to the aristocracy. Howe let the matter slip after casting a probing eye at Della. Bethlyn's sympathy for Della quickly evaporated when she began to openly flirt with Ian, forgetting

Lieutenant Holmes who stood uneasily beside her.

Finally Howe suggested Ian and Holmes join him in a game of whist in the library. Ian's parting glance to her contained confidence and sparked her courage a bit, but moments later when she'd have abandoned the woman to see to the needs of her guests, Della purposely blocked her path.

"It seems you've done real well for yourself, Beth. Married to such a handsome and rich man." Her eyes approved Bethlyn's attire and glanced around the room in admiration. "Real well."

"You've lifted yourself up quite a bit, too," Bethlyn noted. "Lieutenant Holmes must be very generous. I assume you are his kept woman."

Della shrugged a naked shoulder. "For now, but he don't make much money."

"Sorry to hear that."

Della giggled, but her eyes contained no warmth. "I'm going to live in a house like this one day."

"I wish you great success, but now I really must see to my other guests."

"What's your hurry? You seem nervous. Are you afraid I'm going to tell your husband about Captain Hawk?"

"Quiet!" Bethlyn demanded in a hoarse whisper, hoping no one overheard.

A sly smile ringed Della's lips. "We've got some talking to do, Mrs. Briston. May I call on you day after tomorrow to discuss this distressing situation? I'm certain we can come to some sort of an agreement, make an arrangement which will be beneficial to both of us."

Bethlyn had no doubt Della intended to blackmail her. She knew she could tell her that Ian already knew about Captain Hawk, but then she couldn't be certain Della wouldn't go to General Howe. She must let her think that Ian knew nothing. Money was a small price to pay for Ian's safety.

"I shall receive you at three o'clock." Bethlyn started to move away, but she stopped for a second and smiled. "Really, I must compliment you on your manners, Della. Even your speech is much improved. Holmes has done an admirable job of polishing you. Too bad you're still a slut underneath the surface. Good evening." Fluttering her fan, Bethlyn left a red-faced Della, not missing the look of intense hatred mingled with outrage.

"Who is that strumpet?" Cynthia inquired, and took Bethlyn's arm.

"A friend of Lieutenant Holmes, but I don't want to discuss her. Have you seen Molly?"

"She was in the foyer a few minutes ago. I saw her speaking to a private in the Hessian Army. I haven't seen her since."

Bethlyn excused herself from Cynthia and went upstairs to see if Molly was in her room. Perhaps the soldier was sent by Hans to tell her that he'd be unable to attend the party. Poor Molly must be so disappointed.

As expected, she found Molly in her room, sitting on the window seat, gazing down at the garden. At Bethlyn's hand on her shoulder, Molly turned a wet face to her.

"Hans is unable to attend the party?" Bethlyn asked gently, noting how Molly trembled.

The girl's voice sounded choked with tears when she started to speak. "Worse than that, Bethlyn. Hans is gone to New York. He received his orders this afternoon and didn't have time to tell me good-bye. He didn't have time to write to me. I . . . shall die . . . without . . . him."

"I'm so sorry." Bethlyn sat beside her, holding out her arms to Molly, who broke into a gale of sobs.

When Molly's tears were spent, she drew away and huddled against the wall. "I'll never see him again. He'll probably meet some simpering little fool and fall in love, forgetting all about me. I can't bear it. My heart is broken." A fire suddenly blazed in her eyes. "Damn this blasted war!"

Bethlyn almost told her that if not for the war, she wouldn't have met Hans, but she didn't. Things would work out for Molly in time, though now she most certainly wouldn't believe that. Evidently Hans wasn't meant for Molly, and one day Molly would find someone else.

Standing up, Bethlyn bent and kissed the top of Molly's head. "Ian and I love you very much," she reminded her. "If you need us, know that you can always count on us."

Molly nodded solemnly, turning her tear-stained face to the window.

By the time all of the guests had departed Bethlyn felt that she had aged five years. Undressing and dismissing the servants, she collapsed on the bed. Her mind whirled with memories of all that had happened that night. She felt uneasy about Della's visit. Of course the woman would want money, but she was eager to discuss the situation with Ian, and also to tell him about Molly's heartbreak.

She crawled beneath the covers, hoping Ian would come upstairs shortly. He'd barely spoken to her all night, and she craved his arms around her, the security of his love. Perhaps tonight would be the night she conceived their child. She couldn't think of a more perfect way to spend the early hours of Christmas morning than making a baby. She smiled happily into the darkness.

But when nearly half an hour passed, and Ian didn't come upstairs, Bethlyn went in search of him. Pulling her robe tightly around her body, she headed down the stairs and into the parlor and dining room where the servants cleaned up the remains from the party. She inquired if anyone had seen her husband, but no one had.

Finally, on a whim, she went into the kitchen and out of the back door. The night was bitterly cold. A brisk wind stung her cheeks and flapped the edges of the robe around her legs. In the heavens stars twinkled and the moon cast its sheen upon the snow-laden ground.

Her slippers were thin, and her feet felt cold and wet as the snow seeped in. Shivering, she almost turned to go back into the house, but a low murmur of voices from behind a carriage parked nearby drew her attention. She moved closer, and in the still night air, she recognized one of the voices as Ian's; and the other voice belonged to a man she couldn't name.

She stopped and listened.

"When is the meeting to be?" came Ian's voice.

"Day after tomorrow at the old Simpson House, outside of the city. We can't meet at our regular place in town any longer. Too many noses snooping around, if you know

266

what I mean," the other man said.

"Where is the girl staying?"

"With the Babcocks until the meeting. Fine little lady she is. So brave and a real patriot."

"I'll be there."

A long pause followed, then the other man asked, "Will your wife give you any trouble? Its common knowledge she's as English as a rose garden, and being an earl's daughter and all, well, we've all been rather worried."

"Don't be," Ian quickly assured the man. "My wife's loyalties aren't my own. Besides, I intend to keep her well occupied with the business."

Their voices lowered conspiratorially, and Bethlyn couldn't hear anything else. She didn't want to hear anything else.

Hurrying inside, she almost flew up to the bedroom and buried herself under the covers, cold but seething with fury. Ian still didn't trust her. Would he never stop seeing her as British, the daughter of the man he hated? If he had, she felt certain he would have confided in her about his secretive activities. She guessed that on all of those nights he left supposedly on business, he was really attending some sort of a meeting. Evidently Captain Hawk had exchanged the sea for dry land.

What galled her the most was his attitude that she could be kept busy at Briston Shipping and not realize when he disappeared. Did he believe her to be a stupid, unobservant child?

Her hands clenched into fists. Arrogant man to think she could be put off so easily. And who was this girl Ian and the other man mentioned? Bethlyn's curiosity piqued.

The man had said the old Simpson House outside of town would be the meeting place. She didn't know where that was, but by the day of the meeting she would. However, she must be careful not to arouse suspicion with her question. She comforted herself that Molly would know where the house was and not think a thing about it.

Closing her eyes, she fell asleep in a surprisingly short time, not aware when Ian slipped beneath the sheets to enfold her in his arms.

Chapter Eighteen

Despite the early morning hour the docks bustled with life. A weak sun colored the sky with tentative golden fingers above the Delaware River when Bethlyn and Ian alighted from the carriage in front of Briston Shipping. Instead of going inside the office to escape the cold morning, he took her by the arm and walked to the harbor. Inclining his head towards a large ship, he said, "What do you think of her?"

Bethlyn huddled beside Ian, placing a gloved hand over her chilled nose. "That ship? She's superb, a very nice hull."

"I'm surprised at you, Bethlyn. After all of my tutoring the last month on ships, explaining how Briston Shipping builds and outfits our ships, you don't recognize that one."

"Should I?"

"It's *Nightingale*, or rather used to be." He leaned back on the balls of his feet, pleased with himself. "No one can tell the ship was ever damaged, or that she was ever a ship of your father's line. Thomas Eversley will just have to take a loss on her."

Ian was right. Bethlyn had learned a great deal about ships the last few weeks, but she'd never have recognized this ship as *Nightingale*. Even its color was different. But she had learned to observe, and a bright smile expressed her surprise and pleasure to find her own name in large golden letters on the side. "*Bethlyn B*," she said softly, a

268

warmth flowing through her chilled body.

Ian kissed the tip of her nose. "A beautiful ship must bear the name of a beautiful lady."

"Thank you, Ian. Such a touching gift might be rather hard to repay."

"I can think of a very pleasant way to express your gratitude, but after last night I'm forced to accept your repayment at another time." He grinned at her and took her hand, leading her to the front door of the office.

The rest of the morning passed surprisingly fast. Ian was in and out of the office at least a dozen times. Making an unsatisfactory attempt at estimating the cost of refurbishing a ship, Bethlyn finally admitted defeat and laid aside her paperwork. The thought of meeting Della that afternoon filled her with dread.

She didn't mind paying the money if Ian's safety was assured. Yesterday afternoon Ian had visited an ill employee to wish him Christmas cheer. Bethlyn had sneaked away from Edgecomb and entered the office. Feeling like the thief she thought herself to be, she opened the large moneybox Ian kept hidden in a locked cabinet, taking a small fortune in gold. She intended to replace the money before Ian realized it was gone. The transfer of funds from her London bank would soon be complete, but she needed the money now. Without Ian the wiser, she returned home and placed the gold in the bottom drawer of the large desk in the library.

When Ian returned to the office, he gave her more work to do. Bethlyn realized he wanted to keep her so busy that she'd be too exhausted that night to comment on his comings and goings. She smiled smugly to herself, on to his game.

"What's so amusing?" he asked.

"I'm quite happy. I wish Molly could be as happy." Molly had spent all Christmas Day in her room, brooding.

"She'll be fine," he said brusquely, but his tone softened. "I love her but can't forget that she's in love with an enemy." Bethlyn worried that he still considered her his enemy. Maybe he needed to believe he loved her to make their marriage bearable. She shivered at the thought.

Arriving home that afternoon a servant told her that Miss Della Trammel waited in the library for her.

Della was early, no doubt eager for the money she'd collect. Let her wait, Bethlyn thought and went upstairs, taking her time in freshening up. When the grandfather clock chimed three, Bethlyn entered the library.

Della rose from a chair by the fireplace, clutching a velvet reticule. Her pretty face contorted into a sneer.

"You kept me waiting on purpose. I heard you come in more than thirty minutes ago," Della complained.

"My, what a little timekeeper you are. Perhaps I should hire you on at Briston Shipping, but knowing you, Della, you're not cut out for work. I distinctly told you three o'clock. You were early, I wasn't late." Bethlyn gestured to her to sit while she purposely sat in the large chair behind Ian's desk, which took up almost half of the room, hoping to intimidate Della.

Her ploy worked. Della licked her lips, the anger left her eyes, and she almost timidly sat down. Toying with the black collar on her ruby-colored gown, she waited.

Bethlyn leaned forward in her chair, placing her hands together on top of the desk. "I believe you wanted to speak to me."

"That I did."

"I'm waiting."

"Don't play coy with me, Mrs. Briston. You may pretend to be an uppity lady, but I know what you are. You ain't no better than me."

"You're wrong there, Della, I am."

"Hmph! I ain't going to debate that with you. I'm here because I think you owe me something. If not for you, I'd have been Captain Hawk's lady. But he took a fancy to you and never looked at me again. You owe me for the trinkets he'd have given me, the money I could have gotten out of him. Besides," she lowered her voice, "your fine husband might be itching to know about you and Hawk. But I don't have to tell him anything if you reimburse me for my losses."

"How very considerate of you, and you're right, you do deserve something for your losses, as you so eloquently put it."

Della's mouth dropped open in surprise. "I do?"

"Certainly, Della. I won't intend to argue with you about anything, nor will I dicker over a price." Opening the library drawer, Bethlyn pulled out a woolen knit bag and placed it on the desk. "This should more than adequately compensate you."

Narrowing her eyes, Della rose and inched her way to the desk, drawn by the bag. When she opened it, she braced herself on the desk for support. Her face paled.

"There's so much—money." She sounded breathless, disbelieving.

"It's all in gold. There's enough money there to last you for a number of years, that is, if you don't live too high of a life-style. I think you should be able to buy a nice house, have nice clothes and tasty foods until the day you die. I'm being more than generous." Bethlyn placed her hands on her lap, unable to keep them from shaking. Would Della refuse this? Would the silly woman want more money? So much depended upon Della's absolute silence. "You may count it, if you wish."

"No . . . no. I can see this is a great deal of money."

"Are you satisfied then?"

Della truly looked baffled and shocked, but her hands burned to close the bag and run. "Yes, Mrs. Briston."

"Fine. I have some stipulations which you will promise to honor before you leave here."

At Della's raised eyebrow, Bethlyn continued. "First, you will never tell anyone that I was Captain Hawk's lady or mention that you've ever seen me before. Understand, you are to tell no one, for if you do, you shall regret your ready tongue. I have a great deal of money and power, and I know many powerful people who'll be only too glad to stomp on someone like you. Secondly, you will leave Philadelphia no later than tomorrow and never return."

"But, but," Della stuttered, "what about Lieutenant Holmes?"

"What about him? Do you love him? Are you willing to give up enough money to last you the rest of your life for a soldier? Think, Della, what you're giving up. Imagine all of the jewels, the fine clothes you'll be able to buy. And who knows? You may attract a very wealthy man one day."

Della grabbed for the bag, a large wiley smile on her lips. "I was getting tired of Holmes anyway. All right, Mrs. Briston, I agree to everything."

"You promise to adhere to all of my terms? Every one of them?" Bethlyn held her breath, not certain still she could trust the woman.

Della grew serious. "I promise. I may be a doxy, anything you want to call me, but I do keep my word."

Bethlyn rose from the chair and extended her hand to Della, who took it. "We have an agreement then."

"Yes, Mrs. Briston. Good day to you."

The moment Della sashayed from the room Bethlyn sunk into the chair again, and finally took a deep breath. She trembled so much she poured herself a brandy. Soon she felt steady enough to mull over what had happened, coming to the conclusion that Della would keep her word.

Her spirits lifted.

She went upstairs to rest before supper. A long night stretched before her.

Shortly after supper, Bethlyn pleaded tiredness. Not unexpectedly, Ian told her he had a great deal of work to do in his library and that he probably wouldn't go to bed until quite late. He'd sleep in his own room that night rather than disturb her.

A sly smile lifted the corners of Bethlyn's mouth as she left the dining room. So, he thought he could keep his comings and goings from her. Such a feeble excuse. No doubt he'd sneak out of the house as soon as the library door closed behind him. But she'd be ready long before then.

Dismissing Annie after she helped her undress, Bethlyn went to her wardrobe. Hidden in a corner on the floor were some breeches, a linen shirt, and a pair of well-worn boots she'd gotten from the stable boy who was her same size. Within minutes she'd changed into the clothes and had pulled back her hair with an ebony ribbon and threw a dark-colored velvet cloak with hood over her shoulders.

A noise outside her door perked up her ears. It was Molly's footsteps heading in the direction of her own room. She heard Annie's voice mixed with Molly's, then ten minutes later the door opened and closed again, and Annie padded down the hallway to the backstairs.

All was silent.

Bethlyn went to the window which overlooked the rear of the house. In the murky darkness she made out the black shape of the stables; the only point of light came from the lantern on the windowsill. She strained her eyes to see, wishing a moon was out to provide some illumination, because traveling in the dark would be perilous, but at least there would be less chance she'd be spotted.

The clock in the foyer chimed ten, and she grew edgy. Why hadn't Ian left by now? Perhaps the meeting had been postponed and she waited here like a dark specter for no good reason. She hoped it hadn't been canceled. The desire to know what Ian did with his time was too strong for her to resist. She hated spying on him, but his love for liberty was a part of his life he refused to share with her, and she wanted to know everything about him.

Half an hour later, she yawned, trying to decide whether to go to bed. A slight movement outside caught her attention, bringing her to full alertness when a shadowy shape crossed the yard to the stables. By the long, purposeful strides she knew it was Ian.

Seconds later a horse and rider left the barn and proceeded across the snowy landscape. Luckily the snow had melted some that day, allowing the stallion to gallop at a steady pace. She watched Ian turn onto a winding path which would take him through a forested area and then onto a back road to the Simpson House.

Glancing at the clock on the mantelpiece, she noticed the time and waited twenty minutes more before leaving to give Ian and the others sufficient time to assemble.

When Bethlyn finally did leave her room, she treaded quietly down the hallway to the back stairs, praying none of the servants saw her.

Soon outside, she breathed a deep relieved sigh, her breath freezing and hanging on the air. Entering the stables she saw Amos, the stable boy, waiting with the reins in hand beside a black, spirited mare.

"I done just like you said, Miss Bethlyn. I waited till Mr. Ian was gone before I done saddled Star here for you. I kept my mouth shut, too, just like you asked. I won't tell a soul about you running off."

"Thank you, Amos. I'm pleased I can trust you." She mounted Star, placing her hood over her head, and smiled at the thin red-haired lad who was no older than fourteen. She'd told the boy she needed his utmost cooperation and silence. In the morning she'd make certain that he received new clothes for the old ones she'd taken from him, and also send a fat goose home with him to his mother.

"Be careful, Miss Bethlyn," he cautioned her.

Assuring him that she would, she rode out of the barn, following the same route Ian had taken.

Cantering into the heavily wooded area, she carefully guided the horse beneath an endless canopy of bare-limbed trees. The darkness was so thick she could barely see the horse before her, but Star seemed to have little problem finding her way.

A shiver slid down Bethlyn's spine, suddenly aware of her vulnerability. Anything or anyone could be hiding in these woods. She'd never ridden this path before, having taken Molly's word that this was the fastest way if one wished to take a leisurely jaunt in the general area of the Simpson place.

Wanting to discover what happened at the secret meetings was one thing, but to traverse through the woods on a moonless night was something else, Bethlyn quickly discovered and wondered at her foolhardy sojourn. For a fleeting moment she almost turned back to the house, but she kept onward, determined to obtain some knowledge of her husband's cause.

By the time she'd reached the back road she felt she had ridden for an hour, but less than a quarter of that time had elapsed. The horse galloped easily now, and before Bethlyn was fully aware of it, the dark silhouette of a large

274

house loomed before her. Halting Star, she took shelter behind a cluster of bushes, surveying the situation.

From her vantage point, she saw no one and nothing unusual, and wondered if the meeting place had been changed. She almost decided to turn Star in the direction for home, a bit upset with herself for traveling all this way on a bone-chilling night and aggravated with Ian for keeping secrets from her. But a flicker of light from a downstairs window spurred her to tether Star to a small oak tree and investigate.

The darkness of her attire blended in perfectly with the ebony night, and she was more than glad to have the warm boots as she silently trod through the snow, her figure clinging to the shadows of the massive oak trees which lined the long drive.

At one time Simpson House had been quite grand, but now the gray stone dwelling was deserted, the Tory family who'd lived there having returned to England. Bethlyn well understood why the house had been chosen for secret activities. Far from the main road, the property fronted an infrequently traveled back road, the Simpson House being the only residence for miles around. The chance of discovery was slim.

About halfway from the house, she stopped, scanning the front. Two massive pillars graced the portico, and four windows ran the length of the house. She saw nothing through the windows, no flickering lights. Had she imagined she'd seen something?

Moving closer, a voice cut through the still night air and she jerked, stopping dead in her footsteps. The irregular beating of her heart coincided with her pulse. Any moment she expected someone to seize her, to drag her before the assemblage, before Ian, and she knew she'd be mortified to try to explain why she was there. No one would believe that the daughter of the Earl of Dunsmoor might wish to know the reasons why her husband fought for liberty. They'd no doubt think she was a spy, and she dreaded having to answer to Ian.

But seconds passed and no one pulled her protesting form away from the shadows of the trees.

Suddenly she heard laughter coming from the portico. A candle illuminated two masculine figures, and she saw the unmistakable gleam of a musket.

"Any sign of anyone?" a male voice asked the owner of the musket.

"Nay, nary a peep" came the other voice.

"Good, then get out of the cold and come inside and have a cup of cider with the gents. 'Tis not every chance we get to meet a true heroine of liberty."

The musket man said something else and followed the other man into the house. Bethlyn watched the light, weaving its way into a nearby room, only to disappear as if it never existed.

They must be meeting in the back of the house, she decided, and gingerly made her way through the snow, following the drive and then skirting the entire length of the house until, keeping her eyes and ears sharp, she came upon a well-lighted window.

Fortune had indeed smiled upon her. The window was open a crack, allowing her to hear the mingle and rumble of voices inside before she saw the men assembled in the room.

Peering in, she counted about twenty men, finding Ian with little trouble since he was the tallest and handsomest man there. There were furnishings in the room, probably original to the house, which attested to the fact that this must have been a sitting room. No fire burned in the hearth, but no one appeared cold, seemingly much aroused by an inner fire. Bethlyn felt unbearably chilled despite her warm clothes, but she wouldn't leave until she could understand why grown men would brave a cold winter's night to meet in a deserted and forgotten house.

From her vantage point she identified some of the gentlemen present, already having met them at many affairs. All of them were supposed loyalists, men like Ian, who pretended to be faithful to the Crown but in actuality worked against it. Goodness, she thought, General Howe would enjoy arresting this crowd.

Some of the other men she'd never met, concluding that they weren't Tories but dyed-in-the-wool patriots.

Their voices mingled, and then they fell silent when a white-haired man rose from his chair.

"Gentlemen" came the surprisingly strong voice from such an elderly man, "many of you have known me all of your lives. My ancestors settled here with William Penn, and, ever since, a Babcock has served in local government to do our duty to king and country. However, the day has finally arrived when the Babcock family will no longer serve a king who cares naught for his people. How can any of us serve a tyrant who sends troops to our shores, soldiers who cause destruction to our businesses and manhandle our women. This king regards us as unruly children who are unable to govern ourselves. We're expected not to cry for liberty, for equality. I say to every one of you here that the time is long past for silence. Someone must speak for us in a different way now. Our protests have fallen on deaf ears."

The old man trembled from emotion, wiping a tear from his eye. Heads nodded in assent. Finally he drew himself up tall and continued. "I lost my grandson in battle. He was a lad of seventeen years and the light of my life. So young, but so brave. My heart is broken at his passing, but bursts with joy at his heroism. I'm certain that if he'd lived, he'd have followed our gallant General Washington to Valley Forge and would gladly have endured the cold and hunger our heroic soldiers face each day while His Majesty's finest partake of our bountiful tables and comfortable homes."

An angry murmur rose, many men nodding in agreement.

"I am an old man," Mr. Babcock said. "I do not mind being old, for I've lived a long and happy life. I do not mind that I shall die soon. I accept my state as a part of God's divine plan. I do not accept tyranny." He gestured to a man sitting in a corner chair. "Mr. Thomas Paine has been at Valley Forge. He knows firsthand of the suffering of our men, has witnessed the sickness, and the despair. Some Philadelphians have little hope that we can rally. But I say we can. We must. I am optimistic for the future, because providence has guided someone to us who will bring us together in our fight. Come here, Emmie."

Mr. Babcock turned to a chair away from the window where Bethlyn stood. A tall, willowy young woman rose and clasped the old man's hand. Long hair, the color of silvered moonlight, hung down her back in undulating waves. Her simple blue gown clung to a slim body, and she lowered her eyes in shyness as Mr. Babcock positioned her next to him.

"This is Emmie Gray, gentlemen. She is the reason for this meeting tonight. As you know, the British instigated the Indians to uprise against some of our settlers. Emmie's family was killed; she is the only survivor. This heroic young lady walked miles for days on end through the snow with little clothing to protect her from the elements. It is a wonder she survived at all. But she did. God must have wanted Emmie to live and come within our midst, to fire all of us to continue our fight. Once Philadelphia learns of the atrocity committed by the British, we shall join together, and Emmie shall become our battle cry."

Applause broke free, and the men joined Emmie and Mr. Babcock, forming a circle around them. Bethlyn leaned closer, trying to get a better view, but the windowpane was in her way. She was tempted to open the window further but didn't dare.

Towering above the other men, she saw Ian quite clearly, especially when he and liberty's newfound heroine left the circle and came to stand very near the window, his hand clasped in Emmie Gray's. He bent forward, his head quite close to Emmie's, speaking earnestly to her. Bethlyn couldn't hear a word that he spoke, but it didn't matter what he said. The look on Ian's face, a look filled with something close to adoration, said it all.

Never had he looked like that at her. Never had she remembered seeing his eyes so bright and worshiping. A stab of envy twisted inside Bethlyn at the sight of Ian with this woman. Not only was Emmie Gray docile and demure, but she embodied courage and patriotism, a shining beacon in the cause for liberty.

Emmie Gray was everything Ian wanted in a woman. Everything Bethlyn wasn't.

Unable to watch Ian practically fawning over the woman a second longer, Bethlyn wrenched away from the window and trekked through the snow back to Star, who waited patiently for her.

The return trip to Edgecomb was just as dark as an hour earlier, but she wasn't frightened any longer. Bethlyn kept seeing Ian and Emmie, hearing Mr. Babcock's speech revolving in her mind over and over again.

She hadn't known about some of the things Mr. Babcock had mentioned. In fact, she'd heard some of the reasons why the colonials thought they should be independent, never having taken them seriously. Most people in England viewed the fight for independence with a jaundiced eye; the whole situation was so far removed from most of them, especially the people in Bethlyn's circle of acquaintances. Everyone believed that the rowdy colonials would bow to British might eventually, regarding them as unruly and brash children who needed a good swift swack to see reason.

Bethlyn had thought the same, if she ever thought about the fight for independence at all. Only after meeting Ian had she spent any time mulling the situation over, still clinging to the hope he'd give up his nefarious life as Captain Hawk. She knew now he wouldn't, and she didn't expect him to.

Ian valued freedom, and she should have known this all along. Hadn't he freed her from her fathery's tyranny when he could have left her at the earl's mercy? Instead, he'd arranged for her to go to Aunt Penny's, where for the first time in her life she'd experienced what it was like to come and go, to control her own life and do as she pleased.

For the first time she understood the reasons behind the war.

"I want to help, too," she spoke aloud to Star as the horse neared the stables, her thoughts centered on Ian with Emmie. She wanted her husband to look at her in that same adoring way, to view her as courageous.

When she slipped into her room, she hastily threw off her cloak and sat by a small writing desk, dipping a quill into the inkpot and quickly set words down on paper.

The words became verses and spilled from her with an

urgency, almost as if some force, unseen and unknown, guided her hand.

When she finally laid down the quill, the soft gray streaks of dawn broke through the heavy drapes.

Picking up the paper, she read part of what she had written.

"If liberty be a dream, then I am a dreamer,
But arise dreamers of dreams and lovers of liberty,
Throw down the shackles, betray the schemers,
Fight for the cause, dare to be free."

The rest of the verses met with her approval, and she wondered what Ian would think if he should read them.

"But if he does read them," she said to her reflection in the mirror above the desk, "he must never know I'm the author."

Never could she show this poetry to Ian or tell him how she had come to feel about the ideals for which he fought. He wouldn't believe her. In his mind he would always doubt her loyalty, because she was the daughter of a man he hated.

She knew Ian had come to love her but had already decided he couldn't trust her. Still, she wanted to help him and his fight with her poetry. Maybe her verse could incite people to claim their independence.

However, Bethlyn couldn't sign her work with her own name. She'd use a *nom de plume*, but which one?

Mulling this over, she again caught sight of her reflection and remembered the day Miss Grosvenor had positioned her in front of the mirror and ordered her to look at herself.

"You're as plump and colorless as a dove," the woman had told her.

Well, she wasn't plump and colorless any longer, but sometimes she did still feel like that lonely, unloved child. She could think of no better appelation.

Picking up her quill, she dipped it into the inkpot. With a flourish she signed the bottom of the paper.

The Dove was born.

Chapter Nineteen

Bethlyn walked into Ian's office humming to herself, a bit triumphant because she'd persuaded Molly to accompany her on a shopping trip. Molly waited in the carriage for her while Bethlyn paid Ian a quick visit to discover when he'd be home for supper. She planned for all of them to sit down to a sumptuous meal that evening, hoping Molly's brooding was at an end. Getting the girl out of the house was an indication that Molly's spirit might be returning.

The door to Ian's office was open, but Bethlyn's entry was blocked by Marc, who suddenly materialized before her.

"I wouldn't go in now," he advised.

"Is something wrong?" Bethlyn diverted her gaze from him and peered across his shoulder. She saw Ian sitting behind his desk, his face flushed with what she discerned as anger, though he spoke calmly to a perspiring Mr. Eakins, who sat across the desk from him and constantly wiped his brow.

"Ian will handle it. Don't concern yourself, Bethlyn."

She reared upward, surprised at Marc's condescension.

"Briston Shipping is my concern, as is Mr. Eakins, who is one of my employees. I have a right to know what's wrong."

Marc smiled apologetically. "It's a rather delicate matter, I'm afraid. Ian believes that Eakins has been stealing."

281

"I don't believe it. Mr. Eakins is a most trusted employee. Ian told me he's worked here for twenty years."

"I find it difficult to believe myself," Marc agreed, "but someone stole a great deal of money from the box that Ian keeps hidden in the cabinet. Only three people know where the key is to unlock the cabinet. Ian, Eakins, and myself. And I assure you that I didn't take the money."

Bethlyn's face turned pale, and for a moment she felt horribly weak-kneed. She'd hoped that she could have replaced the money by now or that Ian wouldn't open the box until the middle of January to meet the payroll. But the London bank still hadn't transferred her funds, and because of what she'd done, poor Mr. Eakins was being accused of thievery.

She started to push past Marc, but he held her back.

"There are four people who know where the key is kept. I know who took the money, Marc."

Marc allowed her entrance into Ian's office. For the first time in her life, as she stood before her husband's desk, she trembled with such fear that she wanted to retch. Having no regard of the circumstances which might befall her, she knew she must set things right and explain.

"What is it?" Ian practically growled at her.

"I must, must speak to you about—a most distressing matter which can't wait." She licked her lips and sank into a chair next to Mr. Eakins. "You may go, sir," she dismissed the flustered and white-faced man.

Eakins looked to Ian for confirmation and Ian nodded briskly. When Eakins scampered from the office, Ian didn't hide his anger.

"What's the matter with you? You sashshay in here and interrupt me. Have you no idea of what has happened or care that I may have to call in the authorities to—"

"I took the money."

Ian winced, his mouth dropping open, no words came out. Several long seconds passed before he uttered a sound. "Why?"

Bethlyn laughed nervously. "I would have thought you'd say that you didn't believe me, but you are a direct man, Ian." Her composure seemed about to crumble, but

282

she calmly explained to him why she'd taken the money.

"I paid Della to keep you safe," she finished, and folded her hands demurely in her lap. "I intended to replace the money with my funds before you realized it was gone, but evidently some of the ships from England are slow or they're not getting through at all."

With a strength of will, she purposely kept her gaze on Ian, hoping she'd see a flash of understanding in his eyes. She saw nothing but incomprehension.

"I beg your forgiveness for not telling you about Della's threats, but I'm not sorry for paying her off. More than anything in the world, Ian, I wanted to keep you safe."

"Really?" His voice broke into hers, startling Bethlyn with its curtness, a hint of suspicion lurking within its timbre.

"Yes, what other motive could I have had? I dislike when you look at me or speak to me like this. It makes me think that you don't trust me."

Ian leaned back in his chair and perused her thoroughly, almost as if he tried to read her thoughts. After a few moments, he said, "Do you have anything else you've done which you'd care to tell me?"

She started. Did he mean Simpson House? But he didn't know about that, and she couldn't tell him. "No."

"I see; then I won't keep you."

"I'm free to go? You're finished with me?"

"Quite finished."

She didn't care for the sound of that. Standing up, she fiddled nervously with the button on her cloak. "I suppose you're very angry with me, and you have a right to be, but try to remember why I took the money. I'll apologize to Mr. Eakins."

"Don't do that. I shall apologize to him, since I'm the one who accused him." He took a deep breath and rose from his chair, then he leaned over the desk, his face dangerously close to hers. "Never again go behind my back, Bethlyn. You should have told me about Della. I'd have taken care of her. Damn it, woman, you gave that wench a small fortune. She'll never have to lie on her back again."

"I'll replace the money."

"That's not the point. Suppose the woman opens her mouth and divulges information to someone about you and Captain Hawk? We were fortunate she didn't mention this to Holmes. I can't afford to pay off every blackmailer who may come along in the future. The worst of the whole mess is your sneakiness. I wouldn't have thought you capable of this."

Ian was right. She had been sneaky, surprising herself. But she wouldn't apologize again. She'd done what she thought was right.

"Molly is waiting in the carriage for our shopping trip. What time will you be home tonight?" she asked, and made her way to the door.

"I'm not certain," he said noncommittally, impaling her with a look which was as sharp as a knife. "A friend of mine was arrested for conspiracy to commit treason. You do remember Percival Forrest."

"I do." Bethlyn recalled meeting the man at a New Year's party at Cynthia's, and she thought he looked familiar to her until she remembered she'd seen him at the secret meeting at Simpson House. Like Ian, Forrest pretended to be a loyalist and now he'd been found out. "I'm quite sorry to hear about him."

"Not half as sorry as I am. Forrest is the second man to be arrested this past week. Jacob Dennery was carted off to the Walnut Street Prison on Monday. I believe you met him at Shippens House."

Why was Ian looking at her like she was some sort of an insect under a microscope about to be dissected? She didn't care for this at all, growing nervous because he believed she was hiding something.

"Yes, I did." Dennery was another supposed loyalist whom she'd recognized at the secret meeting.

"Aren't you a bit surprised, Bethlyn? After all, you have no reason not to believe they weren't loyal to the king."

"I'm very sorry for your friends, but nothing surprises me any longer."

"Ah, then you won't be too surprised or care too much if I should be the next man arrested on the list."

"List? Someone has a list of names?" Her heart jumped

in her chest at the thought. Suppose someone had learned about Ian and he was taken away from her? She wouldn't be able to bear it.

He lifted an eyebrow, his face tense. "Maybe."

"Ian—"

Moving quickly from behind the desk, he opened the door for her. "I have a great deal to do this afternoon. Give Molly my regards. And don't wait supper for me. I shall be late."

Bethlyn uttered her farewell, sensing that he wasn't that busy. He was too angry and disappointed with her to even speak to her another moment. And there was something else which accounted for his brusqueness, the mistrust she read in his eyes. But what?

Stepping into the carriage Molly told her she didn't feel like shopping today and could they please return home. Suddenly Bethlyn didn't want to shop anyway, only too glad to order the carriage back to Edgecomb, welcoming Molly's silence. All Bethlyn could think about was losing Ian.

Thomas Paine glanced up from the papers in his hand, his brows knitted into a frown when his gaze settled on Bethlyn, who sat across the desk from him.

"You're serious about having your poems published, Mrs. Briston."

"Yes, I am. I can see from your expression that you're not exactly pleased. Are they very bad?"

"No, not all. In fact, your poetry is excellent, and I'm quite certain that if the poems are published, the Dove will be a success, and the British will be beside themselves, trying to discover the Dove's identity."

Bethlyn clutched her fox muff in her hands and licked her lips in nervousness. "Thank you for the praise, Mr. Paine. I was undecided whether to approach you on this matter, but having recently read your pamphlet *Common Sense*, a piece I much admired, I decided to visit you. I do hope you aren't upset that I came to your home today unannounced."

Paine leaned back in his chair and smiled a wary smile

at Bethlyn, who made a becoming picture as she sat near the window, the soft sunlight of a late January afternoon highlighting her natural beauty. "I assure you that I welcome your visit, Mrs. Briston, but, if I recall, *Common Sense* was published anonymously. Why do you credit me with the piece?"

Bethlyn looked away, feeling the color rise to her cheeks. She couldn't very well tell the man that she'd overheard Ian speaking to Marc about Paine's pamphlet. In fact, she'd been blatantly eavesdropping, actually pressing her ear to the library door to discover why Ian never stayed at home nights anymore. She knew about his secret meetings, but she doubted the men met more than once a week. So where did he go when he left home?

The eavesdropping hadn't answered that question, but she did hear about Paine and decided to approach him on the publication of her poems after secretly obtaining and reading a copy of his *Common Sense*. Now she felt ungodly stupid, hating to lie to him, so she skirted the issue with a half-truth.

"My husband mentioned you were the author of *Common Sense*," she commented, lifting her gaze to Paine.

"I see, but why would your husband, a noted loyalist, think I'd written such a piece?"

Bethlyn cleared her throat, sincerity etched on her face. "We both know my husband isn't what he appears to be, Mr. Paine."

Paine lifted an eyebrow.

"Simpson House," she said, immediately eliciting a knowing nod from Paine. She hoped he wouldn't ask how she knew about that.

With well-manicured fingers, he tapped the top of his desk. "Forgive me, ma'am, but you're the daughter of a British nobleman. Your roots are firmly entrenched in England. I find it hard to believe that your allegiance is with the American cause.

"But it is, sir," she persisted. "I've come to care a great deal about Philadelphia and her citizens. I've seen the cruelties forced upon some of our people by the soldiers when they wish to meet, to voice their views on liberty. I've heard about the hardships at Valley Forge, and I've read other pamphlets besides your own, enumerating the reasons why we must rid ourselves of tyranny. I freely admit that before I came to this country, I never thought about the war at all. But liberty is important to me now. I hope soon to conceive a child. I don't wish to raise a child in a country which has no say in its government.''

Bethlyn's face flushed becomingly and her eyes gleamed a bright brown. A person would have to be blind not to see her sincerity, and Paine was definitely not blind.

He gestured to the papers before him. "If I agree to have these poems published, you risk danger of exposing yourself and being hanged as a traitor.''

She winced, not caring for the image of herself swinging from a rope, but she'd already considered this possibility. "I'm aware of what may happen to me.''

"Yes, I believe you are, Mrs. Briston," he said, and his face suddenly glowed with warmth. "I'll have these published and distributed for you. Before you know it, you'll be as popular as Emmie Gray.''

"I've heard of her." Bethlyn had, of course, more than heard of Emmie Gray, having recently seen her in an intimate conversation with Ian and not about to forget her. The past month Emmie Gray had become an undisputed heroine. Her name was on everyone's lips, from the servants at Edgecomb to the employees at Briston Shipping, her sad but heroic story recounted with such fervor and tear-filled eyes that Bethlyn had grown tired of hearing it. Truly, the citizens had taken the orphaned waif to their breasts, but for some reason Bethlyn didn't like her.

Bethlyn stood to leave, extending her hand to Paine. "I have one request to make of you, sir. I know already that the poems will be published under the Dove's pseudonym and that you shall keep my identity confidential. But I would deem it a great favor if you would not tell my husband.''

Paine looked a bit flustered. "I thought he knew.''

"No, he doesn't. My husband is a gallant man, a man who fights for liberty in his own way. He wouldn't tolerate any of this and would be constantly fearful for my safety. I don't want him to worry about me, but I must do what I can to help in this fight. I do hope you understand and honor my request."

For a moment Paine looked ready to refuse, but he seemed to reconsider. Taking her hand, he kissed it. "I give you my word, Mrs. Briston. You're a brave woman, a true patriot."

"Such words from you, sir, are high praise indeed."

On the way home Bethlyn almost told the driver to take her to Cynthia's when the carriage rolled onto Spruce Street, being a block away. She hadn't seen Cynthia in some weeks, but she changed her mind, deciding that since Cynthia was newly married she might not appreciate an impromptu visit.

Dusk descended gently over the city, bathing it in a purple-gray light. The carriage had just passed a large, imposing home with two figures huddled together on the porch, causing Bethlyn to blink, unable to believe what she'd just witnessed. It's a trick of my eyes because of the twilight, she thought, but she tapped furiously on the small pane of glass behind the driver and ordered him to halt.

Scrambling unceremoniously out of the carriage, Bethlyn paid the driver no mind when he gawked at her as if she were a bit mad. The cold wind stung her eyes and blew her cape about her legs, but she ran the short distance until she stopped behind a hedge planted in front of the house.

She waited, unaware that she held her breath, until the figure of the man drew away from the smaller one of the woman. To stifle a loud gasp, she covered her mouth with her hands to identify the two people as Ian and Emmie Gray.

His hearty and sensuous laugh drifted through the encroaching dusk, sounding husky and filled with something so intimate that Bethlyn thought her heart would burst from her chest.

For moments she couldn't summon the strength to move. Should she fly up the stairs like a shrew and claw out Emmie Gray's eyes? Or should she vent her hurt and wrath on her husband? Or both of them?

Instead she turned away, and soon found herself in the carriage on the way to Edgecomb.

The darkness outside resembled her soul. Emmie Gray was the reason Ian didn't stay at home at night, why he sauntered into the house after the clock had long since chimed twelve. She knew it. Apparently he visited her at that house, and she was almost positive the home belonged to the Babcocks, the family who'd taken in liberty's newfound heroine.

"Heroine, my eye!" Bethlyn groused. "Emmie Gray is a strumpet."

This was the second time she'd caught Ian and Emmie in an intimate discussion. Now, what was she going to do about it? Tell Ian she knew and risk his learning that she'd followed him to Simpson House to spy on him and his cohorts? Say nothing and pretend everything was fine?

But nothing was all right and hadn't been since Emmie Gray mysteriously appeared. The young woman had somehow survived the hostile wilderness, hunger, and extreme cold for days while Bethlyn knew that soldiers at Valley Forge, men who were larger and stronger than Emmie, died from exposure and starvation with little effort.

Had the woman survived only to find her way to Philadelphia and steal Ian away from a wife who loved him? Bethlyn couldn't bear thinking about it.

Tears formed in her eyes, threatening to spill onto her pale cheeks. Had she lost him already? He hadn't come to her bed in a number of weeks, weeks which were numbered by Emmie Gray's arrival. She admitted that her mistake concerning Della hadn't endeared her to him, either. He hadn't mentioned that incident to her since the day she'd left his office, not even when she'd replaced the money she'd taken.

Ian treated her courteously, but she'd catch him watching her sometimes, a puzzled frown on his face, as if he totally didn't understand her. Once she almost lashed out at him, intent on making him reveal the reason why he didn't seem to care for her any longer. But now she knew.

Had Emmie taken Ian from her? Did Emmie appeal to

the part of him which admired her heroism, their mutual love for liberty? She wished she could tell him about her poetry and prove that she now felt as he did about America's freedom, but she couldn't. Ian would, no doubt, believe she'd composed the poems to gain his attention and wouldn't take her seriously.

She found herself in a potentially dangerous situation and couldn't confide in her husband.

A part of her wished she'd never written the poems or showed them to Mr. Paine. Yet another part found the danger exciting. She doubted her poetry would cause barely a ripple of interest in Philadelphia, and she convinced herself that she was safe from discovery. Thomas Paine was the only other person who knew her identity and he'd never tell on the Dove.

Her momentary sense of elation diminished to think about Ian with Emmie Gray.

Was Emmie Gray her rival? Perhaps not, perhaps she'd built something in her mind which didn't exist.

She had to learn the truth.

"I believe I should call on the Babcocks and pay my respects," Bethlyn muttered aloud, and wiped away her tears, already feeling much better now that she decided to take action and end her torment. "Then I shall meet Emmie Gray and decide for myself if this paragon of virtue truly is trying to steal my husband."

Before noon the next day, Bethlyn already had her answer.

She'd used Mr. Babcock's recent bout with influenza as an excuse to visit. Arriving with Pearl, who carried a pot of chicken soup, her specialty, which she claimed could cure any ill, Bethlyn was admitted into the house by a servant. As the maid ushered Pearl to the kitchen, Bethlyn took a seat in the parlor and awaited Mrs. Babcock.

The frail, silver-haired old woman joined her five minutes later, and it was Emmie Gray who supported Mrs. Babcock by the elbow and helped her to a chair. Emmie, wearing a fashionable but modestly styled green-and-blue-print day dress, sat near to Mrs. Babcock and smiled warmly at Bethlyn. Only Bethlyn was aware when Emmie's welcoming smile dissolved during the introductions or that her bright blue eyes flickered over her in cold disdain for a fraction of a second.

"I'd heard Mr. Babcock has been ill," Bethlyn said. "I'm sorry I haven't been here before today to see if there is anything I can do for him."

Mrs. Babcock inclined her head, her low voice sounding soft but clear. "Thank you, my dear. I appreciate your visit, and I shall tell my husband that you inquired about him and brought that delicious soup, too. However, he's much too under the weather to have guests, I'm afraid. Your husband was here yesterday, but he couldn't go upstairs. Emmie was kind enough to entertain him."

The look of pure triumph which Emmie shot in Bethlyn's direction confirmed her fears. Emmie Gray was in love with her husband, but was Ian in love with her?

"Emmie has been a godsend," Mrs. Babcock continued. "Our dear grandson was all the family we had left until— his death. But Emmie has become the granddaughter we never had." She patted Emmie's hand. "A gift from heaven, to be sure."

Bethlyn thought Emmie Gray was the devil's own. Hidden beneath that pretty countenance, framed by long, silver-gold hair and wide blue eyes which contained an innocence any angel would envy, Bethlyn sensed duplicity. There was no reason why she should feel this way, but she'd come here expecting not to like Emmie, and she didn't. Something wasn't right about Emmie Gray, but she couldn't pinpoint what it might be. Did she feel this way because she'd already decided that Emmie was out to steal her husband?

"How very nice for you, Mrs. Babcock. I can tell that Miss Gray is a wonderful person," Bethlyn said without rancor, and pasted a pleasant smile on her face.

Mrs. Babcock looked tired and very frail. Bethlyn started to take her leave, but the old lady insisted she stay and speak with Emmie, that she must retire as she hadn't felt well the last few days.

The maid appeared at Mrs. Babcock's summons and helped her from the room. Bethlyn and Emmie were left alone, sitting quietly together until Emmie poured them tea.

"I do hope Mrs. Babcock isn't coming down with influenza. She doesn't seem in the best of health." Bethlyn added sugar and stirred her tea.

"I do so worry about her and Mr. Babcock," Emmie declared softly. "They've taken the place of my family."

"Yes, I've heard of your tragedy. I'm very sorry."

"Everyone was killed. My . . . parents . . . and Baby Tad, my little brother." Emmie choked on her words as sobs welled in her throat. "No one but me escaped those . . . those horrid savages!"

Bethlyn decided it was no wonder everyone had taken Emmie Gray to their hearts. A poor and pretty young orphan, Bethlyn judged her to be about eighteen, but there was something about Emmie which caused her to seem older than her years, more experienced than the innocent and naive facade she projected.

After a few seconds she composed herself, apologizing to Bethlyn.

"I understand perfectly, Miss Gray. Tell me, how long do you plan to remain in Philadelphia?"

"As long as I'm wanted."

Wanted by whom? The Babcocks? By Ian? Bethlyn almost asked, but Emmie answered her question for her.

"Mr. Briston has been most kind to me. I do appreciate everything he has done to help me. He has made me feel most welcome and wiped many of my tears away."

Bethlyn placed her cup and saucer on the silver tea tray, deciding to play the Tory wife to the hilt. "That is a puzzlement, Miss Gray. Why should my husband, a loyal servant of the king, take such an interest in you?"

"I suggest you ask him, Mrs. Briston."

"I see no need, Miss Gray. My husband is easily moved by sad tales and pities any unfortunate human being."

Bethlyn rose from her seat, and Emmie followed suit. Almost by mutual consent, they squared off, each eyeing the other in veiled contempt.

"Ian feels more than pity for me, Mrs. Briston. He has developed a deep fondness for me, and I for him. I doubt a

292

man would leave a happy and loving home to travel in the bitter cold because of pity. I suggest you think on this before you ask him anything."

Emmie Gray was more of a threat to her marriage than Bethlyn had thought. What had happened between Emmie and Ian for Emmie to insinuate that Ian didn't love her any longer? She felt extremely shaken by Emmie's attitude, but she'd never allow her to see her unease. Instead, she remained at eye level with the woman, not blinking a lash.

"Our homelife is quite happy, I assure you. As his wife, I know what pleases Ian, and because I am his wife I have a great advantage over anyone else, because I have such ready access to him and can cater to his every want and whim. Husbands and wives develop a silent communication after a while, Miss Gray, something you couldn't possibly appreciate."

Bethlyn managed a tight smile and added, "If my husband has visited you and offered you his friendship and help, you should place great value on them and not be too sad when he doesn't visit you as often. I assure you that after tonight, he'll find no need to visit here unless to pay respects to Mr. Babcock. Good day, Miss Gray."

Twirling around, Bethlyn let herself out and was glad to find Pearl already seated in the carriage. Before they drove away, Bethlyn caught sight of Emmie Gray's face, purple with rage, at the window. For a second she almost swore that the woman's eyes blazed a deep, burning red, and reminded her of a picture of a demonic creature she'd seen in a book once.

Why couldn't Ian see her as she did?

She must win Ian back to her, make him love her again.

A plan formed in her mind, and she giggled aloud. Pearl looked curiously at her.

"Pearl, when we get home I should like you to prepare a wonderful meal and please serve it in my room tonight."

"Are you gonna eat alone, Miss Bethlyn?"

"No, dear Pearl, I should like a cozy dinner for two."

"Oh, yes, ma'am." Pearl winked knowingly.

Chapter Twenty

"Oh, missus, please forgive me and don't think bad of me."

"Annie, whatever are you wailing about?" Bethlyn queried and began to remove her cloak when she entered her bedroom, Annie on her heels. "Well, what is it?" she asked impatiently when an answer wasn't forthcoming, growing aggravated by Annie's constant sniffling.

She didn't like to be short with the servants, but it seemed that the more she questioned Annie, the louder and harder she cried.

"The master will . . . beat . . . me."

"God in heaven, Annie, if you don't tell me soon, *I'll* beat you." An empty threat, but Annie didn't know that.

Finally Annie stopped sniffling and raised red-rimmed eyes to Bethlyn.

Annie sniffed and blew her nose loudly into her kerchief. "I done promised Miss Molly I wouldn't say nothing until after she left, but I'm fearful for her."

"Is something wrong with Molly? Tell me, Annie."

Annie's lower lip trembled. "I'm breaking my promise by telling you, but one of those foreign soldiers came to the door this afternoon with a letter for Miss Molly from that soldier she loves. She made me help her pack. She's leaving with this soldier for New York. Her young man asked her to marry him and that's what she's going to do. It's so romantic and all, missus, and I wonder if any man will love me like that. Running away is so sneaky but sweet . . ."

Bethlyn didn't wait to hear the rest. She immediately headed for Molly's room, startling Molly when she entered without knocking. Molly stood in the center of the room, dressed for traveling in her warmest gown and cloak, her small portmanteau in her hand.

"Annie has a large mouth," Molly noted.

"Never mind her, Molly. I want you to reconsider leaving like this. You may be making a terrible mistake."

Molly shook her head in denial. Her eyes sparkled, her usually pale, tear-stained face positively glowed of late with vitality. Bethlyn hadn't seen her this happy in quite some time.

"I appreciate your cautious words, Bethlyn, but I think you're mimicking what you believe Ian would want you to say to me. I know you don't believe I'm making a mistake. How can I be when I'm going to marry the man I love?"

Molly went to her and the two of them embraced. Tears shone in their eyes.

"I'll write to you and Ian as soon as I'm settled. I love you both very much, and I will be deliriously happy."

Bethlyn didn't doubt that for a second. "Wait and tell Ian good-bye. He'll be upset for you to leave like this."

Molly smiled sadly. "I can't do that. I must leave now. I know that if I tell Ian, we'll get into an argument, and I don't want to be separated a second longer from Hans. He'd have come for me himself, but he couldn't get away. An officer in Hans's regiment is waiting for me with a horse at the back of the house. He's a good friend to Hans and me; I'll be safe with him."

Bethlyn wished Molly would wait until daybreak, but, like Molly, she knew how time dragged when not in the company of the man you loved. Molly had been miserable for so long that Bethlyn didn't argue with her. Instead she hugged Molly again. "Please be careful and write as soon as you can."

"I will. I do hate leaving you to bear the brunt of Ian's rage, but there's no other way, Bethlyn. Please understand."

Bethlyn was about to assure Molly that she did

understand when Annie rushed into the room, breathless and on the verge of tears to announce that Ian had just returned home and was coming up the stairs.

"Oh, Bethlyn, he'll stop me. I know he will," Molly cried, looking almost like a trapped mouse about to be cornered by a large cat.

"I'll stall him somehow. Sneak down the back stairs to the stables, and promise me you'll be happy, Molly." Quickly she kissed Molly on the cheek and left Molly's bedroom only to literally bump into Ian in the hallway.

"What a rush you're in," he said, and placed an arm around her waist, surprising her with his show of affection.

"I couldn't wait to see you. This is the first time you've been home early in weeks."

Ian cleared his throat, but not a flicker of guilt crossed his face. His days as Captain Hawk had forced him to learn to hide his emotions and made him into an accomplished liar. How else could one account for his escaping capture for so long, for allowing the British to believe he was a loyalist? Bethlyn hated his ability to hide the truth, wishing he'd show some qualm of conscience about Emmie Gray. But it was this very thing which allowed her to swallow her nervousness and show a calm demeanor when he asked her where Molly was.

"In her room," she said truthfully, not adding that his sister wouldn't be there for much longer.

"Perhaps I should check on her. I hate for her to hole herself up like a rabbit. It's time she ends this silliness and takes an interest in life. I know of a fine young man who is clamoring for an introduction to meet her, and I warrant that once she gets into the social whirl, she'll forget this adolescent crush."

Ian made a move to grasp the doorknob, but Bethlyn threw her arms around his neck, rubbing her body suggestively against his.

"Do you have something on your mind?" he asked, seeming to forget Molly as he nibbled on her ear.

"Maybe."

"Something lewd, I trust."

A shiver of raw desire slid down Bethlyn's backside when Ian clasped her rounded bottom, bringing her to fit snugly against the bulging spot in his trousers.

"Definitely lewd." She felt breathless, her senses whirling. "Does this mean that I'm forgiven? I meant only to keep you safe."

His fingers placed on her lips stopped her words. "I don't approve, but I understand. I can't live without loving you; you've become a fire in my blood."

With warm hands and heated eyes, he undressed her when she stood beside the bed in her room. He helped her step out of her chemise, her hair spilling across her naked breasts. The sweet, musky scent of her body caused him to lower his mouth to the swelling globes and feast on the jutting peaks.

Bethlyn moaned. Her fingers threaded through the dark strands of his hair. It seemed that such a long time had passed since Ian had loved her. Her body rekindled with desire for him and the memory of Emmie Gray with Ian faded as a liquid sensation, melting and hot, coursed through every nerve and fiber of her body.

She'd intended to occupy him so Molly could sneak away, but with each possessive kiss, each stirring caress, Bethlyn forgot all about Molly. She needed to be loved fully, ached to be loved until she whimpered in satisfaction against his hard, muscular chest.

"You're so beautiful," Ian whispered, his lips scorching each satiny inch of her breasts and stomach before he knelt in front of her. His tongue began an arousing journey downward to tease and taste the tempting bud of her femininity.

Trembling with need, Bethlyn could barely think, her breath coming in tiny gasps. She clutched at Ian's shoulders, her fingers digging into the brown velvet material of his jacket to keep her knees from buckling as each flick of his tongue caused golden heat to gather and swirl within her, threatening to singe her very being.

She didn't think she could survive the mounting pleasure, which was almost painful. "No, Ian, stop," she pleaded, wanting him inside her, to know that he was completely hers. She tried to move away, but Ian's hands clamped on her buttocks, bringing her closer, savoring her very essence.

"Enjoy it, Bethlyn," she heard him whisper. "Enjoy what I'm doing to you."

A tiny whimper of complete surrender escaped from between her lips. Her body grew fluid, molding against him, eager for his pleasuring. A delicious tension coiled within the womanly part of her, writhing like a serpent.

Glancing down at her husband through desire-filled eyes, Bethlyn realized that Ian seemed to more than enjoy loving her, hearing her moans of pleasure. She closed her eyes and gyrated her hips, opening herself more fully to him.

The tension coiled tighter and tighter within her. Her body felt ready to burst, but Ian seemed to know how far to the edge of ecstasy to bring her, how to keep the liquid heat from entirely consuming her.

Never had she felt like this, never had she moaned with such pleasure and abandon, craving sweet release. But still Ian kept her body in check, almost as if he was master of her flesh and her soul. She sensed she waited for some sign from him before she plunged into the deep cavern of exquisite ecstasy.

With fingers trailing into his hair, she grasped a handful of his thick black locks.

"Ian, please . . ." she whimpered, not certain she could stand any more of this slow and delightfully torturous lovemaking.

He seemed not to hear her plea, deepening her pleasure until she wondered if she would go insane with need, but suddenly and without warning, he lifted her from her feet to dangle her legs over his shoulders, his strong arms keeping her in place. Bethlyn gasped with pleasure when his tongue speared her, reaching into the center of her womanhood and not leaving her. His hot breath flowed over her like a tropical breeze. And then it happened.

The tension uncoiled and twirled through her like a spinning top. Finally her body exploded. Wave upon wave of delirious rapture flooded her, only to gather and inundate her again with ecstasy so intense she thought she was dying from the sheer joy of it.

"Oh, Ian, Ian," she whimpered, clinging to him and growing limp with the force of her climax.

Opening her eyes, she gazed into Ian's eyes, so filled with his desire for her that she shivered. With a start she realized that they now reclined on the bed and he held her in his arms.

"I don't recall moving to the bed," she said.

Ian traced her lips with his forefinger and smiled. "You were occupied with something else."

Kissing her, she surprised herself by responding, her desire renewing itself.

Ian's lips broke away from hers, a naughty smile hovering around his mouth. "Don't tell me I didn't do an adequate job of satisfying you, you lusty wench."

She grinned and undid the buttons on his jacket, urging him out of it. "Apparently not."

"Liar," he mumbled, and kissed one of her nipples before getting up and removing his clothes, only to join her again to thoroughly explore each other's bodies with hands and lips.

When Bethlyn writhed beneath him, wrapping her legs around the broadness of his back, she thought never to experience the same intense pleasure she'd known only minutes before. But when Ian slid into her warm and moist center, she opened to him like a blossoming rose. She matched her movements to his, arching and grinding her lower body against him, reveling in the glorious and pulsating sensations with every heart-stopping thrust.

Then Ian's tongue plundered her mouth, demanding the taste of hers, and she was lost.

She stiffened and cried out as a climax, so unexpected in intensity, ripped through her.

"Insatiable wench," he said, his voice husky and his eyes hooded with dark desire. "Have you had enough now?"

"No. I want more of you, all of you." Bethlyn's hands traced his back and wandered to his buttocks, pressing him against her to be filled more deeply.

"God, Bethlyn, God, God . . ."

His voice broke off to capture her lips. She moved beneath him, enticing him to a climax with wanton words whispered into his ear, her hands stroking and kneading his buttocks. Fire once more spread through her, leaving her moaning and aching until Ian plunged into her one last time.

He shuddered, his eyes glazing over, and held her tightly against him. Ian's release became her release when the licking flames of passion consumed her. Their cries of fulfillment echoed as one.

"I'm starved." Ian rolled onto his back when Bethlyn got out of the bed half an hour later.

Pulling on her robe, she nodded, totally unaware of how beautiful she appeared with her tousled hair and flushed face. "I'll ring for Pearl to send something up for us. We can eat in here."

"Maybe we should go downstairs. I hate for Molly to dine alone."

Fumbling with a button, Bethlyn turned her back to him, certain Ian would suspect something was wrong if he saw her face. "I'm certain Molly has eaten already." Quickly she pulled the cord to summon Pearl, and within a minute the woman knocked on the door and Bethlyn told her she and Ian wished to eat in her room. Pearl bobbed a curtsy and fifteen minutes later the food was delivered to the room and placed on a small table by Annie, who gaped openly at Ian as he sat with only a sheet to cover his bottom half.

Bethlyn followed Annie to the door and stepped into the hallway for a moment.

"Mr. Ian is powerful handsome," Annie remarked, her face holding a trace of awe. "Not even in my whoring days have I seen a better-looking man. You're real lucky, missus."

Bethlyn shot her a chastising look, and Annie lowered her eyes in embarrassment.

"Has Miss Molly left?" Bethlyn whispered.

"Yes, missus. She and the soldier been gone a while."

Bethlyn was tempted to tell Ian about Molly, but she'd given her word and wouldn't break it. Morning would be soon enough to tell him, she decided, when, after supper, he opened his arms to her and loved her through the night.

When Bethlyn woke the next morning, she stretched like a kitten, a lingering smile on her face. She should be exhausted, having gotten very little sleep. It seemed that each time she started to doze, Ian woke her with hot kisses. They'd both been insatiable last night, their lovemaking more intense and mind drugging than ever.

For a second, Emmie Gray's image flitted across her mind, but Bethlyn no longer felt threatened that Ian would prefer Emmie over her. She didn't know if Emmie Gray was the reason he'd stayed away from home and her bed the last weeks, but after the hours they'd spent last night making love over and over again until neither one of them could move from exhaustion, Bethlyn knew that Ian belonged to her and would never feel the need to seek out another woman.

Satisfied with herself, Bethlyn sat against the pillows, the sheet barely covering her full breasts. She wondered where Ian had gone, since today was Sunday and the office was closed. Almost making up her mind to get up and dress, the door opened and Ian walked in.

He wore a white shirt, opened at the throat to reveal his bronzed skin, and a pair of brown trousers and black boots. This casual attire reminded her of Captain Hawk. She rose to her knees, the sheet hanging in disarray around her. A lovely smile beckoned him to the bedside, and she lifted her face to his, expecting a kiss. She wasn't prepared for the cold disdain in his eyes, the sneer which crimped the edges of his mouth.

"Ian, what's . . . wrong?"

"Why don't you tell me."

That terrible black look, the icy tone of his voice which could freeze water meant only one thing. Molly!

Somehow Ian had learned about Molly before she could tell him. Bethlyn braced herself, taking a deep breath, and pulled the sheet about her, suddenly and stupidly embarrassed to have Ian view her body. Last night had

301

proved to her how much Ian loved looking at her and touching her, that she wanted him to look at her and touch her, to do the same to him. She had wanted last night to last forever.

Now it was morning.

"I . . . I . . ." She seemed to lose her power of speech, almost reverting to the cowering child who displeased her father.

"Since you're unable to speak, no doubt from guilt, I will tell you." Ian held out a hand to her in which he held a crumpled piece of paper. "I found this on my bureau when I went to my room to dress. It's a note from Molly, and, needless to say, you know what's in it. She cares for you very much, Bethlyn, pleading with me not to think harshly of you for helping her run away."

Ian threw the letter on the floor and bent down, his eyes level with hers. Never had she seen such contempt on another human being's face, except for her father. She shivered, her trembling hands barely able to hold on to the sheet.

"Sad as it is, Bethlyn, I was growing to trust you. Your body is most enticing, and you arouse me as no other woman I've ever known. Foolishly I allowed myself to be taken in by your beauty. You held great appeal for me, madam. For the first time I believed in love."

Ian yanked the sheet from her and pulled her resisting body against him. "You still hold me captive with those innocent-appearing brown eyes . . . your silky hair which smells like a spring garden." One of his hands gently stroked a breast and slid down her leg to caress the soft nest of curls at the juncture of her thighs. Then, with his eyes never leaving her face, his fingers slowly slid inside her, to tease and torment her. He seemed to find some perverted pleasure in touching her when he wished to hate her.

"And this I loved most of all, because you gave yourself to me completely. I loved watching your face and feeling the ecstasy wash over you when I was inside you. I have power over your body, Bethlyn. At this moment I could reduce you to a quivering mass of flesh with a few strokes of my fingers. I know you want that, because I feel you

302

pulsing with need."

"Ian, stop, let me explain," she said, at last finding her voice. She tried to pull away from him, aching for the dark pleasure he promised, but hating his anger and disappointment in her. "Molly loves Hans. She feared you'd stop her."

"I *would* have stopped her."

"But you couldn't have kept her here. She'd have run away to New York eventually. She isn't a child, but a woman in love. She begged me to help her, and I couldn't refuse her. I know how it feels to love deeply. I promised her. Please . . . try . . . to understand."

"Ah, but I do understand. You used your body last night to keep me amused so Molly could run away."

"No, I didn't mean to. I wanted you . . . I wouldn't . . ."

"I also understand about Della and what you did to ensure my safety." Ian pulled her closer, his arm wrapping around her like a rope, stealing the breath from her. His fingers slid in and out of her, never ceasing their tender torment.

"I understand that I panted after you like a besotted fool, falling in with your plan. You used my feelings for you against me. I almost forgot you were a British subject, loyal to your king, and the daughter of a man I detest. I wanted to forget everything but your tempting body, and I did. I forgot who and what I am."

"Let me explain."

"No! I don't want to hear your lies, I want to touch you and force you to listen to me."

She didn't know if she could speak anyway. Her mind whirled. Perhaps she should have tried harder to convince Molly to stay and speak to Ian, or she should have told him as soon as she saw him. But she felt confused, unable to think clearly as Ian's fingers mesmerized her, deftly bringing her to the edge of fulfillment.

"Do you want me to stop, Bethlyn?" he asked in a hoarse whisper against her ear. His hold moved from her waist to the rounded curves of her buttocks, his fingers playing within her flesh like a master musician on a finely tuned instrument.

303

"You're trying to prove something to me—to punish me." She clung to his shirt front, barely able to speak. The world careened, ready to fly free and spin off into a universe filled with bright, exploding stars.

His eyes blazed with black passion, his arousal of her unrelenting. "Yes, for other reasons besides Molly, but do you want me to stop?"

God help her, she didn't. If he stopped now, she'd have to beg him to finish with her. Shaking her head from side to side, her hair tumbling to hide her face, she blocked out everything but the raw pleasure igniting within her. Ian laughed, a wicked sound to her ears, as his finger movements quickened, working to end her torment.

When he lowered his head to her nipple, sucking and tugging on the peak, her body betrayed her. Her cry of ecstasy broke free only to be smothered by Ian's lips on hers, startling her with the force of his kiss. An eternity seemed to pass before he broke away, and she was breathless and embarrassed, burying her face in the soft folds of Ian's shirt front.

For an instant she almost swore she felt Ian place a gentle kiss on the top of her head, but she decided she was mistaken when he cupped her chin and forced her to look at his face, so icy and aloof she felt chilled to her very soul.

"I've been a fool, but no longer," he said. "Your many charms made me forget that our marriage was a business arrangement. I should have left it as such. I'd have been spared the pain of loving you." Ian took a deep breath, holding on to her tighter. "But you're my wife now, and as my wife, you shall perform your wifely duty by me."

"Oh, Ian, I'll do anything you want. I love you so much. I'll never keep anything from you again. I promise."

"Will you?" he asked softly. "Then tell me why you followed me to Simpson House a few weeks ago?"

If he hadn't been holding her, she'd have fallen. How had he discovered her secret?

"I-I, wan—" she stuttered, her childhood affliction surfacing when she was nervous or taken aback.

"Could it be that you wanted to know who took part in those meetings, that the names of loyalists turned traitor might prove beneficial to General Howe? Did you write down the names, or keep them in your head?"

"No, I didn't do that!" she cried at last.

"Stop lying. There were five of us at that meeting, five men who pretended to be Tories and hobnob with the king's own. First to be arrested was Forrest, then Dennery. I received word from Marc this morning that Simon Price was arrested last night. Then there is Mr. Babcock, but nothing shall be done to him since he died in his sleep yesterday evening. So, that leaves me, the last remaining Tory of the group. Am I to be protected because you love me, my dear, or should I prepare for the worst?"

"I'd never turn you in, I'd never do any of that." She was shocked and dumbfounded by his accusation. "You must believe me."

"I don't, Bethlyn. I can never trust you again." He shook his head in dismay. "I wanted to believe you'd explain why you followed me. I gave you the chance. Remember the day you confessed to the robbery. The night of the meeting, I found the horse's tracks in the snow when I returned home. The tracks led right into the stables, and Amos had just finished rubbing down Star. He said nothing, and I didn't ask, because I needed to believe in you."

"Ian, you can believe in me. I never betrayed your friends." Bethlyn threaded her arms around his neck, an urgency in her voice. "I needed to know where you went when you left the house, and when I listened at the window, I understood for the first time about the war. I know now why you're fighting. I even wrote some—"

"Stop it, Bethlyn!" His hands grabbed her arms, nearly shaking her. "Do you think I'm such a fool to believe that you'd embrace my politics? I assure you, I'm not." Suddenly his hands slid to possessively wander across her buttocks. "I do believe that I love touching you and can't get enough of your tempting flesh. You've betrayed my friends, helped my sister run away, probably to be used and abandoned by a mercenary enemy, and, lest we forget, you stole from me. But still I want you. What is this power you hold over me?"

Ian appeared so lost that her heart went out to him. She'd hurt him when she'd only wanted to protect him and to allow Molly to find her happiness. His accusations of betraying his friends cut deeply into her, but in his present state of mind, she doubted he'd hear her out or believe her innocence. He didn't trust her. Didn't it always seem to boil down to trust with them?

"I admit that you're my weakness," she heard him say in a tortured voice. "So, I shall be forced to live with you, or die without you. I can't give you up yet; I shall make a pact with you, as we did when you first arrived at Edgecomb."

"What sort of a pact?" Bethlyn already knew she wasn't going to like it whatever it was.

Ian twirled a long strand of her hair between his fingers. "We shall remain married, and you will not admit to your contacts that I am Captain Hawk or that I am less than loyal to our dear Majesty."

"None of this is true," she broke in, pleading. "I have no contact."

He spoke over her words. "I want a child by you, an heir, as double insurance that you won't turn me in. After all, the child will need a father, and you wouldn't want the stigma of my crimes to blemish him. The fact that I wish to sire a child by you hasn't a thing to do with my feelings for you. I've a large amount of capital and would prefer to leave it to my own flesh and blood, rather than let the Crown take it. Until you conceive, you may dance with your Captain André and beguile your many male admirers with your charms, as it would appear odd if you shunned the season's activities."

His eyes held a warning. "No one is to touch you. I need to know without a doubt that any child you bear is my own. Under the circumstances I'm being more than generous to you. After the child's birth, you may cavort and sleep with whomever you choose. I don't care what you do or with whom you do it, as long as you bear me an heir."

She felt as if he'd kicked her in the stomach, staring in stunned disbelief, in shock to realize that Ian was serious. No matter what he thought she'd done, she wouldn't be able to live such a life-style. He was prepared to use her as a breeder and then to abandon her.

He intended to ignore her, something she wouldn't tolerate. For most of her life she'd been ignored. Did the pompous man also believe she was so naive that any dalliance he may have had or considered having with Emmie Gray had gone unnoticed by her? He must think she was blind. Fury welled within her to be treated so shabbily by the man she loved.

"This is a preposterous proposition, and I refuse to consider such a thing," Bethlyn stated heatedly, barely aware when Ian broke his hold of her, and she crumpled onto the mattress.

"Ah, that rebellious streak must be tamed, sweetheart."

"And how do you intend to do that?"

"Need you ask, Bethlyn? I know that I'm as much your weakness as you are mine, and don't bother to deny it."

She couldn't deny it, he was right.

"You really won't want me after I give you a child?" she asked, hoping against hope that he'd suddenly see the folly of such a stupid idea.

He shrugged. "Perhaps I will, then maybe I won't. The possibility exists that if I avail myself of your body as often as I wish, I may grow tired of you. Either way, I'll be occupied elsewhere."

"Occupied with Emmie Gray?" The woman's name slipped out before she was aware she'd said it.

"So you know about Emmie."

"Of course. I saw her at the meeting, remember. I also visited her yesterday. We had an enlightening conversation."

"Now you understand why everyone admires her."

"I don't like the woman, Ian, but my feelings are unimportant. I must know if you love her."

Bethlyn clutched the sheet to her breasts, her eyes wide and filled with pain, but defying him to say he did. How could he love Emmie Gray after the glorious night of passion they'd shared?

A great shuddering sigh wracked his composure. "At this moment, Bethlyn, I love no one. Not even myself."

Chapter Twenty-One

The next few weeks were the most miserable of Bethlyn's life.

She barely saw Ian except when he visited her bed where he took her with little passion. But no matter his treatment of her, he always saw to her pleasure, a bitter pleasure given the circumstances. So many times she was tempted to literally crawl on her hands and knees and beg his forgiveness, somehow convince him that she wasn't guilty of spying. But she didn't.

As much as she still loved him, she had her pride.

Throwing herself into the social whirl, she attended more balls, parties, and soirées than she cared to count. Behind a brilliant smile and witty conversation, she hid her pain. At one such glittering affair given by Cynthia and her new husband, Cynthia ushered Bethlyn upstairs to her bedroom. The woman pointedly inquired what was wrong, why did Ian stand like a statue all evening long while countless gentlemen twirled her around the dance floor.

Bethlyn couldn't admit that Ian didn't love her any longer, that he most probably had never loved her to treat her so shabbily. But Cynthia didn't believe her story that the Bristons had had a minor tiff. "A tiff which has lasted almost two months?" Cynthia raised a finely arched brow. "I think not."

Bethlyn needed to confide in someone, and finally she broke down, weeping huge tears as she explained Ian's

308

displeasure because she'd helped Molly leave, the only part of her problems she could divulge.

"The man is a beast!" Cynthia cried, and embraced Bethlyn. "I shall give him a good dressing down."

"No, you mustn't! I don't want him to feel guilty about his treatment of me. If he forgives me, I want it to be because he loves me. Otherwise, I don't want him at all."

Cynthia contemplated the young woman with red-rimmed eyes and smiled gently. "Sometimes a man must be pushed in the right direction."

Days later, Bethlyn mulled over Cynthia's words. She knew she might be able to use her feminine wiles on Ian and had no doubt that her body was a great temptation to him. More than once she'd caught him casting lustful glances at her when she thought she didn't see him. He couldn't forget their nights together and neither could she. But she refused to seduce him. If he wanted to make things right between them, he'd have to apologize to her.

So preoccupied with her marital troubles, Bethlyn barely registered the fact that pamphlets containing the Dove's poetry swamped Philadelphia. Before February was over, pamphlets had been printed and distributed, eagerly read by all those people who craved liberty and some who expressed sentiments that the Dove, whomever this person might be, should be sniffed out and hung as a traitor.

John André made Bethlyn aware of the Dove's popularity when he dropped in for tea one afternoon with the lovely but shallow Peggy Shippen as his companion.

Ian arrived home early, an unexpected event of late, and took a seat on the sofa next to Bethlyn as John rattled on about General Howe's aggravation over the poems.

John took the pamphlet in question out of his breast pocket and laid it on a side table. "I tell you that Howe is getting a great deal of flak over the Dove. People loyal to the king are demanding that he discover this person's identity and put an end to all of the patriotic prattle which has erupted." John wolfed down a crumpet and grinned in amusement. "I've never seen the old boy so flustered. The Dove is more popular than that wench Emmie Gray."

Bethlyn stiffened, not giving Ian an extra look, when Peggy made a haughty sound of disdain.

"Personally I think the uproar is ridiculous. Poetry can't possibly change the tide of the war. The British will be victorious," she stated emphatically, as if her knowledge about the war extended beyond the parties and dancing with British soldiers into the wee hours of the morning. "I can't imagine life if the colonials win. Things will be so horribly dull."

Peggy smiled at Bethlyn, expecting her to agree, but Bethlyn stirred her tea, not acknowledging Peggy's remark.

"What do you say about all of this, Ian?" John asked. "Have you read the Dove's poems?"

"Yes."

"And?"

"I find her style to be quite refreshing, simple and unaffected. Granted, the work is overlong but never ponderous or dull. She flings herself at liberty as a moth flies into a flame. I can understand how her enthusiasm would capture people's attentions and disturb General Howe."

"You sound like a champion of the Dove," Peggy commented, a hint of slyness in her voice. "What makes you believe the Dove is a woman?"

"Because of the softness and gentleness expressed beneath the surface," Ian explained, pouring a glass of brandy. "This woman is not only a poetess, but a true patriot. I recommend that she be taken seriously." He lifted the glass a bit, almost as if he toasted the Dove.

Bethlyn placed her teacup on the table beside the sofa in fear she'd drop it. Tremors ran the length of her spine, the reality of the Dove's sensation hitting her with full force. Here she sat under the nose of a British captain and his Tory companion while her husband, a hunted man in his own right, favorably commented on the merits of a work she'd anonymously penned, something for which she could be hanged. Even if she'd ever considered admitting to Ian that she'd written the poetry, she knew she could never tell him now.

Though John and Peggy apparently didn't recognize his fascination with the Dove, Bethlyn did. When the conversation switched to gossip about the wife of an officer who was involved with a lowly soldier, Peggy taking delight in disclosing every juicy detail of the affair, Bethlyn noticed that Ian pretended to listen. He commented in the appropriate places, but she could tell his mind wasn't on the discussion.

From the feverish gleam in his eyes, the gleam she'd seen so many times when he spoke about his country's fight for independence, and the way his gaze lingered on the pamphlet on the table, she guessed that Emmie Gray was about to be displaced by the Dove.

Almost tempted to crow her delight, she restrained herself at the irony of the situation.

Ian had found a new heroine. Herself.

Three days later Bethlyn sat beside Ian on the Briston pew in Christ Church for the burial services of Mrs. Babcock. The old lady had died in her sleep, and though she'd been in poor health since the death of her grandson, it was felt that her husband's passing had hastened her own departure from this earth.

Out of the corner of her eye, Bethlyn watched Emmie Gray, who sat on the pew in front of them, dab a finely made linen kerchief to her eye. Her black mourning gown, embroidered in a thin braid of gold at the cuffs and hem, made a startling contrast against the paleness of her elegantly coiffed hair, covered by a gossamer wisp of black tulle. Bethlyn hadn't recognized Emmie at first, taking her for a wealthy relative of the Babcocks until she'd remembered that the old couple had had no living relations after the death of their grandson. Now Emmie Gray resembled a confident and wealthy woman, totally unlike the demure, shy girl Bethlyn had first seen at Simpson House.

And wealthy she was, too. The Babcocks' lawyer had paid a visit to Edgecomb yesterday morning to inform Ian of the terms of Mrs. Babcock's will, which had been changed the day after Mr. Babcock's death. The will stated that Emmie Gray should be judged heir to the Babcock house and fortune, having been regarded as a dear daughter to the old couple in the short time she'd resided with them. Ian was to be executor of the estate until Emmie reached the age of twenty in a year's time, and he would advise Emmie and see to her overall well-being.

Bethlyn had felt some surprise that Ian even bothered mentioning the details to her. Was she supposed to cheer for the poor orphaned darling who wheedled her way into the affections of an old and lonely couple? Did Ian want her to congratulate him on being named executor of the Babcock fortune? Did he want her to give her blessing to the many nights he'd spend advising Emmie?

She'd looked at him as he stood before her in the library, the morning sun highlighting the rugged features of his face, literally willing herself to drown in the beryl pools of his eyes and unable to stop her heart's rapid pounding. She knew she should hate him and treat him with contempt, but she loved him. Cruelty wasn't in Bethlyn's nature.

Somehow, though she felt like weeping because she believed that she'd truly lost him now, she managed to smile and hide her pain. "How very fortunate for both of you. Miss Gray is lucky that Mrs. Babcock chose you to be executor. Now, if you will excuse me."

Bethlyn had risen from her chair to leave the library when Ian made a move and touched her arm. The gentle pressure of his hand nearly brought tears to her eyes, because it seemed so long ago that he'd touched her with tenderness.

"Mrs. Babcock entrusted me with Emmie's future. I want you to know that this is no doing of mine."

"I believe you. Still, the request is a fortuitous pairing for the both of you. Please let me know when the carriage is ready for the funeral."

And with that she'd left the library.

Now Bethlyn wondered if she should have admitted how much she minded this new turn of events. Would a tirade have done any good? She didn't think so. Ian would only have declared that she was jealous of Emmie Gray and couldn't possibly understand the heroic Emmie. But Bethlyn didn't think Emmie was that much of a heroine for escaping being scalped by savages. Any normal person would have run. Yet when the service ended and the coffin containing Mrs. Babcock's remains was buried in the churchyard, people milled around Emmie like she was a reigning queen. They consoled her, held her hand, patted her slender back, and assured her in hushed tones that people loved her and could be counted upon if she ever needed any help.

Bethlyn wanted to retch.

Finally, when she thought she could stand no more, Ian took her by the elbow and escorted her to Emmie. Upon seeing Ian, Emmie's eyes grew bright, and the tears hanging on the tips of her lashes resembled exquisite diamonds.

"My wife and I wish to pay our respects on your loss, Miss Gray. Please accept our condolences."

Emmie's fingers clutched Ian's hand like a piranha's teeth and held on tightly. "Thank you for coming today. I'm so relieved that Mrs. Babcock has put you in charge of my affairs. Could you please come to the house tonight? I hope Mrs. Briston won't mind, but we do have a great deal to discuss and plans to make."

I just bet you do, Bethlyn thought to herself, and hated Emmie Gray more at that moment than she'd ever hated any other person in her life. However, her face appeared serene and she managed to look sympathetic at the same time.

To her unmitigated shock, Ian turned to her and said, "Do you mind, Bethlyn?"

For the second time that day Ian had thrown her off balance. He didn't have to tell her about Mrs. Babcock's will and certainly he didn't need to ask her if she minded his visiting Emmie Gray. Ian was the sort of man who did whatever he pleased. Yet she was flattered that he'd thought to ask her at all.

She didn't want him to see Emmie Gray, but she knew she'd appear small if she admitted to this. Or perhaps Ian wanted anyone who happened to be listening to believe that he was a kind and considerate husband, to protect Emmie's reputation by making it appear that his wife had given her blessing for him to visit the woman's home on business concerns.

Anger roiled within her at this notion, but no other choice was left to her. "I don't mind," she said softly, but her tone was frosty.

"How wonderful," Emmie breathed, and shot a smug smile in Bethlyn's direction. "I shall see you this evening at seven, Mr. Briston, and would you care to dine with me?"

"Thank you, but no. I'll dine at home."

Emmie released Ian's hand when a friend of Mrs. Babcock's appeared to cluck over her like a mother hen. At this point Bethlyn shrugged off Ian's hold on her elbow and headed for the carriage. When inside, she didn't glance at Ian, but she knew he watched her—intently.

"Are you jealous of Emmie, Bethlyn?"

She turned her head from the window and glared at him. "My feelings about Emmie Gray are unimportant to you. No matter what I'd say about her, whether good or ill, you'd find some way to belittle me by comparing me with her. And I warrant that I'd come up lacking. No one can possibly be as noble, heroic, and beautiful as the image of Emmie Gray you've built in your mind."

"You shouldn't be jealous of Emmie. You're much more beautiful than she could ever hope to be." And with that remark, he retreated into silence, not saying another word.

Ian had never kissed Emmie Gray.

When he sat in the Babcock parlor that evening while a servant he'd never before seen in all his visits to the Babcock house went upstairs to tell Emmie of his arrival, he wondered why he hadn't. He'd held her against him many times, had kissed her hand, and, more often than he cared to count, Emmie's full and sensual lips had tempted him to possess them. Why didn't he just take the girl in his arms and kiss her? He sensed that Emmie would eventually surrender herself to him if he wished to make love to her after, no doubt, entreating him to be tender with her and have some regard for her maidenhood.

He'd made love to countless women in his life. Emmie appealed to him, but she was young and untried in the ways of love. She was also liberty's heroine and he'd been forced to put her on a pedestal, which he deemed her rightful place.

Emmie's innocence and bravery, her recountings of the horrible night her family had been killed, sparked a protectiveness within him which he'd only felt in relation to Molly. He might be attracted to Emmie, but in his mind she'd become like a sister to him, and a man didn't desire his sister. And then there was Bethlyn. Bethlyn with the honey-brown hair and bright brown eyes which glowed when he made love to her. It hurt him to think about her and her treachery.

He still suspected she might be the spy about whom General Washington had warned him months ago, but he hadn't turned her in. The thought of Bethlyn being executed as a spy was too horrible for him to contemplate. Yet something nagged at him that he might be wrong, but who else could he hold accountable for the arrests of the men like himself who posed as loyalists? What had Bethlyn hoped to gain?

He'd poured and finished drinking a brandy when the servant girl appeared. "Miss Gray isn't up to coming downstairs tonight, sir. The funeral today has undone her and she's grieving. She requests that you join her upstairs in Mrs. Babcock's sitting room."

Poor Emmie, he thought, and climbed the stairs. She'd been through a terrible ordeal the last few months, first to lose her family and, now, the deaths of the Babcocks, people she'd grown to love. He decided not to take up too much of her time. Emmie needed to rest.

The servant opened the sitting-room door and closed it after he entered the room. The white walls and the blue-and-green floral rug on the floor impressed him, as did the feminine and graceful furnishings. A perfect place for

Emmie to seek solace, he realized. But where was Emmie?

He called her name and heard her answer from the adjoining room. Walking through the doorway, he discovered himself in a white-and-pink bedroom. A large tester bed stood in the center of the room, the white hangings tied to the posts by dainty pink ribbons. Within the center of the bed sat Emmie. He moved to the bed and stopped short at the foot, somehow stupidly embarrassed to find her covered by a thin sheet, her bare shoulders looking soft and alluring in the candlelight. Waves of silver-gold hair cascaded down her back, and never had he noticed that her eyes were so translucent a blue.

Ian stood transfixed.

When she spoke, the sensual and seductive quality of her voice heightened the spell. "Thank you for coming upstairs, Ian. I do appreciate it." She patted the spot next to her on the bed. "Please sit here. I don't feel well enough to get up. The day has been most draining."

Like a fly in a spider's web, he sat next to her, feeling the pressure of her thigh against his. He couldn't look away from Emmie. Her eyes, her voice, her face captivated him in some strange and perverse way. He'd never seen her like this before. Usually she dressed in a maidenly, almost childish manner. The Emmie reclining in the bed, and who suddenly took his hand and brought his fingers to her mouth to gently kiss and then seductively suck with her lips, was no child.

"You taste like I always knew you would. Masculine and musky and warm." Her voice was a gentle breeze, lifting him up and floating him toward her.

He cleared his throat. "I noticed a new servant downstairs."

"What a thing to say at a time like this," she laughingly chastised. "Yes, I have a new servant. In fact, the whole household is composed of new servants. I let the ones who served the Babcocks go." Her mouth trembled a bit. "It was too painful to have them around me. I wish to forget all my pain and start a new life. Will you help me, Ian? I do need your strength so very much."

"I'll help you in any way I can."

She smiled and kissed the tips of his fingers. "I'm glad."

Ian pulled his hand away, not quite certain what to make over this less than modest Emmie.

"Emmie, I think you need to rest. You're not yourself."

"But I am myself. Look at me and see me, a flesh-and-blood woman, not some untouchable icon the people have made me out to be."

Icon? Wherever had Emmie heard that word? He knew she spoke well and had been educated some despite her backwoods upbringing, but this child-woman who suddenly spoke like a duchess but behaved like a wanton totally mystified him.

"You're overwrought," he said, and began to rise to his feet, but Emmie grabbed at his velvet jacket with one hand and threw off the sheet with the other. "Look at me, Ian!" she demanded.

Being only a man, Ian looked. Emmie's nude and very slender body reared upward to him. Her breasts, which were small, rounded globes and so utterly touchable, pressed against his chest. Her slim hips fit against the lower part of his body, moving against him in a primitive rhythm which caused his loins to fire and his manhood to harden.

Her hand snaked to his lips, gently running her index finger across them.

"I'm a woman, Ian. I want you, need you desperately. I've loved you since the moment I first saw you. Remember, it was the day Mr. Babcock summoned you here after I'd escaped. I was ill and no doubt looked wretched to you. But you were the most handsome man I'd ever seen. Each time you visited after that I cherished every second with you, going over all you'd said to me, imagining that each touch was special. I know you're married, but I don't care. Make love to me, Ian. Make me yours."

Her luscious mouth graced his in a whisper-soft kiss, which she promptly deepened into something wild and fierce, her tongue forcing his lips to open so she could seek and mate with his. Ian found himself kissing her back, more than aware of the moaning sounds of passion

Emmie made. He felt her hand slip to his aroused shaft and caress him through the material of his trousers.

His body was on fire for her. He'd unwillingly fantasized about being with Emmie, but he'd placed her above other women and decided early on that she was untouchable. Now, however, he realized that Emmie was what she claimed to be: flesh and blood, a woman who desired him. She was his for the taking, and even when she whispered something obscene into his ear, he was still prepared to lower her to the bed and take her.

But something stopped him.

In his mind flashed the image of Bethlyn's face, flushed and shining, her eyes hooded with desire whenever they made love. Lately he'd been curt and much too hasty in his visits to her, but for all his suspicions about his wife, he still wanted to please her physically and to see her face when she climaxed. He'd never felt this need to see passion consume any other woman's face. Ian considered himself to be an ardent and considerate lover, but the other women had meant very little to him, except for Cynthia, of whom he was very fond. But he'd never loved Cynthia or experienced the pain which love can bring before now.

Despite Emmie's hand upon him and her scorching kisses, she couldn't alleviate his pain. For some reason she intensified it. He wanted to go home, ached to be with his wife again and see the ultimate passion flit across her beautiful face and know that he was the cause of it.

Ian drew away from Emmie, but she clung to him. "Ian, come to me. I'm ready for you."

Pulling her arms from around his neck, he managed to lower her to the bed. Perspiration beaded his brow. "Emmie, you don't know what you're doing. You're much too young and inexperienced. I can't do this."

"Don't worry about taking advantage of me," she responded. "I'm not a virgin, if that's the reason you're pushing me away. I know what will please you, Ian. Let me try and make you happy."

If this had been any other woman but Emmie admitting to him that she wasn't a virgin, he wouldn't have been shocked. He was, however, and felt numb by her admission. He'd thought her virginal and innocent, a sweet, trusting young girl. Suddenly, to his eyes, she didn't seem all that young and certainly not an innocent virgin. He sensed that Emmie Gray was more than well versed in the ways of passion.

"Emmie, you're a tempting woman, but someone has to stop this before it goes any further. I have a wife—and I love her. I suggest you forget about me . . ."

"And find someone else?" she broke in, her face distorted in a sneer which was less than becoming to her. "I don't want anyone else but you."

"The Babcocks appointed me to look after you, to see to your needs. I don't want to besmirch their request and memory by doing the unforgivable with you." Was that Ian Briston, notorious womanizer and the infamous Captain Hawk, making such an insane statement? What had happened to him? But he knew the answer when Bethlyn's face once again invaded his thoughts. He loved her, no matter what she'd done.

"You will be looking after my needs if you bed me," Emmie retorted. "I need you, Ian, need you inside me."

At that moment, any infatuation Ian held for Emmie withered away. He realized that something other than Bethlyn kept him from making love to Emmie. Emmie had turned from a shy flower into a vulgar woman. Where was liberty's heroine?

He wondered if he'd built up Emmie in his mind as something she wasn't. This was the real Emmie, the woman who sat nude on the bed, stroking her breasts in an attempt to excite him to take her. The demure and shy Emmie was how she wanted him and other people to perceive her, but that Emmie wasn't real.

She'd lied to him all of these weeks.

He couldn't trust Emmie Gray, either.

Her moaning as she touched herself disgusted him. He wished he was home with Bethlyn, loving her, making a child with her. Not here with this woman, a woman who'd deceived him. He felt like a complete imbecile.

"Good evening," he brusquely intoned, and started for the door. Emmie catapulted from the bed when he stepped into the hallway, not caring that any of the servants might see her, naked and holding on to Ian's coat sleeve, begging him not to abandon her.

"I have no intention of abandoning you," he told her. "I promise to look after you as the Babcocks wished. When you reach twenty, you may do as you want with your money, but until then I'll make certain that you're well cared for, that your bills are paid, and I'll advise you in any capacity you deem necessary. But I won't become your lover."

"You don't mean that. I know you don't. Your conscience is bothering you, that's all. You'll change your mind eventually. I know you will."

He disentangled her hand from his sleeve. "Good night."

For a moment he thought Emmie was going to follow him down the stairs, but she stood on the landing, her eyes filled with some emotion he couldn't name. He shivered.

Seconds later, he climbed into the carriage and closed his eyes, grateful to have escaped Emmie's clutches. He nearly laughed. Emmie's clutches. What an absurd choice of words, but after a few moments' thought, he decided they aptly fit the situation. He'd felt cornered, more than eager to flee her and those grasping hands.

Emmie had deceived him and others into thinking her an innocent. But why?

Ian had meant it when he told her he wouldn't abandon her. He'd do his duty by Emmie in the way the Babcocks had requested, but an uneasy feeling nagged at him. Something wasn't right about all of this.

He silently vowed to himself that somehow he'd discover the mystery of Emmie Gray.

Emmie had just returned to her room, flinging toilet articles to the floor in an unbridled rage when the servant girl arrived to inform her that a gentleman wished to see her.

"Ian has returned!"

Her hope was dashed when the girl said it was Lieutenant James Holmes.

"Tell him I'm asleep and can't—"

Holmes broke off her words by appearing in the doorway, and he dismissed the girl.

"You look quite awake to me," he said, and leered at her, his eyes taking in every aspect of her body.

"What do you want, James? I'm quite exhausted."

"Not too exhausted to risk dallying with a married man."

"Ian Briston isn't happily married. I think he might be having trouble with his wife."

James Holmes reclined on the bed, delighting in watching her. "Ah, yes, I remember the vixen. Bethlyn Briston is a most beautiful and desirable woman. It's no wonder you're jealous. She isn't the sort of rival you can match, Annabelle."

Emmie swiftly turned from the mirror where she stood, admiring herself. "Never call me Annabelle again!" she hissed at him. "Annabelle Hastings is dead, but Emmie Gray is alive and quite ready to do battle with the haughty Bethlyn Briston. I know a few tricks which I doubt she can match."

James laughed. "Yes, I'm certain you do and that Ian Briston will appreciate your special talents, talents you learned from your stepfather, no doubt."

Her face paled, and her mouth trembled. "Don't mention him to me ever again. I hate him."

"Come now, Annabelle. Don't lie to me. I know the truth about you, got it straight from my mother's mouth before she breathed her last breath. She told me how sorry she was for you after she married your stepfather. She wanted to be a good mother to you, but you hated her. At first she thought you disliked her because you thought she was trying to take your own mother's place, since you'd been caring for your stepfather and running the tavern during the time he was widowed. Almost like a proper wife, too." He laughed at her reproachful look.

"I don't want to hear any more of your lies."

"Now don't put your hands over your ears, love. My words can't block out your memories of the nights the old

321

man sneaked into your room and your bed."

"He wasn't old," Emmie denied. "Luther was thirty-eight."

"And a randy thirty-eight he was, too. Or so my dear mother told me. At least he was until you started catering to his baser needs. Tell me, did old Luther teach you everything you know? Or can I take some credit for your ability?"

He was actually salivating, his gaze feasting on her breasts and darting to the light-colored triangle of hair at the juncture of her thighs. She always had this effect on James, whether clothed or not. He wasn't the best of lovers, in some ways Luther had been better, more able to please her.

She now realized that she had enjoyed bedding Luther because he was her stepfather, someone forbidden to her. But she hated him for making her a woman at only thirteen, for changing her from an innocent child to a wanton the day her mother was buried. During the two years when her mother and Luther were married, she knew Luther had looked at her in an odd way, but she'd been too innocent to know what those looks meant.

The night she cried into her pillow for her mother, she learned. It had all started when Luther came into her room and sat beside her on the bed, pulling her into his arms and consoling her. She had wanted to think of Luther as her father, but he was nothing like her real father, who had been kind and gentle.

Luther wasn't always nice to her mother. Sometimes he hit her, leaving bruises on her face and arms. He never hit his stepdaughter. It almost seemed that he went out of his way to please her, but she couldn't forget those strange looks.

That night Luther pleased her in a way she never thought possible. One moment he'd held her like a father would, the next his lips had claimed hers. She remembered trying to break away, growing frightened and confused. But Luther had held her, telling her that she belonged to him now and must do whatever he said or he'd have her carted off to London where there was a school for bad girls who didn't listen to their folks.

Having no other relations and no place to go, she didn't balk when he laid her on the bed and removed her thin nightrail before taking off his own clothes. She didn't know what to make of this hairy but well-built man, and Luther was well endowed in all ways. She didn't know what to make of Luther's hands and lips moving across her body, touching her in places she never knew could feel. But feel she did, and she moaned her pleasure while Luther's fingers buried themselves deep within her. Even now, years later, she blushed to remember how wonderful her body felt when Luther finally entered her. The pain of joining dissolved with each thrust, and every time he kissed her budding breasts, fire grew within her, and with the subsequent explosion, she became Luther's willing slave.

Perhaps she'd been destined to be wanton, but she hated him for making her a woman. He had destroyed her image of herself as a nice little girl, yet she couldn't get enough of him, sometimes teasing and seducing him three or four times a day, until Luther was physically incapable of lovemaking. When he married James Holmes's mother she was jealous of the woman because she was rather pretty and seemed genuinely fond of Luther.

At fifteen, Annabelle's body was alluring and beautiful, and many a young man had vied for her attentions. But she didn't want any of them. She wanted Luther, because he was so smitten with his new wife. Sex gave her a sense of power, and finally she wore down Luther's resistance.

Then James arrived to visit his mother, and she decided she wanted to captivate this handsome young soldier. Being her stepbrother, he was forbidden to her, too. But the two of them made love in the barn on the first night of his arrival. Things, however, turned ugly when Luther found them together and raised his pistol. James was quicker, and tackled Luther to the ground, knocking Luther unconscious. James picked up the pistol and, before the disbelieving eyes of Annabelle Hastings, he killed her stepfather.

His mother died of a heart attack that night, and from

that day on Annabelle belonged to James Holmes.

Even now, it seemed that her body knew he was her master. She moved closer to the bed, hating herself for wanting him, but the man she saw before her wasn't James Holmes any longer but Ian Briston. Ian, Ian, her heart cried when James pulled her down to him, swiftly and violently making love to her. I love you so!

"That was good, wasn't it?" James asked, and lit a cheroot as he leaned against the pillows.

Gritting her teeth at the absurdity of such a question, she agreed it was. Why did he have to ask her? Didn't he know if the sex was good or not? She bet Ian would never have to ask something so stupid.

"You promised me the fifth name," he reminded her.

She sat up and wrapped the sheet around her. "I told you that there is no fifth person. I was wrong."

"I don't believe you, Annabelle, or Emmie. I think there is a fifth man who betrays his king behind a loyalist cloak. General Howe is much impressed with my information and is considering making me a major. You wouldn't want me to lose my promotion by keeping such a valuable secret from me."

"There is no one else," she retorted.

His fingers dug into her arm. "All I need do is arrest Ian Briston to learn the truth."

"No! You're wrong. I swear you are."

"Stop lying. You're an expert liar and actress, my dear, but I know you well. You forget that I'm the one who tutored you in speech and proper manners. You were a countrified little dolt when I took you away from the tavern. You may have all of Philadelphia eating out of your hand with your poor waif story, but I know differently."

"Sometimes I wish you never had involved me in all of this." Emmie gritted her teeth and pulled away from him.

"Liar! Without me all of this luxury wouldn't be yours today. How fortuitous that the Babcocks were old and ill. You don't actually think that I'm going to allow you to live like a queen while *I* can't live in high style. Their deaths and the will, leaving all to you, took me by surprise, but you're going to marry me so that I may profit from your windfall."

This was the first she'd heard of marriage. Never would she marry Holmes, not when she'd fallen so in love with Ian Briston.

"Tell me the fifth name."

"James, you're utterly tiresome. I wish that little strumpet you kept for a while hadn't taken off the way she did. At least she kept you amused so you wouldn't have the time to pester me about a man who doesn't exist."

"Della was amusing," he agreed, and eyed Emmie warily. "But she was grateful for everything I gave to her and taught her. She was more ignorant than you were, but she never lied to me."

Tossing his cheroot on the carpet, he grabbed her again, hurting her. "Ian Briston will never want you. You're too far beneath him. He's married to the daughter of an earl, a woman who can no doubt trace her ancestors back hundreds of years and tell you every little detail about them. I won't allow you to fancy yourself in love with Briston. I demand that you tell me he was the fifth loyalist who was at Simpson House."

"I can't—Ian wasn't there!"

His voice held an ominous threat. "Oh, no? Well, let me see how I can remedy this sudden loss of your memory. Maybe I should pay Briston a visit and tell him how his heroic Emmie Gray is nothing but a whore, that she seduced her own stepfather and then used her wiles on me, her stepbrother, tell him that you're not as young as you look. Perhaps I should also inform him that the real Emmie Gray died during the Indian attack, an attack which I planned to wipe out the settlers on the frontier, that you've spied for me many times, but this time you came to me, begging me to use you as a spy, and assumed Emmie Gray's identity. Do you think he'd even think of bedding you after that?"

"Those are half-truths. I never wanted to spy for you."

"Maybe not at first," he admitted, and leered at her, "but

325

the thought of all you might gain from spying piqued your interest. As it is, you're less than an innocent. I don't want to hurt you, dear Annabelle-Emmie, but I can arrange to have your pretty face ruined so that neither Ian Briston nor any other man will never look at you again except in disgust and pity. I have a great many unsavory friends who take delight in harming others."

"You're a coward, James. You can't do your own dirty work."

"Tell me the name," he demanded, and this time, by the way his hands tightened on her arms, she knew that he might decide to leave her with his own handiwork for a remembrance.

"Ian was there," she said, her voice breaking on his name. "He is the fifth man."

He let her go, and he smiled as he started to dress. "I shall look quite dapper as a major, thanks to you. And don't forget our wedding. I think next week should be soon enough."

When he finished dressing, he kissed the top of her head and left. Emmie's lips curled in disdain, but she flashed her own smile and spoke to the closed door.

"I have some unsavory friends, too, dear James."

When Ian arrived home, he intended to go to Bethlyn, but Annie came out of his wife's room and told him that Bethlyn was fast alseep.

"The missus ain't feeling too good, sir," Annie volunteered. "She done got her monthly and took some of that medicine the doctor gave her for the pain last month."

Never let it be said that Annie wasn't straightforward.

Surprisingly, he wasn't tired, though his mind had dwelled on Emmie Gray's astonishing transformation. He went downstairs to the library and sat at his desk. A piece of paper was opened, and at the bottom of the letter he saw Molly's signature.

A letter from his sister. He couldn't believe it and eagerly scanned the contents to discover it was addressed to him and Bethlyn. Molly stated that she was deliriously happy.

She adored Hans, loved him fiercely. Their wedding had been a quiet but beautiful affair. New York was exciting and there was always a party to attend, though she and Hans preferred staying home together. She ended the letter by saying that she had just learned she was pregnant and hoped her dear brother and sister-in-law would visit when the baby was born.

Ian groaned, unable to believe that he'd soon be the uncle of a child fathered by a German Hessian. Good God, what had Molly been thinking to marry such a man? Then again, he couldn't blame his sister. He'd never told her how he felt about liberty, pretending he was a loyal subject of the king. He supposed it was inevitable that Molly would fall in love with one of his enemies, since he had allowed her to consort with them, having felt that her ignorance protected her.

Well, as long as she was happy.

He examined the letter, noting a spot near the part where Molly wrote about her pregnancy. Was this a tearstain? Had Molly been crying when she wrote this? But no, the spot was fresh.

Bethlyn must have read Molly's letter. Annie had told him about Bethlyn's condition, and now he realized that upon learning of Molly's baby, she had wept in despair. He knew how much she wanted a child and feared she was barren.

A great sadness entered him. He longed for a child, too, but he'd treated Bethlyn with such contempt that day he demanded she produce an heir that he worried she might not want a child of his. What was going to become of them? He didn't think they could go on living in the same house as intimate strangers for much longer.

Another piece of paper on the desk caught his attention when he put down Molly's letter. Recognizing Bethlyn's penmanship, he saw that she was in the process of writing Molly a reply, but near the end of the letter, she'd written a poem expressing the love of a parent for a child.

The verse was two stanzas long, and he felt a bit astonished that Bethlyn's poem was so good. In fact it was superb, filled with a sweet, lovely quality and the right choice of words to convey a mother's adoration and awe for her baby.

"Such a simple and unassuming style, but each word was carefully chosen for the overall effect," he mumbled aloud, having always considered himself to be a fair judge of the literary arts.

Ian shifted in his seat and placed the letter to Molly on the desk; then he opened his desk drawer and withdrew the pamphlet which contained the Dove's poems.

He'd read them many times before, but this time as he read, he paid particular attention to the cadence and choice of words. When he finished reading, he sat far back in his chair, a wide grin on his face and mused aloud.

"I think it's time I meet the Dove. We have a great deal in common."

Chapter Twenty-Two

"Captain Hawk wants to meet the Dove."

Bethlyn's mouth fell open, her face registering surprise and a bit of shock. Her chair creaked when she leaned forward, and she shook her head in bafflement at Thomas Paine. A devilish glint sparkled in his eyes, and he seemed to enjoy her reaction at his announcement.

"But . . . but why?"

"Why not?" Paine answered, adjusting his spectacles. "I can't but wonder why you never thought that Captain Hawk might want to meet the Dove. You are aware, Mrs. Briston, of the sensation your poetry has created in Philadelphia. Suddenly Emmie Gray is nothing more than a passing fancy, while your poems excite the populace with the idea that liberty is within their reach. Apathy for our cause is lessening, and all because of the Dove. I visited Valley Forge recently, and believe me when I tell you that the Dove is a great favorite of the soldiers, as well as General Washington."

Bethlyn's head spun. She knew that her poems were fairly popular, but she had no idea of their impact until this moment. General Washington had read her poems and liked them. This was all too much for her to take in at once, especially the news that Ian was so moved he wished to meet with the Dove.

"Just what did my husband tell you when he saw you, Mr. Paine?"

"Only that he realized that all of the people in

Philadelphia I would be the only one bold enough to have such inflammatory material printed and distributed. Ian and I became friends upon my arrival in Philadelphia a few years ago, and he trusts me to keep his secret, as he and Mr. Gibbons keep mine. After all, someone had to be aware that he is Captain Hawk. In case he never returned from a mission, I was to inform his sister. He wanted me to divulge the Dove's identity to him, but I resisted. That Ian is a rogue to even ask me such a thing.''

Bethlyn breathed a relieved sigh. "Then Ian has no idea that I'm the Dove.''

Paine nodded. "Correct. Trust me when I tell you that he is all fired up to meet you, or rather, the Dove.''

He would be, Bethlyn thought resentfully. First, Emmie Gray and now the Dove had captured his attention, while as for herself, Bethlyn Briston, she might as well not exist. Too caught up in his own obsession, she decided. And why did he need to meet the Dove anyway when he had dear Emmie Gray to fuel his love of liberty with her heroism and her kiss?

Jealousy poked sharp talons within her breast at the lengths Ian would go to find a woman who thought as he did. Why couldn't Ian want her for herself?

"The Dove doesn't want to meet with Captain Hawk.''

Paine looked disturbed. "But you must, my dear. Ian has no knowledge of your identity, so I don't see the harm in meeting him. Personally, I think this situation is most intriguing. Consider the possibilities, if you will, and I guarantee that you'll change your mind.''

She had considered the possibilities, that was the problem. Ian was probably so smitten with the Dove, someone who saw things in the same light as himself, that he'd be more than ready to sweep the Dove into his passionate embrace. Over the last weeks she'd imagined Ian in Emmie Gray's arms; now to think of him with another woman caused her to grit her teeth.

"But the woman is yourself, you silly fool,'' a voice cried in her head. "Make Ian desire the Dove and then reveal your identity. He'll be so mortified and humiliated that he'll give you anything you want, even your freedom if you wish it."

Her freedom. Why had she thought about that? Months ago she'd have given practically anything to be free of Ian, but she'd changed her mind, admitting her love and glorying in his love for her. Then Emmie Gray entered their lives, changing everything. She'd realized that Ian couldn't totally give his heart to her, because he mistrusted her, and would no doubt mistrust her for the rest of his life. She felt very tired of being ignored, of having Ian not see her as a person in her own right but associating her with where she was born and her father. He deserved some humiliation for his callous treatment of her, his disregard.

Coming to her bed each night to get her with child was one thing, that was her duty as his wife. But to touch her, to make her mewl with pleasure like some wanton woman and cause her to think he might still love her, and then leave her to her own devices the rest of the time . . . Well, she'd had enough!

She wasn't like Emmie Gray, thank God, and didn't intend to be. She was herself and also the Dove. As the patriotic poetess, she'd make him want her fiercely and desperately, then she'd prove to him how he'd misjudged her.

She'd have a great laugh at his expense, hurting him the way she'd been hurt. She'd turn and walk away from him, leaving him panting after her, begging her to stay. But she wouldn't look back. At that moment her freedom, if she wanted out of this disastrous marriage, appeared more than assured. If she'd learned one thing about Ian Briston during their time together it was that he was prideful. And a prideful man hated to look foolish.

The corners of Bethlyn's mouth turned upward into a smile, intrigued by the whole scenario she'd played out in her mind, and she directed her attention to Thomas Paine.

"Kindly inform Captain Hawk that the Dove will meet with him, wherever and whenever he chooses."

Bethlyn should have known that Ian would choose Simpson House as their meeting place. Mr. Paine had passed this information to her, telling her that Hawk wanted to meet her at midnight.

331

She'd waited two days to learn this news, growing more than frustrated with the whole charade. They lived in the same house, ate at the same table, and shared the same bed when Ian visited her room, but they inhabited separate worlds, only allowing the other to enter on occasion. Such an existence wasn't to her liking, reminding her of the life-style her parents had led. The only difference was their lack of children.

As she dressed in her room, watching the clock's hands inch toward midnight, a great sadness consumed her and shadowed her eyes. Once again her flux had come and gone. Probably Ian would be more than glad to be rid of her when he realized that she undoubtedly was barren. Not conceiving a child must rest on her shoulders, she decided, having years ago overheard her father rant to her mother that the woman was always to blame if she didn't conceive. He'd screamed to his wife about the lowly girl she'd given him. Where was his son?

Even now the memory tugged at something deep within her, causing tears to form in her eyes which she willed not to fall. She'd been no more than five when her father's harsh words had inflicted a deep, raw wound which had never properly healed.

Where is my son? The words rolled around in her brain, but it wasn't her father's voice she heard, rather Ian's.

Shaking herself to drive away the tormenting thoughts, she pulled on her dark cape and adjusted a black wig she'd found in Molly's wardrobe, one Molly must have worn at a costume ball. Her reflection showed a dark-cloaked and ebony-haired figure, but she still thought Ian might recognize her. It was when she placed a mask, silver and white, on her face that a wide smile expressed her pleasure. Ian would never be able to identify her as his wife now.

She'd fashioned the mask, which she'd also found among Molly's things, into a dove's features, extending the nose outward a bit, shaping it and then covering it with a piece of white satin. Deciding to appear more mysterious, she had sewn silver beads, slanting them at an angle, at the eye holes. Taking in her reflection she saw that she was more than a perfect foil for the black-masked

Captain Hawk.

A giggle escaped her and then when she looked at the clock she saw it was twenty minutes to twelve. Sailing out of her room, she didn't worry about the servants. All of them were asleep at this hour. Ian presented no problem, either. He'd spent last night in Philadelphia, supposedly with Marc and Mavis, because he'd had problems with the design of a new ship, but Bethlyn presumed he was staying at Babcock House with Emmie Gray for company.

Jealousy, tempered with pain, ate away at her.

As she headed into the yard, she mumbled, "Only a few more minutes, Emmie Gray, and then the Dove will steal him away from you."

Before reaching the stables, she pulled off the mask, not willing to endanger young Amos's life with her secret. Seconds later, she mounted her horse and nodded to the loyal stable boy.

"Mayfair is a fine horse," the boy said, and patted the taupe-colored filly's nose. "But you be careful riding at night like this. Your friend who lent her horse to you may blame me if you get hurt or lost. Or worse."

His concern touched her, and she assured him she'd be fine. Cantering out of the barn, she felt grateful to Cynthia for allowing her to borrow Mayfair. Cynthia practically doted on the animal, but when Bethlyn expressed her need of a horse, Cynthia hadn't hesitated though Edgecomb had a stable of fine horse flesh. Bethlyn admired Cynthia for not probing. She hated to lie to her but she couldn't tell her about her plans tonight or admit that she needed a different horse because Ian would recognize a mount from Edgecomb.

The ride to Simpson House was easily accomplished this time because there was no snow. When the house loomed in front of her, she felt uneasy, but she pushed onward and finally halted at the rear. She tethered Mayfair to a hitching post and carefully replaced her mask.

Glancing around, the full moon illuminated the surroundings. She didn't see Ian, and grew apprehensive that he may have decided not to come. But one of the French doors to the parlor blew gently in the cold night

333

breeze and pulled her attention to the interior. A glowing candle beckoned to her, and through the thin lace curtains she made out the tall muscular frame of Captain Hawk.

Entering through the doors, she waited, the light casting flickering shadows across the black-clothed figure and the equally dark hawk-shaped mask. It had been a long while since she'd stood in the presence of Captain Hawk, and she somehow forgot that Hawk and Ian were the same man. All she knew was that the pulse at the base of her throat thrummed like a kitten's purr and her body tingled in his presence, a perverse reminder of all those nights she'd spent in Hawk's arms. For a split second, she longed to throw herself into his embrace but resisted. To him, she wasn't the woman he'd thought was a prostitute or the woman he called his wife. She was a stranger and must remember this.

"You . . . you are Captain Hawk." Purposely she lowered her voice to a husky whisper, emulating Hawk's vocal disguise.

"I am, and you are the Dove." He made a slight bow, and gestured for her to take a seat on the divan while he seated himself across from her.

They sat in silence for a few moments, steadily perusing each other. Finally he shifted in his seat and a smile tipped the edges of his mouth.

"I'm sorry at the strange circumstances involving our meeting, but it is imperative I keep my identity secret."

"I understand, Captain Hawk."

"I'm certain you do now that your poetry is so popular. I heard today that many young lads are enlisting in our fight because of you. The British are less than pleased."

Bethlyn clutched her throat, upset that nameless, faceless young men, probably no older than fourteen, were joining the colonial ranks because of her poetry. She felt responsible for pulling them away from their families at so tender an age to fight, possibly to be killed. The burden of being the Dove was becoming oppressive.

"You should be quite proud of your ability to stir men's souls with your words. You have a rare gift," she heard him say.

"It wasn't my intention to cause children to leave their play for the battlefields, Captain Hawk."

"I appreciate your concern, but nevertheless you are a driving force in our fight for independence. Tell me, why did you write your poetry? What caused you to honor the cause with your talent?"

Bethlyn swallowed, feeling a bit silly to be sitting here in this strange house and speaking to her own husband as if she didn't know him. But what good would it do if she pulled off her wig and mask as she was sorely tempted and prove to him who she was? She'd only make him angry and more convinced than ever that she wasn't to be trusted.

"Someone I love very much opened my eyes to the truth of the war. His cause became mine." Your own cause, you infuriating man! she silently railed.

A long silence greeted her remark. After a while, she fidgeted under his direct and probing gaze. "I wish you'd say something. I don't like being stared at."

He cleared his throat, seeming to come out of a self-induced trance. "Pardon me, but I was thinking how very fortunate this man is to have you on his side."

God help her, she wanted to cry! He hadn't said anything so kind to her in a long time, but she quelled the urge by remembering that Ian didn't realize he complimented his wife, but the Dove.

Rising quickly to her feet, Bethlyn clutched her riding crop in her hand. "I fear I must leave. The hour grows late."

Ian rose and stepped nearer to her and gently lifted her chin to cradle it in his hand. "I should like to see you again."

She nearly refused, but then she remembered her plan to bring Ian Briston to heel. When she spoke, her voice fanned his cheek like a seductive summer breeze. "Yes, Captain, I look forward to our next encounter."

"Tomorrow night at midnight. Here. I eagerly await you, my Dove."

My Dove! Heavens! Didn't the man have a conscience? But she flashed her most seductive smile and hurriedly left. During the ride home she ached to scream her frustration with Ian Briston/Captain Hawk, feeling the cries rise in her throat.

And finally she did.

The next afternoon Bethlyn poured tea for John André in the dining room. She was genuinely fond of André, but this fondness was tempered by her existence as the Dove. He regaled her with stories about how people claimed to know the Dove's identity, and how harried and furious General Howe was over his inability to ferret out the poetess.

"I was charged to investigate the wife of a minister last week, because someone in the congregation saw her scribbling on a piece of paper. Turned out she was only writing a shopping list and the poor woman nearly fainted dead away at the sight of me. This hysteria is doing more harm than good, and in the long run the Dove will regret ever writing a word of poetry whether her identity is discovered or not."

Bethlyn stirred her tea, deeply troubled by what John told her. "I fear you may be right, John," she said after a few moments.

"I've news which may be of interest to you, Bethlyn. Do you recall that loutish Lieutenant Holmes, the one who couldn't keep his eyes off of you at the Shippens's soirée some months back?"

"Yes."

"His body was found yesterday morning in an alley behind an ale house. Knifed through the heart and not a farthing on him."

"How very distressing. Are there any clues as to who killed him? I never liked Lieutenant Holmes, but I do feel sad that he came to such an end."

John shook his head. "No one saw anything or anybody suspicious. Probably murdered for his money by some desperate and hungry colonial."

After John left, Bethlyn forgot about Lieutenant Holmes's unfortunate demise. She had something else to think about today, namely the midnight tryst with Hawk.

*   *   *

She arrived at Simpson House earlier than usual that night, but the candle already glowed in the parlor, inviting her inside. To her pleasant surprise, she found the fireplace had been lighted, bathing the parlor in a warm glow which grew when Hawk presented her with a cup of sweet elderberry wine. The wine tasted delicious and made her think of Tansy Tolliver's brew, which had undone poor Sparrow. Bethlyn chuckled at the memory, amused and a bit guilty for how they'd dealt with her bodyguard on Windhaven.

"I like your laugh," Hawk complimented her.

Bethlyn reddened beneath her mask. When she was alone with Hawk, she almost believed Ian Briston didn't exist. But he did. Ian and Hawk were one and the same, separate identities which completed a whole man. And man he was. That she couldn't forget no matter how she tried.

"Are you always so free with compliments, sir?" she asked somewhat flirtatiously, but her voice held a slight edge.

"I say only what is in my heart."

Arrogant bounder! She turned away from his heated gaze on her so he wouldn't see her pain, then faced him with a brilliant smile on her lips.

"It seems that you don't wish to discuss politics tonight," she said.

"By all means, madam, I do." He'd been standing near the fireplace all of this time, but now he took a Chippendale ladderback chair and placed it before the divan where she sat. Straddling the chair, he folded his arms across the top rung and watched her in all seriousness. "Please tell me your views on the war, from the heart and not some political lip service everyone so freely spouts today."

Taken aback, Bethlyn froze. What did he want her to say? She'd already expressed to him how she felt. She knew precious little about the war other than the reasons behind the fight, a fight she found herself supporting more and more each day.

"I . . . I . . . I feel the war was a long time in coming."

She inwardly cursed herself for stuttering, somehow finding her composure again. "America should have asserted her independence long ago rather than remain tied to a heartless and uncaring country."

Ian nodded. "All true, but you mentioned that someone had changed your thinking. I profess that something else caused you to heed the cry of freedom. What might that have been?"

What did he want of her? She didn't like the way this conversation was progressing. It was almost as if he wasn't interested in her views as much as her personal life, or rather the Dove's personal life. As much as she would like to ignore the question, she wouldn't. She'd tell him flat out what had changed her mind.

"To put it simply, Captain Hawk, I like to think of myself as a bird, a dove, if you will. A creature who is totally free, unhindered by human bonds. In my life I've known many restrictions, and I feel people in America are different than Europeans. There's a delightful wildness about them, they're not afraid to try their wings and fly. Only people with an innate sense of self can dare to rebel against injustice. You are one of those people and must understand how I feel."

"Yes," he said softly. "I do understand. We're very much alike, madam, more alike than I first realized." Reaching out, he took the wine from her and kissed the inside of her wrist before his tongue swirled like a gentle mist on the sensitive flesh, tasting her and branding her as his.

Her silly heart pounded so hard that she was deafened. She ached to glance away from him, to pull her hand away, or make some sort of remark to still the sexual tension which suddenly oozed around them like red-hot lava from an erupting volcano. Feeling desire well within her wasn't what she'd planned. Oh, she had wanted to entice him, to arouse him, but somehow the tables had turned and she found herself falling into a sensuous trap of her own making, because she was weak where Ian Briston was concerned. Weak and too aroused to resist him.

Her jealousy and all of the reasons for coming here fled

when he rose from the chair and willed her to her feet with his piercing gaze. Her will was gone. He held her spellbound as he had done from the first moment she saw him on the *Black Falcon*. Nothing mattered at that moment, nothing but having him love her again. And she didn't care if the man who loved her was Captain Hawk or Ian or King George himself. She only knew that she couldn't hate this man who slowly drew her to the fireplace and undressed her with such arousing skill that, as each piece of clothing slithered down her naked flesh to fall at her feet, she whimpered and clung to him, unaware that they both were still masked.

"Easy, my love," he said, and undressed quickly. "Our need is great and will soon be replete."

Lowering her to a layer of animal furs on the floor, he kissed her like a starving man, devouring her with his lips. His hands upon her naked flesh scorched her in their quest to reach and fondle the lush velvet mound of her womanhood.

Bethlyn's arousal peaked, driving her into a frenzy of wanting when he placed his hard and throbbing shaft into her hand. She stroked him and knew she pleasured him by his husky moans in her ear.

Mind-shattering ecstasy was but a few strokes and touches away. She couldn't wait a moment longer, her body craving his complete possession.

"I . . . I need . . . you now." She could barely speak, but it didn't matter because her body had already conveyed to him her desire.

Skillfully, he parted her legs and slid into her, plundering the soft satin folds of her body. The breath died in her throat. By instinct she arched towards him, clutching him to her, knowing that the end was near, regretting it and aching for it at the same time.

Glorious rapture for both of them came with a sudden powerful thrust. Nothing prepared her for the throbbing surge of his release or for the intense mind-drugging pleasure which washed over her, leaving her drained and suddenly defeated when he gathered her in his arms.

"Next time, my dove, we shall take our time. I promise I

339

will bring you to heights of pleasure you can barely dream."

She closed her eyes, blocking out the masked visage of Captain Hawk. She didn't want to see him or the man behind the mask. A tear fell from the corner of her eye and dribbled down her cheek to land on the fur beneath her.

Her husband, the man she had loved so desperately, had been unfaithful to her. With herself! Dear God, she was jealous of herself.

The worst part of the whole mess was that she still loved him. No matter his treatment of her, she would always love him, but she knew with no uncertainty that she would have to leave him and make a new life for herself. She'd be unable to look him in the face now without remembering this night, of how he had made love to the Dove. Herself!

She waited until he fell asleep, unwillingly memorizing every bronze angle of his handsome face. Then she quietly dressed, slipped outside, and returned to Edgecomb.

Chapter Twenty-Three

Annie removed Bethlyn's gowns from the wardrobe and laid them on the bed. A flurry of activity descended upon the room when Sally ordered the two servant boys who followed behind her, lugging a large trunk between them, to set the trunk on the floor.

"What do you suppose has happened?" Annie asked Sally in a worried whisper after the boys had departed. "The missus ain't said a word about returning to England before today."

Sally shrugged her plump shoulders. "I don't know. The comings and goings of the rich are a mystery to me."

"Pearl said that the master has a woman he meets on the sly. I ain't certain why he'd want another lady when his own wife is so beautiful and kind."

"Ah, just kitchen gossip," Sally uttered, and began to fold the gowns for packing. "I don't believe a word of it. Now hush and get on with your work. I hear Mrs. Briston coming."

Like a small tornado, Bethlyn streaked through the room, issuing orders to Annie and Sally, finding fault with each and every thing they did. Finally Annie burst into tears, unused to being chastised by Bethlyn, and fled before she could disgrace herself further.

Bethlyn looked askance, then she realized she'd been acting like a dictator since early that morning. She hadn't meant to hurt Annie's feelings, or anyone else's, but her pent-up frustration and hurt over what happened at

341

Simpson House the night before had turned her into a miserable and shrewish woman.

A heavy feeling in her heart forced her to sit down on a large, cushioned chair. "You may go for now," she said to Sally, and managed a small smile. "Please tell Annie that I didn't mean to scream at her."

"She knows that, ma'am. Annie will get over her hurt feelings and will have forgotten all about it by day's end. Is there anything else you'd like?"

"Nothing for now. Just please have all my belongings packed by tomorrow night. The ship leaves early the next morning."

"I will, ma'am." Sally curtsied and left Bethlyn to her thoughts.

Day after next she would leave Edgecomb and never return. She planned to visit Mavis before she left, but right now she didn't have the strength to walk down the stairs. Ever since last night she'd felt emotionally and mentally drained, pushing herself to supervise all of the packing and to discover when the first available ship left Philadelphia for London.

She grimaced because the ship wasn't owned by Briston Shipping, a good omen in its way. At last she'd be free of everything that had to do with Briston Shipping and Ian. Before the day was over she'd see a lawyer about contacting Ian for a divorce. She felt cowardly, not wanting to see him and tell him in person. But she didn't think she could bear looking at him again.

Suddenly a great sleepiness overtook her, having not slept a wink last night. Closing her eyes, she drifted off to sleep, and sometime later she dreamed she woke to see Ian standing over her, his arms placed on either side of the chair, imprisoning her.

"Wake up, sleeping beauty."

Instantly she started at the sound of his voice, coming to the realization that this wasn't a dream. The lines on the sides of Ian's eyes crinkled into a heart-stopping smile.

"You've been a busy little bee this morning," he noted, his head inclining to the dresses and her trunk. "Going somewhere?"

342

The frosty contempt in her eyes chased her sleep away. "Please move so that I may get up. I've quite a lot to do, so I'd appreciate it if you wouldn't bother me."

When she reared upward, Ian drew away and watched as she wrenched her toilet articles off of her dresser top to throw them into a small wooden and porcelain-inlaid case.

"You're going to break something," he warned.

"If I do, I'll replace it."

"Well then, have at it."

"What do you want?" she snapped. "I have a great deal of packing to do before the ship sails in two days."

"Bethlyn, where are you going?"

"To London and I shan't return."

Ian quietly studied her, his face showing no expression. "Why didn't you tell me you were leaving?"

Bethlyn chunked the case down on the floor, not caring that her expensive perfume bottles clattered and broke with the fall. "Oh, you horrid man! Why should I tell you anything I plan to do? Since I'm unimportant to you, then my leaving you will have no effect upon you whatsoever. Go to your darling Emmie for comfort when I'm gone, go to the D—" She broke off, feeling ridiculously foolish to even think of saying it. He couldn't possibly seek out the woman he'd been with the night before because she'd be long gone. She hoped to soon stop being jealous of an identity she herself had created. Instead she gave him her back and said, "Find a woman whom you can love."

"But I already have found that woman. Do you want to hear about her?"

He'd come up close behind her, his breath warm on her neck, ruffling a few strands of honey-brown curls. A knifelike pain seared through her at his words. Ian loved another woman. Was it Emmie? The Dove? She didn't want to know, and like a child she placed her hands tightly over her ears and shook her head from side to side. "I don't want to hear any of this!" she cried.

Ian pulled her arms down, clamping them to her sides with his own. "No! I don't want to hear such filth!"

Her protest and the subsequent wriggle to break free met

with the stonelike resistance of his chest. He'd ensnared her with his superior strength. It wasn't fair of him to do this to her, to humiliate her in this way, but she had no choice. Hot tears scalded her eyes to believe how much he truly must hate her.

"You shall listen to me, Bethlyn. What I have to say is of great importance."

"I hate you."

"Right now you do, but hear me out." She heard him take a deep breath, and for a second she wondered if he was going to speak at all, but when he did, his voice trembled for an instant before coming out clear and strong.

"I will tell you about the woman I love. I hasten to speak about her, because she has brought me unbridled happiness and passion, two things on which a man places merit."

"How thrilling," she broke in, feeling his chest shake with suppressed laughter.

"This woman," he continued, "is beautiful and loving, filled with such warmth that she melted my cold heart. I never thought to feel this way about any woman, but, alas, she owns me body and soul. Her lovemaking can be gentle or filled with fire and her total abandon in my arms makes me feel strong and tall and humble. I am her willing captive. Of course, we've had our problems, but I still love her and will always love her."

"Please, Ian—"

"Shh, let me finish. This woman who stole my black and frozen heart sometimes thinks the way I do. Then again, I appreciate her intelligence to make up her mind and follow her own path. I've begun to realize that loving her doesn't mean we must think alike. In some ways her differing views make her all the more appealing to me. I've discovered that two people don't have to be alike to complement the other. For instance, her soft body, her warm essence complements my hardness and cynical view of life. Sometimes it is a man and woman's differences which make them fit together, come together in love. Don't you agree, Bethlyn?"

His voice was warm on her neck, but she felt horribly

344

chilled. Couldn't he see she was dying here? Didn't he care?

"No!" she spat out defiantly, hoping Ian would end this sick game.

His arms tightened on hers like two lengths of steel, rushing the chill from her body. "Ah, I hoped you would agree, but, if not, I hold your opinion in deep regard. You see, Bethlyn, sometimes we are of the same thought, but not always. Still, we're good together. In fact it is our differences which complement each other, because something in you fills a void in me, and you need parts of me to make you whole. We're so opposite that in a perverse way we do complement each other like—" He paused.

"Like what?" she babbled, hating the words for spilling out because now he'd know she was listening to him.

"Like a hawk and a dove," he whispered huskily into her ear.

Bethlyn sucked in her breath. Had she heard him correctly? Dear God, had Ian known all of the time she was the Dove?

She didn't realize that Ian had turned her around until she saw his face, smiling down at her and wreathed with so much love and desire that she started shaking.

"How . . . how did you know that I . . . I was the Dove?"

"I didn't know at first. I read your poems and was impressed," he explained, and gently kissed her forehead. "Then I found a letter you were writing to Molly, and you'd made up an endearing and sweet poem. Well, then I knew that you and the Dove were one and the same. Your style is very easy to recognize, Bethlyn. I decided that I hadn't truly known you. I arranged to meet the Dove because I was curious about why you'd changed your views. Somehow I knew you'd open up to Hawk. I had closed my mind and wrongly accused you of spying."

"And now?" her voice sounded small and weak.

His expression was gentle but filled with pain. "Now I know you weren't guilty, and I can never forgive myself for hurting you. I beg your forgiveness, my darling."

She did forgive him. Nothing seemed to matter any

longer, because she knew he loved her as she'd always known she loved him. Still a doubt nagged at her.

"Are you certain that you knew when you made love to the Dove that she was me?"

"Of course."

"But I disguised my voice and wore a wig. How?"

Ian tilted her chin. "Because of your delicious stutter, my love."

"I really must try and curb my nervousness," she said as Ian pulled her into his arms, ready to claim her lips with a kiss. However, she stiffened and peered suspiciously at him. "What about Emmie Gray?"

"Emmie who?" he asked and, like the hawk he was, he swooped down and kissed her, stilling any further questions and driving any lingering doubts from her mind.

He belonged to her, they belonged to each other. Nothing would ever separate them again.

Carrying her from her cluttered and dress-strewn bedroom, Ian kicked open the door into his and laid her on the large bed.

For the rest of the day and late into the night, the Hawk and the Dove touched and soared together, ever higher, into a bright and brilliant dawn.

Happiness. What a wonderful feeling, thought Bethlyn many times over the next few weeks. She was totally, completely and deliriously happy. Her world revolved around Ian. Each evening she waited for the sound of his footsteps coming up the stairs, and each day she met him on the landing, laughing and clinging to him as he lifted her from her feet and carried her to the bedroom where they didn't come out until the hunger pains grew too strong to resist the tempting delicacies on the dining-room table.

Visiting Mavis, however, was the thorn in her perfect world. She loved Mavis, more than pleased about her friend's pregnancy, but she couldn't help but wish she were the one who waddled around the house and laughed

346

at her own clumsiness as Mavis did. Mavis and Marc reveled in each added pound, each added inch to her waistline. Every slight change in Mavis's figure heralded that glorious moment when she and Marc would welcome their first child into the world and their lives.

One night Bethlyn lay in Ian's arms. Their bodies were still flushed with passion, but both of them knew that their rest would be brief. The fires still flared within them, and with each act of love, the flame intensified instead of dwindling.

But Bethlyn was unusually quiet, and Ian was troubled. "Don't you feel well?" he inquired, and kissed the tip of her nose.

"Yes, that's the problem." Her voice shook. "I'm in perfect health, and I shouldn't be. By now, I should have morning sickness and be growing as large as a toad, but I'm not. I've . . . failed . . . you."

She gulped back a sob, and Ian gathered her closer to him while he looked into her eyes. "Bethlyn, I love you, love you. A child would be wonderful, but when the time is right, God will grant us this gift. You haven't failed me. Perhaps I'm the cause of your inability to conceive."

"Oh, no," she quickly disagreed. "Not you, never you. You're so virile and masculine that the fault must lie with me. My father said—"

"Forget your father! The man was wrong about many things, and I don't want to know what he said. He was wrong not to love you, but I'll make up to you for all those years he ignored you, and for the ones I had a bride and didn't care. God, Bethlyn, I love you more than life itself. I want you to conceive our child, but I want you more." His mouth moved to her lips. "I know something we can do." His voice sounded silky smooth.

"What?" she asked, already seeming to know.

"We can practice making a baby until we get it right."

"Hmm, I've always heard that practice makes perfect."

"Let's see if there's truth in that old saying." With that, he brought her atop him, and she immediately straddled his thighs. Her body was ripe and ready for him, and within seconds, he slipped effortlessly inside her.

"I'd like to practice a long time tonight," Bethlyn whispered thickly, her body catching fire.

"Ah, my dove, nothing would give me greater pleasure." And nothing would.

"I'll be gone for a few months, Marc, so I'll leave the company in your care during my absence. Remember to contact Eli Templet about that matter I briefed you on the other day."

Marc nodded and stood up, shoving his hands in his jacket pockets as he waited before Ian's desk. He looked less than thrilled. "I wish I was going with you."

"Mavis needs you. You should be with your wife at this time, not off sailing the seas with me."

"God, but I miss the *Black Falcon*!"

"So do I, but within the week I'll be at Windhaven, ready to set sail. The sea is in my blood, and I've been away for too long." Anticipation glowed on Ian's face.

"What about Bethlyn?" Marc asked. "How will she take this decision to leave?"

Ian grinned. "She's coming with me."

"How did she talk you into that?"

"She didn't. I asked her. I guess I'm just smitten with my wife and can't bear to leave her for too long a time. Needless to say, she'll remain on Windhaven when I take out the ship."

Marc regarded him with a bit of awe. "So the notorious and fearsome Captain Hawk has finally been tamed."

"Seems that way," Ian capitulated and flashed a smile. "Now if only I can tame my rebellious bride."

Informing the house servants that they were going on an extended holiday, Bethlyn and Ian sailed away from Philadelphia on the *Bethlyn B.* with a skeleton crew of Hawk's most loyal men.

With the wind blowing in their faces, and their hearts filled with the exhilaration of love, they clung to each other and watched the setting sun bathe the island of

348

Windhaven in brilliant golds and reds as the ship drew nearer to land that afternoon.

Ian met her gaze, and his face was filled with strength and an inner peace. "We've come through troubled waters, but nothing can harm us ever again, Bethlyn. Nothing and no one can hurt or separate us."

Though he'd soon leave her to take out the *Black Falcon*, risking his life for his country, Bethlyn somehow knew he would return, and unsurpassed joy burst within her.

Leaning against him, she raised her head and looked into the eyes of the man she loved more than her own life and said, "We'll be together always. Forever."

A dark cloud suddenly appeared and skidded across the sky, but Ian and Bethlyn were unaware of it. Their attention was centered on each other.

Chapter Twenty-Four

Thomas Eversley rammed himself into the woman who writhed beneath him on the bed. Instantly he spilled into her, so overcome by the notion that he made love to Bethlyn that he couldn't control himself. But all too soon he opened his eyes and reality intruded. The woman staring up at him didn't possess brown eyes whose centers were rimmed with gold. He saw not Bethlyn but Grace, a young woman he'd picked up off a London street and taken back to Woodsley in the carriage which bore the Earl of Dunsmoor's coat of arms.

Rolling off her, he didn't bother to stifle his groan of disappointment at his bed partner, unwillingly recalling how the wench had gazed in awe at the lavishly appointed interior of the carriage. Her awe was nothing in comparison to her astonishment when her eyes beheld Woodsley.

"I'm really going to stay here with you?" she'd asked as he led her to one of the many lavishly appointed guest rooms. He'd told her she'd stay as long as she did what she was told, advising her that anything she wanted, whether clothes or food, would be hers. She had only to ask. However, she must please him in all ways.

Thomas shifted to his side, silently admitting that Grace did please him only because she resembled Bethlyn and eased his physical needs. He'd been more than astonished and happy to discover that Grace was a virgin when he took her, and this somehow endeared her to him.

He never questioned her about her past or even if she had a family. He didn't want to know anything about her, caring only that she avail herself to him when his thoughts centered on the Earl's daughter. But now he was growing restless and bored with Grace for the same reason he'd originally bedded her. She wasn't Bethlyn Briston.

"You were very good," Grace said, and snuggled near to him.

Lying wench! he thought to himself. He'd come too soon for his own liking, but he was never able to control himself when he imagined that Bethlyn was the woman beneath him.

"We should see to our guests." Thomas rose from the bed and began to dress, missing the flicker of hurt which passed across her face. "I want you to be especially nice to Lord Detweiller. His purse is very large, and he is known for his generosity to beautiful women."

Grace sat up in alarm, her eyes wide. "But, Thomas, you told me I'm not like the other women here. I don't want to be nice to him, as you say. I only want to belong to you."

"And you do, pet." He stroked her cheek, his touch calming her. "I would prefer the women I bed not to have lain with too many men. Sexual diseases are repugnant, and I dread contracting one. However, you can be accommodating to men in other ways, Grace. Men like Lord Detweiller, who have a preference for variety in their lovemaking, want something a bit more stimulating and will pay handsomely for a woman to please them in a way their prim and proper wives will not."

Thomas stopped speaking for a second and traced her lips with his fingertips. "Your mouth is lovely and finely made. I'm certain you'll please His Lordship with the special talent you reserve for me."

Grace immediately understood and tensed. "I'll do whatever you want, Thomas, but I won't like it."

"As long as you do it well, my dear."

While he dressed, he stood by the window and glanced down at the garden and grounds below him. Superbly dressed men and fashionably attired young ladies strolled prettily in the springtime sun, sipping champagne and

351

eating canapés presented to them by well-trained servants. Mentally he calculated how much richer he'd be after dark. That was when all of the young ladies would parade into the sumptuous drawing room where the Earl and his wife had entertained in grand style at one time.

Thomas couldn't help but to smirk at the look of horror on the earl's face if the man rose from his grave and saw what changes had been wrought at his beloved Woodsley. The house and grounds were still unbelievably beautiful, but Thomas had added gambling in the ballroom and turned the drawing room into an auction room of sorts.

Each evening wealthy and titled gentlemen traveled from London or other distant cities to partake in a game of faro and then to bid on the beauty of his choice. Thomas wondered why he hadn't thought of such a delightful and easy way to increase revenue sooner. Grace had mentioned the auction part to him, having read about how the barbaric Americans auctioned off their slaves. She made some sort of a comment about how awful that must be for the women, and, thus, the idea took root in Thomas's brain.

He'd enlisted the help of Bartholomew Perkins, his able secretary, to search for the most beautiful and willing women he could find. Within a matter of days, Perkins appeared at Woodsley with twenty women, and Thomas slapped the man on the back, declaring he had wonderful taste where beauty was concerned. Of course many of them were young, some no older than fourteen, having lived most of their lives in abject poverty and brutality. A few looked wretched as they stood in Woodsley's drawing room in their raggedy clothes and patted down strands of hair which hadn't been washed in months, maybe even years. Others were from decent but financially strapped families, but Thomas had a keen and perceptive eye. Once these girls were thoroughly washed and dressed and tutored in the art of conversation and manners, any man, be he a duke or a prince, would pay a high price to bed them.

Some old crone of a serving woman had refused to follow Thomas's orders to clean them up and see to their rooms. His fist on her face turned her into a most docile creature.

He had Grace explain to them what was required, and no one expressed horror or outrage. Evidently these girls had had some experience with men, because after they'd been auctioned off to the highest bidders that first time, Thomas heard no complaints from them or from the esteemed gentlemen they serviced.

The general public didn't know what happened at Woodsley. Only the richest and most discreet gentlemen, those with a penchant for unusual entertainment, ever entered Woodsley's doors. Woodsley had been transformed into a high-class brothel for two months now, but the money garnered from this enterprise had already made Thomas into a very wealthy man. No matter that he'd forced the earl to sign over all of his holdings and wealth to him, Thomas could never get enough money.

When he went downstairs his manservant informed him that a gentleman waited in the study for him.

"He doesn't seem to know about what goes on here, sir," the servant whispered.

"Who is he?"

"Sir Jeremy Smithers."

Thomas didn't suppress his groan. Milksop Smithers, the grandson of Penelope Evans, wanted to speak with him. God, what now? Thomas wondered. But a spark of hope ignited in him that if Jeremy had returned, then Bethlyn might have come back also.

Without hesitating further, Thomas greeted Jeremy and offered him a seat.

"I suppose you've heard about *Nightingale*," Jeremy said and placed his hands on his knees.

Thomas nodded. "I was informed that the ship was captured. You seem no worse for wear, considering the ordeal. How is Lady Bethlyn? Shall I see her soon?"

"When I last saw her, she was fine and quite happy in the arms of her husband. Bethlyn and Ian Briston are very much in love with each other."

"How nice." Thomas was far from pleased over this news. He'd expected Briston to send Bethlyn back to

353

London post haste, already having divorced or annulled the marriage. Then Thomas would be free to pursue the girl and marry her. Thomas couldn't stand thinking about Bethlyn with that barbaric colonial.

"I would like to speak with the earl and tell him how Bethlyn fares," Jeremy told him.

Thomas turned a concerned face to Jeremy. "I should like to grant your request, son, but His Grace isn't up to seeing guests. His health varies from day to day. And today is one of his poorer days."

"But what about all of the people who are here? I know a great many of the men, but the women are strangers to me. If the earl is ill, then why does he have guests milling about the place?"

Thomas silently cursed Jeremy for his probing questions. Why didn't the milksop return to his grandmother and leave things alone? He hid his aggravation behind a polished but cool smile. "His Grace had invited them before he took ill. He expressed his dismay over his illness, but he wants the gentlemen and ladies to enjoy themselves."

Jeremy didn't question Thomas, because he knew that Nathaniel Talbot had been ill for some time, but still he didn't trust Thomas Eversley.

"Now, Jeremy, my lad, I hate to cut short our conversation, but I must look after the earl's guests."

Jeremy stood up, and Thomas took him by the elbow, literally steering the young man from the room and into the Entrance Hall. "I do hope you visit again," Thomas told him, and shook his hand.

Suddenly Jeremy found himself outside, vaguely aware that a servant had appeared from seemingly nowhere to open the door for him.

"Strange, very strange," Jeremy mumbled, still in a daze when he got into his aunt's phaeton. But he didn't know what it was that bothered him.

After Jeremy's departure, Thomas wasted no time in ordering his man to pack a trunk for him. He didn't know how long he'd be gone, but he summoned Perkins and advised him on how to handle Woodsley and the office during his absence.

He'd just pulled on his warm gloves when Grace appeared in his room.

"Finished with Lord Detweiller so soon?" he asked nonchalantly as if Grace performed such an intimate act for men every day.

"Thomas, I did what you asked, but I hated it." She shivered, overcome by the memory of the obese man's florid face when he climaxed and the way she'd been so disgusted that she almost threw up on him. "I knew nothing about sex when you found me. You taught me everything. I want to belong just to you. What I did for Lord Detweiller has cheapened what we do together. I want to love only you in that way."

Thomas glanced sideways at her, barely raising an eyebrow. "Did Lord Detweiller pay you well?"

Grace took a large bag of gold and laid it on his bed. Thomas opened the bag and emptied it. A shower of bright round coins spilled onto the counterpane. He grinned his satisfaction. "I see he was more than generous, Grace. As long as you received such a bountiful reward, then you have nothing to complain about."

"I don't want the money! I want you, Thomas."

The desperation he heard in her voice angered him. Grace was going to present a problem, and at the moment he didn't want to deal with her. She'd become too dependent on him, that was it. He must sever the ties thoroughly and completely, force her to accept her lot in life, otherwise, she'd be of little use to him here.

He was totally unprepared for Grace to throw herself at him suddenly, holding on to him as if she were about to drown. He'd warned her over and over that she wasn't to touch him unless he told her to. Apparently, Grace was so overwrought by the service she'd performed for Detweiller that she wasn't thinking clearly.

"Take me with you," she begged. "I don't want to stay here without you. I can't bear for any man to touch me but you."

Thomas detested pleading of any kind, and this was the last straw as far as he was concerned. Pulling her off him, he went into the hallway and shouted for Perkins, who immediately appeared.

Grace had followed after him, and Thomas yanked her forward, causing Perkins to break the woman's fall by latching his arms around her waist.

"See that this wench is kept busy," he ordered Perkins. "I have other things on my mind but a clinging, sobbing bitch who fancies herself more than a whore."

"But, Mr. Eversley, I thought Grace belonged exclusively to you."

"Not any longer. She belongs to any man who'll pay the price for her 'special talent.' And I warrant there are many men here today who'll seek her out on Lord Detweiller's recommendation alone. Take her to the gold room and strip her to make certain she doesn't run away. And, Perkins, when she's finished with her many patrons, you may avail yourself of her service for nothing."

Thomas saw that Perkins was already aroused by this generous gift. "Come on, Grace, let's go," Perkins ordered, and almost had to drag her along the hallway.

"Thomas, please, no!"

Grace's pitiful cries didn't move him. She'd suited his purpose and now she must earn her keep. He turned a deaf ear and headed down the north corridor to the Painted Hallway and into the open colonnade of the Entrance Hall. His trunk was already in the large coach, and he sank into the thick velvet upholstered seat, heaving a huge sigh.

Women were a great bother, he decided. His late wife had nearly driven him out of his mind, always complaining about various and sundry things until he felt immense gladness at her death. He hadn't lived with a woman again until he brought Grace home like a little kitten in need of food and attention. But he hated clinging, whining women, and after today, he didn't doubt that Grace would ever cling to him or expect preferential treatment again.

However, he didn't mind in the least if Bethlyn Briston clung to him. The image of her beautiful face and body as he lowered her to a bed and drove himself deep within her caused him to instantly harden. He wished Grace was there to relieve him of his desire, but he did the next best thing and fondled himself.

He vividly pictured Bethlyn on her knees before him, pleasuring him the same way Grace always did, and it was this image which undid him.

A large shudder of absolute ecstasy intensified his release, and he moaned in pleasure, forgetting everything, until a warm stickiness seeped into his pants.

Thomas muttered a profane curse at his loss of control. He wanted to change clothes, but in the coach that was impossible. He felt appeased somewhat that his cloak would cover the wet spot and hide his weakness from inquisitive eyes.

"I'll have you yet, Bethlyn Briston," he vowed aloud, feeling Bethlyn was to blame for his problem. "And when I do, your body will be the willing receptacle of my lust."

Chapter Twenty-Five

The next few weeks on Windhaven were the most wonderful and memorable of Bethlyn's life with Ian. They were never separated for long, and when they saw each other, even after an hour's separation, it was as if they had been apart for months, delighting in touching and feasting their eyes on the other's face.

"You two are the most lovey-dovey pair I ever did see," Sparrow commented one afternoon, finding them wrapped in a tender embrace on the beach. "If you stop hanging all over each other, you might be surprised to find that you can walk by yourselves."

"Haven't you ever been in love, you old sea dog?" Ian asked, barely taking his eyes from Bethlyn's face for a second to pose the question.

"Aye, I have, but sometimes a man has to do other things besides sitting in the warm sunshine and making cooing noises to a beautiful woman. Eh, Captain Hawk?"

Ian turned his full attention on Sparrow, a great sadness stealing across his face at the hidden meaning behind the man's words. Nodding at Sparrow, the older man turned away and meandered down the windswept beach. When he was a dot on the horizon, Ian tenderly kissed his wife's mouth.

"You're leaving soon." Bethlyn's voice caught in her throat.

"Yes."

She gave a trembling sigh, finding herself held more tightly against Ian's chest. "I knew things couldn't go on like this much longer. Such a paradise can't last forever."

"I'll be back before you've had sufficient time to miss me," he assured her.

"I shall miss you five minutes after the *Black Falcon* leaves Windhaven." She was silent for a few seconds. "You want to go, don't you?"

"Yes, I want to go because I've missed the sea, but no, I hate leaving you even for a minute. Let's not use our last hours together talking about my going away." His lips caressed the lobe of her ear, then trailed to the tops of her enticing breasts which swelled above the thin orange-and-white calico dress's bodice. A warm, wet mouth sensuously grazed her flesh, and Bethlyn felt her body responding to his.

Without a further word, Ian lifted her from her feet and carried her into their small cottage, which had become more of a home to them than Edgecomb. Up the stairs he carried her, his lips in contact with hers. As one, they fell upon the bed and, in each other's arms, they found heaven.

Two days after the *Black Falcon* sailed away, Bethlyn had explored every inch of Windhaven, baked four pies, and watched young Nate consume two of them by himself, visited with Tansy and Jack Tolliver, then returned to the cottage, and, like a whirlwind let loose, cleaned and mopped the three rooms until they shone. She even rearranged some of the furniture. But when the third day arrived, she had nothing to do and was so bored she wanted to scream—and so lonely for Ian she felt like dying.

Tansy arrived and found her sitting listlessly on a chair in the kitchen. "You look as happy as a seagull who's lost its wings."

Bethlyn barely racted to Tansy's comment except to say, "I feel lost."

"Goodness, child, you're much too young and pretty to sit here moping over your husband. Captain Hawk is tied to the sea, and you're going to have to accept that. He's a lot like my Jack, who can sit at home during the long months of winter, but when the frost starts thawing and the sun comes out, I can see him getting restless. I never say anything to him, because Lord knows I can't stop him from getting in his boat and taking off somewhere. One time I screamed at him that if he went off again, I wouldn't be here when he got back."

"Did he go?" Bethlyn asked, growing interested.

"Got right in his boat and sailed off, never said a word to me."

"And you were here when he returned."

Tansy laughed. "Of course I was. Where else would I go after I'd been married to that man for thirty years? I'd be lost without him."

Sitting on a chair next to Bethlyn's, Tansy patted her hand and gave her a motherly smile. "You'll do fine, Beth. Before long, Hawk will be back. His privateering is important to our country."

"I know, but I still miss him."

A devilish gleam danced in Tansy's eyes. "Sometimes I used to imagine stowing away on Jack's boat, hiding somewhere until we were far out, and then popping up to surprise him. But knowing how calm Jack is, he probably wouldn't flick an eyelash, but ask me to help with the rigging." Her gaze grew soft. "Since he's older now and only goes to Philadelphia a few times a month with the fish, I see enough of him. Sometimes too much, because, like most men, they get underfoot now and then. But I love him and accept that wild streak in him which needs to break free, the same way you must do with Captain Hawk."

Bethlyn's spirits lightened suddenly. Tansy had placed the seed of a most intriguing and interesting suggestion in the fertile garden of Bethlyn's mind. Now all she had to do was wait until the *Black Falcon* returned to bring it to fruition.

Ian returned home within three weeks. The moment he and Bethlyn embraced, they walked along the beach to the cottage and didn't appear again until three days later. During one of their hours together after their bodies were satiated from lovemaking and they'd drunk a bottle of

360

wine by candlelight, Ian told Bethlyn that the *Black Falcon* had captured one of the British Navy's most prestigious and well-outfitted warships.

He gloated that his crew had no trouble capturing the heavy *Jupiter* because the *Black Falcon*'s lightweight and sleek lines accounted for swiftness on the high seas.

"Do you think you'll ever give up privateering?" she asked, struck by Ian's animation as he explained the ensuing battle. She remembered how frightened she'd been when he'd attacked *Nightingale* and decided that fear mustn't be as great when you're certain of victory. His excitement was contagious, and she found herself not dreading the moment he sailed away from Windhaven again.

"One day when this war is over," he answered.

Ian pulled her against him, and she buried her fingers in his chest hair. Kissing the top of her head, he said, "I missed you so much, Bethlyn. This seemed the longest mission I've ever made. I hate leaving you again so soon, but I have to set sail day after tomorrow. There's a large amount of British ships crossing the Atlantic suddenly, most probably because I haven't been as active for the last few months, and we both know why."

A gentle laugh fanned the strands of her hair. "England is transporting a great deal of arms and supplies for her men and they must be confiscated. Sometimes it seems we're fighting a losing battle against so much might and ready munitions. If we win this war, it will be by sheer willpower and self-sacrifice."

She'd never heard Ian sound so discouraged. "Didn't you just tell me you'd confiscated an important ship? Why do you doubt victory now?"

"Because for each ship I take, two slip by me. I can only hope that other American privateer ships get a crack at them. I've heard a rumor that the French may offer help to us and pray it is true. Otherwise, this war may drag on indefinitely."

Lifting a hand, she tenderly stroked his brow, wiping away his frown and his doubt. "Let's forget about the war for now, Ian. I don't want to think about it at all."

"Hmm, I don't, either," he agreed, and kissed the pearly

tip of one of her breasts. "I want to forget that I have to leave you soon."

Bethlyn gave a little moan of pleasure, aching to tell him that they weren't going to be separated again. But all thought died when he parted her legs and she welcomed him inside her.

They had agreed that he'd leave without telling her farewell.

In the hour before dawn, Bethlyn felt Ian kiss her and leave the bed to dress in the darkness. As he dressed, she could feel his eyes on her, watching her sadly, but she wasn't sad this time. She felt a mischievous grin tugging at the corners of her mouth and joyous laughter welling inside her, but she willed herself to lie quietly.

When she heard the bedroom door close, she waited a few minutes before getting up and hurriedly pulled on a thin dress for the warming days and threw on a shawl to protect herself from the cool nights. Then she grabbed a small carpetbag she'd hidden beneath the bed and left the house.

She knew the way to the cove where the *Black Falcon* was hidden by heart, having no trouble finding her way in the darkness. She also knew that before a voyage Ian and his men ate a hearty breakfast in the galley. This would give her time to sneak onto the ship and stow away in the captain's quarters to hide in the smaller adjoining room and make her appearance when the ship was a great distance from Windhaven.

Would Ian be angry with her? she wondered, and decided that he would be, but when she'd kiss him, her lips promising future delights, he'd be more than pleased she'd stowed away.

Nearing the ship, Bethlyn saw in the torchlight and lanternlight that all was deserted on deck. No one was about when she made her way onto the ship and down the darkened corridors to Ian's cabin, but she could hear male voices and laughter coming from the galley.

As she entered the room in which she'd spent so many wondrous and love-filled nights in the arms of Captain

Hawk, her mouth twitched with delight, and her gaze immediately centered on the unrumpled bunk.

Hearing a noise down the corridor, she quickly scooted into the small room where she'd stayed when she nursed Ian back to health after stabbing him and settled herself on the small cot. She knew she wouldn't sleep in here tonight.

Ian was indeed angry. He'd just entered his cabin to have Bethlyn pop out of her hiding place, scaring the wits out of him. "What in the name of God are you doing here?" he cried, and his tone of voice sounded less than warm, but Bethlyn ignored it.

She smiled, unwittingly beguiling him with her beauty and the sweetness of her kiss when she rose on tiptoe to reach his lips. "I couldn't stand to be parted from you an hour longer, Ian. I hate upsetting you, but aren't you just the teeniest bit pleased to see me and know that tonight you won't have to sleep alone in your cold bed?"

He wanted to be angry, she could tell. But a grin stretched across his handsome face, and in a moment she found herself ensnared in his arms and then in his bed.

"Our agreement is that when an enemy ship is spotted, you're to come into the cabin and stay in here, even if fighting starts." Ian gulped down his morning coffee and buttered a biscuit before devouring it. "You do understand, Bethlyn."

Bethlyn lazily stirred her tea, too contented and still flushed from last night's lovemaking to concentrate on anything but Ian's face and hard, bronzed chest. She was fascinated at the way his muscles rippled with each movement, growing aroused again. "Hmm, what did you say?" she asked, her eyes a smoky brown.

"You're to stay in the cabin if fighting breaks out."

"Ah, yes, I will."

Ian rose from his chair and stood beside her and cupped her chin. "Chase that wanton look from your eyes, wench. I have a great deal of work to do today and can't make the time for another toss in the bed with you."

"Why, such a thought never crossed my mind." Pretending to be offended, she made a mock pout.

"Insatiable hussy. You're going to be the death of me yet, but never let it be said that Captain Hawk ever turned down a willing woman, even if she is his wife."

To Bethlyn's surprise, Ian lifted her from the chair and falling to the bunk with her amid husky and seductive laughter, he somehow managed to find the time.

Almost four weeks later, the *Black Falcon* had captured three British frigates. Two of the battles had been unsettling for Bethlyn, who waited them out in the cabin, but they amounted to brief skirmishes. The ships's goods were confiscated and the British crew set adrift in longboats.

However, three days after the last attack, Bethlyn was still shaken and offered a prayer of thanks that two of Ian's men were only wounded in the foray. The British crew wasn't as lucky and didn't survive. It was only now that Bethlyn began to realize how awesome was the *Black Falcon*'s sea power, and that Captain Hawk gave no quarter to his enemies.

Ian, sensing her disturbance over the last sea battle, had decided to return to Windhaven. He'd just given the command to head for the island when Sparrow spotted a ship in the distance.

"Damn," he muttered softly, feeling rather unsettled himself and not eager to engage the enemy so soon after the last confrontation. Raising his spy glass, he located the approaching ship. "She isn't a warship," he shouted up to Sparrow in the crow's nest. "Still, she is British, and if she comes closer, we must take her."

"Aye, aye, Captain," Sparrow called and slithered down the pole as Ian ordered his men to prepare for a possible battle.

The noise of running feet and the sound of artillery being loaded alerted Bethlyn to imminent danger. She groaned and looked out of the window in Ian's cabin, hating the thought of another fight. Ian had told her they'd be returning to Windhaven, and she wanted more than anything to be there now.

Spotting the ship, she watched as the dark speck on the horizon grew increasingly larger, and, with it, her fear. The ship fired a cannon boom at the *Black Falcon*, she supposed in the hope of running them away, but the answering boom which echoed from the bowels of the ship beneath her feet, clearly expressed another sentiment.

Bethlyn braced herself for the inevitable, waiting for the other ship to fire again. It didn't. As the ship drew ever closer, she was finally able to make out the flags on the masthead. She was a British passenger ship for certain, but also something else.

"My God!" she whispered, and wondered if Ian realized that this ship was the *Jessica*, named after the woman who'd stolen her father's heart and the woman who was Ian's mother. Only her father, the earl, ever traveled on this ship. What if her father was on the ship now, at this moment? Suppose he were coming to America to see her, to atone for the wrongs he'd committed against her? Bethlyn didn't dare hope, but hope surged through her nonetheless and she rushed from the cabin onto the upper deck and discovered all of the men had pulled on their masks, and Ian in the guise of Captain Hawk appeared more formidable than any of them.

She pulled at his shirt-sleeve, and Ian didn't hide his aggravation at finding her above deck. "That's my father's ship, the *Jessica*," she exclaimed with bright eyes, filled with anticipation. "You mustn't destroy her. He could be killed and I couldn't bear wondering for the rest of my life what he might have said to me."

"I have no intention of attacking the ship, Bethlyn. In fact, they've raised the white flag. If your father is aboard, then you should hide in the cabin until I hear him out. He can't see you, otherwise, my privateering days will end with me dangling from a rope." Ian sounded patient, and she couldn't argue with him. She turned and left the deck to find a place by the doorway and waited until the *Jessica* drew up to the *Black Falcon*.

The grappling hooks connected the two ships, and Ian and his men nimbly jumped the distance, easily capturing the booty and crew of the *Jessica*.

An hour later Bethlyn was still waiting. What was happening? Had Ian found her father? What would he say to her when they met again after all of these years? Father, I love you. Daughter, I love you. She shook her head. No, her father would never admit his feelings in such a straightforward manner. Still, he must have some feelings to have come all of this way.

Her palms perspired, and she wiped them on the pants she'd borrowed from Amos, perfectly aware that Ian didn't care for her male attire, but she felt more at ease wearing the pants and the white ruffled shirt than a dress on board ship with an all-male crew. The time seemed to drag, and when she didn't think she could stand another moment of waiting, she saw Ian grab a rope from the *Jessica's* masthead and swing across to land steadily on his feet like a jungle cat.

Even behind his mask, she sensed an eager anticipation in his steadfast gaze, which never wandered from the man who now boarded the *Black Falcon* by way of the plank.

Bethlyn's heart sank when she recognized the man as Thomas Eversley. Where was her father?

Apparently the earl wasn't on board, for minutes came and went, and Eversley perched on a water barrel like a frightened bird whose nest has been disturbed. Droplets of sweat rolled down his face and into his fine lace cravat. But then again, not many men could sit, unmoving and unafraid, beneath the ominous countenance of Captain Hawk.

Bethlyn should have felt sorry for Thomas Eversley, but she didn't. He'd been responsible for transporting women to the Colonies, and she thought he was a disgusting man and wanted to face him and berate him for what he'd done, but he'd recognize her. Then the idea hit her and she ran back to the cabin.

Ian surveyed Thomas as if he were a bug about to be squashed by a boot heel, and as he paced, circling the frightened man, he didn't hide his contempt. "Delivering any women this time, Eversley?" Ian asked in his raspy tone of voice.

"No, no, Captain Hawk. How do you know my name?"

"I know the names of all the snakes who inhabit the

366

king's garden. And you are the most loathsome one of them all."

"I . . . I'm sorry you feel that way, Captain Hawk." Thomas's face was horribly pale, and his skin looked pasty and clammy.

Ian bent down, and Thomas quivered for a second at the black-masked bird and the hate-filled eyes behind it. "Are you going to puke, Eversley? Are you afraid that I will end your wretched life here and now?"

Lifting his sword, Ian ripped away the buttons on the front of Thomas's jacket. Thomas flinched, seemingly expecting the blade to tear through his shirt and lance his chest. The terror etched on his face was clear for all to see, and the crew of the *Jessica* did when Sparrow and Ian's men led them to the railing.

"Please, please . . ." Thomas could barely mouth the words.

"Yes, Eversley?"

The blade's tip rested on his pounding heart, a cold sweat broke out on Eversley's forehead, all too aware of the condemning eyes upon him. He'd been the one who'd ordered the white flag to be raised.

"I beg for . . . my life, sir."

"And should I spare you?"

Opening his mouth to speak, he was interrupted by the sensually soft, husky-sounding voice which came from the doorway. "Do spare the man's life, Hawk. He isn't worth killing."

All eyes turned to see the dark-haired woman with the dovelike mask on her face. Surprise rocketed through Ian, but no one but Bethlyn noticed. Thomas sat with his tongue hanging out and cast her a pleading look to save him.

Moving forward, Bethlyn was all too aware of the stares from the crew of the *Jessica*. Ian's men were used to her parading around the ship in pants and shirt. But these men were startled, yet quite unlikely to remove their gazes from the rounded curves of her buttocks. She hadn't known why she'd packed the clothes, the wig, and the mask, before leaving Edgecomb, transporting them to Windhaven and then the ship. Now, however, she was glad she'd hastily thrown them in her carpetbag. All the more fun to taunt Thomas Eversley.

She somehow knew that if Ian's sword hadn't imprisoned Thomas, the man would have thrown himself at her feet, begging for mercy.

"You best stay out of this, Dove," Ian warned in a silky voice. "I have plans for our guest."

I know you do, her eyes seemed to say. And she wanted to avoid Ian's vengeance. She guessed his hatred of Eversley ran deep, probably stemming from incidents related to her father. She wondered if Ian really intended to kill Thomas or just frighten him. She didn't want to find out. Thomas might be a despicable man, a man who loved profit, but most certainly he didn't deserve to die for being greedy.

"I have plans, too," Bethlyn countered and smiled at Thomas, "and they don't include his death."

"Thank you, dear lady," Thomas offered, almost like a prayer.

A low, sultry laugh parted Bethlyn's lips. "Don't thank me too soon, sir." She turned to Ian and whispered something in his ear. Immediately this caused a wicked grin to appear.

He called to Sparrow and some of his crew to lower the longboats from the *Jessica* and to soon begin loading them with the captured sailors. "But first, we shall have some entertainment," he cried and nodded to Bethlyn.

"Your life is saved, Mr. Eversley," she said, "but not without a price."

Eversley's delighted expression disappeared, and he narrowed his eyes. "What is it you want?"

Bethlyn touched the fine lacework on his cravat, then ran her eyes down the front of the well-made gray satin jacket over the black trousers to the tips of his soft leather boots. "I want your clothes."

"My clothes?" he mouthed.

"Yes, every last piece you've got on." She flashed an impish smile at him. "Captain Hawk has need of such finery and will look much more handsome than you, sir. So, strip."

"Now? Here?" Total disbelief.

"Yes."

"But, but—"

"Do it!"

Thomas jumped, and he quickly began to remove his jacket, and then his shirt. Whistles and howls from the *Jessica* caused his face to redden, and Bethlyn wondered if he was embarrassed or angry. That was the only indication Thomas gave that he felt thoroughly humiliated to undress in front of both crews, Captain Hawk, and a strange woman.

When he was down to his drawers, he nearly balked, but a curt nod from Bethlyn hurried him along and he was naked.

Ian folded his arms across his chest and perused Thomas. "Not a pretty sight by far" was his comment.

"Now, now, Hawk. Don't distress our guest further." Bethlyn kicked the discarded clothes aside, not feeling any great urgency to even look at Thomas, but she did so only to prove that his nudity meant nothing to her.

Thomas's eyes burned with a red-hot fire, and he made no attempt to cover himself. He stood as naked as the day his mother birthed him and showed no emotion to be the object of ridicule and laughter from the *Jessica*.

"Lower the boats!" Ian commanded his men, and immediately the boats were lowered and the *Jessica*'s crew was loaded, Thomas following behind them when Ian gestured him forward.

Finally all of the crew and Thomas sat in the boats, heading in the direction of the open sea, at the mercy of the elements and any ship which happened past.

From Bethlyn's vantage point at the railing, she easily spotted Eversley's pale flesh among the uniforms worn by the crew. The man was humiliated beyond belief, but still he presented a stoic facade. The burning hatred in his eyes was the only indication of what Thomas must feel, and that hatred was directed at Bethlyn and Ian.

As the longboats slipped away, Bethlyn shivered from a sudden chill when Thomas pinned her with his glowering gaze. She hoped he'd never discover their identities, not wanting to be the recipient of such fierce, simmering hatred.

Shivering again, she returned to the cabin.

Chapter Twenty-Six

How boring, thought Annabelle Hastings, and demurely sipped her champagne. She wondered why she'd ever agreed to come to this New Jersey country estate with Malcolm Carstairs, a young man who'd been friends with the Babcocks' late grandson. She'd met him a few months ago and, since inheriting her fortune, he'd visited her a number of times.

She supposed Malcolm was considered handsome, and he was rich, an added inducement. However, Annabelle didn't have to snare a wealthy man for a protector or as a husband any longer. Her future was secure.

Glancing around the large parlor of the Potter mansion, she was struck by the beauty of the furnishings, the elaborately laid table—which featured every type of mouth-watering delicacy—and the black-coated servants who hovered with champagne bottles in hand, filling empty glasses. A rotund William Potter had escorted her and Malcolm to his cellar earlier, and they'd marveled at the quality of his stock. Annabelle considered life fascinating. A few months ago, she'd never tasted Bordeaux or had any knowledge of fine wines and champagnes, now she knew quite a lot. My, how a great deal of money will change a person, she thought wryly, and lifted her glass in a tiny toast to the memory of the departed Babcocks.

Malcolm, in conversation with William Potter, glanced her way. He was Tory through and through, apparently not the least bit worried to be seen with a woman thought to be on the rebels' side. But she guessed Malcolm was far from being so smitten by her that such a thing would be overlooked. Her newfound wealth did weigh heavily with him. She could never admit to him that she was, in reality, a British spy. Only Holmes and a nameless contact of his had known.

And now poor Holmes had met his doom, thus eliminating him from the picture. She'd paid an unsavory henchman quite a large amount of money for this service, but the fee was worth it. Holmes wouldn't bother her again, and she'd never have to worry about Ian Briston learning her secret.

Her heart seemed to stop beating whenever she thought about Ian. She'd never been in love with anyone before him, however, the way he'd spurned her when she threw herself at him distressed her immeasurably. The emotions of love and hate for the cad warred within her breast. When she'd calmed down a few days after he'd rejected her, deciding that she'd crawl on her hands and knees to beg his forgiveness—all the while hoping that he'd take pity on her, pick her up, and make love to her—Ian's secretary called on her.

Marcus Gibbons, in his extremely polite way, informed her that he would be handling the estate matters since Briston and his wife had taken an extended holiday. Annabelle had felt shocked and hurt that Ian hadn't told her good-bye, and she ached to inquire where the Bristons had gone and when they'd return, but she'd learned diplomacy over the last few months and didn't ask. Mr. Gibbons didn't offer the information, either.

Now she sat among strangers to ease her loneliness and the pain in her heart for a man who didn't want her but a man she nevertheless was determined to possess.

Malcolm excused himself from William and came to sit beside her on the cabriole-leg sofa.

"Are you enjoying yourself, Miss Gray?" he asked softly, almost shyly, but his reticence and use of her last name didn't keep her from thinking he was interested in her for her fortune.

"Indeed I am, Mr. Carstairs. The gathering is quite nice and my accommodations are comfortable. Thank you for inviting me for the weekend. I know it isn't proper to have come here with you." She purposely lowered her eyes to appear innocent. "But I've been so terribly lonely since my dear friends passed away."

Malcolm patted her hand and shot her a sympathetic smile. "I understand, Miss Gray. They were my friends, too." After a few moments, he said, "I hope you don't mind if I leave you alone for a bit. William insists I join him and some of the other gentlemen in a game of cards in the library. I'm certain the ladies assembled will keep you occupied. William's fiancée should be coming downstairs shortly. I trust you and she will find each other's company pleasing."

The little twerp was leaving her alone. How dare he bring her here and desert her! But she really didn't care for Malcolm, more than eager to have him gone, but the slight stung. Instead she lifted her gaze and said sweetly, "Please enjoy your game. I shall be fine."

Promptly he left her.

For a few minutes she passed the time with a matron who bored her to tears with details of how to make an effective poultice against croup. Another woman's ears perked up and began to give her own remedy. Finally the chattering women took their leave to the buffet table and sat happily stuffing their faces, forgetting Annabelle.

Having decided to go upstairs and crawl into bed, she couldn't move a muscle when a beautiful ebony-haired woman entered the parlor. Her gown was fashioned with the most daring bodice Annabelle had ever seen, and the red satin material was quite expensive. The woman carried a large black fan, imprinted with scarlet roses—a rather garish-looking thing, Annabelle thought, but somehow it suited her and no doubt had cost a pretty penny.

Could it be? she asked herself, and openly stared at the woman who was immediately surrounded by some of the Potter females, twittering and giggling together like a gaggle of geese. Another woman joined the group and

Annabelle heard the older Potter sister introduce the young woman as Della Trammel, William's fiancée.

It was her! Annabelle remembered the time she'd encountered Della Trammel. She'd visited Holmes at the small boardinghouse where he shared a room with the woman, eager to impart information he might find useful. And there was Della, all done up in a frilly orange gown, less expensive than the dress she now wore. The two women had warily stared at each other until Holmes pressed some money in Della's hand and insisted she go shopping, which Della was only too glad to do.

Annabelle hadn't asked Holmes about Della, but she'd been curious. Holmes volunteered that Della was a prostitute and meant nothing to him. He needed a woman to pleasure him, now that she was staying with the Babcocks and was more or less unapproachable—a situation Annabelle found to her liking, not at all upset that Holmes had turned his attention elsewhere.

But now flutters of trepidation settled in the pit of her stomach to realize that Della Trammel was staring at her. Does she remember me? Annabelle worried, and hoped that Della Trammel had forgotten her. She wouldn't be able to explain to her or anyone else why she'd visited a British soldier that day when she was supposedly the brave and patriotic Emmie Gray, darling of the colonial cause.

Get out of here! her mind screamed, and she would have fled, but at that moment, Della blinked as if coming out of a trance.

To Annabelle's chagrin, Della approached her, stopping a few feet away. "Good evening," Della began in a surprisingly cultured tone from the nasal one Annabelle remembered. "We've met once before."

Should she deny it? Her temples throbbed. God, how awful to have her dual identity destroyed by a doxy! She didn't know what to say, so she asked, "How are you?"

Della sighed, her words tumbling out. "I was fine until I saw you." She sat next to Annabelle, who questioningly arched her brown, but Della didn't notice. Her hands trembled as she held on to the gaudy fan, and her lower lip followed suit.

"I hate to beg," Della confessed. "But I've done my share in the past to get what I wanted. When I was little I'd hold out my hand on the street and hope for a few coins to bring home to my mother, who was always sick, and maybe have a bit left over to buy some food for my little brother and me. Usually there wasn't.

"Then I learned a different type of begging, but begging just the same. I sold my body to any man who'd pay my price. Then Holmes came along and treated me like I was a lady. I know he wasn't a perfect man, but he saw that I had food to eat and clothes to wear. He taught me how to speak and behave like a real lady. Sometimes I believed I was one."

Where is all this chatter leading? Annabelle grew more tense by the second. Perspiration dripped from her upper lip, and she daubed at the moisture with her kerchief. "I can understand how you would," Annabelle commented, feeling that she had to say something in regard to this strange outpouring. Was Della playing some sort of absurd game with her? Did the woman plan to blackmail her? She had no interest in hearing about the woman's unsavory past. She had one of her own to forget.

Della bit at her lower lip. "I beg of you, ma'am, please don't tell anyone about me. I'm going to marry William Potter next month, and I care deeply for him. He isn't handsome like some men, but he loves me. Everyone believes that I'm a widow who left England in search of a new life. If any of them were ever to learn about . . . what I did . . . they'd never forgive me. I have money. I can pay you for your silence."

Annabelle was so stunned she could barely speak. Della Trammel was afraid of her! So afraid she was willing to pay her not to divulge her secret past, something which she had no desire to do, because she empathized with Della and understood all too well the circumstances which can drive a person to desperate acts.

A weight dropped from Annabelle's shoulders. "Your secrets are safe with me. I wish you every happiness in your marriage."

"Oh, thank you." A relieved sigh burst from Della's

throat and she vigorously fanned herself. "I am so grateful."

Annabelle studied Della, and finally curiosity got the best of her. "How did you enchant a wealthy and cultured man to such an extent that he wants to marry you?"

Della grinned, apparently eager to talk, and she heedlessly rushed on. "As I told you, Holmes had a hand in tutoring and refining me. But I owe my happiness to Mrs. Briston for the money she gave me—"

She broke off, and Annabelle jumped at the mention of the name Briston. "Mrs. Ian Briston? What does she have to do with anything? What money?"

"Oh, dear." Della put her hand to her mouth in dismay. "I shouldn't have said that. I promised her."

"What did you promise, Della?" Annabelle prodded in a silky soft voice she used with people from whom she wanted information. "Evidently you need to speak about this to someone, otherwise, you'd not have slipped."

"Well," Della drawled out the word and looked about, making certain no one was in hearing distance. A sly gleam danced in her eyes. "I knew something about the high-and-mighty Mrs. Briston that she didn't want her husband to know, so I told her I'd tell him unless she paid me to keep silent. And she paid me more money than I ever dreamed to ask for. That's why I can afford expensive clothes and everyone accepts me as wealthy. She made everything possible for me, but I promised I'd never tell anyone about where the money came from and also that I'd never set foot in Philadelphia again."

Della looked pleased with herself, but Annabelle waited in agitation to hear about the secret for which Bethlyn Briston had paid a small fortune. "What is it you know about Mrs. Briston?" Annabelle burst out in a harsh whisper.

Della was flustered for a moment, then said crossly, "I don't know why you should care."

Ah, so the wench was still a conniving whore beneath all of her finery and pretty manners. Well, she'd make Della tell her. Annabelle placed a finger on her lips and considered the strumpet. Finally she spoke, her voice sounding soft but clipped. "Such information may prove quite useful to me. However, if you don't wish to part with it, I believe that your dear William and his family might be more than interested in your past. And I won't charge them a thing for mentioning it."

All color fled Della's cheeks, and she trembled violently. "No, you mustn't!"

"Tell me Mrs. Briston's secret."

Swallowing hard, Della admitted being transported to Philadelphia on a ship which was captured by the fearsome Captain Hawk. Mrs. Briston was also on the ship and probably a doxy, though some of the women didn't believe she was because of her manners and bearing. Hawk took a liking to her, and soon she was Hawk's woman.

"Is that all?" Annabelle asked, pretending disinterest. It would never do for this strumpet to know just how much value she placed on such startling information.

"I'd think that's enough! Mrs. Briston paid me a great deal of money to keep her secret." Della folded her arms in a huff, practically pouting.

Annabelle rose nonchalantly from the sofa and shook out her gown. She yawned. "Thank you for your company, but I fear I must retire. I am most sleepy. Good night, my dear."

She knew Della watched her depart the parlor, most probably a bit stunned that the news didn't have more of a profound effect on her. But Annabelle's calm demeanor belied the way her insides trembled.

Hastening to her room, she closed the door and locked it, not wanting to be disturbed by anyone. She undressed and slipped into bed but couldn't sleep.

Bethlyn Briston and Captain Hawk. Her mind repeated this like a litany. No matter how many times the names rolled around in her head, she still couldn't believe it. But Della knew this was true; she'd been a witness to all of it.

No wonder Bethlyn had paid Della to keep silent. Such information would damn her in the eyes of the British authorities—and her own husband. No matter where Ian Briston's real sympathies lay, Annabelle didn't think he'd like knowing his devoted wife had slept with the notorious privateer, Hawk.

Annabelle knew how much the British wanted to capture this blackguard, and Bethlyn Briston might be the key to finally ending his reign of the seas. If she told the authorities about Bethlyn's involvement with Hawk, she'd be arrested and hung as a traitor, and Ian would be free. But she discounted this idea, knowing Della would have to admit any knowledge she possessed, and she'd given the woman her word and wouldn't break it. The poor thing did deserve the chance to turn her life around and marry William Potter.

She considered going to Ian directly, but might not Ian resent her for telling him? She wanted Ian, but didn't wish for him to realize she possessed a great deal of information about things to which only a well-trained spy would be privy.

What do do? After hours of tossing and turning, she decided to take her mother's advice. When in doubt, do nothing.

Nothing for now.

The summer months passed in a flurry of ocean-drenched days and moonlit nights. For Bethlyn, having to reside on Windhaven when Ian took out the *Black Falcon*, the moments passed slowly. But whenever he returned, her joy and love knew no bounds. She dreaded leaving this sun-kissed paradise, but the day finally arrived.

Ian had recently come home, having been gone for two months this time. They lay in each other's arms, watching the morning sun color the sky like an artist's palette, Bethlyn nestling in the crook of his arm. Her honey-brown hair flowed across his chest, and he absently twisted a strand between his fingers.

She felt satiated and content, dozing off for a few seconds, barely hearing Ian's voice.

"We must return to Philadelphia tomorrow."

Realizing what he'd said, she opened her eyes and moved her head to see his face. He looked as unhappy as she felt.

"I've been expecting it," she said, and felt a lump thicken in her throat.

Ian held her close. "I happened to cross paths with a privateer out of New York. The British have fled Philadelphia for New York. General Washington and the patriots are in control of the city."

"Oh, Ian, this is what you've wanted for so long." Amber sparks of pleasure danced within her eyes, but she realized he didn't share the same emotion. "What's wrong?"

Heaving a ragged sigh, he sat up. "The war is far from over, Bethlyn, though I'm happy about the news. But New York is still under British control. It seems that Captain Hawk is meant to have no rest."

"You're going to New York."

"Eventually. Not right away. Marc should have some important information for me by now, and I still have to run Briston Shipping and keep up the pretense of being a loyal Tory. I doubt Philadelphia is free of all British spies." He fell silent for a moment, then said, "My trips to New York will, I hope, not involve a great deal of coming and going. I'd much prefer staying at Edgecomb with you." Tilting her chin, he gazed deeply into the fathomless pools of her eyes. "I don't want to neglect you, sweetheart, or have you think I'm not interested in making our baby. Nothing would give me greater pleasure."

Wrapping her arms around his neck, she pulled his head down and whispered against his lips, "Then by all means enjoy yourself."

Thomas Eversley was far from enjoying himself.

He'd arrived in Philadelphia four days earlier from New York on a rickety coach which had been driven by the most surly and arrogant colonial he'd ever met. The man had been rude, not even bothering to help him with his trunk, small thing that it was. All of the clothes and possessions Thomas had packed for this travesty of a trip were probably still aboard the *Jessica*, if not on the backs of some filthy, scavaging privateers.

Even three months after the incident with Captain Hawk and his doxy weren't enough time to wipe away the total humiliation Thomas had suffered. His face still burned at the memory, and more than anything he wanted revenge against the malicious twosome. He didn't know if he'd ever be able to face the crew of the *Jessica* again; their mocking laughter still echoed in his ears.

He'd been lucky that one of the crew had lent him a jacket; otherwise, he'd have suffered a terrible chill out on the ocean when the sun went down that first day. No one, however, had volunteered a pair of pants. He knew he could have ordered someone to undress, but he hadn't wanted to, fearful he'd be forced overboard. The men weren't in the best of moods.

The three small longboats had drifted for two days, and by the time a British passenger ship out of Liverpool had rescued them, Thomas was hungry and filled with such an incredible thirst that he never thought to get enough to drink. Never again did he want to be without food and water.

The ship docked at New York just as General Clinton, who'd taken over General Howe's Philadelphia command in early May, arrived. By the middle of June, the last British troops left Philadelphia, and now New York was the hub of the social scene—something which Thomas didn't get to enjoy.

He felt the fates had cursed him by falling ill with a fever and an aching sore throat which kept him abed for more than six weeks. Thanks to General Clinton's concern for his harrowing experience, and the fact that the man was more than eager to learn facts about Captain Hawk and this Dove person, Thomas recuperated at his residence.

Thomas told him very little, but from a contact of Clinton's, a man who appeared at his bedside one afternoon calling himself Mariah, he learned that the Dove was first heard of in Philadelphia. How the Dove, a rebel poetess, came into contact with Captain Hawk was unknown. But this man had heard that Thomas was interested in gaining revenge, and having been a contact of a British officer who'd met with an early and ignominious end, he could perhaps gain a foothold by going to the city of brotherly love and seeking out a Miss Emmie Gray.

And this was exactly what Thomas decided to do on this very warm September afternoon.

His step, despite his recent illness, was spry as he climbed out of the carriage before the imposing white house. Upon arriving in the city, he'd made inquiries at Briston Shipping about Bethlyn and Ian Briston and discovered that they were on a holiday. Much perturbed by their absence, he decided to pursue the information he needed from this woman named Emmie Gray. He could never bring himself to query Ian Briston about the notorious Hawk and his whore. Though he knew that as a businessman in the shipping industry, Briston might possess some information about the pair, Thomas would never suffer the final humiliation of revealing to the arrogant young bounder about his run-in with Captain Hawk. Wouldn't the nervy Briston just adore hearing every nasty, juicy detail?

Minutes later, Thomas found himself ensconced in the Babcock parlor and watching the very lovely and innocent-appearing Emmie Gray pour him a cup of tea. But Thomas wasn't fooled by her demure appearance in the high-necked blue gown or those downcast eyes. His New York informant had spoken to him at length about Emmie Gray, or rather that Emmie Gray was a fraud.

She was a trained British spy who had been intimately involved with a certain late Lieutenant Holmes, but she'd lost her value to the British now, because her face was too widely recognized by the Philadelphia citizenry to mingle among them and gain information. And since inheriting a large fortune, which Thomas learned was controlled by Ian Briston, she'd lost interest in the spy business, preferring to be a woman of leisure.

This Emmie Gray was most suited to leisure and other things having to do with soft beds, Thomas thought, and felt himself harden. Her full, sensual lips belied her innocent act. The slight brush of her hand against his when she handed him the cup aroused him, and he didn't miss the glimmer of lust in her eyes. He sensed she'd been without a man for too long. She needed to be kissed and bedded—very soon.

He couldn't imagine a more enjoyable way of spending his time in Philadelphia than having Emmie Gray's slender body writhing beneath his—that was until he decided how he was going to entice Bethlyn Briston into rushing back to England and into his large, imposing bed at Woodsley as his wife.

"I hope you find our fair city to your liking, Mr. Eversley," Annabelle said in a satin-smooth voice.

He hated it, but he smiled. "Most charming."

She sipped her tea and set down the cup on the low table in front of the sofa and hesitated. "I know, sir, that you mentioned you were connected with Briston Shipping, but I fail to see why you would choose to visit me."

"Don't you, Miss Gray?" Thomas cocked an eyebrow at her, his cup poised in midair. "The connection should be obvious, since Ian Briston is executor of your estate. I enjoy knowing every interesting facet of Briston's life. His wife is the daughter of the Earl of Dunsmoor, my employer. I hope to be able to give the earl a favorable report on his son-in-law."

It had been a shot in the dark, but Thomas took the gamble by purposely mentioning Briston. He hadn't known what this woman looked like before he met her, just that she was connected to Briston and she was a spy. He desperately needed something to pin on the man if he were somehow going to pull Bethlyn away from him. And he believed that Emmie Gray was it. An emotion of momentary pain and—could it be love—flickered across her face at the mention of the man's name.

Perhaps all wasn't paradise in the Briston household. Why else would Ian and Bethlyn take an extended trip if not to put distance between Ian Briston and this delectable spy?

"Mr. Briston has been quite accommodating," she said.

I bet he has, thought Thomas, and stifled his lecherous smile. "You're very fortunate to have such a prominent man as an adviser. In fact, you've been quite lucky the last year. I heard about your near escape from bloodthirsty savages and your dangerous trek through the wilderness to safety. And now you've inherited this beautiful home. I wonder if there isn't anything you can't achieve, Miss Hastings."

"I—" She broke off. "What did you call me?"

Thomas put down his cup and smiled, a crafty expression in his eyes. "Your name is Annabelle Hastings, I believe."

Annabelle swallowed hard. "How . . . how did you learn about me?"

Thomas silently applauded her for not lying. "I have my sources." He leaned forward, placing his elbows on his knees. "Now what can we do about it?"

Annabelle didn't flinch from the probing stare. "Pray, tell me, sir."

"First, you can tell me all you know about the Dove."

"I'm sorry, Mr. Eversley, but my information about this person is sketchy, at best." Annabelle settled herself comfortably against the sofa cushions. "A pamphlet of poems was published and the citizens went quite mad over the Dove, and he or she became a great favorite."

"My dear Miss Hastings, I was led to believe you were a more than adequate spy, but I must change my opinion. You seem not to know this person's sex."

Annabelle hid her affront behind a sweet smile. "No one knew for certain, sir."

Thomas smirked. "I can tell you with no hesitation that the Dove is a woman, a most beautiful and well-formed woman, I may add. I had a run-in with her and her cohort, Captain Hawk, some weeks ago. However, both of them wore masks to conceal their faces."

Annabelle leaned forward, her interest piquing. "And you escaped with your life? That is most intriguing, Mr. Eversley."

"Call me Thomas."

"Thomas. Tell me about this Hawk and Dove."

She listened intently as Thomas recited the incidents after the *Jessica* was seized, leaving out the part about his release in the buff. He ended it by saying, "I'd be most grateful if you happen to stumble upon any information at all. I want to trap this Hawk and his ebony-haired whore."

"I can see why you would," Annabelle commented. "If I do find out anything, where may I reach you?"

Thomas sighed, waving his hand in aggravation. "I have a room above Crosskeys Tavern, but needless to say, I'm quite put out by not finding the Bristons at home. That secretary fellow of his told me they're on a long holiday. I had hoped to be invited to stay at Edgecomb."

"Well, I trust they'll return soon and will offer their hospitality."

Bitch, thought Thomas, you could invite me to stay here. But he realized after a few silent moments that Annabelle Hastings didn't intend to say anything else on the subject.

Finally he rose and kissed her hand.

"I trust that I may be allowed to call upon you again, Miss Hastings."

Annabelle quickly withdrew away her hand, and she frowned. "Refer to me as Emmie Gray. For all intents and purposes, Annabelle Hastings is dead."

Thomas reached out a finger and stroked the smooth line of her jaw. "Ah, my dear, I believe that she is very much alive." He laughed at her look of rebuke. "I shall see you again, and I will call you Annabelle when alone. The name suits you. Good afternoon . . . Annabelle."

Closing the door behind him, Annabelle leaned against it. She trembled and hated herself for being shaken by Eversley's visit. The man was handsome and she'd felt drawn to him at first because he resembled Luther, her stepfather, bringing back bittersweet and sensual memories better left forgotten. But then he'd mentioned Ian, and she sensed that he knew she loved him. Yet it wasn't this knowledge which unsettled her.

Eversley's recounting of the incident with Captain Hawk and the Dove had interested her, and she'd fleetingly wondered how this ferocious sea pirate had connected with the Dove, a woman whom Thomas professed to be a raven-haired beauty and was last heard of in Philadelphia.

An intriguing puzzle, but one which Annabelle only pieced together when he'd mentioned the long absence of Ian and Bethlyn Briston. Ian—a man who ran a shipping enterprise and spent a great deal of time at sea. A man whom she knew pretended to be a loyalist but was in actuality a patriot. And then there was his wife—the daughter of an earl, the woman who had been Captain Hawk's whore. She'd been blackmailed by Della Trammel, supposedly to keep the fact of her status as a privateer's doxy from her husband.

Might she have paid a small fortune to Della, not because she didn't want her husband to know about Hawk, but because she was protecting her husband who was Hawk?

Annabelle felt her knees buckling and held on to the doorknob. God in heaven, that was it! The Bristons weren't on an extended holiday at all, not unless one considered capturing and raiding British ships as holiday amusements.

Ian Briston was Captain Hawk, and his wife was the Dove. She knew information for which the British would pay dearly and which Thomas Eversley wanted with a zealousness only rivaled by religious fervor.

Annabelle felt rather powerful at that moment as the life flowed back into her limbs, and she retired to the parlor to gaze out of the lacy curtained window at the street scene outside. The Bristons' fates rested in her hands. Ian's fate. Bethlyn Briston meant nothing to her.

She didn't have to ask herself what she should do. She'd already made up her mind. Most certainly she didn't need any more money even if she was of the mind to leak information. For one thing, the rebels controlled Philadelphia, and she doubted anything would be done to Ian here if she did contact General Clinton in New York, or that dark specter of a contact Holmes had used named Mariah.

Another reason, and this was the most important one in Annabelle's mind, was that she loved Ian Briston and would never betray him. However, she couldn't get rid of Bethlyn as the Dove without incriminating Ian as Captain Hawk.

384

"A rather touchy situation," she mused aloud, but knew also that she'd never tell Eversley. Let him think that the Dove was dark haired. He'd never suspect that the earl's brown-tressed darling wore a wig to confiscate British ships. But she'd deal with Bethlyn soon enough. And Hawk . . .

She'd deal with him in the most pleasurable way possible.

Ian glanced at Marc, who'd just entered his office. On his desk lay a great deal of paperwork which required his signature, though Marc had been quite efficient in running things during his absence. However, the last week the man's mind had been taken up with thoughts of Mavis and their new son, a fine, healthy little lad who was destined to grow up to be a handsome heartbreaker.

"Any news yet from Eli Templet?" Ian asked, and frowned when Marc shook his head. "That's odd," Ian mused aloud. "We should have heard something from him long ago."

"You're right," Marc agreed, and sat down in the chair on the other side of the desk. "I've wondered the same thing myself, but the wilderness is a hazardous place. Anything could have happened to Eli. You know, Ian, he isn't a young man any longer."

"I know, but Eli, for all of his seventy years, is still an able spy and proficient scout. Something must have happened to him."

"Shall I send someone to search for him?"

Ian considered for a moment before saying, "No, I'll give him another month or so. But I had thought to have this business with Emmie Gray resolved by now."

Marc left him to his paperwork, but Ian found it difficult to concentrate on such mundane matters. What had happened to Eli Templet? It was unlike him to take such a long time investigating matters which could prove crucial to the war. He'd left for the Pennsylvania wilderness around the time that Ian and Bethlyn had gone to Windhaven. That was months ago. Eli should have returned by now. He had a good mind to search for Eli himself, but he couldn't leave Philadelphia at the moment.

An undercurrent of tension ran through the city. Since the rebels were now in charge under the command of Major General Benedict Arnold, and the Continental Congress and State Government returned to Philadelphia, the city had been in the throes of a severe inflation and wheat shortage. The citizens blamed the loyalist businessmen who remained for these predicaments, claiming that their prices were too high. For years inflation had presented a problem, but now with scarcity of goods and the public outcry for Tory heads, Ian felt an unrest and a forboding. Some of the men he'd known for years, men loyal to the Crown, were being charged with treason against the American government.

Would someone come for him one day and cart him off to a trial where he'd be found guilty of treasonous conduct because he gave all the indications that he was a loyalist? Would he be hung? The way things were going, Ian wondered. He'd never be able to admit he was Captain Hawk or a patriot. On one hand, he could count those people who knew that Captain Hawk and Ian Briston were one and the same. General Washington knew, but he wasn't in Philadelphia and wouldn't help him anyway. Long ago, they'd agreed that if he ever got into some dire situation, Washington would avow no knowledge of him or raise a finger to help him. Otherwise, he'd be of no use to his country if he happened to escape.

And now he feared not only for himself but for Bethlyn. She, too, was thought to be a loyalist. For a moment he considered sending her to stay with Molly and Hans in New York but decided against such action. He'd miss her unbearably, and for now he had to stay in Philadelphia. At least until he heard from Eli Templet.

That afternoon Ian visited the Babcock House. At his knock, he was a bit astounded to find Emmie opening the door.

"I saw your carriage drive up," she explained, and looked very fetching in a light pink silk gown with a tiny rose pinned on each side of her long silver hair. "Do come in, Ian. I've missed you so very much."

She hooked her arm with his and led him into the parlor where she poured him a glass of his favorite brandy. "I didn't forget what you like to drink," she said, and laughed softly. "I could never forget anything about you."

Watching him with adoring eyes, Ian thanked her but felt uncomfortable. Apparently she still wanted him, and that passion seemed to have increased rather than abated. If he didn't love Bethlyn so much and trust Emmie Gray so little, he might be flattered enough to make love to the wench. But he didn't want her, and he'd never want her. Yet he couldn't break all ties with her. Not yet.

He'd come to discuss estate business with her, but she wasn't the least interested. She'd been brazen the last time he'd seen her, but now she sidled up to him on the sofa, and her hand rested on his knee until her palm possessively fondled his crotch.

Without a word, he removed her hand, not missing the lust-filled eyes change to express a deep hurt and then anger. It was almost as if the wench thought she had the right to touch him anyway she damned well pleased!

"A gentleman wouldn't treat me so shabbily," she cried, her lower lip trembling.

"A lady wouldn't have done what you just did."

Standing up, she placed her hands on her hips and glared at him. "So, I take it I'm not a lady like your highborn wife."

Ian placed his paperwork in his breast pocket and stood up. "Emmie, I'm not going to debate with you or bandy words around. I don't want to bed you . . ."

"But I want you, Ian, I love you," she interrupted and clutched at his shirt front.

"Nor do I love you," he said, and softened his words with, "We're just too opposite, Emmie."

"Ian, please don't return to your wife. You must love me as I do you. Why else do you keep coming here?"

Her anger had turned to pleading, and he hated to see a

woman beg, even if he did have doubts about her. But he didn't love her, and she'd realize this fact before long if what he thought about her turned out to be true.

"We have business to discuss and that's all. I have a wife whom I adore. I suggest you look elsewhere for your bed companions."

Her hands slipped away from him. "How cruel you are, Ian Briston. I shall not forget what you just said to me."

Was that a threat? Ian wasn't certain because her words were low and uttered without emotion.

"I have no desire to hurt you," he told her, and headed for the door. "But I also have no desire to love you, either. Good evening, Emmie." And then he left.

Bethlyn met Ian in the hallway when he returned home, growing breathless and more than a bit pleased when he pulled her into his arms and kissed her until her head spun.

"Goodness, what a greeting," she exclaimed, her brown eyes dancing with sparkles.

"I've missed you. You've been on my mind all day. I can't wait to get you upstairs and to be alone with you." Ian nuzzled her ear, but Bethlyn pulled away a bit.

"We have a guest for supper."

"Who?" he asked, and wished the guest would leave.

"Thomas Eversley."

Ian groaned and almost imagined that the earth had shifted beneath his feet.

Chapter Twenty-Seven

A late-summer breeze gently flickered the candlelights attached to the huge chandelier which hung above the dining table. The meal passed in silence except for the noises of spoons and forks clattering against the Sèvres china and the slight rustling of the servingwomen's gowns.

Thomas Eversley's presence at Edgecomb disturbed Bethlyn. The man's manners were impeccable, his bearing quite gallant, and his grooming couldn't be faulted. Bethlyn doubted if a more refined and well-dressed guest had ever partaken of a meal at this table. But she didn't like Thomas, and her dislike had gone beyond the fact that he'd used her father's ships for doxy transportation. She couldn't name what it was about him that caused her such unease. Apparently he didn't associate either her or Ian with the humiliation he suffered at the hands of Hawk and Dove, and she felt quite safe he never would. Still, whenever he looked in her direction, which was often, and asked a question or informed her about matters at Woodsley, a cold shiver ran up her back.

She silently berated herself for her reaction and put on a pleasant smile, but she couldn't shake her discomfort until she remembered how Thomas had looked as he stood naked on the deck of the *Black Falcon*. Gales of delighted laughter escaped from her, causing Thomas to look askance and Ian to stop eating his custard tart to snicker knowingly.

"Whyever are you two laughing like hyenas?" Thomas asked, seemingly much affronted, and tilted his dark brown hair inquiringly in Ian's direction.

"Nothing, Thomas, old man," Ian finally said after his amusement subsided. "A private joke between Bethlyn and me. Now, you never did tell us why you're here in Philadelphia. And how long do you plan to stay?"

Eversley's lips curled in disdain, but he quickly smiled. "I wished a trip abroad. Working for the earl keeps me extremely busy, and I suppose the long hours I've been working have made me a bit tired. The earl insisted I take an extended holiday, so I chose to visit here. I wanted to check on Lady Bethlyn for her father—to make certain she is being treated well."

"I assure you, Thomas, that I am well and happy. Please convey my regards to my father when next you see him." Bethlyn managed to smile politely, but somehow she doubted Thomas's reason for being in Philadelphia."

"There is also another reason for my visit," Thomas offered. "I have come to your fair city to seek my bride."

"What!" Ian nearly choked on his coffee. "You're going to get married? Who is the unfortunate woman?"

Thomas grinned a Cheshire-cat grin, ignoring Ian's slur. "I'm in the marriage market, and I hope to meet all of the eligible young ladies and choose one to return home with me. I trust that the alliance will be satisfactory to the both of us." He shot a meaningful glance at Bethlyn, one she didn't fail to miss.

Ian, however, didn't see the interplay here or notice that Bethlyn's face flamed a deep shade of crimson. He continued the conversation with Thomas, but for the rest of the meal Bethlyn's hands trembled. She tried to convince herself that the way Thomas had looked at her meant absolutely nothing. She was a happily married woman for God's sake. He couldn't mean to marry *her*. But no matter how hard she tried to shake the memory of those cold eyes, trained on her face and filled with hidden meanings, she couldn't.

Finally she managed to convince herself that she was imagining things, because for the rest of the evening,

Thomas was most gracious. Before he departed, he kissed her hand in an almost cousinly fashion and told her he would be most grateful if she'd introduce him to some of Philadelphia's reigning belles. She'd agreed, convinced that he had no hidden motives even if he was the sort of despicable man who profited from transporting women across the seas in one of her father's ships. However, later that night as she lay in Ian's arms, she shivered again.

Thomas slipped into his bed above Crosskeys Tavern and listened to the sounds in the ale room downstairs. The lone candle on the nightstand illumined his grin as he silently congratulated himself on the story he'd told the Bristons about seeking a wife. The inspiration for such a tale had sprung easily to his lips, but in all truthfulness he hadn't lied. He did intend to find a wife; in fact, he'd found her already. Bethlyn Briston was going to marry him one day. Of that, he had no doubt. He'd always been a patient man, and this situation would merit a great deal of that virtue.

Bethlyn and Ian loved each other deeply, and he couldn't help but to be jealous. The arrogant cad was no doubt making love to her at that very moment, and the mental image of their mating caused a tortured groan to escape him as he hardened beneath the thin sheet.

"Just thinking about the damned haughty bitch always does this to me," he groused aloud and believed he'd have to end his own torture since he hadn't been able to seek out a prostitute yet. Never in his life had he wanted a woman as much as Bethlyn, and he vowed that when she was his, he'd imprison her in his bed and not let her go until he had slaked his lust. If that was even possible.

He'd just placed his hand beneath the sheet when a no-nonsense knock sounded on his door.

"Who is it?" he called.

"Annabelle Hastings" came the reply.

Having forgotten to lock the door, Annabelle entered at his summons. Closing the door, she leaned against it, her pale blue eyes taking in the fact that he was already in bed, and from the looks of things beneath the cover, he was in need of a woman's touch.

She moved forward, a knowing smirk on her face which caused Thomas to snap, "What in blazes do you want?"

"Don't act testy," she chided. "I might change my mind and decide not to . . . ah . . . help you with your problem." Her gaze lingered on the evident bulge which the sheet barely concealed.

Thomas's eyes flared with ill-concealed lust, and he nodded. Annabelle flashed him a beguiling smile and quickly threw off her fashionable and expensive dress, leaving it on the floor beside the bed. When she was completely and beautifully naked, her long silver hair curling to her waist and hanging like gossamer across her small breasts, she slipped beneath the sheet.

Her hand immediately found his warm, pulsing shaft, large with desire. "Oh, Thomas," she moaned, "I had no idea you were so well endowed."

Pulling away the sheet, he pushed her downward. "Pleasure me, wench, in the way only a whore can."

Annabelle licked her lips almost like a starving person who awaits a feast. "You know, of course, that in my mind you aren't the man I'm making love to."

"I know," he said, and watched her lower her head to him, her hair a bright shiny curtain across his thighs. "In the dark all women are the same." But he meant to say that in the dark, he could better imagine that Bethlyn was the woman who now worked her magic on him.

With that, he blew out the candle.

"Mavis, little Marc is the most beautiful baby I've ever seen. He has your eyes, and Marc's nose. But he would have to be beautiful, because you and Marc are two of the most perfect-looking people." Bethlyn placed her finger in the baby's fist, feeling the child's strength as he closed his tiny hand. She'd arrived two hours ago and still sat in the rocking chair, holding this precious little bundle. It seemed she couldn't stop staring at him.

"Well, you should be here at two in the morning when

that most perfect baby wakes and wants to eat," Mavis grumbled good-naturedly, slowly moving around the bedroom. The baby was three weeks old, but Mavis still hadn't recovered completely from the long, arduous birth. As if to prove her point, Baby Marc began to fuss and root at Bethlyn's breast. "You better hand him to me," Mavis said, and laughed. "I don't think you have what your godson requires."

Reluctantly Bethlyn handed him to his mother, giving Mavis her seat. She watched in fascination as the baby suckled at his mother's breast. A large sob welled within her at the sweet sight and sounds the infant made. Never had she seen anything so beautiful, but the baby reminded her of her own inability to conceive. At that moment she doubted she'd ever have a child. Mavis read her thought.

"You'll bear a beautiful and healthy child one day, Bethlyn."

Bethlyn shook her head, her fingers dashing away a lone tear in the corner of her eye. "I doubt it. I fear I'm barren and will never bear a child for Ian. I want to have our baby so much that I ache."

"Perhaps if you stop thinking about it and trying so hard to conceive a baby, you'll become pregnant."

"It seems a baby is all I ever think about," Bethlyn said, overwhelmed by her own hopelessness.

"Then find something else to dwell on. I guarantee that when you do, you'll find yourself pregnant."

"I wish it were that simple."

An hour later Bethlyn headed for Edgecomb, but before leaving the city, she stopped at a dressmaker's shop to order a christening gown for little Marc in honor of the christening which was to take place in two weeks. She was so happy that Mavis and Marc wanted her and Ian to be the baby's godparents. She consoled herself with the thought that even if she never had children, Baby Marc would be the recipient of all of her maternal devotion.

Upon leaving the dress shop, she saw a group of people assembled at a bakery across the street. The citizens grumbled and some raised their fists when the baker, a stooped old man named Mr. Clement, appeared at the window and lowered a curtain.

"Now ain't he the high and mighty Tory," a man in the crowd shouted. "We ought to smash his shop to bits for charging so much for a loaf of bread."

"Yeah," another man cried. "I bet there ain't a wheat shortage at all. The blasted king lovers just want us poor people to pay their prices."

Many in the crowd agreed, and Bethlyn, who had stopped to watch some distance from where her carriage waited, hoped that no violence would ensue. She'd patronized Mr. Clement's bakery often, and she knew that he was a kindly old man who had probably given many of these people credit over the years, never expecting the bills to be paid during hard times. Now, because there was a shortage of wheat, the populace blamed him for his loyalty to the English government, instead of realizing that the war was the cause of lack of bread. Even at Edgecomb they were forced to do without many things which had been in abundance during the British occupation.

"Come on, let's storm him!" came a cry from a bedraggled-looking man who stood near Bethlyn.

She didn't know why she interfered at that point, but she couldn't stand the thought of Mr. Clement being hurt.

"Wait!" she screamed loud enough to be heard above the din. "Please don't harm that poor old man. He has done nothing."

At first she wondered if anyone had heard her at all, but suddenly the silence dimmed and became almost church-like, and all eyes turned to her.

The man who had ordered the storming peered at her and said, "Just who are you, missy?"

Bethlyn didn't care for the tone of his voice, and she squared her shoulders. "I'm Bethlyn Briston."

Her name apparently didn't mean anything to him or to some of the others, but a shrill female voice shouted from somewhere within the crowd, "That's a Tory bitch! She's married to a loyalist, and look at her, lording it all over us in her fancy gowns. Ain't she the one to open her mouth to protect her own kind."

"By God, you're right," the man agreed with the

woman, and the others nodded their heads, their faces wreathed in hatred.

All Bethlyn could think as the people in the crowd progressed upon her was that she would soon be lying on this street, probably torn and bleeding—perhaps dead. She'd never see Ian again, would never have a child. The thoughts whirled in her mind, but it seemed that the hardened hate-filled faces and bodies approached her in slow motion. Yet she couldn't move, so overcome by fear. From the corner of her eye, she saw her driver's frantic face, then arm movements as he flagged down a soldier who approached on a horse. Then she saw nothing else but towering bodies as the crowd of people surged towards her like a plague of black locusts.

Their breaths were hot on her face, and clawing fingers dug into her flesh as they pulled her forward into the street. She expected to be mauled then, but with her fear came a surge of anger, and she struck out at the people nearest to her, but to no avail. Someone grabbed her by the arms and held her, yet she kicked out, determined not to be a docile victim. She'd fight to the death.

Then, like a deafening peal of thunder, a gunshot exploded above their heads. Immediately all turned, rage and terror in their eyes to behold the angry visage of the man whom Washington had placed in charge of the military government. His prancing stallion broke into the crowd, and instantly soldiers on horses surrounded the throng with raised muskets.

The man's assessing eyes in his pockmarked face took in the situation. Glancing about the populace, he sneered, "Have you all become such rabble that you'd attack a defenseless woman on the street?"

"But . . . but, sir," a male voice began to explain, "she be a Tory . . ."

"So? You're a colonial. Do you see her holding any of you down, showing no mercy for your fears? Release her," he ordered the man who held her. "And all of you go home; otherwise, I'll arrest each and every one of you."

With little care for her person, the man behind her let her go, and she crumpled to the ground like a dead weight.

As the crowd dispersed, there was great deal of muttering and head shaking.

Bethlyn's driver suddenly appeared by her side and helped her up. "Oh, Mrs. Briston, are you all right?" he asked in a quivering voice.

She could barely speak, because she wasn't all right, and the man on horseback seemed to realize this. Sliding from the horse, he limped a bit as he came towards her and took her arm. "Madam, you're deathly pale. May I escort you home?"

"I . . . I . . ." There was her stutter again, and she couldn't form any words; she didn't know what to say anyway, so overcome by fear that she was in a state of shock.

Without hesitation, he ordered one of the soldiers to tie his horse behind the Briston carriage and for the driver to start for home after he helped her into the vehicle. Sitting across from her, he pulled the shades for privacy and watched her in the semidarkness for any signs of collapse.

None came. When they were very near to Edgecomb, Bethlyn sighed and composed herself. She was safe now, no need to be frightened, when she suddenly remembered the soldier sitting across from her. The man had saved her life.

"Thank . . . thank you for rescuing me, sir. I can never repay you for what you did."

He smiled. "Your safety is payment enough, Mrs. Briston. That is your name, isn't it? I heard your driver call you that."

Bethlyn nodded. "And may I have the name of the most gallant gentleman who saved my life?"

"Major General Benedict Arnold, Mrs. Briston. Your servant and admirer."

Annabelle waited supper for Thomas in her bedroom in a huff. Damn, she'd been so close to her goal today, so close that she almost imagined Ian's arms around her. She'd just happened to come across the mob at the bakery when she noticed Bethlyn Briston watching from across the street.

Knowing that the crowd was out for blood, she'd turned their attentions to her own aim by declaring Bethlyn to be a Tory bitch.

She'd watched in fascination, wondering if the woman would be maimed for life or killed, which was her true objective. Instead Arnold had intervened and ruined everything.

Would she never have the man she loved?

Throwing herself on her bed, the diaphanous material of her gown barely covering her, she mulled over her relationship with Thomas. As far as sex went, the two of them were well matched. Both were insatiable and liked unusual ways of making love, even inflicting a bit of pain. Thomas was a good lover, even better than Luther, Holmes, or any other man with whom she'd ever lain. At first he'd been a bit stingy about her own pleasure, wanting all of the fun for himself, but Annabelle refused to be aroused and then left hanging. When she'd made her wants known in no uncertain terms, Thomas had obliged almost happily.

Her release had been glorious, rivaling anything she'd ever known with any man. But she didn't want Thomas and would never settle for him as long as Ian was alive. She sensed that Thomas used her for pleasure, but that she didn't fit into his long-range plans either. He wanted someone else, but she wasn't certain whom.

"Things would be so much simpler if that bitch had been hurt or killed today," she mumbled. "I'll go insane if I can't have Ian soon."

Her monologue was interrupted by a slight noise outside her door, and then Thomas entered, looking extremely handsome.

"My, my, Annabelle, you're a delicious sight."

Annabelle didn't bother to cover the parts of her anatomy on which his eyes lusted. "And you need to undress," she ordered in a husky whisper.

Thomas was only too pleased to accommodate her.

Later, moments after their cries of completion had faded from the room, Thomas turned to her and wrapped a long strand of silver hair around his fingers.

"I saw the most horrifying sight this afternoon, Annabelle."

"Hmm. What?"

"Bethlyn Briston was nearly mauled by an unruly mob."

"Oh?"

"Yes, but luckily a Major Arnold rescued her."

"How fortunate for her."

"I agree that it was. Annabelle?"

"Yes, Thomas?"

He yanked on her hair, causing her to shriek with pain.

"Why did you do that?" she asked, and tried to pull away, but he wound the strand tighter, hurting her more.

"As a warning, my dear. If you ever try to harm Bethlyn Briston again in any way, I will pull each and every strand of hair from your head—one by one. And if you succeed in killing her, I shall make absolutely certain that you join her in the Great Beyond. Do you understand me?"

He looked diabolical, and Annabelle knew Thomas meant what he said. "Yes, yes, I understand."

"Good," he said, and smiled before sucking one of her nipples.

God, she should refuse him, but with each flick of his tongue, each burning caress upon her flesh, Annabelle's resolve melted. No matter what she thought of Thomas or how much she might fear him at times, she couldn't resist his savage brand of lovemaking. When she opened her legs for him, she was more than ready.

No one was more grateful to Major Arnold than Ian. Upon learning of the ordeal Bethlyn had faced, Ian ordered her straight to bed. Bethlyn, who was still overwhelmed and a bit upset over what had happened, went without question like a dutiful child.

Ian invited Arnold to partake of a whiskey, and to express his appreciation, he invited the man to dine with him and Bethlyn in a week's time. Considering that Arnold had no reason not to think that Ian wasn't a British sympathizer, Ian was extremely surprised when the

398

American major agreed and requested if he could bring Miss Peggy Shippen.

Soon Arnold left and Ian went upstairs to see to his wife, finding her huddled on the bed and crying into the pillow while Annie stood helplessly by. Dismissing the girl, he enfolded Bethlyn in his arms and held her until her tears ceased and she fell asleep.

Watching her, he noticed that in sleep she frowned, and he wondered if he should send Bethlyn to New York. He didn't want another incident like the one that day to happen again.

Weeks later, when the pleasant winds chased away the hot sumertime breezes, Annabelle woke one morning and dressed for her usual shopping jaunt. Thomas, who it seemed spent more time in her bed than his own at Crosskeys Tavern, had already departed. She had no idea where he went during the day, but many nights he attended parties in the company of Bethlyn and Ian Briston, supposedly to meet the young eligible ladies of Philadelphia.

"Silly lecher," she muttered, and threw on her lightweight cloak. "You want Bethlyn Briston for yourself." Which was perfectly fine with her. She wished Thomas would steal the woman away so she could work her wiles on Ian. No matter that he didn't love her, she was determined to win his affections somehow. Blackmailing Ian into coming to her bed had crossed her mind, but Annabelle wouldn't do this. There would be little triumph in conquering the man by assuring him she'd tell he was the notorious Captain Hawk and that his wife was the Dove.

Besides, the spy business was behind her.

She'd just walked onto the back terrace to admire the beauty of the morning when she felt that she wasn't alone. Glancing around, expecting to see a servant, she startled at the black-garbed figure of a man standing behind her. His low tricorn hat obscured most of his facial features, but Annabelle recognized him as Holmes's contact, Mariah.

"What do you want?" she asked, her voice quavered.

Mariah made a slight bow. "I've come for you, Annabelle. I suggest you pack a few things. I have a job for you."

"What job? I'm not a spy any longer. Go away."

She'd have run into the house, but a long, black-gloved hand on her arm stalled her. "You've led quite a pretty life up to now without my interference. Be grateful that I didn't inform General Howe about your hand in Holmes's death. No matter what you thought about Holmes, he was a valuable tool to me. As you are."

"Well, I won't go," she insisted, and tried to pull away. "No one will believe you. I have a great deal of money and can buy my freedom. I don't need you."

"What a scoffing, ungrateful wench you've become." His voice lowered to a growl. "Nothing belongs to you. You seem to forget that you're Annabelle Hastings, not Emmie Gray. All of the Babcock estate was left to Emmie Gray, not to you."

"I *am* Emmie Gray." She lifted defiant eyes to him.

"Not for much longer, Annabelle. I happen to know that some months ago Ian Briston sent an investigator to check into your story. He will shortly learn that Emmie Gray is dead. So, then what will you tell him?"

Annabelle blinked in bafflement and felt utter shock to realize that Ian, the man she loved so desperately, hadn't trusted her. Somehow going away with Mariah didn't seem as horrible as facing Ian after he learned the truth. He'd detest her, and she couldn't bear his hatred.

"Thomas will wonder where I've gone," she conceded, knowing she'd leave.

"Write him a note and say you had to go away, and give him the run of the house. I sincerely doubt if he'll mind not having you around."

Mariah was right. Thomas didn't care for her except to bed her like all of the other men she'd known. Nodding her head, she woodenly turned and went to her room to pack a few clothes and pen a note to Thomas. The servants were busy in the other wing, and no one saw her head down the stairs and meet Mariah in the garden. Following him to the street, they entered a large black carriage and soon Philadelphia was but a memory. But in Annabelle's mind, Ian Briston's image would always be clear and vivid.

Eli Templet limped into Ian's office, looking older and more frail than Ian remembered.

"Sorry not to have been able to get here sooner," Eli apologized, and sank into a chair, placing his cane on his lap. "But I got snake-bit and nearly died before I could check on this Emmie Gray person. Some Indians nursed me back to health."

"I've been worried about you, Eli," Ian told the old man, and poured him a glass of brandy which Eli downed in one gulp.

Minutes later, after drinking another glassful, Eli elaborated on the Indian raid which had killed the Gray family and some other families in the Pennsylvania wilderness. "Yep, the British stirred them Indians up with liquor and all sorts of talk. I found the Gray farm and the graves, but there weren't no headstones. A farmer named Fisher had lived nearby, but he left after the raiding party. He and his wife escaped to Lancaster, and I caught up with them only two weeks ago. I asked him if he remembered Emmie Gray and her people."

"And did he?"

"Yep," Eli intoned in a deep voice. "Fisher told me that Emmie's folks were killed, then the little brother. Finally Emmie was raped by one of the braves before her throat was cut. Mr. Fisher buried all of them himself."

"So Emmie Gray is dead."

"Been dead for months. Fisher claims she was a little red-haired gal with huge green eyes and freckles. No more than fifteen she was. I hope I got you all the information you needed, Mr. Briston."

"Eli, you've been most helpful," Ian admitted. As soon as he shook hands with Eli and they parted, Ian knew who he was going to see that afternoon.

401

Chapter Twenty-Eight

During the next eight months Bethlyn's life settled into a peaceful routine, broken only by the nights of intense passion with Ian. She no longer worried about Emmie Gray. The woman had mysteriously disappeared, giving no clue when she might return, which was fine with Bethlyn, because she dreaded that fateful day.

Thomas Eversley, to both Bethlyn's and Ian's surprise had remained in Philadelphia. Since the Babcock House was empty, Ian found no reason to deny him when Thomas inquired about leasing it. Thomas had accompanied them to a number of parties and made acquaintances with noted Tories, but was especially friendly with, and the Bristons thought oddly, the American major, Benedict Arnold.

Ian had explained to Bethlyn that Arnold lived a rather expensive life-style in the former dwelling of General Howe, and there was much speculation about his income. At more than one social affair, Peggy Shippen had flashed expensive jewels, hinting that they were from a dear admirer.

The announcement of an engagement between Arnold and Peggy came as no surprise to Bethlyn. Peggy, as flighty and seemingly empty-headed as ever, had had the thirty-six-year-old besotted suitor dancing to her tune for some months. But Bethlyn had always wondered if Peggy's shallowness was only pretended. During the British occupation she'd danced and flirted nightly with

John André and the other officers, beguiling them with her prettiness and less than deep thoughts. No sooner had the Americans returned than she was knee-deep in invitations to social functions and extending her own, and once again she was the belle of Philadelphia society. Most probably she'd have continued on this way except her sights had settled on the widowed American major who suffered a hero's wound at the Battle of Saratoga, his limp making him an irresistible and romantic figure to the youthful Peggy.

However, given Arnold's penchant for his Tory friendships, Ian wondered at Arnold's loyalty to the American cause. He'd confided to Bethlyn more than once that the patriots were less than thrilled at Arnold's intimacies with loyalists, Ian among them. Only a handful of patriots knew of Ian's pretense, and Arnold wasn't one of them. Arnold had sought out Ian's friendship, and Ian had much admired the man until recently when Arnold resigned his command in Philadelphia in the face of accusations that he had misused public property and his authority.

General Washington was to soon set the date of his court-martial, but Arnold shocked all of Philadelphia by going ahead with his marriage to Peggy Shippen and arranging to buy one of the most beautiful and grand estates in the area, hardly the sort of home he could afford on his military salary, and considered a foolhardy purchase in the face of the charges leveled against him.

As Bethlyn dressed for the wedding on that April morning, her thoughts weren't on the coming nuptials, but Ian. He'd been called away a month before on a secret mission, and she had no idea when she'd see him again.

"You look so beautiful," Annie complimented her, and stood back to get a better view of the rose-and-white silk gown with elbow-length sleeves which dripped layers of white lace down to the center of the dress. "I think you'll outdo the bride."

Bethlyn didn't reply, her heart not in the coming festivities. She missed Ian so much and wouldn't cease worrying until he was home. When a servant announced that Thomas Eversley waited downstairs to escort her to the wedding, she forced a smile which didn't reach her eyes, but Thomas didn't seem to notice or to mind when she barely responded to his questions or comments during the wedding party and afterward as they rode home in his carriage.

She'd never seen the usually serious and dour-faced Thomas so animated, but thought nothing of his high spirits when he followed her into the parlor, causing her to feel obligated in offering him a glass of brandy for escorting her to the wedding. In reality, she wanted him to leave so she could go to bed.

"When will Ian be home?" he asked Bethlyn, and settled himself in a comfortable chair for what Bethlyn feared was going to be a long visit.

"I don't know. I suppose whenever his business is finished."

"This isn't his first mysterious absence," he commented, and swirled the brandy, his eyes intently studying her. "Don't you wonder at these out-of-the-blue departures?"

Something in Thomas's words alarmed her, putting her on her guard. The man was subtly prying. Could it be that he suspected that Ian's absences weren't related to business but spying? Had he already somehow connected Ian to Hawk? She didn't believe Thomas was brilliant enough for such an assumption. So why did he stay in Philadelphia and escort her to parties when Ian was gone?

"Certainly I wish Ian was home," she said, and weighed her words. "I miss him."

"Is that all you miss?"

"What do you mean?"

Thomas actually snickered and rose from his chair to sit beside her on the sofa. Taking her hand in his, he didn't seem to care that this bold action had stunned her.

"My dear, you've tasted, shall we say, the fruits of the marriage bed, and like all healthy young women left alone for long periods of time, you must be ravenous to taste them again. I offer you my assistance."

Before Bethlyn was fully aware of Thomas's intent, his mouth swooped fiercely down upon hers, and his arms

404

pinned her against him with such unbridled strength that she was left gasping and vainly struggling to break free.

For a second his lips broke away and he whispered something incredibly obscene in her ear. Her surprise gave way to anger, and suddenly his ear was near her mouth allowing her access to his lobe. With teeth bared she bit down as hard as she could, feeling the instant taste of blood spring into her mouth.

Thomas's yowl of pain deafened her, and when his hand grabbed the injured ear, she broke away and ran to the fireplace and grabbed the poker. Brandishing it, she made a vicious jab in the air, but close enough to Thomas that he realized her intent.

"Get out of my house, you filthy swine! If ever I see you again, I'll puncture that hideous bulge in your trousers."

"You're mad!" Thomas screamed at her, and his usually calm and nondescript eyes burned with hatred, pain—and lust. For a second, he almost lunged towards her, not at all worried about the poker. But he stopped when all of the servants rushed to the doorway, their voices shrill with fear that their mistress was in danger.

"Madam, may I assist you somehow?" the butler, a large and powerful man, inquired in his best teatime voice.

"Yes, you can show this blackguard out and remember never to allow him entry again." Bethlyn pointed to Thomas with the poker, but she was shaking and she knew that this flimsy thing wouldn't have saved her from a determined man. And she could see now that Thomas was determined to have her. Why hadn't she realized this before now?

The butler made a move to grasp hold of Thomas's arm, but Thomas wrenched away. He looked at Bethlyn, his gaze burning through hers. "You hate me, don't you, my lady? You've always hated me, never thought me good enough for an earl's daughter, if you thought of me at all—"

"You're a disgusting individual," she interrupted, and didn't bother to hide her contempt. "I don't know how my father has stood you all of these years. I discovered what sort of cargo you were transporting on *Nightingale*, and I

405

wrote to my father. By now he knows everything."

The little chit looked so self-satisfied that Thomas felt an ungodly urge to throttle her backside. But he'd received the letter she'd written to Talbot and destroyed it. Not that it mattered, for the man had died a short time later. Yet he wanted to wipe that self-righteous disdain from her face.

"You are still a stupid, silly child. The earl only laughed at your juvenile letter and threw it away, bemoaning the fact that he hadn't sired a son instead of a priggish daughter. Your only claim to his affections, my dear, was that you married Briston and did your wifely duty by opening your legs for him. All your father wants is a grandson to inherit. He has no use for you." Thomas stopped speaking, seeing the liquid well in those hauntingly beautiful brown eyes. No matter how much she claimed to hate him or how much he liked humiliating her, he still wanted this woman and vowed to have her.

He expected her to surrender to her tears. Instead he felt surprise and grudging admiration when she straightened and, with a great deal of calm, replaced the poker by the fireplace. Then she said without a quiver in her voice, "I suggest you return to England and my father, sir. Whatever your motive was for staying in Philadelphia for so long is indeed gone. I can assure you that if you bother me again, you shall be unfathomably sorry."

"Oh, I suppose you intend to sick your absent spouse upon me, to have him pummel me to death?" Thomas sneered.

"No. I shall delight in killing you myself."

The servants behind him tittered and giggled into their hands. More than anything in the world Thomas hated to be laughed at, and his face flamed brighter than a cherry tree. With as much dignity as he could muster, he left the room and the house of his own free will.

Once outside, he strode into the carriage and slammed the door behind him, but his gaze stayed centered on the parlor window, seeing the servants buzzing around Bethlyn like bees until one of them resolutely closed the drapes.

He decided he'd have to hide for the time being, not

caring to leave Babcock House, but he knew that the hot-blooded wench would tell Briston, who'd feel it his duty to seek revenge. He'd take a room in a nearby town and would be quite circumspect. The Bristons would never know that he was aware of their every movement.

In fact he might just have a bit of fun at Briston's expense, he decided, his eyes lingering on the house a bit too long.

"But I'll break your spirit yet, Bethlyn Briston. I'll break you and delight in the doing," he whispered hoarsely and ordered the driver to return to Babcock House.

The fire started in the dark of night.

Ian and Bethlyn were wakened by the sound of breaking glass and the servants' screams from downstairs. Young Annie, whose forehead was covered in blood, ran wildly down the hallways in her nightgown screaming, "Fire, fire! They're gonna kill us all."

Bethlyn grabbed her robe and Ian pulled on his trousers and ran shirtless and shoeless down the long staircase to the bottom floor, pulling Bethlyn along with him. From the open door of his study, they saw orange-red flames lapping at the drapes and the walls. One of the women servants rushed to them, crying that the kitchen and dining room were afire.

Ian ordered everyone to leave the house, and within seconds the entire staff with mistress and master watched the stately Edgecomb go up in flames. It was no use to fetch buckets of water from the pump. The fire was spreading rapidly, and the heat was intense.

Many of the servants who'd worked for the Bristons all of their lives cried openly. Tears ran down Bethlyn's face to see the house she'd come to think of as her home burn away. Ian, however, stood with his arms around her, and shed not a tear, but Bethlyn could feel his pain and knew that it was immense.

In the morning Edgecomb was a smoldering mass of rubble. Only the stone porticoes, like inefficient sentinels, still stood. The servants told Ian that some of them had seen two men lurking around the property before the fire, and deciding they might be hungry travelers had gone outside to offer them food, but the men had turned and run away. About an hour later, after everyone was asleep, the fire had started. Annie, who had been unable to sleep and wanted to borrow a book to practice her reading, was nearly knocked senseless by a flying brick as it crashed through the study window, followed by a lighted torch which instantly set the drapes ablaze.

Ian nodded at the information, the bright sunshine emphasizing the small lines which fanned out from the corners of his eyes and the furrowed line above his brows.

"We're leaving," he said, and turned to Bethlyn, his look expressing that she not argue. "Tonight we'll stay at Babcock House, since Eversley is gone, and I'll find you some clothes. Perhaps Cynthia will lend you something to wear, because I'm taking you to New York in the morning to stay with Molly where you'll be safe."

"All right," she agreed. "But why can't we stay in Philadelphia?"

His eyes resembled green glass, hard and without reflection. "Because someone burned Edgecomb as a warning to us. I don't know who it was. The arsonists could have been rebels who resent my loyalist views or someone who wishes to control us by driving us from our home. Either way, the servants' lives were in danger. You could have been killed, and I would be unable to bear that, my love. New York is the safest place for you right now."

Splaying her fingers across his bare chest, she lifted her head to look at him and studied him intently, somehow fearful of losing him. "What about you, Ian? Aren't you going to stay in New York with me?"

He pulled her close and shook his head, thrusting out his jaw defiantly. "I thought my last voyage would be the end and that I could live peacefully and contentedly here with you, but I see that Captain Hawk will have little rest until this war is won."

She knew what that meant, and her heart cried.

*   *   *

New York was a most exciting place to live. There was much hustle and bustle and a myriad of stores to occupy one's time. Nothing, however, was as wonderful as being with Molly and Hans and their baby daughter, Greta, named after Hans's mother.

Ian and Bethlyn found the charming old Dutch house in which the Grubers lived to be quite lovely, and the countryside outside of New York where the house was situated was a welcome relief from the busy city and the red-coated British soldiers who traipsed about. Ian also made friends with Hans, though Bethlyn knew Ian would never approve of his brother-in-law's mercenary soldiering for the Crown. However, Ian couldn't admit this was the reason for his distant attitude to either Hans or Molly. Bethlyn finally had noticed how Molly hid her pain at Ian's rejection of her husband, and Bethlyn intervened, telling Ian to see Hans as the fine young man that he was, and not as America's enemy, for one day the war would be over.

The week before Ian left New York, insinuating that Briston Shipping took him away, he and Hans had parted on friendly terms. Parting with Ian tore at Bethlyn's heartstrings, and she silently cursed the cause for which Ian so ardently fought. For his sake she managed not to look crestfallen and to smile and wave as the carriage taking him away rolled down the tree-lined lane. But his passionate farewell kiss still lingered on her lips, and this was all she had for comfort when she cried herself to sleep that night.

The days, the weeks, and months dragged by endlessly. A week before Christmas, Mavis and Marc arrived with their curly-haired imp of a son. Nothing was more heartwarming than the sight of little Marc and Greta stretched out side by side on a blanket in the cozy sitting room before the blazing hearth. Everyone was so happy and filled with the spirit of the holidays, but Bethlyn wasn't. Mavis noticed her forced gaiety, as did Marc. When Molly and Hans left the room, Mavis took her hand. "Ian will be all right," she said encouragingly. "He'll return to you soon."

"Mavis is right," Marc agreed, and smiled, looking boyishly handsome. "No one has ever been able to capture the Hawk but you, Bethlyn."

Tears of gratitude, mixed with fear and longing, sparkled in her eyes, and Bethlyn clutched both of her friends' hands. "I love you both for trying to cheer me, and I know in my heart that Ian is safe. But I haven't seen him in seven months. I miss him so much."

"He'll be with you soon," Marc assured her.

"I hope so, I do hope so."

That December Benedict Arnold was found guilty of using army wagons to haul private goods and of illegally granting a pass to a trading ship. Bethlyn received a letter from Peggy Shippen Arnold, elaborating on how her husband was much maligned and also that she had been corresponding with John André, who begged to be remembered to Bethlyn.

Somehow the memory of John's kindnesses to her and the warm hours they spent at Edgecomb seemed a long time ago. Bethlyn suddenly felt very old and alone.

One evening Bethlyn sat in the garden behind the house and plucked a wild daisy from the earth. Her fingers stroked the fragile petals before pulling each one off and saying as she did so, "He loves me, he loves me not, he . . ."

"Loves you very much."

She spun around at the voice behind her, and in an instant Ian had wrapped her trembling body in his arms. She cried, sobbing out her happiness. "Promise me you won't leave me again," she pleaded after Ian had led her to sit beneath a spreading elm tree.

He kissed away a tear. "I'd like to promise that more than anything else in the world, sweetheart. But I can't. You do understand."

Yes, she understood, and that was the reason for the

gnawing ache in her heart. She wanted to beg him to choose between her and his country, but knew that wouldn't be fair. Ian loved both of them, and once he'd given his love, he didn't relent or would ever think of being unfaithful. Wasn't this the very reason she loved him?

Nodding, Bethlyn let Ian raise her to her feet and then they entered the house and headed for Bethlyn's room, which was away from noise and household traffic. Soon snug and engulfed in passion in the large, soft feather bed, the war seemed a long distance away.

Ian found a beautiful fieldstone house on an old country lane whose banks were dark with wild violets. Bethlyn fell in love with the place instantly, enchanted by the high ceilings in every room and the view from the bedroom which overlooked a running stream.

The house wasn't grand or large like Edgecomb, but to Bethlyn and Ian, Wild Violets, as they'd come to name the place, represented their love and the cherished moments of being together. But all too soon their idyllic existence ended on a warm summer afternoon when word came that Benedict Arnold, who had somehow convinced friends in high places to put him in command of West Point and its garrison, had intended to surrender his post to the British for twenty thousand pounds. Arnold had escaped before he could be arrested.

The courier who'd arrived out of nowhere seemed to leave the same way. From the way Ian hung on to the message Bethlyn knew something serious had happened, and a cold fear clutched her heart. Ian told her before she even asked.

"Poor Peggy," she mumbled.

"There's more," he said, and cleared his throat. "John André has been captured with the incriminating documents on his person. It is assumed that he'll be hung as a spy."

Bethlyn rose abruptly from her chair and dropped her knitting onto the floor. She clutched her throat. "Not

John. Oh, Ian, he's such a sweet, kind, and gallant man."

His hand massaged his forehead. "I know. I remember those nights he dined at Edgecomb."

"You must help him some way." She grabbed onto his arm, her eyes pleading.

"I'll try," he said, but from the despairing tone of his voice she knew already that it was hopeless.

Bethlyn received word from Ian, who'd gone to General Washington's headquarters to plead for André's life. The General, for all his great regard for the young English officer, refused to back down. André was going to be hung as a spy.

Bethlyn crumbled the letter in her hands and wept her utter hopelessness. She felt that André, as did many other people, was being made to be the scapegoat for Arnold's treason. André was a British officer, doing what any other officer would have done in a like situation. Arnold had contacted André first about handing over West Point, not the other way around.

She felt helpless, but she wanted to do something for John André, the man who had been her friend and admirer. The thought of directly begging Washington to save his life crossed her mind, but she discounted it. If Washington wouldn't budge for Ian, then he wouldn't listen to her. What could she do then? What might possibly have a lasting impact on the populace and General Washington?

The Dove.

The answer was so simple she felt startled, but she knew the Dove could arouse people to take a stand whereas Bethlyn Briston could not.

Sitting at her desk, she reached for a quill and began to pen what she felt was the most important poem of her life.

"This is a stunning surprise," the spy known as Mariah commented and sipped his wine.

"What is?" Annabelle Hastings stirred, her sleepy eyes

coming awake. She found Mariah sitting against the pillow, reading a pamphlet. Her fingers traced the curve of his thigh. "Oh, that's one of those rebel pamphlets, espousing drivel about independence. Why do you bother to read such trash?"

Mariah cocked a dark eyebrow over one of his equally black eyes at her. "Because this one is most intriguing. It seems that the Dove is in New York and bemoaning the capture of André. Her poem is quite a tribute to him, but rather a strange turn of face, don't you think. Months ago she was a patriot and now she is in André's corner."

Annabelle clutched the sheet. The Dove was Bethlyn Briston, and Ian's wife. She'd thought she'd forgotten Ian Briston, but now warring emotions stirred within her breast. Hatred was the more powerful, but the love she felt for him vied for the upper hand. She mustn't allow Mariah to see she might still desire Ian Briston. He'd never understood her obsession for the man even after she'd learned Ian had had Emmie Gray investigated and had never trusted her. More than once Mariah had told her she should consider herself lucky to escape Briston. But Annabelle didn't feel lucky at all.

She'd lost the only man she could ever love.

Mariah, she discovered, for all of his covert dealings, was a basically kind and generous man. A handsome man, too. She didn't know his ancestry or his true name. He was so dark that she wondered if he might be part Indian. He never told her about his past, but he always told her that he loved her. And Annabelle believed he did.

No man had ever been so wonderful to her or treated her like she was so fragile she'd break. Mariah made her feel feminine and beautiful. He adored her and worshiped her body with his masculine and finely shaped hands. Her pleasure was his pleasure, and Mariah introduced her to gentle but sensuous lovemaking—nothing coarse or crude as she'd known with Holmes and Eversley. The man was everything most women could ever hope to find in a lover.

Why didn't she love him?

"What do you make of the Dove and this poem?" she heard Mariah ask.

413

Annabelle shrugged and sat up, her long hair reaching to her waist. "Perhaps she likes stirring up trouble."

"She? I didn't realize you had any inkling the Dove was a woman."

"Eversley told me."

Mariah leaned forward and cupped her chin in his hand, causing her to look at him. "Annabelle, do you know who the Dove is?"

When his eyes probed hers, Annabelle found it impossible to lie to Mariah. Sometimes she wondered if the man held her in some sort of thrall. "Maybe," she reluctantly admitted.

"Thomas Eversley would pay dearly for that information, and the British have been most eager to catch this woman for months. Why didn't you tell someone? Why didn't you tell me?"

A note of hurt was in his voice and his eyes expressed his disillusionment with her. "I believed we had no secrets from each other, Annabelle."

"God, Mariah! You can't expect me to tell you everything I know or all I've ever done in my life. You certainly withhold information about your past."

"That's different. There's money to be gained with this information."

"Yes, but I was under the impression that you were a spy because you were loyal to the Crown. Do you mean to tell me that all you really want is money?"

Mariah sighed and leaned against the pillow, folding his arms behind his head. Such a hardness appeared in his eyes and such ragged pain shadowed his face that Annabelle flinched.

"Suffice to say that money is all in life when trust has been displaced."

"You're saying that you don't trust me."

"Not any longer," he admitted, and those eyes gleamed with raw hatred. "I don't trust any woman, least of all you. I think you're still in love with Ian Briston."

"You're wrong." Her vehement protest sounded hollow to her own ears. "I don't give him or that bitch he married a thought."

"Annabelle, Annabelle," he crooned sadly. "When will you ever realize how much the man loves her? I could have given you so much love and joy if you had only let me. But your insides are festering with jealousy for Bethlyn Briston, and this shall be your downfall. You never had Briston's heart, his wife did and does. Believe me, I've done some despicable things in my lifetime, things I sincerely regret, but I've been smart enough to let go of an obsession, whereas you have not. I feel sorry for you. I truly pity you."

Mariah rose from the bed and started to dress in his usual black garments. "Where are you going?" Annabelle asked, fearing she knew the answer.

"Away." He took his ebony cape from a wall peg and twirled it around his shoulders. Coming to the bed, he leaned over and gently kissed her lips. "I wish you good fortune, but I doubt you'll be sensible enough to seize it if it comes your way again."

She watched his broad and masculine frame fill the doorway, and then he left.

For the first time in a long time Annabelle wanted to cry. Mariah was gone and she'd miss him, but she would never rush after him and beg him to stay. She just didn't love him.

Ian, however, she would always love. But he didn't want her, and he was the only man who hadn't wanted her. She hated the rejection more because he'd chosen his wife over her.

But she hated Bethlyn Briston more than anything, and if she never could have Ian as her own, then Bethlyn wouldn't either.

General Clinton's aide was most grateful for Annabelle's information about the Dove. After her departure, he notified the general because of the gravity of the situation. Clinton mulled over all he'd been told, but shrugged and leaned back in his chair.

"Arrest the wench," Clinton stated, and the aide instantly obeyed.

Chapter Twenty-Nine

Bethlyn told her inquisitors nothing, and for that she earned a cell with a mildewed feather mattress and a cracked chamber pot for amenities.

No one had harmed her. In fact, General Clinton had been most accommodating by pouring her a cup of tea which she hadn't been able to swallow, and inquiring after her husband's health. However, his smarmy smile had faded when his aide had no luck in gaining an admission from her that she was the Dove. So now she sat on the cold stone floor of her cell rather than sit on the foul smelling mattress which she felt certain must be crawling with bugs.

She wanted to cry but wouldn't give her captors that satisfaction. However, she did pray for Ian to learn of her arrest and come to her. Her body literally ached to see him again, but since he'd left for Washington's headquarters nearly a month ago, she'd received only the one message about André. And André had been hung on October second, more than two weeks ago.

Where was Ian? Why hadn't he returned by now? She felt so alone and frightened without him. Yet even if he did receive word that she'd been arrested, could he help her? At the moment her only hope was that Hans and Molly would soon receive the message she'd sent by a servant to them when she was arrested at Wild Violets. But even that hope was dashed when Hans and Molly appeared by her cell some two hours later.

Molly dabbed at her eyes with a kerchief and held on to Bethlyn's hands which reached through the bars to hers. "What a travesty this is," Molly noted in high indignation. "You're the wife of Ian Briston, a loyalist, and Clinton dares to treat you like a criminal. I shall have my say with the man, believe me!"

"Hush, Molly," Hans warned, his concern for Bethlyn clearly expressed on his face. But it was the glimmer of knowledge shining in his eyes which conveyed to Bethlyn that he knew she was the Dove. His thick accent sounded harder to understand when he sadly shook his head and said, "I can't help you. You're not to be released under any circumstances until your trial proves your innocence. I'm sorry, Bethlyn. Forgive me for not being able to do anything."

Bethlyn sighed, fearing as much. "Then I shall be in here a very long time."

After Hans left and Molly had parted tearfully from her, Bethlyn knew such intense isolation that the tears she had suppressed all day finally ran free. Huge gasping sobs tore from her throat, and she wondered if she'd ever see Ian again.

"Please keep Ian safe," she prayed after she'd wept so hard and long she couldn't squeak out another tear. "Keep him safe so that he can come for me, and we can be together again. Is that so much to ask?"

Somehow she feared it was.

Ian watched as General Washington's tall figure settled into the chair behind his desk. The man's weariness was evident by the sloping line of his shoulders and the dark circles beneath eyes which had had little sleep. Yet a spark of determination flowed through him as he waited for Ian's response to the secretive plan he'd just put forth.

"I need you for this mission, Ian. I've chosen only the best and never have you been a disappointment to me. You see, I'm so positive you'll accept that I decided to inform you of what has been planned for a number of weeks. The only hitch was that André confessed to everything, and I

417

was forced to hang him." He tiredly rubbed his eyes. "If he wouldn't have said anything, then he could have been exchanged with the British for Arnold."

"You must want Arnold quite badly," Ian noted.

Washington's face hardened. "I confess that I do. The man not only betrayed his country but our friendship. So often I took up his cause when he wanted to advance himself, even writing to discover why he didn't receive some commissions. And his treason is my reward. I even believe that his wife was in on everything and pretended to be hysterical the morning I visited their home and learned of . . . this . . . this travesty. Arnold has ill used me, and I want him returned to me. Alive. I need your help."

Ian fairly groaned under the knowledge that he had no choice but to accept the mission to kidnap Benedict Arnold. If Washington had gone so far as to brief him on secret plans, then he knew the seriousness of the situation. Arnold was leading an army of American deserters who'd taken up the British cause. Such an influence could be damning to an American victory.

As much as Ian wanted to help, he also wanted to return to Bethlyn. Yet he'd already vowed that his country would have to come first until the war was won, and he hoped that Bethlyn truly understood. Still, this fight wouldn't keep him warm at night. He missed Bethlyn so damned much!

"I'll do anything that's necessary," Ian finally responded.

"Good, son. I knew I could trust you. The man in charge of the operation is Sergeant Major Champe."

"I thought he was a deserter."

"Champe's desertion was a finely tuned deception. He has since made contact with Arnold and been offered a position as one of his officers. Major Light Horse Harry Lee and three of his men will be hiding nearby on the night of the kidnapping with horses in readiness for Arnold, Champe, and yourself. You and Champe will kidnap Arnold in the garden of his home, gag him, and drag him through the streets. If anyone questions either of you, you're to say that "the soldier is drunk and is being

418

taken to the guardhouse." Another associate will wait with a boat by the Jersey shore for transportation to Hoboken where Arnold will be delivered to Lee, who will in turn bring the traitor to me. Any other briefings between now and the kidnapping will come from Champe." Washington's gaze penetrated Ian's. "As always, I avow no knowledge of activity. Your escape is entirely up to you."

Ian nodded and stood up to shake Washington's hand. "Don't fail me, lad," the general requested softly.

"I promise that Arnold will be in your hands before long, sir."

On his way out of Washington's office, Ian nearly bumped into a man who was sweeping very close to the general's door. He nearly stopped, wondering if he should say something to Washington about the man. One never knew who might be listening. But the man who resembled an Indian with his coal-black hair and bedraggled clothing shot Ian a very bright smile and said something in an Indian dialect which Ian didn't understand.

Inclining his head, Ian mumbled a good day to the man and walked on, deciding that he was no threat. Apparently he couldn't speak English.

The Indian man disappeared from his mind as he conjured up Bethlyn's image. He wanted to see her again, but there wasn't time. For the Arnold kidnapping to be carried out, he had to make immediate contact with Champe to arrange the details. But he decided that when this mission was over, he'd settle down at Wild Violets with Bethlyn for a long rest. Maybe a permanent one.

Thomas Eversley was livid at the news from Mariah that Bethlyn Briston was the Dove.

What a fool the little tart had made of him! He'd never forgive her for humiliating him in front of his crew, for the innocent way she'd gone along with nary a clue after his arrival in Philadelphia. How she must have laughed at him. But now he'd have the last laugh. The bitch was in prison, most likely suffering horrible indignities. No Captain Hawk would come to her rescue now.

His head bolted up, no longer seeing Bethlyn's face in

419

the bottom of his empty ale cup. The loud voices and bawdy tales from the sailors and men who surrounded him in the seafront tavern ceased to exist for Thomas, and he barely saw Mariah, who sat across the small wooden table from him. Instead, he pictured the masked visage of Captain Hawk and wondered how he'd been such a stupid jackass as to not realize the truth before this. If Bethlyn Briston was the Dove, then wouldn't it figure that her paramour, Hawk, was, in reality, her husband?

The sudden knowledge rolled over him like a thunderbolt, deafening him with the implications. Finally, after all these years, Thomas had Ian Briston backed into a corner, a cage to be exact, in some filthy hole of a prison if he had his way, and he relished the sense of absolute power.

But a sense of frustration welled within him. Briston wasn't in his grasp.

"Has Briston been to visit his wife yet?" Thomas asked Mariah.

"No. Only the Grubers."

Thomas didn't hide his downcast look, and Mariah gulped down his ale and laughed. "My friend, I thought you were most eager to learn the identities of this couple."

"I could have put the pieces together once I knew Bethlyn was suspected of being the Dove," Thomas reminded Mariah sharply. "Most certainly I'm not stupid, man."

"Ah, but you're not a spy and you don't think like one or know how to obtain the information you seek. At this very moment you want to know how to lay hands on Ian Briston."

"Yes."

"Then I shall help you do this. For a price."

"Of course I'll pay you, but don't expect a fortune from me."

Mariah stood to leave, his large frame bending over Thomas. "If that's your attitude I will keep the information to myself. Good night, Mr. Eversley."

"Wait!" Thomas hissed, and Mariah sat back down. "I'll pay your price, no matter the cost. I want Ian Briston."

"I think you want his wife more," Mariah noted, and there was a bit of dislike for Thomas and loathing for himself in his tone of voice. "But I tell you what I know only because I need the money, a very large sum of money, Mr. Eversley."

"The damn money is yours," Thomas grumbled, running out of patience. "Just tell me the plan to capture Briston and be done with it. I've waited long enough in these godforsaken colonies. Heaven only knows why we're fighting to keep them. I say good riddance to the lot of them, and to you, Mariah. Before this month is over, I'll sail for England—with my bride beside me."

Mariah felt no satisfaction when he started to reveal the plan he'd overheard outside the door of Washington's office. As a trusted British spy, he'd make certain that Benedict Arnold wouldn't be the man kidnapped that night. But a pang of guilt twisted through him at what he was doing to an innocent woman.

No woman deserved the distinction of being the object of Thomas Eversley's lust, but to realize that he was helping to place her in Eversley's keeping pricked the last vestiges of Mariah's conscience. When Eversley left the tavern, much pleased with the plan, Mariah sent up a prayer to the creator and begged forgiveness.

Bethlyn dozed as she leaned against the damp wall of her cell. Dusk filtered in through the small, barred window and no lanterns had been lighted yet. She thought she must be dreaming when she heard someone softly call her name from outside, but being too fatigued from her weeklong stay in the prison, she nodded off again.

"Bethlyn!" The voice cut through her sleep, and she woke to stare at the window, seeing a figure silhouetted against the darkening sky. Blinking back her disbelief, she rose on unsteady feet, the hem of her gown dragging along the dirty floor, to grasp the bars and feel the warm pressure of Ian's fingers in her own.

"My God!" he whispered in a ragged voice. "What have they done to you?" If his hands had been small enough he'd have slid them through the bars to wipe away the dirt streaks on her face and the dark smudges beneath her eye from lack of sleep and worry. Yet those beautiful brow orbs which swirled with golden specks shimmered wit joy at seeing him.

"I thought I'd never see you again." She choked on he words as tears slid down her cheeks. Increasing th pressure of her fingers on his, she gazed wonderingly a him and hoped she wasn't dreaming.

Ian could barely speak from the sense of dismay an guilt which clutched at him. Just that afternoon he' learned about Bethlyn's arrest from a house servant whe he'd returned to Wild Violets, hoping for a few hour alone with her until he had to leave. As he'd viciousl spurred his horse towards New York, he'd blamed an cursed himself a hundredfold for not being there to protec her.

Arnold's kidnapping was scheduled for midnight allowing very little time to tell her how much he loved her that would take days. He knew that at that very moment h should be going over last-minute plans and changing int the uniform of a British officer. But he knew Bethlyn mus be frightened, and he must convince her that he would fre her as soon as he was able and to cling to his love for her

"I haven't much time, my love," he said, and memorize every inch of her beautiful face. "I learned what happene just today. Has anyone wondered why I haven't visited yo yet?"

"Yes, but I told General Clinton and his aide that yo were away on business. Oh, Ian, I'm frightened."

Her fear transferred to him, but he must soothe her unti he could free her. "Listen to me, Bethlyn, and understand I've been preparing for a mission which will take plac tonight. As soon as it is ended, I'll be back here an demand your release. When this night is over, Captai Hawk will no longer exist. We'll go home and never worr about espionage again."

"What if General Clinton doesn't release me?"

Ian had considered the possibility. It seemed that th evidence against her was damning, but that wouldn't stop Ian. "Be prepared for anything, even an escape. Can yo be brave until then?"

She nodded. "I can stand anything as long as we're together again."

For a few silent seconds they gazed at each other with so much love that the sound of footsteps and the sudden brightness from a wall lantern along the corridor nearly went unnoticed until the jailer's shuffling step grew louder.

"Ian, you must leave," Bethlyn whispered in a rush.

Ian kissed one of her fingertips. Before he disappeared into the gathering darkness, he whispered, "Remember, I love you, and be prepared."

A nagging torment ate away at Ian's vitals as he stealthily neared the arranged meeting spot where he expected to find Sergeant Major Champe. He couldn't forget Bethlyn's face, streaked with dirt and tearstains, when he told her good-bye. Already he reasoned that Clinton probably wouldn't release her, so an escape was the only way to free her. They'd head for the safety of Windhaven and would stay there until the war was over, but he'd have to somehow arrange to bribe a guard to glance the other way when he sneaked into the prison to spirit Bethlyn away to freedom. He couldn't wait to have her in his arms again, to know she was safe.

First, however, he must put all his energies into completing this mission.

The Arnold residence glowed with but a few lights when Ian neared the back fence of the property. He found the wooden boards which Champe had quietly loosened weeks ago to make removal a simple task when they entered the yard to capture Arnold. The space would allow enough room to accommodate Ian and his fellow conspirator when lugging the hapless Arnold away.

Champe had discovered in his investigation of Arnold's habits that the man always used the privy late at night, thus eliminating the presence of servants. And on such a dark and cloudy night as this one, the abduction should be quite easy.

Feeling a bit warm with his black cape thrown over the scarlet officer's uniform, Ian skulked into the bushes to await Champe. He knew it was nearly midnight, and wondered where the man was. They had decided to meet at a quarter before the hour, and Champe was too much of a professional not to be punctual.

Had something happened?

Minutes dragged past until suddenly a door opened at the back of the house. Ian stiffened in response, melting into the darkness to peer over the fencetop. Suppose it was Arnold going to use the privy? He couldn't attempt the kidnapping on his own—otherwise, he'd be disobeying orders—but he sighed in relief to see that the figure silhouetted against the lamplight was Peggy Arnold's. In her arms she held a cat, which she promptly let loose and closed the door. All was silent except the wild pounding of Ian's heart.

When moments passed, Ian grew edgy, instinct warning him that something wasn't right. Champe should have arrived before then, and having seen no sign of Arnold he began to wonder if Arnold was even at home. Should he abort the mission? He wanted to leave but he'd given his word to Washington and decided to wait fifteen minutes longer.

The time passed slowly, and Ian grew more agitated, knowing that no kidnapping would occur tonight. The realization of this simultaneously annoyed and elated him. He'd wasted a great deal of time, but now he could concentrate on freeing Bethlyn.

Leaving the shadows of the bushes and trees, he quietly trod away from the house, but he hadn't gone far when his sense of danger alerted him to the fact that he was being watched. He'd barely halted in his tracks before he felt hot breath fanning the back of his neck.

He spun around, going for his pistol, but before he could even raise a hand to defend himself, the shadowy figure knocked something rock-hard against his temple with such unbridled force that Ian staggered, willing himself not to fall.

But the stunning dizziness won, and he barely realized that he'd dropped to his knees. Blood streamed freely down the side of his head and into his eye, but he wouldn't relinquish his hold on the pistol despite the incapacitating weakness which overpowered him.

Somehow he managed to lift his gaze to the dark-shrouded man before him who wore a black tricorn hat. "Who?" he rasped, losing strength as he tried vainly to rise to his feet.

"No one of importance," the man uttered in a somewhat sad tone of voice before hitting him with the hard, blunt object again.

Falling forward onto the grass, Ian lay totally defeated and unprepared for the black fog of unconsciousness.

An hour before dawn Bethlyn was awakened by the rattle of a key in the lock of her cell. A tall man wearing black gestured to her to be quiet, and he waved her forward.

Remembering what Ian had said about an escape, she stiffly stood up from the corner where she huddled and felt an immense delight that soon she'd be with Ian. Following behind the broad-shouldered man in the tricorn hat who stalked down the dimly lit and abandoned corridors, she wondered why Ian had sent this man.

As they made their way to a back door, Bethlyn noticed the place was empty of guards. During her time in the prison she'd heard a great deal of talking and activity when the soldiers changed shifts, and she knew it was very near that hour. Where was everyone? Not that she cared, but an uneasy feeling pricked at her.

"Who are you? Are you taking me to my husband?" she whispered to the man.

He said nothing as he opened the door and took her by the elbow to steer her into an alleyway which led onto the dark and deserted street. She almost balked, knowing that it was stupid to do so when the man was helping her to escape, but something wasn't right about this. Where was Ian?

"Come," he ordered, and dragged her along with him, not giving her the opportunity to say anything at all.

Reaching the street, a black carriage suddenly appeared, and by the gold markings on the side she recognized it as the one in which Briston Shipping conveyed important clients about the town.

Ian had come for her!

As soon as the door was thrown open, Bethlyn lunged a
the carriage only to be pulled unceremoniously onto the
seat by the man inside when the carriage started off at a
thunderous pace. Her delighted smile faded when it settled
on Thomas Eversley, sitting smug beside her.

"How kind of you to join me, my dear."

"Thom—Thomas, what are you doing here? Where i
Ian?"

The downward turn of his mouth belied the bold
pleasure in his eyes. "Ah, I hate to be the one to have to tel
you this, but your husband is quite dead. He was killed
tonight in an escapade of derring-do. But I shall comfor
you during your time of grief. Indeed, I will." Patting her
hand and holding it pinned beneath his own, Bethlyn
could barely move.

The absolute shock was too great to be believed. Ian
wasn't dead. He couldn't be dead!

"You're—lying," she heard herself say.

"My dear, he is gone. The man who led you out of the
prison is a British spy. He caught your husband, a man
who pretended to be a loyal servant of the king, by the way
committing a treasonous act. He had but one alternative
and killed him. Please don't screw up your face like tha
and start wailing. I can assure you that the end Briston me
by that man's hands was much more merciful than the on
the authorities had in mind for the notorious Captain
Hawk."

The fact that Thomas knew about Ian's other identity
didn't register in her mind. All she could see was her
beloved Ian lying dead somewhere.

The tears which welled in her eyes to stream down her
cheeks blinded her to everything else, even the lecherou
grin of Thomas Eversley.

An unbearable pain had centered in her heart, robbing
her of the desire to fight Eversley and throw herself from
the carriage to meet Ian in death. She was unaware when
the carriage finally stopped on the docks and didn't realiz
that Eversley led her like a whipped and docile puppy onto
a waiting ship where she was soon placed in a luxuriousl
furnished cabin.

She was vaguely cognizant that he stood before her unti

426

he said, "I trust you shall be fine for the next hour or so. I have business to attend to, but I shall be back soon and we can leave for England—and Woodsley. Wouldn't you like that?"

Saying nothing, because she was overcome by her own torment and grief, he bent down and kissed her firmly and possessively on the mouth. "I won't have sulking, Bethlyn, or wailing over Briston's demise," he commanded none too gently. "Understand when I tell you that I will brook no disobedience from you or teary eyes during this trip, which means a great deal to me. Listen to me!"

His piercing cry brought her head up sharply, and his words finally began to sink into her brain.

"I am leaving now, but when I return you will meet me with a loving smile on your beautiful face. Pretend I'm Briston for all I care, but I expect you to be amenable and sweet—like a good wife is to her husband."

"Wi-wife?"

Thomas flashed her a cruel grin. "Yes, my stammering darling, that's what I said. The captain of the ship will marry us shortly after we set sail, and I expect that delectable body of yours to satisfy me in every way. Do you hear me?"

Yes, she heard him. She watched as he left the cabin, heard the bolt which locked her in, but she didn't care. She cared about nothing, not even that he planned to marry her and most probably intended to assert his husbandly rights. Her mind felt unable to function or to even project herself into a future which no longer held any joy or mattered at all. Nothing was left to her except a gnawing pain and a horrendous ache which tore at her soul. Such a pain was far more excruciating than anything Thomas Eversley could ever do to her.

Ian was dead, and once the ache left her, she knew she would be, too.

Thomas spoke to Ian, who rested upon a hard-planked floor and was chained by the hands and feet to the wall of the British prison ship. Glad to see he was conscious now but no doubt in great physical pain, Thomas pricked his chest with the point of his walking stick and was more than eager to see the arrogant Briston suffer torment which went beyond the physical. He didn't fail to miss the burning hatred in the green eyes of his enemy. In fact, he relished that hatred and knew that one day Briston would be consumed by it in his own private hell.

"I know that Bethlyn shall make an admirable wife and that she'll enjoy mounting me as much as she did you," Thomas said. "However, I do intend to teach her things probably lacking in your tutorship of her. I shall enjoy her often and in many different ways."

Ian kicked out at him, but the leg irons prevented him from reaching Eversley. "Touch her, and I'll kill you!"

"Man, she'll be my wife. You are as good as dead to her now. Once you're in Mill Prison, there you'll rot for the rest of your life. I have no fear of your pitiful threats. No one ever escapes from there, but I wish your mind to be active when your body craves sweet death. For the rest of your miserable existence you'll suffer knowing that Bethlyn is mine, mine to do with as I please. Think about the two of us together, writhing in passion on the state bed at Woodsley. Think on it," Thomas bantered. "Grow impotent with rage against me and your imprisonment. I gladly thrust you into a living hell."

"I'll find you, Eversley, and I'll kill you. You won't be safe from me. Never safe!"

Thomas turned away from the sight of Ian straining at the chains, pretending not to hear his threat of vengeance. Even after he'd gone on deck of the frigate to bid the captain farewell and had settled in his carriage for the short ride to his waiting ship and was warmed by the morning sun which streamed into the window, a cold feeling of dread had taken root within him.

"Briston can't possibly harm me," he remarked, and sniffed his nose in disdain. "The man is mad, mad indeed to think he'll ever have the chance."

But his dread persisted until he chastised himself for being foolish and simply wouldn't dwell on Briston any longer. He had the man's wife to think about, and the cold feeling vanished to be replaced by the heat of lust.

Chapter Thirty

Once the ship was well away from New York, Bethlyn stood beside Thomas and was married by Captain Sterling in her cabin. The only reason she didn't slide to the floor during the ceremony was because Thomas's arm was firmly wrapped around her waist, seemingly defying her to move. Before the captain and Dr. Hanover, the ship's physician, had arrived, she'd told Thomas she felt ill. However, he'd ordered her to be quiet and do as she was bid, that she wasn't about to feign illness and interfere with his marriage plans.

She'd rebelliously lifted her face to him, but the menacing way Thomas had raised a hand to her quelled her momentary surge of defiance. He reminded her of her father at that instant, and the little girl inside her surfaced enough that she allowed Thomas to docilely introduce her to Captain Sterling.

The pain of Ian's death and all she had endured the last week, plus the fact that she felt close to retching, caused her to barely comprehend the words which united her to Thomas Eversley. When the ceremony ended and Thomas turned to place his lips upon hers, she did the unthinkable again. For the second time in her life on the day she was married, she vomited.

She heard Thomas's screech, vaguely aware that he'd been her target when she slipped to the floor. Dr. Hanover, the only one who seemed to have expected such an occurrence, positioned a chamber pot beneath her face and waited with her even when Captain Sterling and Thomas had departed the cabin.

When she'd finally heaved her last and her stomach began to settle into place, she found that Hanover's eyes were filled with pity and felt his comforting hand on her back.

"Here now, Mrs. Eversley, let me help you to the bunk."

The middle-aged and kindly man lifted her from her knees as if she weighed nothing, and soon she was lying down while he placed a cool washcloth on her forehead. "Are you ill like this often?" he asked.

She almost told him that she'd been ungodly sick on the morning she married Ian, but resisted because the memory was too bittersweet to even speak about at that moment. Instead she said, "I haven't eaten very much the last week. But I suppose my stomach has been queasy even before then."

"I see," Hanover said. "When was your last flux?"

"My last—what does that have to do with this?" She moved the washcloth from her forehead.

He smiled and patted her hand. "Mrs. Eversley, hadn't you considered you might be with child?"

"Child?" she repeated, and knew the man must believe her to be a simpleton. Somehow the retching had cleared her fog-shrouded brain, and she began to mentally calculate. Her last flux had been three months ago, but since she'd always missed some months she didn't question the long absence. Bethlyn had come to doubt she'd ever conceive so she no longer worried over not getting her flux. But she'd never gone this long before now, and her heart began to beat out a steady tempo along with her brain. Baby. Baby. Baby.

"I'm having a baby," she said in disbelief.

"Probably. Would you care to be examined? I promise to be most gentle with you," Hanover assured her. "The voyage to England may be long and rough going for a lady of your delicate upbringing. But if I know for certain you're with child, I can keep a close watch on you and the little one."

"Oh, yes, Doctor, please," she eagerly voiced, and the shock of Ian's death abated a tiny bit. "I need to know if

430

I'm having a child. I have to know."

Thomas was disgruntled and disgusted. Just like the chit to throw up all over him! He'd changed from his stained jacket and shirt, having to borrow one of Sterling's shirts, which was less than fine. He gulped down more than his share of the captain's whiskey while he waited for Hanover to finish with the girl.

"What in the deuce is taking so long?" he queried in a voice which sounded like a growl.

Sterling shrugged, more than soothed by the whiskey's effects as his eyes grew heavy.

Thomas, seeing that Sterling would soon be snoring, stalked out of the man's cabin and headed down the hallway to his own. His face was mottled in rage to think that Bethlyn was going to pretend illness to keep him away from her. Well, she was his wife now, and he'd spent too many damn aggravating nights thinking about her body and imagining how it would feel when he entered her. She wasn't going to deny him this pleasure. He'd see to that!

He very nearly bumped into Hanover as he came out of the cabin. The man shook his hand, beaming at him. "Congratulations, Eversley. They're both fine!" And then Hanover left him. What in the hell was he jabbering about? Thomas thought, pushing open the cabin door.

Before his eyes was the most unbelievable sight he'd ever seen, rivaling his most intimate dreams and fantasies about Bethlyn Briston. Waiting in the doorway, with mouth agape, he could barely swallow when Bethlyn turned towards him. She wore an exquisite nightrail, one of the elaborate creations he'd purchased in New York for her and placed in the cabin wardrobe, fashioned of the sheerest pink chiffon and white lace at the low neckline and long, flowing sleeves. Honey brown hair cascaded down her back and over her shoulders in abundant waves, and the centers of her brown eyes danced with amber sparkles. Her lips resembled wet and luscious strawberries, and they seemed to beckon him near to her.

431

"You're . . . too . . . beautiful," he gasped, unable to realize that this woman, the woman of his erotic fantasies, was dressed like this to please him, and that she was going to give herself to him without a fight. He felt himself hardening, incapable of controlling the lust which shot through his very body like thousands of arrows.

"Thank you, Thomas." Holding out a glass of wine to him, he took it from her like a mesmerized mouse under the watchful eye of a cat.

She lifted her own glass. "What shall we drink to?"

"Us, my dear. Only to us."

Their glasses clinked in a toast, but Thomas could barely drink his wine. Already he felt drunk, not from alcohol but from the beauty of this woman.

Bethlyn's perfume drifted to him, enveloping him within her scent. Her fingers grazed his when they placed their glasses on the table beside the bunk, and her hair slid sensuously across his lips. He had to have her, needed her with such a fierceness that for the first time Thomas was frightened by the intensity of his need. But still he grabbed for her and pulled her to him, delighting in the feel of her swelling breasts against his chest, loving the way his hardness rested against her abdomen.

Kissing her, he was more than a bit surprised to discover that she kissed him back. "Don't you intend to fight me?" he asked, suspicion coating his voice.

"No, dear Thomas, I don't. And before you ask why, I shall tell you." Moving from the circle of his arms, Bethlyn pirouetted before him, the sheer and lacy creation she wore swirling around her in a sea of pink-and-white froth. "This gown is most beautiful, as are all the other ones in the wardrobe, and I applaud your taste. I find that I love pretty clothes and a man's attentions. And you seem quite willing to accommodate me."

"Be assured that I will," he said, sounding smug.

Bethlyn flashed him a beguiling smile which made his already fast-beating heart nearly gallop out of his chest. "I do hope that you mean that," she observed, "because in the coming months I shall need you more and more."

"I don't understand."

"I shall show you then."

Before him, she removed her gown, allowing him to see all of her radiant beauty. She was more beautiful than any woman he'd ever lain with, more glorious in her nakedness than his own wanton imaginings. Her breasts were high and deliciously full and kissable. No wonder Briston had been enamored of her, so besotted he'd finally fouled up a mission. Who would be able to think straight when this woman, whose small waist and rounded hips, which tapered to perfectly lovely legs, was home waiting for him? But now Bethlyn waited for him and his eyes feasted on the hidden center of her womanhood, openly licking his lips in anticipation of tasting her delightful sweetness fully.

"Bethlyn, show me how you love, my sweet." Thomas began to remove his pants, but her words stopped him.

"Don't you see, Thomas? Didn't you notice the bulge here?" She placed a protective hand on her abdomen.

"Yes, so?"

"So, I'm carrying a child. A child the world will believe is yours. Aren't you quite thrilled?"

His hand reached for her wrist and he held it in a taut and painful grip. "You're having Briston's bastard? Is this some sort of a trick to keep me from touching you?"

"No, why would I trick you? Ask Dr. Hanover. He confirmed my pregnancy, and my child isn't a bastard."

He could tell she spoke the truth. Pregnant with Briston's child. Good God! He couldn't stand it. He thought he was free of the man, but now Bethlyn was going to have a child to remind him of Briston for the remainder of his life. For an instant he thought about causing her to abort the baby, but he wouldn't do that, realizing he needed this child to cement his future. Marrying Bethlyn Briston wasn't enough. The legal ramifications of his claim as head of Briston Shipping had been questioned by some of the attorneys who represented the company, and he'd decided that a marriage to the earl's daughter would ensure his claim. Yet the child might indeed make all of the difference, and no one would ever have to know he wasn't the father.

"Thomas," he heard her voice. "Don't you want me any longer?"

"Yes, I want you, Bethlyn, but not until after you deliver Briston's whelp. I'm disgusted to even think of taking you with his child growing inside you. I hated the man, hated him more than any man on this earth. He had everything I've ever wanted and he never had to work for it. All was given to him. He thought he could dismiss me as unimportant, but he'll remember me. Believe me, he'll remember me. And as for this child . . ." He stroked her abdomen with lazy fingers and delighted to feel her flinch. "When it's old enough, I'm going to send it away to school, anywhere, as long as I don't have to see the little bastard. And as for you, well, you've gained some time, but when you've recovered from the birth, I shall take you in violence and pain for what you've done to me."

"I've done nothing to you!"

"Having Briston's bastard is enough! I don't even want to look upon you."

Pushing her away, Thomas didn't care that she'd stumbled and fell onto the bunk. He'd had his fill of her—for now.

The tears streamed freely down Bethlyn's cheeks as she huddled on the bunk. She cried from fear, from desperation, loneliness and sadness, but also joy. Finally after months and years of longing, her dream was going to come true.

And for the next seven or eight months she didn't have to worry about Thomas claiming his husbandly rights. She'd gambled on the assumption that he'd leave her alone once he knew she carried Ian's child. Thank God, she'd been correct about the man hating Ian so much that a child growing within her would dissipate his lust. Yet she'd live in dread, knowing that Thomas intended to send away her child one day. If only Ian hadn't died . . .

"If only he'd known about you," she whispered to their unborn child.

Seven months pregnant and growing larger every day, Bethlyn finally arrived at Woodsley. Not the least bit sad to be off of the ship, she did regret arriving home, married to Thomas. In fact, she hated it, but Thomas had kept his word during the long voyage and never touched her, finding quarters for himself in another cabin. His absence allowed her time to think, and she decided that once her father realized what a monster Thomas was, that he'd threatened his grandchild, the earl would save her from this madman.

Seeking her father's help was uppermost in her mind when servants she'd never before seen lined up in the Painted Hall for introductions. She barely listened as each servant curtsied or bowed and curtly stated his or her name. Her hope-filled gaze was on the stairway, waiting for her father to appear and somehow make things right for all of the years he'd ignored her by rescuing her from Thomas. But when they neared the end of the long line, which seemed even longer because of the lack of personal warmth, she realized he wasn't coming downstairs.

"My lady, I'm so happy to see you again."

Bethlyn noticed for the first time the old, plump woman who was last in line when she grabbed her hand.

"Tessie, Tessie, is it really you?" Bethlyn joyfully cried, and immediately embraced the Woodsley housekeeper. Finally there was one servant left whom she remembered and could call her friend.

"Indeed it is me, my lady." Large tears gathered in the corners of Tessie's eyes.

"We have much to discuss," Bethlyn said. "First off, you must tell me how my father fares and advise me on running the household."

"Oh, oh—my lady," Tessie made a muffled sound and clasped Bethlyn's hand tighter.

"Enough of this prattle!" Thomas broke in, having watched from a distance. "All of you are dismissed."

Immediately everyone left, silent as snowfall, except for the choked sobs from Tessie which grew fainter as she made her way to the kitchen.

"Thomas, I wished to speak with Tessie. She was my friend and . . ."

"The woman isn't housekeeper any longer. I found her to be impertinent and brash, and much too old for the strenuous duties involved, so she helps the cook. Mrs. Pemberton has the job now, but I gather you didn't hear when she introduced herself and stated her job. Your mind was wandering." It was almost as if Thomas could read her thoughts, and she didn't hide her resentment.

"My father thought highly of Tessie. Surely he didn't agree to sending her to the kitchen," she persisted, not about to let the matter drop. "As mistress of Woodsley I insist she be made housekeeper again. If not, I shall petition my father."

Thomas shook his head, devilment shining in his eyes. "If that is your wish, then please do 'petition' your father, but you will have to do it in the cemetery. The earl died nearly two years ago."

The room spun precariously around her, but Bethlyn managed to make it to a chair alongside the wainscotted wall. She couldn't believe her father was gone. She'd known he'd been in ill health, but she never thought she'd arrive home to discover he was dead. But Thomas had known this for some time. He should have told her, but he delighted in playing games, even more so when he possessed a trump card as he did now with no one to save her.

She grudgingly realized that had her father been alive, he most probably wouldn't have lifted a finger to help her. Truly, he had hated her, and she must come to terms with this once and for all. Finally she lifted dry, condemning eyes to Thomas.

"You should have told me long ago. Your silence in the matter was extremely cruel."

"I'm a cruel man, as you shall soon discover once you're delivered of your brat."

Bethlyn winced, but raw courage filled her at a new thought. "I remember, as you've told me often enough. But since Father is gone, then I've inherited Briston Shipping. It seems you're at my mercy, Thomas."

"Does it?" he remarked, his voice sounding much too pleasant. "My dear Bethlyn, looks can be deceiving. Do you imagine that I traveled to America on a solicitor's salary? If so, you're more naive than I imagined. But I shall clear all of this up now. Before your father died, he turned over all of his fortune and the company to me. You are at *my* mercy."

Bethlyn rose up, fury in her face. "You must have tricked him! He'd never have disinherited me like that."

"He hated you."

"Not that much."

"Believe what you will."

She didn't know what to believe. No matter how much her father may have disliked her, hated her even, he'd never have turned over his entire fortune to Thomas, a mere solicitor, no matter how indispensable. Thomas must have manipulated him. But how?

Squaring her shoulders, she shot him a look of dark rebellion. "As Ian's widow I own the colonial end of Briston Shipping. And I don't intend to turn it over to you."

Thomas sighed his aggravation, but he looked more than pleased when he said, "I'm your husband now, Bethlyn. We signed no agreement as to property before our nuptials, so whatever you own is mine. Without my say-so to withdraw funds, you're as penniless as a church mouse."

He'd duped her again!

Rather than stay there and argue further, she turned headlong and rushed up the stairs to the security of her room. She ached for a good, long cry.

The good, long cry was denied her. When she entered her bedroom she found a brown-haired woman brushing her hair by the dressing table. A sheer white lace nightrail barely covered the woman's bosomy figure, and with her hair hanging past her waist, she looked ready to go to bed, though it was barely past four in the afternoon.

"Well, can't a person have any privacy?" the woman cried, and stood upon seeing Bethlyn. She held the brush at an angle, almost as if she intended to hurl it.

"Who are you?" Bethlyn asked, taking in the open wardrobe, which contained expensive and elaborately beaded gowns.

"I could ask the same question of you," the woman

retorted, her gaze settling on Bethlyn's pregnant form. "But from the looks of you I doubt you're here for the entertainment. No gentleman would want to bed a pregnant woman, but then again, some of them are most peculiar."

"Whatever are you talking about?" Bethlyn grew exasperated. "Who are you?"

"My name is Grace."

"Well, Grace, what are you doing in my room?"

"Your room? This is my room. Has been for a long time. You better speak to Perkins about accommodations. Maybe he can put you in with one of the other girls, but I don't share my room with anybody."

What was this woman jabbering about? Who in God's name was Perkins and what other women did she mean? None of this made any sense to Bethlyn, but she'd been through hell the last few months and she wasn't about to let this woman take over her room—the last remnant of her life.

Standing very close to Grace, she made her face quite bland, her voice frosty when she spoke to the woman as if she were a common servant. And for all Bethlyn knew, she might have been one who'd gotten uppity ways during Thomas's absence. "I am Bethlyn Bris—Eversley," she corrected, and very nearly choked on the name. "My father was the Earl of Dunsmoor and this is my room. I demand that you collect your personal items and leave, otherwise, I shall have you bodily removed."

Grace stood quite still, almost as if she were in shock. "Are—you—married to Thomas Eversley?" At Bethlyn's quick nod, Grace paled. "Thomas got married and you're having his baby." It was more of a statement than a question, and the true situation of Grace and Thomas clicked in Bethlyn's brain. Grace, evidently, was Thomas's mistress.

"I don't want to cause you distress," Bethlyn managed to say gently, seeing that conflicting emotions whirled within Grace's eyes but not correcting her about the child's sire.

"Would you mind leaving me alone while I dress and gather my things together?" Grace burst out. "I—I have

438

much to do."

"Of course," Bethlyn mumbled, and gladly left the room to enter the large, drafty hallway. She felt sorry for Grace, knowing that the woman loved Thomas, but realizing that Thomas didn't love her. If he had, it wouldn't have mattered to Bethlyn, because she hated Thomas Eversley.

She wandered down the corridors, familiarizing herself with the house again. Woodsley was still beautiful, but something wasn't right here. The portraits of her illustrious ancestors still hung on the walls, and the house was still spotless as far as she could tell. What was it that caused her unease?

She began to realize what it was when she passed a bedroom with door ajar and heard flutey female laughter coming from inside. Quietly peering into the room, she saw three very pretty young women, lounging around in skimpy attire on the bed and a chaise longue. They were talking among themselves about Lord Barrett and the Duke of Ellingsworth, both men whom Bethlyn remembered. It seemed the conversation was centered on the gentlemen's prowess in bed. Bethlyn found their conversation, plus the fact that these women were there at all, almost as stunning as the transformation of the bedroom furnishings.

Remembering the simplicity of style and the muted colors of the room, she found the garish bed and accompanying furniture, as well as the thick red velvet and gold-fringed drapes, to be mind-boggling. What was going on here? she asked herself, and quietly moved down the passageway. If she didn't know better she'd swear Woodsley had become a house of ill repute.

"I'm going to find Thomas," she mumbled in determination under her breath. "I want some explanations."

The explanations weren't forthcoming until she sat near Thomas in the state dining room that evening. A great oval wine cistern of silver gilt rested on one of the gilt side tables, and was near to overbrimming with ruby red wine. Bethlyn wondered who was going to drink such a large amount as she nibbled at the portions on her plate. A man named Bartholomew Perkins dined with them, and from the sketchy introductions Bethlyn assumed he was somehow connected with Briston Shipping and appeared to be so at home that Bethlyn felt like an intruder.

Thomas ate with gusto, and it wasn't until the servants had quietly cleared the table and he sat smoking a cheroot after Perkins had departed that she finally asked the question which had been burning a hole in her tongue for the last two hours.

"Who are those women upstairs?"

"Friends of mine," Thomas answered blandly and sipped his wine.

"Why are they here, Thomas? I demand an explanation. Woodsley is my home, and I don't like it resembling a . . . a . . . a . . ." She couldn't say the words.

"Tsk, tsk. You really should do something about that stammer, my dear."

"As if they're here for foul purposes!" she blurted out.

Thomas laughed, his amusement turning his face red. He angered her to such an extent that Bethlyn threw down her napkin on the table and rose quickly to her feet.

"That is what's happened here, isn't it! My God, you've turned Woodsley, my home, into a brothel. Well, I won't stand for it, I won't. Get those harlots out of here. Now!"

Barely moving a muscle, Thomas grabbed her wrist, twisting it painfully. "Woodsley belongs to me just as you do. Don't get high-handed with me. Remember you've been reprieved from my attentions until you've recovered from your brat's birth. But rile me and I just might decide to overlook your delicate condition. Perhaps you'd like to join in the festivities tonight."

Fear of that very thing caused Bethlyn to blanch. Finally, seeing the fright on her face, Thomas released her.

"You're a disgusting, evil man," she said softly before leaving the dining room.

"I know," he countered, not hiding a smirk. "And I wouldn't have it any other way."

From her window in her room Bethlyn watched as the

first of the elaborate carriages began arriving one night, days later. Torches on the front of the house illuminated the silk and satin clothes worn by the gentlemen who left the vehicles to enter the house. She couldn't help but to shake her head in disbelief. Many of these men she recognized, knowing they were all of the peerage and extremely wealthy—wealthy enough to openly partake in debauchery, and Thomas preyed on their vices, no doubt making a grand profit. Didn't he ever tire of his lust for money? He had so much that he couldn't possibly want for more.

A discreet and gentle tap on the door drew her attention away from the events transpiring downstairs. At her summons to enter, Tessie silently slipped into the room.

"My lady, I wish I could have warned you," Tessie apologized after a few moments of conversation. "Woodsley is the home of the devil now."

"Is Thomas more of a devil than my father was, Tessie?"

"Oh, yes, my lady. The earl had his faults. He was a cold, proud man who couldn't unburden himself of his pain. He truly loved you, miss. I just know he did. But he wasn't like Eversley or that lackey, Perkins."

Bethlyn smiled sadly at Tessie, not able to believe her father loved her. "Was he very ill at the end?"

"Your father, you mean. I suppose he was. Mr. Eversley had just a few servants looking after him. They saw to his personal cleanliness and his food, but His Grace never left his room after Mr. Eversley moved in. Mighty strange it was, too."

"Why, Tessie?"

Tessie cocked her head, deep in thought. "Well, His Grace seemed to be in fine form for a while, then all of a sudden he grew weak and feeble. This was shortly after Eversley came to live here. I never did like that man ordering His Grace's servants around. But what was I to do? I needed the work, my lady."

"I understand." Bethlyn placed an arm around Tessie's shoulders. "What happened after Eversley arrived?"

Tessie bit down on her lower lip. "Everything changed. His Grace stayed in his room while Eversley ruled the roost. Then one day the earl took bad and died. Eversley

441

ordered the state bedroom shut up and locked. No one's been in the room since the day His Grace died."

"Not even Eversley?"

Shaking her head, Tessie said, "No. It was almost like he feared to go in there. That wing of the house is always locked."

"I see," Bethlyn mumbled, but shot Tessie a sly smile. "Would you happen to have a key to the wing and my father's room?"

Tessie grinned and took two keys out of her ample pocket and handed them to Bethlyn. "His Grace always liked to have extra keys, just in case they might be needed one day. But you be careful going there at night like this. Mr. Eversley and his guests and the fancy tarts will be busy with their sick goings-on, but, my lady, please take no chances."

"I won't," Bethlyn assured her. The desire to see her father's room again and somehow feel a closeness to him which they lacked in life, squeezed her heart like an iron fist.

The candle glowed eerily upon the walls as Bethlyn climbed the stairs to the third floor and her father's suite of rooms. Opening the locked door which guarded the wing, she smelled a musty odor and saw that the usually spotless carpets were threadbare and dirty. Apparently Thomas had forbidden the servants to clean this section much less enter it. She thought it a bit odd that for a man with Thomas's greed, a man who longed to own everything the earl had possessed, didn't choose to sleep in the state bedroom or use any of the other rooms.

Walking down the long hallway, Bethlyn bypassed her mother's room and the large upstairs parlor where, as a child, Bethlyn had sat in her mother's lap on those occasions when the earl was away. Vague patches of nursery rhymes and songs filtered in and out of Bethlyn's memory suddenly, and she smiled to recall her mother's melodious voice. When her mother held her tightly against her breasts and sang to her or read to her, her mother never stuttered as she was wont to do in her

442

husband's presence.

Soon she stopped at her father's door, her hand shaking when she placed the key in the lock and turned the gilded knob. As a child she'd been in her father's room only twice, and both of those times he'd been absent. But upon entering, she realized nothing had changed except the large state bed had been stripped bare of covers. The gold-and-red hangings surrounding it resembled staunch sentinels with nothing to guard. The dressing table which used to hold her father's personal grooming items was empty, as was the adjoining dressing room.

Moving closer into the tomblike depths, she placed the candle on the night table beside the bed and quietly waited for emotions to wash over her, to purge her of the past. She forced herself to remember that this was where her father had spent his last hours. Yet she felt nothing, not love or hatred. To her mind, this room was as cold and empty as her father's feelings for her. She'd come here, foolishly hoping to find a part of him that she could cherish, something of the warmth he'd always expressed for Jessica. Instead, she felt none of the torment she'd suffered these last months over Ian's death, or any of the deep and abiding love she'd preserve in her heart for her husband until the day she died.

Then again, why should she feel anything for her father, a man who had despised her so much that he bequeathed all he possessed to a malevolent person like Thomas Eversley?

Sighing her defeat, which she knew was a rather odd way to feel since her father had always disappointed her during his life, she began to pick up the candle. The flickering light drew attention to and emphasized a white object on the floor between the massive bed's headboard and one of the hangings.

Bending down, her fingers curled around a piece of parchment. In the dim candlelight Bethlyn read the scrawly and nearly illegible handwriting, vaguely aware when her blood began to race and pound through her head at a sudden truth which hit her like the force of a gale wind at Hallsands.

Her father had loved her!

This letter was proof of that. He must have suspected Thomas was poisoning him, and she knew that his suspicions were correct. Tessie had told her that the earl had been on the mend until Thomas arrived. Why else would a highly intelligent man sign away all of his fortune to a manipulative solicitor if not for his weakened physical state? It was obvious Thomas had preyed upon Nathanial Talbot like a leech.

But for all the horror and shock and sadness which suddenly overshadowed Bethlyn, an immense joy filled her. Her father's last physical effort was spent in trying to warn her, a clear indication that he had loved her, or at the very most, he had felt some fondness for her.

Tears sparkled in her eyes as she folded the letter into fourths and placed it in the bodice of her gown, next to her heart for safekeeping, not only because she would send Thomas Eversley to the hangman with such damning information, but because her father had cared about her.

His energies had been spent penning this warning to her, so the least she could do would be to see that his last moments hadn't been for naught.

Returning to her room, Bethlyn found Tessie still there. "We're leaving here," Bethlyn whispered to her though no one would have heard them anyway above the din of voices, laughter, and music which drifted upstairs to them. "We're running away."

"Oh, my lady, I fear that's too dangerous. What if Mr. Eversley catches us? Besides, you're carrying a child and the night is icy. You could catch your death of cold."

Tessie's horrified look caused Bethlyn to smile as she reached for two fur-lined cloaks from the wardrobe and handed one to Tessie. "Believe it or not, I've braved worse than cold nights and Thomas Eversley during the past few years. The worst of all was losing my husband, and I swear that I now think Thomas had a hand in his death. But we have to leave here tonight. I have proof that Thomas slowly poisoned my father. We must get to the constable."

"Merciful heavens!" was all Tessie said, her face ghostly

pale as she threw on the cloak.

Since Thomas and his guests were apparently being amused by the doxies downstairs, Bethlyn and Tessie weren't spotted as they hurriedly left by the way of the back stairs which led to the rear garden. A full moon brightly beamed down upon them, and they were more than recognizable since the fruit-bearing trees and plants were now naked, courtesy of the first winter frost.

"Shall we take to the stables and get a coach, my lady?" Tessie whispered in a breathy voice as they swiftly hurried away from the well-lighted house.

"No, we shall go by foot along Farmer's Pass until we come to the Stuart home. There we'll beg help and send for the constable. On such a freezing night as this, we'd never be able to walk the distance to the village." Bethlyn didn't say that she feared Tessie might not be able to make it safely because the woman was wheezing. She also doubted her own ability to traverse the five miles in her pregnant condition. Even now, she felt a heaviness of limb and an aching sensation in her abdomen, and she worried she might not get far at all. Yet they had to keep on. Being at Woodsley with Thomas presented a danger upon which her mind didn't care to dwell.

They'd scarcely reached Farmer's Pass when suddenly out of nowhere it seemed the night was alive with bright, smokey torches behind them.

"Up ahead!" a male voice shouted, followed by a chorus of excited, raised voices.

Unable to speak a word, both women shot a frightened glance at each other, knowing they were the prey. In unison they broke into a run, scampering across the pebble-strewn path which was thick with cow manure, since many of the farmers used the well-trod passage to herd their stock to market. Bethlyn silently cursed for forgetting to change her thin slippers, wishing devoutly that she owned a pair of sturdy, thick shoes like the ones Tessie wore, when a foot stepped in the malodorous dung.

But she plodded on, growing out of breath, as if the devil himself was behind her.

And he was.

Chapter Thirty-One

Bethlyn's cumbersome condition was her undoing.

Out of breath with heart rapidly pounding and a strange abdominal ache which grew more intense with each unsteady footfall and terrifying second, she was almost relieved when Thomas's arms ensnared her from behind. "Stupid little fool," he berated her in a hoarse, breathless voice. "I should beat you for this."

"Do, Thomas," she uttered in perverse pleasure to see that he was as out of breath as she. "Slap me, flog me right here."

"Ha! You'd relish that." Cocking his head in the direction of the raised voices which drew nearer, he sneered. "No one can save you, my dear wife, so cease your theatrics. And as for you, you meddlesome old hag," he said to Tessie, who cowered a few feet away and looked quite ashen, "I shall deal with you later. Return to the house and say nothing."

The promise of a dreadful retaliation against Tessie hung thick as smoke in the air when Tessie stumbled towards the house. "Don't hurt her," Bethlyn pleaded. "Please . . ."

"Quiet, you aggravating wench. Be thankful I don't kill the ungrateful hag right now, and let that be a warning to *you*, too, my fine lady. Keep your tongue still. I may not be able to extract my punishment on you physically, but utter a suspicious word to anyone and Tessie's sudden and unfortunate demise will be upon your head."

Bethlyn trembled. Would this man stop at nothing?

The sounds of raucous laughter and running feet drew closer until Thomas's guests and the women surrounded them.

A gentleman laughed and poked Thomas in the ribs. "What a clever one you are, Thomas, for providing such unusual amusement. I adore a good hunt, and from the looks of things you've bagged quite an attractive trophy." The young man forgot his giggling companion as his appreciative gaze settled on Bethlyn.

Despite the ache which threatened to double her over, Bethlyn reared upward at his assumption that she belonged to Thomas's stable of women. "I am no trophy, sir, to be snared for your amusement!"

Thomas's fingers gripped her arm painfully and forced her to silence as she remembered his threat against Tessie.

"Eh? What is that you say? I know of but one woman who was possessed of such a rapier tongue that she took delight in wounding the most hard-hearted. Let me have a closer look at you."

Bethlyn didn't flicker an eyelash when the aristocratic and well-dressed man approached her until recognition flickered across both of their faces at the same moment.

"Lord Augustus Stanhope!"

"Bethlyn? Bethlyn Briston, can it really be you?" Augustus laughed warmly and kissed her cheek. "I haven't seen you since our ball some three years ago, shortly before you left for America. You know, of course, that my sister, Madeline, married Sir Jeremy Smithers. Why haven't you visited? I know everyone would adore seeing you again." He turned and motioned some of the other men forward. "Come see who has returned to us, gentlemen. The brightest star in the ton."

Soon about fifteen men of various ages, men whom Bethlyn remembered from her London years, gathered around her, a bit uneasy at the circumstances of their being at Woodsley. "Didn't you leave to claim that bounder of a husband," one of them said, and guffawed.

"I did," Bethlyn admitted in such a pain-filled whisper that everyone grew silent. "My husband is dead."

447

"But—but I can see you're expecting a child," Augustus blurted out.

"My wife must take to her room," Thomas interjected in an impatient and edgy voice. "She needs her rest."

"Yes, yes, much too cold," someone said, the others agreed.

When they started back to the house, Augustus took Bethlyn by the hand, pulling her a bit away from Thomas. However, Bethlyn was all too aware that Thomas watched her and was close enough to hear each word she spoke. Tessie's life depended upon her silence. She couldn't tell Augustus that Thomas had murdered her father, and most probably her husband and now kept her a prisoner in her own home. But she squeezed his hand tightly, hoping to convey some of her fear and frustration to him.

"You must visit us soon. Both of you," Augustus offered when Thomas began to lead Bethlyn up the stairs to her room.

Thomas solemnly inclined his head to the invitation. Bethlyn, however, spoke in a bright voice despite the worsening ache in her abdomen. "I should adore seeing Madeline and Jeremy again. Please tell Jeremy that after my baby's birth when I am recovered, I shall visit and insist upon riding Fancy Lady. She was my favorite horse and the most beautiful black color . . ."

Thomas's abrupt good night to Augustus broke off her words and she found herself herded up the stairs like a recalcitrant child and literally pushed into her room. The force caused her to grab onto the large post of the bed where she slid to her knees on the carpeted floor.

She could see Thomas's black leather boots as he moved towards her and heard his angry tone of voice but couldn't make out the words. A razor-sharp pain sliced through her belly, stilling all conscious thought save one when she doubled over.

"My . . . baby," she moaned through pale lips in an even paler face.

"Ian. Ian—our baby . . . baby."

The labor pains were so intense that Bethlyn wished to die. She drifted in and out of a hazy netherworld

448

mistaking the flickering shadows on the walls for demons and crying out. Someone bathed her brow with cool water, and she opened her eyes to see Grace bending over her.

"Help . . . me." Bethlyn could barely speak her lips were so parched. She knew then that she burned with a fever. "My baby. If I die . . ."

"Quiet, my lady," Grace demanded harshly. "I'm doing the best I can until the physician comes. Why Thomas sent for a doctor is beyond me. *Ladies* don't need the likes of medical men, but your husband wants you healthy. He wants you to live."

Why was Grace so scornful of her? Was it because she believed that she loved Thomas? She must convince her it wasn't so.

"Grace, you must . . . listen. Thomas . . . I . . ." Suddenly, Bethlyn felt such an excruciating labor pain that she shrieked aloud.

"Dammit!" Grace muttered under her breath. "If that doctor doesn't get here soon I may have to deliver this baby." And to prove that she was up to the task at hand, she rolled up her sleeves and then prepared for the birth.

Ian's son whimpered in his cradle beside his mother's bed. The tiny infant was so small that when Grace placed him at Bethlyn's breast to suck, he nearly disappeared in the crook of her arm. But Grace had helped deliver three of her brothers and sisters and she knew by the greedy sucking sounds that this baby would survive despite his size.

She couldn't say the same for his mother.

The doctor had come and gone; of course, too late to deliver the baby, but he earned his fee by forcing some medicine down Bethlyn's throat. Grace was doubtful anything would help. She'd known a few women who had died with childbed fever, and Bethlyn didn't look like she was long for this world.

Not that Bethlyn Eversley's life mattered to her. The woman was Thomas's wife and now she'd given him a son. A son. A son. A son. The words whirled in Grace's brain until she thought she was going mad.

"Damn you, Thomas Eversley!" she cried out in the quiet room. "Damn you to hell!"

Thomas had visited his wife's bedside only minutes ago, then left, not looking at his own child, not seeming to care as he demanded that she see to the baby and do everything in her power to make certain Bethlyn survived. Who did the fool think she was? God?

But she'd do whatever Thomas asked. Even will his precious wife to live, something the woman didn't seem to want to do for herself. More than once Grace had thought Bethlyn was slipping away, but then she would open her eyes for a second before closing them again.

Grace wanted to hate her, but somehow she didn't. Bethlyn had stolen Thomas from her and had a child— everything Grace had ever wanted. Why then did she wish to die when she should be fighting to live? Why had she been running away?

None of this made any sense as far as Grace was concerned, yet Grace didn't want Bethlyn to die, and not because she cared about her. As long as Bethlyn was weak and the child needed tending, the duties of a nanny greatly appealed to Grace; she wouldn't have to service any gentlemen—especially not that disgusting Perkins.

She made a snorting sound of disgust as she took the baby away from Bethlyn and rocked him to sleep. Perkins was an animal, and for the rest of her life she'd hate him, but not as much as she hated Thomas for handing her over to him. For weeks after Thomas had left for America she had belonged exclusively to Perkins, forcibly participating in the most vile acts imaginable. The worst was having to pretend she liked his depraved play.

But all of that ended abruptly one night when pain shot through her and she started to bleed all over the bed. She thought she was going to die. Perkins sent for a doctor who always examined the women at Woodsley to make certain they and their gentlemen had no diseases and whom Grace knew, performed abortions on the unlucky girls who hadn't taken precautions.

As the doctor administered laudanum to her to deaden

the pain, he told her she'd be just fine with a few days rest. Fortunately for her, the fetus appeared to only have been two to three months along. Shock and dismay nearly suffocated her. She'd had no idea she had been pregnant—pregnant with Thomas's child if the doctor's estimation had been correct.

Hate for Perkins and his foul acts surged through her. She decided then and there that if he ever came near her again, she'd kill him—which was a threat she proved in earnest after she'd recovered. The swine had tried to touch her and she stabbed him. After that, Perkins stayed away from her, and she believed he thought she was crazy.

"Only a little crazy," she muttered to herself, and smiled down at the sleeping baby.

But she hated Thomas more than Perkins—more than anybody. She had loved him and suffered his betrayal. Now he was at Woodsley again, and since his return, she'd climbed into his bed and pleasured him. Her pleasure came not from the love act but from the ways of torture she invented in her mind for Thomas. Sometimes when he'd place himself into her hands, she ached to reach for the sharp paring knife on the bedside table and with one swift, sure swipe . . .

Grace's eyes glittered at the thought, but then she sighed because the timing wasn't right, and she'd learned from Perkins that in such activities, timing was everything.

Continuing to gently rock the baby, her mind was fixed on a distant date in the future.

"Not yet," she promised. "Not yet, dear Thomas. But soon."

"I don't understand any of this, not a single thing you've said makes sense." Jeremy paced the length of the parlor, his hands clasped behind his back as he gave thought to the astounding news he'd just heard from Augustus Stanhope.

"That is what Bethlyn told me, Jeremy." Augustus, seated on the divan, took a long puff on his cheroot. Evidently she felt the need to marry Eversley since she is expecting his child. I suppose the alliance was also a necessary evil, so to speak, since Eversley works so closely with the earl. Strange about that, too, however."

Jeremy raised an eyebrow and stopped pacing. "What?"

"As often as I've been to Woodsley the last year for . . . my visits—" Augustus looked uncomfortable, knowing how much Jeremy didn't approve of his gambling and whoring, and cleared his throat, "in all that time I've never seen the earl. I heard he is quite ill, but I find it odd that he would be prone to allow such behavior in his home."

"Hmph! Such debauchery at Woodsley is unfathomable, and I promise not to chide you on this, Augustus, but Woodsley was the epitome of elegance and beauty. But now, well, I can't imagine why you insist on going there at all. You do have a reputation to uphold, and if Madeline or Grandmama ever discovered this I hate to think how they'd be hurt." Jeremy threw up his hands and waved away the comment which nearly burst from Augustus's lips. "Be that as it may, I won't say another word about your personal life, however, I am quite worried about Bethlyn. This marriage to Eversley is appalling, and for her to actually be living at Woodsley with all of this lewd behavior going on right under her very nose is more than baffling."

Jeremy fell silent and gazed out of the window at the tranquil scene in St. James's Park, but he felt less than calm. The last time he'd seen Bethlyn she was very much in love with Ian Briston and he with her. Had Briston's death unhinged her mind so much that she'd married Thomas Eversley, a man she'd never particularly liked because she'd turned to him for comfort and gotten herself with child, or had she felt she needed him because of the shipping enterprise? No matter the reasons, Jeremy wondered why she hadn't contacted him or his grandmother by now.

"Why do you suppose Bethlyn was wandering around the estate at night? She is carrying a child," Jeremy reminded Augustus, turning to face him.

His brother-in-law shrugged. "That was never ex

plained, and I didn't ask. Eversley looked ready to explode and, before I could adequately converse with Bethlyn, he'd steered her upstairs like she was a naughty tot. Oh, she did tell me to relay a message to you, however. I almost forgot it until now. She said that when she is recovered from childbirth she will visit you and insists she be allowed to ride a black horse named Fancy Lady who was her favorite.''

Jeremy blinked. "Fancy . . . Lady? Is that what she said? Are you sure?''

"Of course. Wait, where are you going?'' Augustus jumped up as Jeremy ran from the room.

"I'm going to Woodsley,'' he cried over his shoulder and rushed into the hallway to retrieve his cloak, Augustus following after him. "I have no horse named Fancy Lady and Bethlyn damn well knows that. She always rode a white stallion called Lancelot.''

"So? Perhaps she made a mistake. I see no reason to rush away like . . .''

"God, you're a mutton-headed dolt sometimes. She lied to you, knowing you'd relay the message to me and that I'd know something is wrong at Woodsley. This was her way of signaling her distress. When was that you saw her?''

"Over three weeks ago. I'd have told you sooner, but you and Madeline only just returned from Paris,'' Augustus explained, his voice nearly drowned out by Jeremy's harsh curse.

"I hope to God that I'm not too late!'' Jeremy slammed the door behind him.

"Is there anything I may get for you, Mrs. Eversley?'' Bethlyn heard Grace ask.

You may help me to escape this monster I married, Bethlyn started to say, but thought better of it. She wasn't certain she could trust Grace. Granted, the woman was considerate to her, having nursed her back to health these last weeks when she had wanted to die, to be lost in a netherworld where one felt nothing. She could also find no fault with her care of her infant son whom she'd named

Nathaniel Matthew, after her father and Ian's. She'd longed to call the dark-haired perfectly formed baby, Ian, but she feared Thomas's wrath if she did. He resented her innocent baby enough without drawing further attention to the man who'd fathered him. Even months after Ian's death, Thomas still clearly hated him, and Bethlyn didn't want her son to suffer because of it.

Her dream was to elude Grace and that horrid man, Perkins, and find Tessie. They'd flee Woodsley and head straight to London where she'd go to Aunt Penny's and seek out Jeremy. Yes, Jeremy would help her, but she couldn't escape now. Perkins or some other male servant, loyal to Thomas, always guarded her door. If only she could smuggle a note to Tessie, the woman could send it on its way to Jeremy, but she hadn't seen Tessie since the night of their attempted escape, and she was growing fearful that something may have happened to her.

Looking down at the sleeping face of her son, his tiny rosebud mouth slack against her breast, she knew she couldn't even try to run now. The weather was much too harsh, and she was still too weak from her illness after his birth. For now she must bide her time and appease Thomas—appease him in all ways until she could decide what to do.

She handed the baby to Grace. "I don't need anything else now. Thank you for taking such fine care of Nathaniel for me."

Grace smiled at Bethlyn's heartfelt compliment and left the room to take the baby to the nursery.

When Bethlyn began to pull the laces of her gown together, she felt Thomas's presence before she saw him. She glanced up to find his eyes resting lustfully upon her full breasts, and the bulge in his trousers was all too noticeable, making her more than uncomfortable.

"I envy your son's good fortune, my lady, but soon I shall engage a wet nurse to tend to him."

She decided this was his way of attempting to break the bond between her and her baby. "But, Thomas, I have a great deal of milk left, and I must feed . . ."

"And so you shall, my dear. I can't think of a tastier

feast." His tongue rapaciously moved across his lips, and he squeezed one of her nipples, allowing a droplet of milk to spill onto the fleshy pad of his index finger before tasting it. He leered at her, seeing her complete repugnance when she understood what fate soon awaited her.

"Thomas, please don't," she croaked.

He bent down and whispered in her ear; his breath felt hot against her skin. "I will give you but three more weeks to recover, Bethlyn. And then, then you shall be mine. I have wanted you for years, and I've waited long enough. Touch me, see how much I want you. Touch me!"

She jumped and he grabbed her hand, bringing it to the telltale bulge which felt as hard as stone. "Now you know what pleasure is in store for you," he told her, and smirked, self-satisfaction in his eyes.

For a second she felt nausea rising within her and grew dizzy. She willed herself not to be sick, but she wasn't certain she could control it until a knock sounded on the door and Thomas broke away with a curse. Swinging open the door, Thomas bellowed at a servant, Bethlyn heard the muffled voices and, to her surprise, Thomas immediately left the room.

Taking deep breaths, Bethlyn forced down the bile in her throat. God, what am I going to do? she worried. She couldn't stand Thomas to touch her, deplored touching him. But somehow she had to do whatever he wanted to keep her child and herself safe until they could escape from here. But for how long could she live as a prisoner, Thomas's virtual slave?

Would he ever trust her enough to allow her to come and go on her own? She must let him think she'd please him in every way possible to gain her freedom and take her father's letter to the authorities. Thomas must never suspect that she knew he'd poisoned her father. If so, he might kill her and the baby, then she'd never gain her revenge upon him.

And had he killed Ian, too?

That was the worst thought of all. For even if she and the baby escaped and Thomas was arrested for his crimes, she'd still have to live life without the man she loved.

Suddenly she found herself unable to breathe in this stifling room and, throwing aside the bed covers, she got out of bed only to lean weakly upon the bedpost. Finally she made it to the window and drew aside the drapes. Finding the strength, she eased open the window and halted, stunned by the sight of a familiar figure emerging from the front of the house to enter a black phaeton.

Blinking back her disbelief, she thought she must be imagining that she saw Jeremy, but as the phaeton moved away she knew it was he.

Her voice came back to her in a straining rush. "Jeremy! Here, Jeremy! Jeremy! Je—re—my!"

But the clip-clopping sound of the wheels flying across the cobblestone drive drowned out her feeble voice like a deafening and ominous thunder.

Penelope Evans dozed in her chair, the book she'd been reading resting upon her stomach. A cold, bitter wind rushed through the usually warm bedroom from the open Palladian-style window and disturbed the crackling flames in the marble fireplace until, finally, the fire went out.

Stirring from the chill, Penelope woke to clasp her thin veined hands around the edges of her shawl and to huddle more deeply into the depths of her chair. Suddenly she opened her eyes to find the window was open and started to lift the bell to summon her maid when what seemed from out of nowhere a hand materialized at her elbow and forestalled her.

"What in heavens . . . !" Stunned and more than a little frightened, she glanced up to find a black-cloaked figure hovering over her. The room had grown dark and she couldn't make out the face of the man, but for all his bulk and brawn, she sensed he wasn't there to menace her because surely if he meant to harm her he'd have had the perfect opportunity to do so while she slept. Still, fear crept into her voice when she said, "Who the devil are you and what are you doing in my room? Can't an old lady be safe from molestation in these days and times?"

She heard him give a ragged sigh, and his voice was filled with pain when he spoke. "I . . . need . . . your help, Aunt Penny."

Placing her lorgnette to her eye, she motioned him to come closer, not the least afraid of the man who she surmised was hurt and in need of some assistance. "Who the deuce are you, young man? Light the candle so I can see you before I ring for my grandson and have you thrown out of here. But I assure you that if you've come here to rout an old bird like myself out of my fortune, you're sorely mistaken. I'm not some silly woman, and I can attest to the fact that I no longer have a nephew."

Following her orders, he lighted the candle beside her chair and held it up to his face. Immediately she saw he was haggard in appearance, seeming to be in need of a good meal, yet his physique under the cloak was quite broad-shouldered. Blinking rapidly, Penny noticed that his eyes were dim, almost glassy, a sure sign that the man suffered a fever. Still, she didn't recognize him, and there was no reason why she should have since she hadn't seen him in a very long time.

"I suggest you leave the same way you got in here, you bounder; otherwise, I shall have the authorities on your head."

"Please, please, help me, Aunt Penny," he said, sounding ungodly weak and starting to sway. "Ring for Jeremy. Please."

Before he fell before Penny's startled eyes, he possessed the good sense to return the candle to the table.

Chapter Thirty-Two

Bethlyn learned that her three weeks were over on the day of a masked ball Thomas intended to throw for his guests' amusements. A "Bacchanalian feast" Thomas had leeringly termed it when he'd told her about it, setting her teeth on edge and her heart to plummet along with her hopes of escape at his obvious meaning.

Over the past weeks she'd spent her days and nights in her room, not allowed a breath of air except for the window. Sometimes despair drove her to consider climbing onto the casement and flinging herself from it, but she couldn't end her own life, not when her child depended upon her. Her only course of action would be to please Thomas in bed and, after she'd gained his trust, she hoped he'd grow lenient with her and not constantly threaten to send her baby away if she didn't obey him. Perhaps she could turn Thomas's lust for her to her own advantage by lulling him into a false sense of security with her body. He couldn't keep her locked in here for the rest of her life. People outside of Woodsley knew of her existence now, and this thought caused her to think about Jeremy.

He was her one grasp at freedom. She surmised Augustus had relayed her message to him; otherwise, he wouldn't have shown up at Woodsley. However, Jeremy hadn't been back, and she wondered what lies Thomas had told him to keep him away, reinforcing her desire to be free. If Jeremy couldn't help her, then she had no one but herself to rely upon. From the unlikely source of Grace she had learned that Thomas had badly beaten Tessie on the night of the aborted escape attempt, and only within the last few days had Tessie been able to get up and help in the kitchen. However, the old woman's movements were closely watched by the kitchen staff and anything she said or did would be dutifully and promptly reported to Thomas. Thus, Bethlyn was prevented from seeking Tessie's help again—not unless she wanted her harmed on her behalf once more.

The sounds of excited and lyrical laughter from the "women of Woodsley," as Bethlyn derisively named them, floated down the hallway and gained her attention. No doubt they were getting ready for the large ball and the later entertainment, both in the ballroom and the bedrooms. Bethlyn grew sick with impotent rage to realize what her home had become and to know that the man who'd caused it all was the man whose filthy, lecherous hands would soon touch her as her husband.

Husband. The word sunk into her brain, hitting her with its intensity of meaning. Thomas was her husband. But no matter how hard she tried, she couldn't relate this word to the man, because in her mind her husband would always be Ian.

"Ian, Ian," she said softly, tears misting her eyes. "We wasted so much time when we could have been together."

The night of Bethlyn's concubinage as Thomas's wife, and this was how she thought of it, arrived.

With each passing hour, a feeling of dread grew within her and threatened to suffocate her. Like a trapped bird, she paced the floor, so agitated that she screeched at Grace when the woman brought her her supper.

As the hour neared eight, Grace came into the room and on her arm was a deep sapphire-blue velvet gown, the color of the ocean. The tight-fitting sleeves ended at the elbow and were trimmed in silver, as was the neckline of the snug and very low-cut bodice. Grace placed the gown on the bed and stepped back to admire it.

"Thomas said you are to wear this dress tonight."

Bethlyn barely looked at the gown. "Is that a command?"

"I fear it is."

Shrugging, Bethlyn began to undress, not caring what she wore for her first night as Thomas's bride. In fact, she wondered why he wanted her to dress at all when clearly he'd made it quite plain that he preferred her naked and panting beneath him.

After Grace had helped her fix her hair into a becoming mass of curls on top of her head, Grace stepped back and smiled. "You're quite beautiful, Mrs. Eversley. Thomas is lucky to have you for his wife; however, I don't think you feel you're fortunate that he is your husband."

"I hate him!" Bethlyn spat out, suddenly not caring if Grace reported to him.

Grace didn't reply. Instead, she turned and left the room, leaving Bethlyn to wonder if she was going to inform Thomas what she'd said. Minutes later Thomas entered the room without knocking, and from the delighted expression on his face, Bethlyn realized Grace hadn't said anything to him.

He circled her like a vulture coming in for the kill as he nodded his head at the beautiful picture she made in the gown he'd had specially designed for her. His perusal over, he flashed her his lecherous smirk which was becoming all too familiar to her. A chill rushed through her, turning her heart and soul to ice, hardly aware when he withdrew a box from the inside pocket of his jacket.

Opening the silk-lined box, he held out an exquisite diamond-and-sapphire choker accompanied by matching earbobs. Not allowing her to touch them, he took it upon himself to place the earrings on her lobes before possessively clasping the choker on her neck. His finger intimately brushed against her skin, but she somehow managed to quell the shiver which sliced through her, praying she could be an expert enough actress to live out the next few hours, days, weeks, or months until she and her child were free.

"Do you like my wedding gift to you?" he asked, and led her to the mirror.

Gain his trust, she reminded herself. Gazing at her reflection, she smiled warmly, but her insides felt as cold a

460

the stones against her flesh. "They're quite lovely. Thank you, Thomas."

He placed his hands on her naked shoulders, seeming pleased with her response. "May I have a kiss of thanks?"

She felt surprise that he asked for one, but she knew now wasn't the time to resist him. When she turned her head in his direction, his lips immediately contacted with hers. The feel of his mouth, the way his tongue creeped between her lips to collide with her own tongue disgusted her. She didn't want to push him away, fearful of what might happen if she displeased him, but her hope of a short kiss dissolved when he forced her to open her mouth to him and pulled her roughly against him.

Not able to breathe and totally repulsed, she began to wriggle. "Thomas, please, not yet. Not now."

"When?" he rasped, and his abrupt breaking away gave her the chance to take a deep breath.

"I'm dressed to go downstairs. I'm not ready . . . now."

He snickered. "I doubt you'll ever be ready. Didn't Briston teach you about passion at all? I don't believe he did an adequate job, but then I always wondered about his prowess. You're like a lump of coal, but I warrant before this night is out, you'll be hotter than one thrown into a furnace. I think you need some inducement, my love."

Grabbing her by the wrist, Thomas pulled her from the room and down the hallway, not bothering to tell Bethlyn where they were headed.

Dragging her behind him, they finally halted by an iron grillwork balcony which overlooked the ballroom. Below, the gaily gowned women of Woodsley mingled with the well-dressed gentlemen, their faces hidden behind colorful masks.

"Notice the women and learn from them," he commanded. His breath and the feel of his hands upon her shoulders felt poker-hot as he positioned himself behind her. "They have no fear of lovemaking or men."

"They're whores."

"Yes, they are, but they're the finest whores in all of England, perhaps the Continent. The men who frequent them are among the wealthiest and aristocratic, as you

461

well know. They pay any price I deem high enough, as each woman is more than adept at pleasing each man, knowing the gentleman's own peculiarities." Thomas pointed to one woman in particular who was being held in an intimate one-armed embrace by a portly man whom Bethlyn recognized immediately as Lord Hoxton despite his mask. Hoxton's coat sleeve was tucked into the front of his jacket, since he had lost his left arm in a hunting accident some years ago, but the whore encircled by his right arm didn't seem to mind.

"That woman's real name is Maggie," Thomas droned on in her ear. "But here, she is called Selina, a name she chose for herself because it makes her feel beautiful. She can forget that she grew up in an orphanage and was initiated into womanhood by a cruel rape, perpetrated against her by a man who was a trustee. When Perkins found her, she was living on the streets and selling herself for pennies.

"Granted, she is a whore. But you see how Lord Hoxton dotes upon her, how he even now offers her his cup of wine and kisses her with such tenderness. If she was only a whore, Hoxton wouldn't bid so highly for her when she is placed on the auction block. Because of Selina's life in an orphanage, she was forced to care for deformed children. Hoxton's loss of an arm isn't repulsive to her. With Selina, he is a whole man and not a cripple, something ladies in the ton will not allow him to forget. So, you see what a needed service we're performing here at Woodsley."

"I see that you've turned my home into a brothel, and that every time one of these creatures is auctioned off you earn a hefty profit!" Bethlyn's breasts heaved with emotion, her usually pale face turning a becoming shade of peach. "No matter what you say, or how noble you want me to envision your women, they are still whores."

Thomas's eyes glittered with rage, but also with such intense desire that he did the unforgivable in Bethlyn's mind by placing his hands upon her breasts and massaging the protruding nipples through her thin gown with his thumbs. "You, my honey-haired aristocrat, are one, too."

462

"Stop touching me like that, you hateful, disgusting man. I don't want you to touch me—ever!"

"I'll touch you whenever and wherever I like, my fine lady," he hissed. "And you can't stop me, because I am your husband. Your master."

This blatant reminder caused her to shake with humiliation and anger, because no matter how much she detested Thomas, no one would intervene if she fought him. She was his wife and was in an all-too-subservient position. She saw the futility of fighting him, deciding to conserve all of her energy and keep her wits if she and her child were ever to escape Thomas's clutches, but she was afraid her own heated words may have ruined any chance to earn his trust.

Taking a deep breath, Bethlyn forced herself to appear contrite. "Forgive me, Thomas. I . . . I didn't mean that."

"Certainly you meant every word of it, my love. However, sometimes I enjoy that flash of fire within you, and it is exactly such passion I wish to see tonight." Thomas smiled suggestively. "The evening's entertainments are about to commence. I trust you shall watch and learn well."

What Bethlyn learned was that men were base creatures at heart. As each woman was placed on the small stage in the ballroom where countless times over the years an orchestra had played for her parents' parties, the masked men bid against each other until the prices were up so high that the lucky gentleman with the most money won the woman of his choice for a night of private entertainment.

Bethlyn couldn't believe that these same men were men she'd known in London, men whom she'd spoken to or admired over the years. To see them in the throes of a bidding war for a woman's body was almost as repulsive to her as Thomas holding her tightly before him and rubbing his burgeoning manhood against her backside. Every so often he'd whisper obscenities into her ear, reminding her of what he planned to do to her, and those things he expected of her, when they were alone later.

Despair shot through her, causing a tear to form in one of her eyes and mark a watery path on her skin as it slipped down her cheek. The second she raised her fingers to wipe it away she noticed a man staring up at her.

She'd been vaguely aware of him when the bidding started, having observed him with two other men. She'd remembered being struck by his tallness and the fact that he was dressed entirely in black as were his two masked companions. However, they weren't as tall or broad of shoulder nor as mysterious-looking. Despite the ebony silk mask which hid his face and the black cape thrown carelessly over one shoulder to reveal equally dark clothes, Bethlyn discerned that this man would be formidable no matter what he wore.

His slitted gaze impaled her, and an electric jolt shot through her. The very arrogance of his stance and his endless staring unnerved her. Somehow she felt she was on the auction block and he was the eager buyer. It was his very rudeness which caused her to cease feeling sorry for herself and she trained her eyes on him to stare him down. Finally he grinned, and motioned to one of his companions. The man turned to Perkins, who was slithering his way among Woodsley's much-honored guests like the snake he was when Bethlyn turned her attention to the stage where the last of the women was being auctioned off.

Thomas placed his hand around her waist just as a hearty cheer went up for the young aristocrat who'd snagged the latest offering with his hefty purse.

"I trust the auction has whetted your appetite for the feast I plan for us tonight." His voice was seductively low and unbearably intimate. "I've waited so long for you, Bethlyn, and I've given you much more time than I intended to have you come willingly to me. Nothing will keep me from you now that the moment is upon us. Not even your own unwillingness, my dear."

She understood his hidden meaning. Rape, as well as murder and kidnapping, wasn't foreign to Thomas, and she didn't wish to be forced or beaten into submission, as any physical violence would weaken her. The strength to endure all for herself and her son drove her to nod woodenly and give her hand to him.

"Sir, I need a word with you." Perkins dashed over to

them, appearing most flustered and out of place in his plain clothes.

"I'm going to retire for the night," Thomas ground out, not hiding his vexation.

"Please, Mr. Eversley, the man downstairs has requested the most unusual and shocking proposition. I know it's quite odd even for the man to suggest it, but he's aware of the situation and still wishes me to ask you."

"What man? What are you jabbering about, Perkins?"

Perkins took Thomas aside and pointed to the black-clad man and his companions. The man looked at Thomas and bowed slightly while Perkins whispered in Thomas's ear.

"He must be insane!" Thomas burst out.

"Quite serious," Perkins remarked. "The information was relayed through Lord Augustus Stanhope. The man is an Italian acquaintance of Stanhope's and speaks no English. I attempted to explain that his offer was impossible, but the foreigner said he'd speak only to you. He promised that you would be unable to deny him when you're aware of how much he'll pay."

At Stanhope's name, Bethlyn raised an eyebrow in acute interest, but pretended she'd heard nothing when Thomas glanced in her direction.

"I doubt any amount of money will change my mind. Stanhope's friend is a lunatic."

"Perhaps," Perkins cautioned. "But Stanhope has led me to believe that the Italian is of noble blood and that to say the man is wealthy is an understatement. No matter how absurd his request, sir, I think you'd be foolish not to court his good will. A man so wealthy might be inclined to take his business elsewhere."

Thomas seemed to mull over this strange proposition in his mind and nodded to Perkins. "I'll speak to the man, but I shall set him straight on this matter. Watch over my wife for a few moments, Perkins." Thomas then sent a penetrating glance to Bethlyn which effectively warned her not to try to escape.

With Perkins standing sentinel behind her, Bethlyn could only watch when Thomas joined the three dark-masked and-clad men on the ballroom floor. She knew one of the men was Stanhope, and from the gestures and the relaying of what the tall Italian was saying to him, she deduced that whatever the man wanted wasn't being taken seriously by Thomas.

Thomas laughed loudly and shook his head, and all too often all four of the men directed their attention to Bethlyn on the balcony. What in the world was going on?

After much more head shaking and translating by Stanhope, Thomas started to look exasperated. Finally he threw up his hands, and he shouted, "Tell the damned bastard that she is my wife and not for sale!"

Somehow this information didn't need translation, for no sooner had Thomas started to stalk away than the tall Italian's voice resounded through the room, causing an instant hush from everyone present.

"Señor Eversley!"

The commanding tone instantly halted Thomas and he turned to face the man.

"I told you no," Thomas declared.

"*Sí*, Senor Eversley."

A sudden battle of wills was going on below Bethlyn, a battle which concerned her. If what she'd heard so far was any indication of the Italian's persistence, he meant to buy her away from Thomas like one of Woodsley's women! The shock of it all left her numb, and she watched Thomas, her husband and a man whom she hated, face a masked stranger who wished to purchase her favors.

Before everyone there the man withdrew a large and heavy purse from inside his cloak. With comparative ease and grace, as if he were used to doing this sort of thing every day of his life, the stranger opened the purse and scattered the shining gold pieces upon the highly polished black-and-white marble dance floor to roll and land before Thomas's feet.

"My God!" Lord Hoxton intoned for all to hear. "It's a bloody fortune."

Hoxton was right, and Thomas knew it. He'd made large profits from selling his women, enough that he'd never want for anything ever again. He was far richer than many of the men present, owing his wealth to the Earl of Dunsmoor. But no gentleman had ever offered him as much for one woman as this foreigner now showered upon the floor. If it had been any other woman but Bethlyn, Thomas would have instantly agreed, but this man wanted to bed Bethlyn, his wife, the woman he'd lusted after for years. God, he was only minutes away from finally making love to her, and now here was this arrogant and persistent upstart with nerve enough to offer for the honey-haired vixen he'd dreamed about ever since the day she asked his help to free her of Briston.

Thomas looked up to the balcony railing, seeing the object of his lust with her beautiful hands pressed to her creamy throat. Why, even her doelike brown eyes were pleading with him not to consider the man's offer, not to sell her to a stranger. Some protective instinct, long buried, lurched within Thomas's chest. He didn't want to sell her away. More than anything he wanted to kiss her sweet lips, to enter her softness with his hardened manhood, and to finally know that he possessed the unattainable. At that second he could read her thought: You aren't that depraved, are you, Thomas?

But the gleaming and glittering multitude of gold by his feet caused him to focus his gaze on it and away from her. Money had always been his first concern and love, long before Bethlyn was ever born. Old habits and wants die hard, he knew. So much money for only one night. His palms itched to pick up the shining pieces, to caress them as he counted them. Their sparkle and cold appeal was becoming too much for Thomas to resist.

He heard the Italian say something, then Stanhope translated. "He wants your answer, Mr. Eversley."

Thomas, unable to stop staring at the money which beckoned like a golden Circe by his feet, decided that he could have both the money and Bethlyn. She wasn't a virgin, and if one other man had his way with her, then waiting an extra day to bed her wouldn't matter. Maybe the experience with this Italian would be good for her, he rationalized. Maybe when he finally did bed her, she'd be all the more grateful and accommodating to him, and also a bit fearful he'd sell her again.

"Sir, your answer," Stanhope said again.

Thomas bent down and scooped up a handful of gold. "Tell your friend that my wife will await his pleasure in her room."

Thomas didn't hear Bethlyn's frantic screams of "No, Thomas, no!" as Perkins led her away or hear the disgusted snorts of the gentlemen present. He saw nothing except the gold, totally unaware that the gentlemen and ladies had deserted him. He was alone in the ballroom, crawling on all fours while he gathered the object of his desire into a large serving dish.

"Quiet, you mouthy wench!" Perkins warned Bethlyn and pushed her into the confines of her room. "I don't want to hit you to quiet you. The gentleman spent a fortune for you and he doesn't want his purchase marred, I'm certain."

"I won't be quiet! I hate you and that depraved wretch of a husband I've got! I won't do anything with that man. I'll fight him, I'll bite him, I'll . . ."

"You'll do what you're supposed to, Mrs. Eversley. Your brat is still down the hall in Grace's care. And I know for a fact that Mr. Eversley would be only too glad to pay Grace to take the child away from here. You'll never see your son again if you don't cooperate."

Any reference to her baby made Bethlyn instantly silent. She never said another thing to Perkins, but watched him with burning hatred shining in her eyes until at the knock on the door Perkins was only too glad to leave her presence.

When Perkins left, the tall, masked Italian entered the room and closed the door behind him.

The flickering candlelight emphasized his tallness and broadness, making him look stronger up close than when she'd viewed him in the ballroom. She was horribly frightened, knowing what sort of monster Thomas was and almost wishing he was the man standing before her. She had no idea what sort of brute she'd find beneath the silk covering on this man's face or what tortures and depravity she'd be forced to endure. No one was going to help her; she was alone. Once again, she must rely on herself to get through life, since Thomas had decided to make a whore of her.

But she wouldn't let this man think her weak and frightened, and she wouldn't cower before him and beg him to gentleness as she truly wanted to do. She'd put on a brave facade and pretend she enjoyed his lovemaking, but since he didn't know English, she'd curse him threefold in soft whispers when he took her.

"Well, señor, it seems that we're to be bedmates tonight," she said boldly and licked her parched lips. "My cur of a husband sold me to you, and like the docile wife I am I shall endeavor to do Thomas Eversley proud."

Walking brazenly towards him, she stopped and placed her arms around his neck and rubbed her breasts against the front of his muscular chest and smiled up at him. "But since you can't speak my language, I can be blunt when I tell you that I have as much regard for you as I do for my husband. I . . . I . . . should like . . . like to kill him, and before this night is over, I will hate you enough to want you dead, too. So, let's please . . . please get this disgusting interlude over." Her voice cracked a tiny bit. "I wish . . . wish that you could help free me, but . . . but you can't."

"You never did get over your sweet stutter, did you, my dove?"

Bethlyn tensed, but the life force drained from her body. "What?"

He raised an arm and lifted the mask from his face, causing Bethlyn to gasp and almost swoon, but his arms locked around her, and he revived her by pressing his hungry lips firmly against hers.

Familiar longings swept through her in tidal-wave fashion, carrying her out of the darkness into the blinding light of clarity. She'd thought she was dreaming, but now instinct and the feel of Ian's mouth against her own and the wondrous way their bodies fit together, convinced her that the man she loved was very much alive. She doubted that a ghost or a figment of her mind could kiss with such unbridled passion.

469

"Ian, Ian" was all she found the strength to say, and kissed his handsome, wonderful face as the joyful tears spilled freely down her cheeks to mingle with those of the man she loved.

"Bethlyn, I'm here," he told her, his voice choked and filled with emotion while his lips explored and familiarized himself with the curve of her throat, the swell of her breasts.

She allowed him greedy plunder while she savored the feel and smell of him. Ian was definitely alive, and she should have realized that Thomas had lied to her about Ian's death. She didn't know where Ian had been, knowing that she had years to discover everything. But for right now, she wanted him with such a ferocity that when he lifted her from her feet and carried her to the bed, she tore at his clothes, and he at hers, until nothing covered them but the sheen of their perspiring bodies.

Coming slickly together, no preliminaries were necessary. Bethlyn opened her legs to him, and Ian entered her quickly and without tenderness. But physical gentleness wasn't what either of them craved as they rode to fulfillment on a wave of hot molten lava.

Nothing prepared either of them for the torturous heat which spread through every nerve of their beings with such swiftness that when the glorious and merciful end came, their bodies arched and pulsated in rapture.

While they dressed, and in between heart-stirring kisses, Ian told her how Thomas had sent him to wallow away his life in Mill Prison. He skipped the tortures he'd endured, but he told her how he'd escaped with the help of a guard he'd learned to trust before making his way to London and to Aunt Penny's.

"Penny was quite startled when I fainted on her carpet," he said, and smiled disarmingly. "But she forgave me."

"I'd forgive you anything, too." Bethlyn found herself swept half-dressed into his arms, wishing they could make love again, but knowing they had the rest of their lives now. "I love you so much. I should have realized Thomas

470

hadn't killed you. He hated you too much to allow you to die, but he did murder my father. I have the proof."

"I wouldn't put anything past him, Bethlyn, and I'm not surprised that he killed your father. The man's weakness is money, and I gambled on that when I came here tonight. I knew he wouldn't be able to turn down such a large offer for you. Without Jeremy and Augustus's help, we might not be together right now. Augustus was most instrumental while I was ill at Penny's the last few weeks. He learned who could and couldn't be trusted here at Woodsley."

"I had no idea Augustus was nosing around." Bethlyn buried her fingers in the soft hairs on Ian's chest. "I wish I'd known."

He shook his head and kissed the tip of her nose. "There was no way to get a message to you, and we felt it was best that you be in the dark."

"Ian, we have a son," she said, her eyes shining with pleasure.

Ian laughed and merrily swung her about. "I know. Augustus told me, and Jeremy knew when he came to visit you, but Thomas said you were too ill for visitors."

After he placed her on her feet, she looked worried. "Somehow we must get the baby from the nursery. Grace is always in there."

"I know about Grace," he admitted, and completed dressing. "We weren't certain about her, since she was Thomas's mistress at one time. But by now Jeremy has taken care of her, and our son is safe and snug in Tessie's arms and waiting in the carriage at the back of the house. Perkins has been dutifully bound and gagged and locked away somewhere by Augustus, who I must say has a penchant for intrigue and would serve Captain Hawk quite well."

"Oh, Ian, I can't believe any of this. Its all too wonderful—Tessie and the baby and you, especially you."

Her beautiful face, shining with love and devotion, was inches from his. Pulling her towards him, he couldn't resist placing a tender kiss on each of her nipples. But when he lifted his face, there was no gentleness there.

471

"Bethlyn, I want you to tell me about Eversley. I mean—the man would have to be made of iron not to have touched you in all of this time, and I don't hold you responsible for his doings. But I have to know if . . ."

"Thomas never touched me. Tonight was to be the first time."

He sighed a ragged, relieved sigh which seemed to come from the very center of his soul. He helped her dress and then he said, "I'm glad for that, because I didn't want to have to torture him first for violating you after I find him."

"Why would you do that anyway, Ian? Aren't we going to leave here now? I don't care about Thomas. I want to go home before he realizes we've gone."

Even when Ian was Captain Hawk, she'd never seen his face filled with such black loathing. Placing his hand on the hilt of his sword, he gave her a thin but determined smile.

"I'm not leaving Woodsley until I find Eversley, and when I do, I'm going to kill him."

She didn't bother to plead with Ian not to kill Thomas. Somehow she knew that Thomas's ending was pre-ordained, and if the utter contempt and hatred Ian held for Thomas was any indication, then that end wasn't going to be a pretty one.

Leaving the room, she placed her hand in Ian's and knew that only by Eversley's death would their lives truly begin.

They found him in the Grotto Room, staring into the stone-faced image of Diana. At their entry, Thomas turned and smiled. "Welcome back to the living, Briston. I should have known you'd find some way to escape, but not killing you when I had the opportunity was my fault."

Ian appeared as nonplussed by Thomas's greeting as Thomas did at seeing a man whom he had sent to a hellish existence.

"I promised you that I would return and kill you, Eversley. As you well know I'm a man who keeps his word." Ian placed Bethlyn behind him, much too aware of

472

Thomas's close scrutiny of her.

Thomas's laugh mocked him. "Yes, I remember how you kept your word all of those years ago when I read the terms of your mother's will. You promised to marry a plain, shy little girl and you did. But you deserted her, cast her adrift for seven years before you claimed her again. But, of course, you'd want that which I most coveted, wouldn't you, Briston? The ugly goose had grown into a beautiful and elegant swan, much too good for the likes of me. And now you believe you have won, but no. Bethlyn is my wife now. She is mine."

"Thomas, you're insane. I'm still alive, and Bethlyn is my wife. Her marriage to you isn't legal."

Bethlyn saw Ian's hand tightening on the sword and heard the warning in his voice. She drew back into the room's shadows, waiting for what seemed an eternity for the final battle to begin.

Thomas withdrew his own sword and held it aloft. "Then I shall remedy that situation permanently."

A muscle twitched in Ian's jaw when he unsheathed his sword from the scabbard.

Before Bethlyn's terrified eyes, the two men began to parry, each testing the other's expertise. Thomas surprised her with his skill, but Ian was a master swordsman and constantly managed to sidestep Thomas's swipes.

"I'm going to kill you, you blackguard," Thomas retorted. "You cost me endless humiliation that day on your ship when you strutted in your hawklike guise. But this day, I'll rip out your heart and feed it to your namesake." Thomas perspired, his breath coming in small gasps which led Bethlyn to wonder if he was growing tired of parrying and would soon commence in earnest.

"You'll be denied the chance, Thomas," Ian commented, moving swiftly away from the point of Thomas's weapon, and not seeming to be at all out of breath or tired, considering his long, grueling months in prison and his recent recovery.

"Cocky young pup!" Thomas spat.

"Insolent, depraved bastard!" Ian rejoined.

Around and around the room they went until Bethlyn grew dizzy and wondered if she should run for help. However, when Thomas nicked Ian's arm, drawing blood and knocking him off balance for a second, her heart fell to her feet. But it was at this precise moment when Thomas looked his smuggest and relaxed his sword arm that Ian lunged and struck the sword in the center of Thomas's chest. Immediately crimson liquid stained Thomas's white shirt front as he fell to his knees.

Kicking Thomas's discarded sword out of reach, Ian towered over his nemesis like a hellish specter—something Ian intended Thomas to see for all eternity.

With arms cradled around his middle, Thomas managed a painful grin. "I always thought you were an arrogant son of a bitch. Now I suppose you'll finish the job."

For all his hatred of Thomas, Ian sensed that Thomas was frightened of a painful death, and he couldn't bring himself to be anything less than merciful even to this man who was his enemy. "Your end shall be most swift," he assured Thomas.

"Thank you for that."

Bethlyn looked away when Ian raised his sword, but a shriek echoed through the Grotto and Grace ran into the room. With her hair all atumble around a face which framed wide, haunted eyes, she resembled a madwoman.

"Don't kill him!" she pleaded, and came to a sudden halt beside Ian.

"Grace, my fair Grace," Thomas said in a suddenly triumphant voice. "I should have known you'd not desert me."

"Quiet, you sniveling excuse for a man," Grace commanded Thomas before turning all her attention on Ian. "I beg of you not to kill him, sir. Take your wife and child and leave here. Please grant me this one favor."

Ian shook his head. "I can't. You'll nurse Thomas back to health. I want him dead."

"As do I, sir," Grace confessed, and for the first time Ian noticed that she held a bloody paring knife at her side. "I escaped from the room your friend locked me in and

474

warned Thomas about you, not because I loved him. No, never love. Not any longer." Fastening her gaze upon her wounded lover who was fast losing blood, she suddenly sounded as demented as she looked. Her voice was a chilling hiss. "I hate him even more than Perkins. I found Perkins bound and gagged in the pantry. I killed him in a most merciful fashion, considering how he ill used me. But for Thomas I have something else in mind—something he should expect as his due."

"Grace?" Thomas sounded weak, unsure.

Grace didn't seem to hear him when she turned to Ian. "Believe me, sir, he won't escape. I'll not allow him to be a bother again to you or your wife and precious baby. If not for Thomas and his depravity. I'd have borne a child to love. I beg of you to allow me to finish him off. I've dreamed of his end for so long. Please, please."

Ian realized Grace was insane. Whatever end she planned for Thomas would probably be totally horrifying and torturous for a man who yearned to die quickly. He believed she would kill Thomas, but in her own way. And perhaps she had more reason to want Thomas to suffer than he did.

"I give you my word," Grace persisted, holding tightly to the blood-smeared knife, lifting it for Ian to see.

Ian sheathed his sword. "The honor is yours." Calling to Bethlyn, he grabbed her by the arm and hurriedly they ran from the Grotto, ignoring Thomas's pitiful cries that they return.

Grace laughed, a wicked sound even to her own ears. In Thomas's weakened state she was able to push him easily onto his back and pull off his satin breeches. She was obsessed by the sight of his shriveled manhood, not hearing his pleas for mercy. She saw nothing but his limp organ, and as in her daydreams of just this event, her mind repeated the action over and over again when she took him into her hand and raised the knife.

With one swift, sure swipe . . .

In the carriage which raced to London a sense of

jubilation prevailed. After hugging and kissing Tessie, Jeremy, and Augustus, Bethlyn handed the baby to his father.

"He looks like you," she hesitantly explained, "but I named him Nathaniel Matthew after our fathers. I discovered my father may have loved me a little, because he tried to warn me about Thomas in a letter." She gripped Ian's hand. "Am I foolish for naming our child after a man you disliked, for hoping that his good points may instill themselves in his namesake? Was I wrong to name the baby after two men who loved your mother?"

Clearing his throat, all Ian could do was shake his head, too overcome to speak by the sight and feel of this perfectly formed child, his son, and the almost childish hopefulness expressed by the woman he loved. Even after all that had happened between their families and this business with Eversley, Bethlyn still clung to the naive hope of a wonderful future.

Was he so jaded by life in general, by the accursed events of his own life, that he could no longer feel as she did? While in prison he thought he wanted to die, sometimes considered ending his life by his own hand, but he kept thinking about Bethlyn and about the life they'd shared. Seeing her face in his mind, filled with winsome hope, always instilled that emotion in himself and gave him the courage to continue and find a way to escape. He realized that before he met her, he had had nothing, and, without her, he'd always be unfulfilled.

If at this moment he was dreaming, then he didn't want to awaken. But the cooing child was real, the people staring at him so strangely were real. Most of all the woman beside him, squeezing his hand, made the reality more magnificent than any dream.

"Ian," he heard her say, "are you all right?"

"I'm fine, my darling." Kissing the furrowed brow of his son, he handed the child back to Tessie then he took his son's mother in his arms.

Now he had everything.

Epilogue

Windhaven
Ten months later

An afternoon breeze ruffled the strands of Bethlyn's hair as she stood on the beach with Ian beside her and watched Nathaniel toddle off with Mavis, Marc, and their child.

"I do hope Nathaniel won't miss us too much," she worried aloud in a motherly fashion. "This is the first time he'll be apart from us."

"For goodness' sakes, Bethlyn, the boy is only spending the night with them at a cottage not a half mile away. You can't keep him tied to your apron strings forever."

"I know, but he's still a baby."

"And likely to remain one if you don't give the child a bit of freedom. Remember, he's soon to have a baby brother or sister." Ian patted the slight bulge of her abdomen. "It's time Nathaniel gets a taste of life without you constantly hovering over him."

"I know," Bethlyn admitted, and dug her toes into the sand.

Ian touched the honey-colored wisps of her hair which blew so becomingly around her face. "Of course, you may hover as much as you like around me."

Bethlyn laughed and impetuously threw her arms around his neck, her lips inviting the kiss which Ian was only too happy to bestow. "Carry me inside the house and ravish me, Captain Hawk," she whispered in his ear.

"Why, you're a saucy wench even to suggest such a thing. And here I thought I had tamed you for the domestic life, and you're always thinking about that rebel Hawk. What am I to do with you?"

"Take me inside and I'll show you."

With a lustful grin clinging to his mouth, Ian gladly picked her up and carried her into the cottage. For the next three hours, until the evening shadows streaked the room in lavender and gold tones, they made love and reveled in their still-hot passion for each other which seemed to grow stronger with each passing day.

For all intents and purposes now, Windhaven was their home until Ian decided to return to Philadelphia and take over the running of the company from Marc's able hands. He'd long since retired Captain Hawk and had no desire to return to his privateering ways, hoping to spend as much time as possible with his wife and child. At the moment, he didn't want to return to Philadelphia with Edgecomb in ruins. The memories of that house were still too painful, but when he decided he was ready, he'd build Bethlyn the grandest and most elaborate house Philadelphia had ever seen. Still, he worried he wasn't being fair to her. Perhaps Bethlyn would prefer to go home now, to have a house with plenty of room for Tessie and the children. Or maybe she'd rather live in New York and be near Molly.

Reaching out, he twirled one of her honey-brown curls between his fingers. "Do you want to go home to Philadelphia?" he asked.

She snuggled against him. "I thought I *was* home."

Lifting her chin, he gazed deeply into her eyes. "I mean, when do you want to return? I can build you a wonderful house with large rooms, anything you'd ever want in a house."

"Ian," she said softly, "you don't understand. Home isn't a place. Most assuredly it isn't a grand house, as I well know. I grew up in a museum, a house so large that I never saw some of the rooms. There was no love within its beautiful gilded walls or the rooms which contained only the finest furnishings and paintings. Right now, my home is here, and I don't mean the cottage."

478

"What are you saying?" Ian looked baffled.

"Open your arms, silly, and hold me."

Immediately he embraced her, drawing her closely against him, and Bethlyn sighed in contentment. "Now I'm home."

For the first time in his life he understood what it was she had yearned for all of those years ago when he'd carelessly and foolishly abandoned her on their wedding day. He thanked God that she had given him another chance, because he'd be nothing without Bethlyn, their son, and the coming baby. But a question burned at him, and he knew he had to ask it of her or go insane with wanting to know the answer.

"Do you think my mother made a mistake in ordering that we marry?"

"Never," she declared, and sat up on her elbow to gaze down at him. "Jessica must have known that we were meant for each other. I like to think that she looks down upon us sometimes and smiles at a task well done. If not for your mother falling in love with my father, and I know this subject has always pained you, but if not for that love, we wouldn't be here at this moment—naked and together. I shall thank your mother every day of my life."

Bethlyn never ceased to amaze him. Images of her over the years whirled in his mind. The plump, sick little girl he'd married, the beautiful woman he'd captured and loved, the feisty and heroic poetess, the woman who nursed his son and then clung to him in passion afterward. How could all of these personalities be housed in this exquisite mind and sexy body? But he no longer questioned his continuing fascination with her. Bethlyn was his now and forever, and he must never take for granted his rebellious bride who'd tamed him with her love.

"I think I'm grateful to her, too, my darling," he said, and finally added, "to them."

After a few silent moments, Bethlyn traced her fingernails over his bare chest, delighting in the way he grew aroused with only a touch from her. "Ian, do you remember what I said outside a while ago?"

"Was that when you pleaded with me to carry you inside and have my wicked way with you?"

"Yes, but I mentioned Hawk. I wondered if he might come visit one night soon. I've missed the scoundrel."

"Wanton witch! You want me to wear the mask."

With a bold smile curving her perfectly shaped lips, she reached beneath her pillow to withdraw the hawklike facade she'd fashioned from some black cloth Tansy Tolliver had given her. "Making love to a masked man is most exciting."

Ian's eyes spilled over with mirth, but he pretended outrage. "In that case, my faithful wife, turnabout is fair play. Do you think the Dove might show up one moonlit night and ravish me?"

With a graceful and sensual movement, Bethlyn again reached beneath the pillow to lift the Dove's masked visage to her face. Before placing a totally tantalizing and utterly beguiling kiss upon Ian's lips and feeling the mounting heat of his desire settle between her legs, she said, "I believe it would be her profound pleasure."

And it undeniably was.